I0760165

Absolutely Free!

Sign up NOW on

http://www.tomvetterbooks.com/join-us/

for my email updates and offers.

I cherish my readers, and I'm thrilled you have become one of them.

As thanks for signing up, I'll send you my FREE e-Books, and offer you special discounts on my novels and e-books for as long as you like.

I hope that's forever!

BOOKS BY TOM VETTER

Historical Fiction:

The Siege Master Series: The Recollections of Lord Godric MacEuan on the First Crusade:

CALL TO CRUSADE—Volume One
THE SIEGE MASTER'S SONG—Volume Two
MARCH TO NICAEA—Volume Three [Coming Soon]

Undersea Adventure Memoir-Anthology:

[Writing as LCDR Tom Vetter, USN (Ret.)]

30,000 LEAGUES UNDERSEA: True Tales of a Submariner and Deep Submergence Pilot

Travel Adventure Memoirs:

Travels With Gabriela: A Lover's Tribute [Coming Soon]

Guido's Bus of DEATH and Other Misadventures
Hello Again, Europe! [...Now, Where Can I Pee?]

Find them all online at:
Amazon, Barnes & Noble, Apple, Kobo, Hoopla and
http://www.tomvetterbooks.com/bookstore/

The Siege Master's Song

The Siege Master's Song

The Recollections of Lord Godric MacEuan on the First Crusade: Volume Two

✠✠✠

Tom Vetter

TOM VETTER
BOOKS, LLC

Tom Vetter Books, LLC
Dumfries, VA

Published by Tom Vetter Books, LLC
15685 Thistle Court, Dumfries, VA 22025
Orders: 540-295-8929 and tomvetter@tomvetterbooks.com.

Book cover, interior design, imprint and maps by Thomas Vetter.
Copyediting by SilverJay Editing.
Cover photo by VIPDesignUSA, used under license from BigStock.com.
Printed by Lulu.com.

Hardcover edition: ISBN-10: 1-941160-19-0; ISBN-13: 978-1-941160-19-0.
Softcover edition: ISBN-10: 1-941160-20-6; ISBN-13: 978-1-941160-20-4.
Mobi edition: ISBN-10: 1-941160-21-3; ISBN-13: 978-1-941160-21-2.
Epub edition: ISBN-10: 1-941160-22-0; ISBN-13: 978-1-941160-22-0.
PDF edition: ISBN-10: 1-941160-23-7; ISBN-13: 978-1-941160-23-9.
Library/Institutions: ISBN-10: 1-541380-18-5; ISBN-13: 978-1-541380-18-9.

First Edition.
Printing:
1

Dedication

For my friends, John and Diana Pagan:

This book sprang from your valuable critique.

✠✠✠

CONTENTS

MAPS

The Siege Master's Song:

We've brought up the army.
We camp at your door.
Our peace terms you refuse,
So now you'll get war.

Come out now and fight us,
We'll entertain you.
And many will die here
before we are through.

Climb over, dig under,
Or pound a way through.
We'll use every weapon
To bring death to you.

Your towers will tremble,
Your garrison fall.
Your ramparts will tumble,
Starvation for all.

We'll cave in your rooftops
With boulders we cast.
With fire we burn all
So nothing will last.

Your loot we will plunder
And your daughters too.
We'll give them fat bellies
So as to spite you.

Your castle can't save you.
We'll never withdraw.
Until you surrender
We stay at your wall.

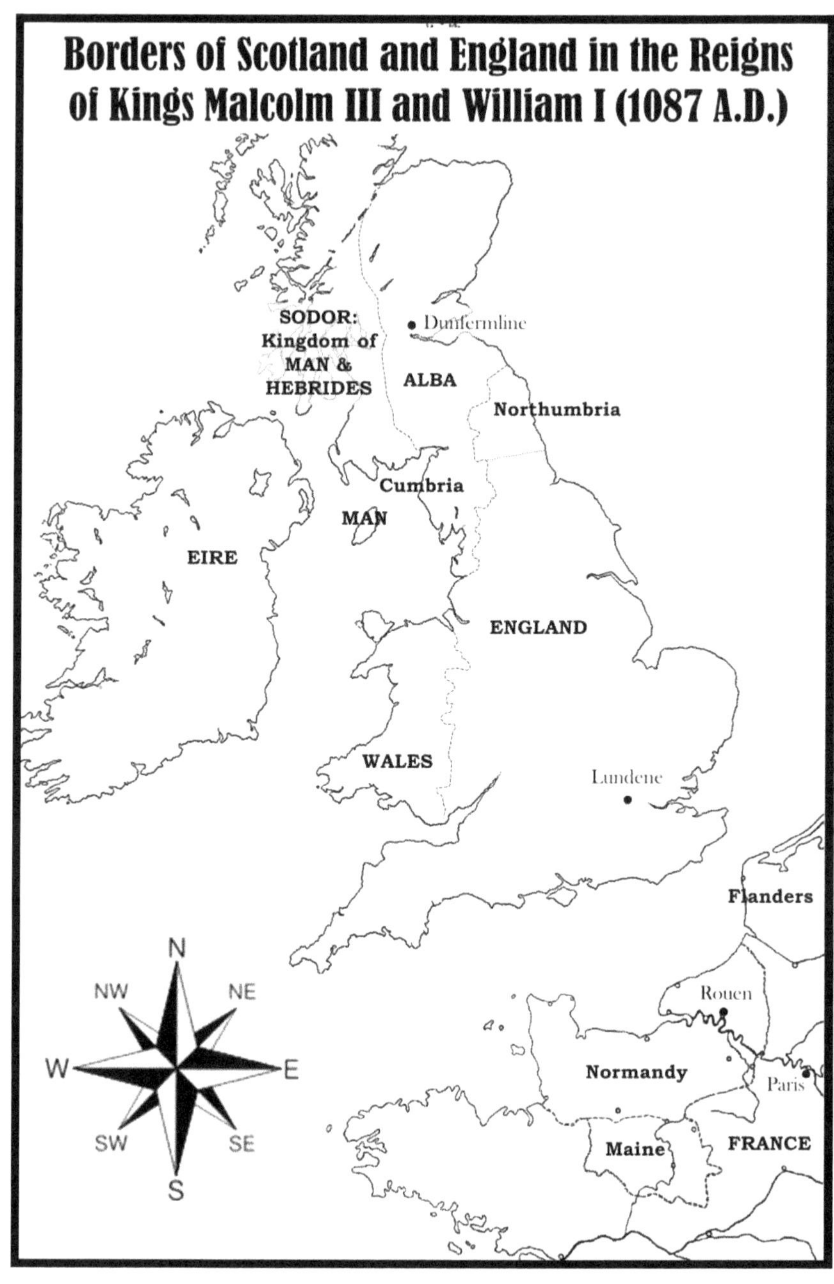

Figure 1: The borders of Scotland and England in the reigns of Kings Malcolm III and William I (1087 A.D.)

PREFACE: The Manuscript

✠✠✠

Forty years ago, while working a summer job to pay for college, I was hired to clear junk from the house of a professor of medieval history, a deceased bachelor who left all to his college. The contents of the house had already been auctioned and the executor wanted the place cleaned for sale. In a dark corner of the attic, I found an overlooked trunk. The executor told me to trash it, but when I asked for it to haul my stuff to and from college, she demanded ten bucks. I stuffed the receipt in my pocket and the trunk in my old station wagon.

The weekend I finished that job, I dragged out the trunk and went through the contents. Underneath heavily edited drafts of papers on the First Crusade, I found a manuscript on old parchment, the Latin text written by a shaky hand. This was not the professor's work but someone else's, composed long ago. And thanks to an executor's greed, I owned it.

I could not understand much of it then, except to discern that it was a memoir of some kind, written by one Godric MacEuan, Baron of Cenachedne, wherever that was. I had no time to go through it, so I put it in the trunk and packed books and clothes on top. It stayed in the trunk, forgotten, for a very long time.

Only recently did I come across it again. Now the trunk was a box of nostalgia with a mystery at the bottom. I thought it would be interesting to learn what Godric was so determined to tell.

It took me years. Thanks to Latin translation software, I could glean the gist of his narration, and then wrestle out the nuances. In the end, I was able to relate Godric's memoir in colloquial English.

It is an astonishing tale. Godric MacEuan was a master of siege warfare. He built the nuclear weapons of his age and used them in the First Crusade to conquer Nicaea, Antioch, and Jerusalem.

✠✠✠

In Volume One Godric told us of his early life—how he became a slave, a baron, a squire and a knight. He told of his experiences with Count Robert I "the Frisian" of Flanders on a pilgrimage to Jerusalem, during which he learned of the construction and use of siege engines during a prolonged stay in Constantinople. And he told us how he employed those engines to destroy the brigand MacanFhirMhóir—"Son of the Devil."

In this volume we learn of Godric's adventures as sheriff-at-large for King Malcolm III during the years 1090-1095, of the troubles that befell the Kingdom of Alba, of Godric's growing experience with siege machines, and how he innovates to build and use the first counterweight trebuchet. And this expertise solidifies his reputation as a siege master, and pulls him into the First Crusade.

Godric MacEuan was a remarkable man. This is his story.

✠✠✠

ONE

✠✠✠

Most of my life is spent now, and I must think myself fortunate to have lived as long as I have—especially amid all the dangers I have faced. But that good fortune must run out soon, so I am writing with unsteady hand, setting down here what I can recall of my adventures before and through what some now call the "First Crusade," for benefit of those who would know of my times.

That it might please God, I would have it be as true as I can say. But as I have come to discover I am flawed with over-pride and too old to change, I confess this: What I write is true; yet it is not all, but only what pride will allow. I have my flaws, and confess pride, but the others you must discover for yourself. For that I beg forgiveness—of both you who read this, and Almighty God.

✠✠✠

I have known much of death. I lost both of my parents when I was eleven, and with them every good thing I had known in life until then. I killed a rapist at fifteen, and felt no remorse for its doing, for the girl I saved is now my wife, dearer to me than life itself. But by then I had tried to kill my mother's murderer, and suffered for my failure. I saw people I loved killed, and I killed their killers in turn.

Since then, I have killed many men, most of them in battle or trial by combat, some by execution. But none by murder, for I am a baron, knight and sheriff-at-large, an officer of the law appointed by my king to serve justice throughout his kingdom. Murder I must not.

But death I know well. I am over-acquainted with the stink of a battlefield—the overwhelming stench of the corpses of men and animals, the gut-wrenching malodorous mélange of rotting meat, shit, blood, piss and vomit—like a blanket of fog over the place, and with the busy bustle of carrion birds, the snarls of scavenging dogs and wolves, the deafening buzz of an uncountable cloud of flies that get in your mouth, your ears, your eyes. The stink forces you to breathe through your mouth, and leaves there the taste of death, but the flies invade every opening, so wearing a cloth over nose and mouth is vital.

Nothing could be worse, you think. But you are wrong. Far worse is a mass grave filled with people you love. I know.

That mass grave happened because I failed to protect the people in it from the vengeful fury of MacanFhirMhóir, the evil brigand who murdered them by locking them in my manor and burning them to death. To be fair, I had already killed him once, and he did not exist when I left on a pilgrimage to Jerusalem. But it's damned hard to kill a devil, and he returned all the worse for my efforts. He is dead once again now, by my own hand, and I keep his skull to be sure of it. But my people still lay where they fell, buried in the burnt ruin of my manor hall.

I will never forget that grim first day. It was January of 1090, just after the Feast of Epiphany that marks the end of Christmastide, when I kissed my bride, took with me Cedric and Carrick, and rode to Cenachedne, where my manor had stood. It was time to begin rebuilding our home.

It had been three months since I was there, and nine months since the manor was burned. The manor hall was a wreck, its plastered walls and blackened timbers collapsed into the raised earthwork that outlined the undercroft, the expanse below the manor house in which my domestic folk dwelt. Once it had been warm with fires and bright with candlelight. Now it was a horror-filled hollow of ashes and death, a gaping mouth open to weather as it screamed at the sky.

As we surveyed the sight in silent sorrow, to Cedric and Carrick I said, "Go now. Leave me here. Go find and gather in the men of Cenachedne. We need their help with what we must do, and the dead here were their loved ones. They deserve to be part of this. I will stay here and start the burial work, for this is my fault."

Carrick, my father-in-law, mentor and at one time my master, would have argued the truth of that last statement, but my squire Cedric pulled him away, and they left me to my work.

In penitence then I set about my grim task alone, digging into this pit of death to remove the bodies of my people, and prepare them for a proper Christian burial.

Enclosed in the stone-flanked earthwork walls of the undercroft they lay, dozens of them, mostly women and children, buried in the sodden ash and charred timbers that fell on them from the manor above when it burned. First fire and then the wee crawlies of the earth had done their work, so it wasn't as terrible as the stench of the newly dead. It was worse.

I began by wrenching free and pulling out the charred timbers, using rope and horse to move those too big to lift or drag alone. They still stank of wood-smoke and rot long after they burned.

When the timbers were cleared, I began digging. Carefully, reverently, and often with my hands, I dug to extract the bodies of my dead. The sights and smells I encountered sickened me again and again, I confess, so that I retched my insides dry within the first hour.

Mostly I found them huddled in the corners and clustered at the only door—mothers and children together, trying to hide from the smoke, heat and flames. They died there that way and lay there still, clinging to each other, pain and anguish plain in the frozen screams on their ruined faces. This it was I found so horrifying.

The great fire above and around them had killed them, but not by outright burning. Smoke and heat had done it instead. The dead were charred in places, cooked in others, but often largely intact. Skin had become blackened leather, dry and stiff like wet boots left too close to the hearth, or slimy supple like wet deer-hide, the bones enclosed within. Their clothing was sodden with winter's rain, and the stink of decomposition told me the wee beasties in the ground still feasted upon them; indeed, when I was not gentle enough, skin tore open and crawly things wriggled forth, setting me to retching until my own insides hurt.

As carefully as I could I extracted them, laying each upon one of the many hides we brought from Dunfermline, the horror of it all making me weep as I did. Many I could not recognize, but those I recognized—by hair color, garments or a possession—those hurt me most, much worse than a sword thrust could.

Nessan, my steward, I identified by his chain of office. Derrick, the carpenter who had taught me woodworking while I was a slave, by his leathern bodkin. And sweet little Moira, the serving girl, and only nine—her flaming red hair still clung to her head, and mercifully covered her face. For that sweet child I wept most.

In the hides I hauled them to the site of our chapel—now just ashes as well. There I marked the site where the altar once stood—holy ground, indeed. There we would dig a burial crypt.

Over the next three days I worked, eating and sleeping in the old smithy, the lone survivor of MacanFhirMhóir's fury still standing inside the ruined palisade.

As I worked, the men of Cenachedne began to appear. Singly or in small groups they returned. And when they saw what I did, they joined me unbidden. Some began digging the vault, others bringing in rock with which to floor and wall the crypt.

But recovering the dead I did alone. My sin, my penance.

When the crypt was ready, we solemnly filled it with our dead, laying mothers and children together, side by side, layer upon layer in their hide shrouds, just as they came from the earth. Many men recognized loved ones, and all of us wept without shame as we did, weeping for lives cut short and deaths so cruel.

As we interred them I made a record of the names of each, so I could memorialize them on a carved stone atop the crypt, and so our priest would remember them at each Mass.

When we finished, we gather in solemn silence around the crypt. Slowly together we recited three paternosters and three ave-marias for the sake of their souls. Then we roofed it over with crossed layers of thick planks taken from the palisade walls. We covered these with flagstones and earth to keep out weather and beasts until the new chapel was built, and marked the crypt corners so the new altar would be placed above it. Henceforth, every Mass there would remember the souls of all those below.

Our grim duty was done. We could do no more for them. So we commended them into God's hands. He would care for them best.

✠✠✠

It was upon my return to Dunfermline that a surprise awaited me, in that good King Malcolm, not only my sovereign but also my godfather, sent for me. As ever, I attended him sitting upon his gilded chair upon the dais in the great hall of the palace.

"Baron Godric, you have returned! How did you find things in Cenachedne?"

"Painfully sorrowful, Your Grace. I have spent days digging up my dead and laying them to rest. They are at peace now, but for what he did to them I hope MacanFhirMhóir writhes in agony."

My old tutor Father Thomas would have taken me to task for that, but my Christianity was weak when it came to forgiving the men who murder the innocent. I shall suffer for it, I know, but I will bear it gladly if it means they endure much, much worse.

Malcolm gave me a wry smile. "Strangely, it is MacanFhirMhóir who has led me to summon you here today. I rejoiced in your victory over him and his band of renegades, but it has since caused me to realize the flaw in our governance that made his rampage possible. You are here today to help me remedy that."

I confess, I was baffled. Malcolm read my puzzlement well, and smiled at the effect it had had on me.

"MacanFhirMhóir was able to raid with impunity all over Alba[1] for years because he rode far, stuck suddenly, and fled the sites of his crimes before the bailies in those jurisdictions learned of the attacks. And since their jurisdictions are local, they had no power to pursue him beyond their counties. Indeed, no one in Alba other than I have that power—until now."

I was lost, and wondered where this was leading.

"Godric, you did something no one else in this kingdom has ever done. You gathered information on MacanFhirMhóir's attacks regardless of jurisdictions, used it to determine where he might be hiding, and then went and found him. It nearly killed you to do it, but you did not flinch from the duty you took upon yourself. And you skillfully used the force I gave you to defeat the monster in his own fortress. You brought me his men, his treasure and his head. I could not be more proud of you for that."

"Thank you, sire," I said. "I was motivated by the murder he did to avenge himself on me."

Malcolm nodded and said, "I understand that. But it matters not. The point is this: renegades like MacanFhirMhóir cannot be dealt with by local bailies and sheriffs, who are skilled in enforcing law as long as the criminals are local. But when criminals strike

---

[1] In the eleventh century, Scotland was called the Kingdom of Alba.

swiftly and flee the region as fast, they are helpless. Something else—something new—is required. And that is you!"

I shook my head. "Sire, I hear, but I do not understand. What would you have of me?"

Malcolm smiled; he was enjoying this. "It is this: I am appointing you to a new office, one that has not existed until now. I am making you a sheriff-at-large. You will have both the powers of bailie to investigate and arrest, and the powers of a sheriff to judge guilt and impose the required sentence. You will have the power to act anywhere within Alba and in those lands I hold title to elsewhere in England. Where possible, bring malefactors to face my justice. But this will not be often, for the matters I will ask you to pursue will be those situations like MacanFhirMhóir, in which you will have my authority to act in enforcement of my laws and my justice. Do you follow me in this now?"

I was stunned. It was an awesome office, one with tremendous power, terrible responsibility. I could only nod comprehension.

Malcolm smiled again then. "I know this seems overwhelming. This ought to be an office I assign to an earl or mormaer twice your age, but none of them have the wit, the drive, or the talent to do what you have proven you can do. For that reason, I choose you as my first sheriff-at-large. Can you do this for me?"

I understood at last. My king wanted me to do what I had done with MacanFhirMhóir whenever such a renegade arose. I could manage that.

"Aye, sire, I can do that."

"Splendid! You will serve me and Causantín mac meic Duib[2], the Regent of Fife, and my chief judge."

At this I rejoiced inwardly, for I knew Causantín, and as this is complicated to follow but important to my tale, let me explain.

As a baron of Fife, I owed a vassal's fealty to the Mormaer—or Earl—of Fife. Traditionally the highest lord in the land, the Earl of Fife had the hereditary right to crown new kings. The previous earl, Giric mac Cináeda meic Duib[3], had died in 1085. As his successor, King Malcolm had named Ethelred, his third son by Queen Margaret, then aged twelve, to be the new Earl of Fife.

Now traditionally the Earl of Fife is also Alba's high sheriff—that is, chief judge. Ethelred was too young to fill that role, so King Malcolm had named Giric's son Causantín Regent of Fife to act in all matters for Ethelred until the prince was old enough to assume those duties. That gave Ethelred both an income and future, but also honored macDuib's heir by making him de-facto earl.

Causantín was perhaps five years older than me, and by 1090 had already filled the role of regent for five years. I first met him as a young new baron. He held lands and had his manor on the coast four miles south of me, making him my closest neighbor. Like me, MacanFhirMhóir had burned his buildings, stolen his wealth, and brutalized his people. So when I tracked down and beheaded that devil and recovered much of Causantín's wealth, I won great favor with him, and we became friends.

---

[2] Constantine MacDuff, first chieftain of Clan MacDuff, and early Earl of Fife.

[3] Giric mac Cináeda meic Duib = Giric, son of Kenneth, grandson of Duff.

As regent, Causantín acted for Earl Ethelred, so I regularly met with him to pay taxes and transact business usual between vassal and lord. But as high sheriff, Causantín was the chief officer of law for the king, judging criminality and settling disputes.

So I realized my new office as sheriff-at-large was created in service of his: to enforce the law and dispense justice. By rights of rank and role, the high sheriff had the power to capture and punish rogues like MacanFhirMhóir, but as a judge, he could not be roaming the kingdom to do it. Hence, the king had decided to create sheriffs-at-large to do it instead: knights with capital power to act throughout the kingdom on behalf of the high sheriff and king and deal with men like MacanFhirMhóir. This was what Malcolm wanted me to do.

"Sire, you honor me," I said. "I will do my utmost to uphold and justly enforce your law, wherever you send me."

Malcolm smiled broadly at that. "I expected I would hear nothing less from you, Godric. Yet another proof of my wisdom."

So that is how I came to be a sheriff-at-large: a knight with the power of life and death who rode the kingdom dealing with the worst men and greatest perils the kingdom faced. I am proud of what I did. I did not do it alone, but no one did it for me. Nor could they.

Through the four years that followed, I led men throughout Alba in Malcolm's name to enforce his laws, quell disturbances, end threats, execute the king's orders and dispense justice. My friend Cormac he also knighted, and Sir Cormac and Sir Hamish were given similar commissions. And thereafter we three rode the land, both apart and together, as the needs of justice required.

✠✠✠

You will recall Lady Aleine and I were wed at Christmastime 1089 in the abbey in Dunfermline. A month prior, on our return from Dunnottar after destroying MacanFhirMhóir, I sent my new squire Cedric by fast ship and faster horse to Normandy with my news and a wedding invitation. I was gratified that my good friends, Baron Jean de Bethencourt and his wife Lady Isabeau, traveled as quickly to attend. Their first son, a cute pink little lad named for his father, and his wet-nurse, accompanied them.

The abbot presided over our nuptials and the entire Scottish royal family attended. Mary, the youngest princess, was our flower girl, a role she sweetly fulfilled and greatly enjoyed. The Baron and Baroness of Bethencourt stood as man and matron of honor.

Since my manor had been burned the previous spring, we remained in Dunfermline following the wedding, where Aleine and I had quarters. Baroness Aleine remained Queen Margaret's lady-in-waiting and companion, and I was now King Malcolm's man. After the festivities concluded, I would need to rebuild my manor as my first priority. But it was Christmas at the palace, and we were regarded as family, so we celebrated for the fortnight, with naught but feasting and revelry occurring during that time. Isabeau had spent the night before the wedding with Aleine, and by her the secrets of the harem became ours. And while the others feasted and reveled, Aleine and I were much too happy in newlywed seclusion to much join in or care.

But my old friend, master, mentor, and now my father-in-law, Carrick the Bailie, was still not himself. MacanFhirMhóir's cruelty and its aftermath had taken a deep toll on him, and left him depressed and morose with internal wounds. Only the demise of the Horned One had helped him move beyond the deep sorrow he felt; yet something else still held him fast. So during a rare foray from the bedchamber I sat with him while he was well-wetted with wedding ale and mead, and we had a much-needed conversation.

“Son,” he began—from affection, ‘Baron’, ‘Sire’ and all other titles I had long ago banned from our private speech—“it’s like this. I’m ever so grateful for your efforts to elevate me ‘n Alice, and especially Aleine. I wouldn’t want yer ta think we wasn’t grateful or honored. But to speak true, I wasn’t ever much suited to be a bailie, though I did my best. A smith I am, and in that role alone do I feel right. Release me from it, I beg you. Alice may be disappointed, for she loves the honor. But she’s a good soul at heart, and knows it’s killin’ me.”

“I understand, Carrick. Let me think a bit on it,” I said, and he nodded. We sat awhile watching the frolic. Baronesses Isabeau and Aleine were dancing to melodies played on harp, lute and fife, each with a wee child who danced with them by standing on their feet. Queen Margaret clapped time in her genteel way. And as we watched, I had a new idea.

To England William the Conqueror brought the idea of guilds—companies of highly skilled craftsmen, each led by a true master of the art—as an innovation borrowed from France and Flanders where guilds were the newest mercantile fashion. In Flanders I had encountered guilds of bladesmiths and learned that guild masters were highly regarded, acknowledged for their skills, and rewarded for the use of that skill in the products they fashioned with prestige and the right to command higher fees. The weapons these master bladesmiths made had to be purchased with gold.

So I took a rare private moment with the king, telling him about what King William had done with guilds in England and then shared my idea.

"Sire, I see you ever wear the sword Carrick and I made for you. Has it served you well?"

King Malcolm gave me a steady look, and I knew he could read my thoughts. He was never one to allow England to remain the foremost in anything. He also knew a good idea when he saw it.

"I have never had, nor seen, a better one," he replied. "Yes, it is truly a fine weapon."

"Then would you consider creating a bladesmiths' guild and naming Carrick as Master of Bladesmiths, since he has proven his worthiness with your own words?"

To my mind this honor would rightly give Carrick the elevated position he had earned through his great skill, and replace an unwanted position with one much more suitable. Malcolm too understood and quickly assented.

So he made it official. Alba would also adopt guilds, and allow them to organize, develop standards of craftsmanship, and appoint guild masters of their own. But Carrick he named himself, as the first master of the first guild.

With that, Carrick Bailie became Alba's first Master of Blades—the title itself a treasure he cherished. And in restoring his sense of honor and self-worth, it truly restored the man. Carrick had at last come into his own, and Alice retained the pride of position she cherished.

✠✠✠

The ten-thousand-pound bounty I was awarded for the destruction of MacanFhirMhóir, added to the silver and gold I had hidden in the forge, now totaled two hundred pounds of gold and twelve thousand pounds of silver, wealth such as a duke or earl might have. And now I had great need of it, for these funds would enable me to rebuild Cenachedne—not only my manor, but also the village and several new enterprises: a market fair, a tavern and inn, a new mill, and a true foundry.

With the debris cleared, I marked out the new manor, a splendid place in which I would build things I had seen in Constantinople and Jerusalem. And not only the manor house, but also a new stable-barn and chapel. Nearby Carrick and I marked out the foundry and mill—these latter two both to be powered by flowing water from a millpond we would dig in the stream. With the potential to create a guild center for blade-smithing, I had ideas about how to do it on a larger scale.

We also laid out the plan for a new village, where I put to work ideas I brought from Constantinople. We would now build not hovels but houses, along as many as nine streets, laid in a square grid, with room for more on the ground beyond should need arise for more. We staked the ground for shops, an inn and even a church. Those might be long in coming, but we had faith there would be need for them someday.

Beside the streets we dug ditches that would serve as sewers. Long had I hated the rivers of filth flowing down the streets with each rainstorm—so frequent in Alba that we only took notice of clear weather. And long had I vowed that, if ever I could, I would banish the dung and muck into channels I could avoid rather than wade through. This was my chance—and I was not going to miss the opportunity!

From neighboring nobles I hired men and bought building material. And I paid my men, although as their lord I did not have to and other lords typically did not. But we all had to eat, and we were too busy building to earn a living otherwise. Later, when the weather improved, we would farm, but now we needed to build. So all worked with a will, and for that reason, the building went quickly.

And so we began rebuilding Cenachedne. We did not do all at once. We built the barn first as our temporary home, for the weather was hardly fair. Then the mill and foundry, for they would help feed us. And my old smithy once again belched smoke and rang with hammer blows, for the first time in a long while. Carrick and I worked again together to produce all the nails and fittings needed until enough other smiths I sent for arrived to share the workload. The best of these we would recruit into the guild.

Do you think it odd a baron would stoop to work at forging iron, digging, hewing, and building? Perhaps. But I was building for myself, and I would see it done the once and right. Besides, it took the place of our daily combat drills, keeping me strong for war. Hammering iron uses muscle as much as does swinging a sword.

Then, too, I would need these skills honed sharp to build my siege engines. Dunnottar had taught me the value of powerful standoff weapons, weapons that defeated an enemy even while keeping my people safe. War was all around us, and war was changing—from gangs of men with edged weapons having at each other, into something more organized and much more lethal. Our castles might today be built of wood and earth, but I had seen fortresses of stone, and realized that soon they would rise here too, even as great churches already did. And only great engines could defeat those stone castles.

Since Constantinople I had in mind a plan to build large-scale versions of the siege engines I had earlier built as miniatures in Constantinople and brought home in my baggage. Those tiny engines fascinated King Malcolm when I showed them to him, and he was as keen to see them in action as I was. So as time and treasure allowed, I would build one of each until I could test each and learn to use them well. The future of a siege master looked to me to be most bright—and very profitable!

And in truth, I loved it. Working in wood and iron was personally satisfying, for when you finished you had something tangible, something of value that sweat and skill had crafted from nothing. I *liked* doing it—as dogs enjoy chasing wagons, and falcons stooping to the kill. So building wasn't a waste of my time.

To my way of thinking, I was making the most of it.

TWO

✠✠✠

Once the rebuilding of Cenachedne was well underway, I turned to my next problem—people! As a wedding gift—given, I believe, at the king's suggestion—in gratitude for ridding his earldom of MacanFhirMhóir, my lord Causantín, Earl of Fife, had expanded my lands around Cenachedne to five times my original, and included the land from Cenachedne south and east to the mouth of the River Leven. But people to work the land were missing.

"Sire," I told the earl, "grateful as I am, I have a problem. I have land, but no people to work it. MacanFhirMhóir murdered many of my people, and left the area so destitute that the folk fled, unable to survive. I need people to work the land if it is to be of any value to you and me."

"Heavy lies the crown, Baron," said the earl with a smile. "Think on it, and I am sure you will find a solution. Let me know what you think best, and if possible, I will support you."

So think on it I did.

To be precise, my problem was that I had men without families. They had been off elsewhere chasing MacanFhirMhóir with Carrick when he and his band of renegades rode through Cenachedne and its surrounds, and took revenge on me, trapping the women and children in my manor and burning it to the ground.

Now, men without families are not really men. They are more like wild beasts, motivated by their bellies for want of greater concern. It is *families* that bring society into order. My men needed families. And to create families I needed women—willing women. I felt it would only be just recompense for all they had suffered to help find them new families as a means to rebuild their lives.

So with the earl's support, the king's blessing, and the help of the abbey, I began a tour of the country's convents, seeking out widows and maids, victims of war sheltered inside, who would be willing to become wives to my Cenachedne bachelors and widowers.

At each convent I would present my charter to the mother superior and request an opportunity to address the marriageable women abiding there. The king's seal served me well—I was never refused.

"Good women of Alba," I would say, "I have a village of good, strong and hardworking men. They lost their wives and children to war, and would gladly take others willing to wed—especially such women as lovely as you!" All would giggle at that and blush, for a little flattery goes far, and I was wooing them all on behalf of my men.

I told each gathering that I would hold a "marriage fair" in early spring, at which they could meet and marry a man they chose. And when the time came, I pledged to send a wagon to each convent to collect all the willing brides-to-be and convey them in safety to Cenachedne. I promised as well a safe return to their convent to those who decided not to wed.

Always was I well received, for of widows and spinsters there were, alas, always too many. And for most of them the convent was their only refuge from utter privation.

So too in the towns I passed through in the regions MacanFhirMhóir ravaged, I spoke to all the freemen I could find —tradesmen, farmers, shepherds and smiths—recruiting them to come live in Cenachedne and help me make it thrive. And given the chance, many came most willingly—enough to rebuild anew my missing population and replace our much–needed commerce.

✠✠✠

In March, as promised, I held my "marriage fair." By then, we had a number of houses built. Those about-to-be-newlywed men who had lost homes would initially share these while we built more.

The wagons arrived, bearing several score of women—some young, others life-worn, but all eager with hope for a new future. To incline them favorably to make Cenachedne their new home, I had the wagons first driven through the village on a brief tour, and rode along on my warhorse CiùinLùth to promote what was there and describe what we yet planned to build. Again, I was wooing would-be brides on behalf of my menfolk, in this case by wagonloads. And as they looked about, they nudged, pointed, and murmured. I could see they liked what they saw.

Good for us! I thought.

After an initial stop at a screened privy—for some wagons had come far—we brought them then to the fair. We had raised canopies in the meadow beside the village to protect against rain, screened them from wind, and built low fires of charcoal to offer warmth. And to ease social interaction against the awkwardness of a mass courtship, I supplied ale, mead and food aplenty. Squire Cedric, who had somehow achieved some musical ability in his yeoman years, had found yet others with similar skill, and they played us merry tunes on fifes, harps, lutes, and tambour drums[4].

So it was there the future of Cenachedne first met its men. All of these latter worthies had scrubbed themselves red with sand in the cold waters of our stream, and had dressed in their best.

At first the men and women lined the sides, eyeing each other for likely mates. More murmurs, nudging and surreptitious pointing occurred on both sides.

As lord of the village and sponsor of the fair, it fell to me to begin the event. So I addressed the assemblage.

"Gentle ladies of Alba, the men of Cenachedne bid you welcome! Come meet and break bread with us. You have come hoping for good husbands. I assure you, there are no better men in the land. And they can see for themselves, as I can, how fair and comely are you! Do step forward and meet the man you fancy."

The women curtsied or nodded acknowledgment of my invitation, but no one moved. I was tempted to do something more, but held my peace—and my breath.

---

[4] All of these are musical instruments the documented pedigrees of which begin later in the Middle Ages. I use them here as commonly-known names for their earlier extant but undocumented ancestors.

Finally, a wise old widow made up her mind, and, pulling in a deep breath, pasted on a bright smile and strode across the great battlefield to speak to the man who returned her gaze.

And with that, the contest—as 'battle' seems harsh—was on. The two sides surged forward and a melee ensued, as men and women met, spoke, courted, flirted, and stuck fast or moved on.

Mostly the proceedings were festive, fun and most successful. Indeed, I had a booth beside the main canopy to house a flock of friars I borrowed from the abbey at Dunfermline. As couples came to terms, I had them avail themselves of the priests: first to confess their sins separately and obtain absolution—a guard against bigamy—and then to wed. Brother David, too, I had borrowed as clerk, and he was kept busy recording the new unions and approving each with my seal. Afterward, the newlyweds returned to the great booth, rejoining the revelry as man and wife, meeting their new neighbors and basking in the cheers and bawdy suggestions of their friends.

Before the day was out, most who came had found a new mate. We had just one heated argument over a woman, and a catfight over a man. Those I broke up—and then drowned the hard feelings in mead.

So the wedding fair proved a vast success, for both the women and men there were well-inclined to seek fresh happiness in new marital unions. Not one woman did I have to return to a convent. As one man told me after much more ale than he needed, "Aye, milord, some ain't as pretty as others, but they're all prettier than the sow I'm sleepin' aside for warmth these cold winter nights!"

Prettier, indeed!

✠✠✠

With my affairs off to a good start, I returned to Dunfermline. In truth I had often been back and forth as often as I could, for the ride was short and I missed my lovely spouse. But she had her duties to the queen and I had to rebuild our home. So by this I mean I returned to my duties to my king.

My first assignment was a patrol through Fife on behalf of the earl. I rode accompanied by Cedric, of course, and a mounted squad of picked men-at-arms. Spring's improving weather brought with it renewed wrong-doing—petty thefts of pigs and lambs; capital theft of cattle and horses; violent disputes between neighbors over land or crops; theft and resale of relics; accusations of pagan worship and sorcery; house-breaking and robbery; waylaying of pilgrims traveling to abbeys to supplicate favor of God; and so on.

All these I dealt with at one time or another—usually by finding the accused miscreant and delivering him to stand trial and judgement in the court of the lord with venue. That my prisoners generally arrived alive, I take pride. A few who fought me I delivered also—wrapped in sailcloth and tied over a pack-saddle.

I used these patrols to develop sources of information valuable to the king—men who traveled, heard things, and would for some consideration—silver, usually—relate or report them to me. My preferred sources were ship captains—smart, worldly men whose travels took them great distances. Much of what they reported was only of nominal interest, but it kept us connected to happenings in distant lands and events, and sometimes these became all too relevant with frightening speed.

And it was a captain of a trading vessel that told me, "Sire, one bit of news that may interest you is that King Rufus is short of money. He's been fightin' his two brothers to seize their lands in Normandy, and it's proving very expensive. He's already taxed his lords and lands to the breaking point, 'n can't get more. So needing a new source of funds, he's appointed his court favorite, Ranulf Flambard, as Justiciar[5], 'n had him levy heavy taxes on the Church. The churchmen don't like it and say it isn't legal, but that won't stop Rufus. He's a bad 'un, sire!"

✠✠✠

We were at last housed at Cenachedne—still in temporary quarters, but as I traveled back and forth between Dunfermline and Cenachedne, I would often bring Aleine with me, to visit her parents and view the progress we were making.

My king and earl were satisfied with me, my people were beginning to thrive once again, my manor was well underway, and my affairs in hand. Finally I had the chance to begin something I had been aching to do since Constantinople: I would build my own helepolis!

From the chest in which I kept the tiny copies of the siege engines I'd built in Constantinople, I took the drawings I'd made of the little helepolis I'd built and given to Demetrius. And working of evenings, often with Aleine or Carrick curiously watching at my elbows, I built another. Long used as they were to my love of tools and building, they still found amusement and pleasure in watching me work. And when I finished, I took joy

[5] The Justiciar was the chief judicial and political officer of the kings of England from 1066 to the 13th century. His modern equivalent is Britain's prime minister.

and pride in their amazement as I employed it to hurl acorns across the hall at the serving girls.

Carrick said with some admiration—and just maybe a hint of envy—"That's a clever plaything you've built, son."

"Clever perhaps, Carrick. But this is no toy. This is the most terrible weapon in the world."

"What? Acorns?"

"When those acorns weigh what you do, my other engines will seem the toys!"

I could see he was dubious. But I had no doubts.

✠✠✠

A week later, its bigger brother stood in a pasture outside the palisade. It was but half the size of the machine I wanted to build, but I'd never built any machine this large, so I thought I'd better begin small. And "small" was still three times my height.

A square of four timbers formed the base, with two more timbers set inside them to divide the frame into thirds. Above the two central horizontals, four other timbers formed two parallel upright triangles supporting an axle for the long throwing arm. The upper three-quarters of this arm pointed skyward, while the lower quarter bore a large wooden barrel filled with several hundred-weight of earth. A wooden floor filled the space between the two triangles.

From the upper end of the arm hung a rope hawser, which widened into a mesh sling at the middle and tapered back to an eye at the free end. Using this we could haul down the arm to cock the machine, using a stout strap over the arm to hold it down. Then, once the arm was cocked, the sling was laid out to enwrap a boulder, and the eye placed over a pin on the end of the arm.

This much was easy, just as it had been with my little engine. Now, with this huge monster, trying to release the strap and loose the arm was terrifying.

Just once did we try pulling the strap off its peg with a lanyard. The arm tore the lanyard from our hands, and we were lucky no one had fingers torn off as well.

I then tried a release pin I could drive home with a mallet. That worked; but after a boulder went straight up and crashed to earth within inches of me, I could see that was a most perilous place to stand. We needed a much better release mechanism.

Carrick combined the two ideas then, cutting the strap into two parts we spiked to the frame, one free end an eye that fit over a peg on a block attached to the other—so that a tug on a lanyard attached to the block could pull it open from a distance. This worked well, to our great relief, so we set about seeing what this new engine could do.

It was far more terrifying than any of my other machines. The great triangles wobbled frightfully side-to-side as the great arm swung—clearly side-braces were needed. But we learned much from it, hurling a score of head-sized boulders as far as a hundred feet before the engine gave a great *crack* and collapsed.

✠✠✠

It was early in this term of mine that King Malcolm came into serious conflict with King William II of England, second son of the Conqueror, who inherited the crown and ascended the throne of England following his father's passing in 1087. The conflict was solely William's doing, and before long, it brought war. But so you may understand both the conflict and the reason I have an enduring hatred of the man behind it, I must tell you of the man.

For fifteen years King Malcolm III of Scotland and King William I—called "the Conqueror" of England—had ruled their adjacent kingdoms in relative harmony, with little but rogue border raiders from one country to vex the other.

It had not always been so. Malcolm was already the King of Alba when then-Duke William of Normandy invaded England in 1066, seized its crown by defeating King Harold Godwinson in battle at Hastings, and forced his rival Edgar the Ætheling to renounce his claim on the crown and submit to his authority. Over the next six years William fought everywhere, to consolidate his power and push his borders with neighboring kings, William contesting with Malcolm over the lands comprising our southern border. William defeated Malcolm at last in battle at Abernethy in 1072, and in the subsequent negotiations, the two men finally came to terms both could accept, dividing the disputed lands between them[6]: William secured Northumbria and gained a hostage in Malcolm's oldest son, Duncan, who would be reared in the English court.

[6] This was the Treaty of Abernethy, signed in 1072. No copy of it survives, and so its exact terms are disputed to this day. Much of the conflict between King Malcolm and William's successor, King William Rufus, that followed arose from dispute over whether it was homage or fealty that Malcolm pledged William, and so the terms by which he held his lands in Cumbria and Northumbria. To this day Scotland maintains it was fealty, while England holds it to be homage.

Malcolm kept traditionally Scottish Cumbria and his personal estates in Northumbria, in return for a pledge of fealty to William done in the manner accorded to kings: with the pledge of fealty performed on the border and witnessed by the principal nobles of both kingdoms. This ensured that each king retained a recognized sovereignty over his realm and that the parties most affected by the pledge—the high nobility of each nation—witnessed the event.

And with that treaty, each kingdom left the other in peace.

But the Conqueror died in 1087, and his will divided his lands among his sons Robert, William, and Henry. Robert, the eldest, inherited the Dukedom of Normandy. William was given England, and Henry monies and lands in Cotentin, France. Robert and Henry were content with their inheritances. William was not.

He was crowned King William II of England. But it wasn't long before his court and commoners began to call him "Rufus" and "The Red King" because of his florid face and red hair. I quickly came to despise him—for good cause, as I will relate—but no more than almost all of his own countrymen. Indeed, I know of no monarch anywhere more hated than was Rufus, and he deserved every bit of it. For this reason I call him only Rufus in this, my story. "Satan" would be more fitting, but that name is reserved for another who is but little worse.

Now Rufus was unlike his father in every respect but one. Where his father was tall, strong, and comely, Rufus was short, pot-bellied, and gaseous—indeed, his lords and nobles mocked him, and called him "Puffbilly" behind his back. He was naturally florid, but this coloring was further heightened both by excessive drink and a continual attitude of irritated outrage—as if life itself were a crime against him.

Where his father had respect for the Faith and the Holy Church, Rufus had none. He hated both Church and churchmen, stole all he could from churches and monastic houses, and withheld his appointments of bishoprics so that he could instead collect all rents and proceeds due them for himself. Beyond a thin façade of faith that Rufus pretended solely for appearance's sake, he was actually atheist, vain, dissolute, immoral and ever-grasping.

Moreover, Rufus was an unnatural. He despised the company of women, entirely preferring companionship of like-minded men. He filled his court with other unnaturals, all of whom dressed with outrageous extravagance, minced about with lisping speech and feminized antics, indulged in unspeakable acts, and sought always and in all things to flatter the king. In turn Rufus preferred them over moral men, promoting them for looks or in reward for unnatural favors, rather than merits. He would not take a wife, he never married and he left the throne without heir—that was left to his brother Henry in the end.

It was only in ambition that Rufus emulated his father; and indeed, there he far surpassed the Conqueror. He quarreled with the Church over possession of its lands, fought yearly with his own brothers to take what they had inherited from their father, and invaded all the neighboring kingdoms, seeking always to take more. And if he was thwarted in one attempt or region, he did not cease—he simply shifted his attention to pursue gains in another.

Exceedingly ambitious and ever-eager to expand his lands, Rufus had no scruples about whose lands he stole or how. But initially he was little trouble to Alba because he was so busy elsewhere, first warring with Duke Robert over Normandy, and then with the Church to seize its lands as well. Only when he was successful in some ways, and completely thwarted in others, did he finally turn his attention north. And it was there our troubles began, at the start of the year 1090—just as I began riding for King Malcolm.

Understand: it was not for these flaws that I came to hate Rufus. I have known other men, just as flawed, whom I loved: his brother, Robert, for one; Tatikios; Demetrius; even some of my brother knights of the First Crusade. I know I too share some of these flaws with Rufus. It was not them that made me hate him.

I came to hate him for what he *did.* For what he did to my king and his family—in truth, *my* family, for they become so after my parents died when I was still but a boy. And for what he did to my country. In both cases, Rufus brought us war, brought us trouble, brought us all anguish and grief—and all just to serve his unquenchable greed.

It was for his many deeds of greed that I came to hate Rufus. For his greed, I wanted him dead—so much so I became willing to raise my own hand against him in order to bring that to pass.

But more of that later. Let me resume my tale as it happened.

✠✠✠

In May of 1090 I led a patrol through Cumbria. It should have been straightforward, a relatively uncomplicated expedition against cattle thieves. It proved to be anything but that.

On these patrols I routinely spoke to thanes and churls living in the area to gather any information they had about cattle thieves.

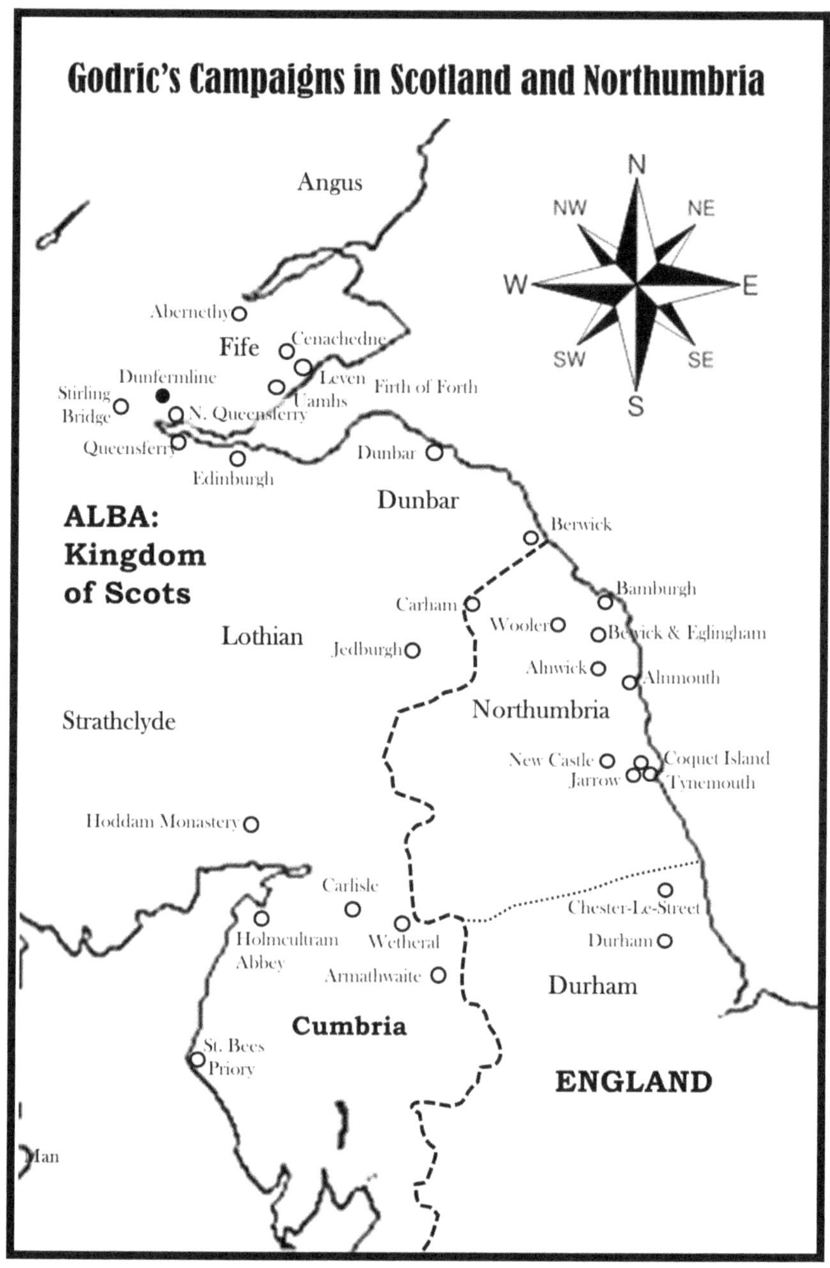

Figure 2: Godric's campaigns in Scotland and Northumbria

And it was they who first told me of the English newcomers. I heard tale after tale from them, all more or less in the same vein.

"Aye, Lord Godric, they've come among us an' onto our lands—land where we've allus grazed our cattle and sheep. They're buildin' houses and manors on land to which we have title from King Malcolm. They gather up our beasts, and when we confront 'em, they claim 'em as theirs under a charter or grant from King Rufus or one o' his earls proclaimin' the land is theirs. An then they back it by aimin' crossbows at our bellies and orderin' us off our own land. 'Tis infuriatin! When is King Malcolm goin' ta help us?"

In each instance, I told those outraged Scots this: "I will promptly report to the king these intrusions, thefts, and claims on your lands. I have no doubt he will protest these acts to King Rufus. You in turn must help me. Mark all your animals with distinct earmarks so we can identify your stolen beasts. Whatever you do, do not give them grounds to use their weapons on you. The king will attend to them."

✠✠✠

As promised, I did indeed investigate the intrusions and thefts, riding into each new manor to speak to the newcomers there. I demanded to see their documents and duly recorded their names.

When I informed them that they were illegally occupying Scottish land, most of them blustered, pretending they were on English soil, and swearing that their charters were valid because they bore Rufus's seal.

"There was no one here when we came! The land is wild and empty. We have a valid title from King William. This is our land. We intend to stay and make homes on it!"

Part of that was true. Cumbria *was* sparsely populated, and the land appeared empty and wild because it was poor ground for farming. But it was good land to graze cattle, and all of that land was already owned by Scots.

So these English charters only made occupancy legal if this was England, not Scotland. And that was the crux of the whole issue.

I warned them that their titles were false because Cumbria was a part of Alba, not England, that they were trespassing on Scottish land, and that I would report them by name to King Malcolm. I warned them that theft of Scottish animals was a hanging crime, that all Scottish beasts not returned to the rightful owner and found in their possession would be regarded as stolen, and that when next I came, I would hang every trespasser and cattle thief I found.

I gave them an alternative, however. "If you are not violating a valid Scottish charter, if you will surrender this false title, swear fealty to King Malcolm and acknowledge his authority, I will see that you are recorded as his liegeman and bring you a clear Scottish title."

Some assented then and there. Others blustered in pretended outrage and disbelief. A few tried to scare me off with threats. And one was so foolish as to pull his sword. I gained a scar from him I wear to this day, but he died an instant later with my Damascene blade in his skull.

✠✠✠

When I reached Dunfermline and reported the trespassing, false charters and deeds, and the general unhappiness of his subjects at the usurpers, Malcolm was furious.

"Damn Rufus to Hell!" he shouted. "His father and I settled all this fifteen years ago. King William and I agreed that Cumbria is a Scottish land by culture, by tradition, and the treaty between us. All Cumbria was ceded to me as dowry when I wed Margaret, and William guaranteed Cumbria as mine in return for the oath of fealty I swore to seal our treaty at Abernethy; never would I otherwise. And now this greedy little boy, this little red worm, seeks to sneak in people to take it from us with false deeds and charters? By God, he will hear of this! And the language I use will hardly be Christian!"

In a calmer tone he said, "Lord Godric, I thank you for this news, though it is hardly good. You did right with your warnings and your offer. I will grant valid titles to those who will swear me fealty, and my clerk will accompany you to issue them.

"And I give you this order: Return to Cumbria. Obtain from each of my vassals there—my clerk will have their names—obtain from each their renewed oath of fealty. Demand the same of all of these English newcomers. Make careful record of who swears fealty and supports us, and who will not recognize our authority. I would know who is a true subject and who an English usurper. And we will treat them accordingly."

✠✠✠

True to his word, Malcolm contested the false charters and protested the incursions with letters of protest he sent to Rufus. The letters availed nothing, since it was Rufus who had issued the charters, and he did so to create an excuse to seize Cumbria in the guise of protecting English "landowners" in residence there. King Malcolm knew this also, but his letters of protest were necessary because they underpinned his legal right to take subsequent action against King Rufus and his usurpers.

I saw to it personally that those who had given Malcolm oaths of fealty supported Malcolm's authority and feudal rights. And on several long rides over the next six months, I built for King Malcolm two lists: Those who pledged new or renewed fealty, and those who foreswore their oath or refused Malcolm fealty.

Oh, and those I found with another Scot's cattle—those I hanged.

✠✠✠

In this way we learned Rufus had found a new scheme to take for himself yet more land. It seemed he thought that if he could surreptitiously fill those regions with Englishmen, their loyalty purchased and anchored with those false titles, then as their feudal lord, he could then claim the region as English.

Now these were lands Malcolm had always ruled—indeed, Malcolm ruled them before the Conqueror gained the English throne, and although Malcolm had pledged fealty to William as overlord to avoid war in 1072, the two had men agreed on the border between them, and Cumbria was Malcolm's. That pledge of fealty was also personal between Malcolm and William, and expired with William. It did not convey to his heir, so Malcolm owed Rufus no fealty whatsoever. Nor did the pledge give Rufus right to any lands Malcolm ruled.

So Rufus's actions were both completely illegal and deliberately provocative, in that they created title disputes between Scottish and English landholders where there should have been no doubt. It was Rufus's personal greed to gain these lands that began this new conflict between Scotland and England. And when monarchs contend, their peoples inevitably must go to war as well.

So with this act Rufus began to sow the dragons' teeth of war between England and Alba. The invasion of Cumbria by these English land-grabbers brought new troubles into southern Alba, kindling flames of conflict that would grow into a bonfire of war.

✠✠✠

My second machine was like the first, but much more strongly built, better jointed with iron straps around heavier timbers. Its uprights wobbled far less under the swing of the arm after I added side-braces. These were essential if I wanted to build the engine any bigger. And after all, that was the whole point—my onager was just as effective, and much more robust, than was this—as yet. But I was learning.

In an effort to see if a heavier counterweight would allow us to throw farther, we filled the barrel with the heaviest rocks we could get—and the next throw nearly killed us when the barrel tore free, arced high, and burst on impact, with rocks and splinters flying in all directions.

"Shit!" we cried as one, and dove for cover.

As we picked ourselves up and checked for damage, Cedric said with a grin, "Something else to fix, I believe."

✠✠✠

By fall, Cenachedne was much rebuilt—twenty small houses, a new water-driven mill, and the just-started new foundry, both these last fed by a millpond formed by digging wide the stream above a dam we built to retard the outflow of water. And the new tavern would soon be ready as well.

To enable the building we did, we let the land lay fallow that year. Without men's labor we could not grow more than gardens. But cattle and sheep grazed all about us, ducks and hens hunted food everywhere, and piglets grew fat in pens These were tended by happy new wives, many with swelling bellies. We bartered the fruits of our agriculture—meat, milk, eggs, wool and garden produce—with our neighbors for their grain and other staples for our subsistence. Next year our planting could resume. For now, houses, barns and buildings were our greatest need…

…because Cenachedne was at last growing once again.

✠✠✠

My third machine was larger and much improved, with better braces to withstand forces I now realized were far greater than anything seen in my onager or ballista. Hoping that a longer throwing arm would impart greater force to the projectile and longer distance to the throw, I increased its length, and indeed, we did get greater distance. But after a dozen throws, the next snapped the arm and threw it instead, a terrifying timber whirling downrange like a thrown blade.

Carrick said, "Well, son, you were so right when you said this was a fearsome weapon. I'm fairly terrified of bein' anywhere near it!"

I was irritated until I realized he was jesting. But he was also right.

So I grinned and said, "Let's go get ale and think of something even worse to try with this thing."

✠✠✠

By Christmas of 1090 my new manor was still incomplete, but it was well along—the undercroft for my manor folk had been completed and it was very habitable. The roof was in place, and the building was walled to keep out wind and wet. The braziers and firepits were ready to hold glowing embers or low fires for warmth, and the great fireplaces in kitchen and main hall roared to cook our food and burn wood into coals. Aleine and I had a bedchamber for ourselves, and the hall was usable, if unfinished. We could live in it, call it home.

Even unfinished, it was already a splendid place. I had added things I had seen on pilgrimage to Constantinople and Jerusalem, things unlike anything in Alba. For example, we dug a small canal from the burn[7] right through the manor grounds and back again, lining it with stone to channel flowing water. Upstream, I built a weir to guide fish into the canal. The flow conveyed them into a rock-lined pool in the kitchen, and a grating across the outflow stopped escape downstream.

---

[7] Burn: Scottish term for a freshwater flow, in size from a large stream to a small river.

By this method we had an endless source of live fish to eat and preserve by smoking. Soon my smoked salmon and trout were renowned in Dunfermline and among my noble neighbors.

A year later a terrific storm swelled the river and sent a flood of water down the canal and into the kitchen, so I built floodgates of stacked timber stoplogs at each end of the canal. Thereafter, when torrents threatened, we could wall off the canal and confine the heavy flow to the burn. Otherwise, we had flowing water inside the palisade to water my horses and livestock in the manor yard without hauling water, reserving the clean well water for the manor folk.

Our new home pleased Aleine much, especially after the queen dispensed with her services for a fortnight of each month I was home from patrol so that we could enjoy the place together.

I found great comfort there. And at my manor door sat Andrew's skull, long cleaned to gleaming white bone by the wee beasties. As I had promised him, I used it to scrape the muck off my boots.

THREE

✠✠✠

I had learned much from my first three helepolis designs, but they weren't any more powerful or effective than my onager, and I was starting to lose hope in my ability to build an actual improvement. The smaller ones worked well, once we developed solutions to the hidden flaws that surprised us with dramatic new ways to kill us and destroy themselves instead of their targets. But as I tried to build them bigger, even more alarming problems revealed themselves.

We had outgrown our counterweight—it simply couldn't hold enough weight to power a larger machine, no matter what we filled it with. So at the close of Christmastide, I tested a fourth engine, the barrel counterweight replaced with a bigger open-topped box on the lower end of the throwing arm.

That looked like a good solution—until the first time we fully cocked it, and half of the rocks fell from the box into a huge pile in the middle of the frame. We added a hinged lid but the weight of the rocks just tore it off—to keep the rocks in it the top would have to be nearly as strong as the heavily-built bottom. At that moment, I realized we needed to articulate the box, so that it was attached but not inverted by the action of cocking the arm.

Ah, well. Father Thomas always said, "Trial and error is how we learn."

✠✠✠

Just after Epiphany of 1091 I rode to Leven and North Queensferry to speak to the ship captains in each port for news. I wanted to learn what King Rufus might be intending to do in the new year, and from that, try to divine what the new year might portend for Alba. A little silver could buy a goodly amount of useful information, and what I heard I would report to Malcolm, who was just as keen for such news.

At North Queensferry I sought out my old friend Thorsson, one of my best sources—intelligent, reliable and far-traveling through all the northern seas. He had just returned from a trading voyage to Lundene, and said he was preparing to return. I asked him what he knew of where King Rufus was, and what he was about.

"Well, let me recall, sire… All the talk among the captains is that early next month King William will take an army into Normandy, with aim to seize lands from his brothers, and he's offering to pay well for ships to haul his men, beasts and gear across the Channel. He wants them landed at the mouth of the Somme. And he needs every ship he can get because his army is huge—perhaps a thousand knights, all told, and ten or more time that in yeomen and men-at-arms at least. I aim to return, as soon as I can offload this cargo and take more aboard—I wouldn't want to miss that opportunity."

I told him, "Thorsson, you are a true fount of information once again. Whenever you have such news, send word to me—I would hear it, and pay well, for it is well worth the price." I handed him a purse of silver.

"Hefting it, he nodded thanks. "The pleasure is mine, sire."

✠✠✠

And I was not wrong. Upon my return to Dunfermline I sent a page to the king that I had news of King Rufus's plans, and soon stood before him. "Baron! You have news of King Rufus?"

I reported what Thorsson told me, and he nodded thoughtfully.

"Thank you! I have had no such intelligence, and this is news indeed. I have not forgotten what Rufus has been doing against us in Cumbria, nor do I think he will stop there. And if he would war against his own brothers to take their inheritances, he won't hesitate to steal from his neighbors. While he rules in England, no lands of ours are safe. And with an army of ten thousand, and a thousand knights, we will need allies when he brings them against us."

Malcolm thought a moment, and then asked, "Do you think Duke Robert of Normandy would be willing to aid us? And would he be reliable?"

It was unlike Malcolm to ask for counsel, so I took it as a mark of respect that he would voice such thoughts with me. Unused to thinking thus, I had to admit my inexperience.

"Sire, I do not know the man. Many English lords, particularly in the north, thought Robert should be king rather than Rufus, and the two have fought over land before—indeed, Robert lost all his landholdings in England in consequence. So he is a rival with cause for grievance against Rufus. That he might welcome a pact of mutual support I think most possible. Perhaps one who knows him well could offer you better advice. The queen's brother, Edgar Ætheling, knows Duke Robert well, does he not?"

Malcolm nodded. "He is the very man, and the last I knew he was with Robert in Normandy. I dare not commit a proposal for a pact to writing, but I'll request he come, seek his advice, and ask he act as our emissary. Do tarry a bit while I have a letter written and confer with the Benedictines. They will know where he can be found, though I don't know how. Angels or demons it must be who keep them so informed. Either way, I ask you to arrange its delivery. Would your ship captain be willing to make a voyage?"

"I believe he would, sire."

"Then choose a squire well-suited to entrust with it—this is too delicate a task for monks, and possibly dangerous."

"I'll go myself, sire," I offered.

Malcolm shook his head. "I need you to take a patrol into Northumbria to see what Rufus may be doing there. After discovering what he has done in Cumbria, I cannot trust the man."

"I understand, sire. I would send my own squire, who is most able, but perhaps this is a mission a knight should perform—and a lord. Since the Duke's support depends upon Edgar's emissary, it is imperative he undertake it, and it may take some persuasion to convince him to do so."

Slowly, the king nodded. "Yes, I think you are right. Very well. Go make your preparations, Baron," he said.

And I was in the midst of a flurry of tasks to do just that when a breathless page pounded on our quarters door.

"Sire, the king says to hold! Edgar Ætheling has just come here!"

✠✠✠

Later that day the king sent for me. Ordinarily, the king would not have included me in a discussion of this nature or magnitude. But as I was to have been his messenger to Edgar, and said there might be need again, he wanted me introduced to the man. For my part, I was eager to meet a man who had nearly been King of England—until William I usurped his crown.

I found Malcolm and Edgar seated together—a sign of Malcolm's regard for Edgar as family and a peer. Malcolm was telling Edgar of his children—they were, after all, brothers-in-law.

"Ahh, Baron, come! Brother Edgar, this is Baron Godric MacEuan, son of Margaret's companion, Lady Mildred, and my battle brother, Baron Euan MacDougal, now grown to be my best sheriff-at-large."

Edgar was Margaret's brother. He and Malcolm were long-acquainted, having had much contact around the time I was born. Indeed, had Edgar not fled to Scotland in 1069 to escape William after a rebellion he had led failed, and brought with him his mother, his sister Margaret and my mother as her lady's companion, my parents would never have met and I would not exist. I had not seen Edgar since I was four and did not remember him, yet he knew me—or pretended to.

"Baron! You were 'little Godric' the last time I saw you. Now you are nearly as huge as your father, but have your mother's color. You have turned out well, I think."

"Thank you, your grace. 'Tis most kind of you to remember me." Edgar was not a king—and not even a landed lord of late, thanks to Rufus—but he still rated the honorific, and in any case, the flattery would not go amiss. And I saw Malcolm wink his quick approval.

"Please remain, Baron—this will involve you, too, all too soon. Lord Edgar was telling us of Duke Robert."

Edgar nodded. "Let me repeat that Duke Robert has asked me to come as his emissary to seek the help of Alba against his brother William…"

Well, I thought, *here is a strange twist of events! I was about to fetch Edgar from Normandy to so we could persuade him to induce Robert to support us. Yet before I can even pack for the journey, Edgar appears as Robert's emissary to Malcolm to seek our help against Rufus. Angels and demons, indeed!*

Edgar was saying, "…we have heard that Rufus is mustering an army to invade Normandy and seize Robert's lands. Robert has sought the support of France's King Philip, who may or may not decide to intervene on Robert's side, as he worries this may induce William Rufus to contend for Philip's lands, also. Robert is levying every man from every lord owing him fealty, but fears he cannot match Rufus. So he entreats you to come to his aid."

Malcolm frowned at this and said, "If he wants me to send knights and men to save his Norman lands, I would be hard-pressed to spare them. I have forces enough to hold Alba against the Celts in the highlands, the Danes in Argyll and the Hebrides, the English to the south, and Danish raiders from Eire and Daneland. But to send a large portion of these into Normandy would invite all of these to exploit the opportunity and seize yet more Alban land. I cannot risk that."

Edgar shook his head. "Nay, brother, I told him as much, and he does not seek this. But we thought that if perhaps you were to venture south with raids in strength into the northern regions of England, Rufus would be forced to return home and defend his northern flank, and abandon this war upon Robert."

Malcolm was cautious in his answer, even though he and I had just discussed doing this very thing—the reason he wanted me to ride through Northumbria.

"It is true that Rufus has given me cause to retaliate. Last year, he began sending English into Cumbria to occupy it and usurp our rule there. I have not yet acted against him beyond protest in letters, and to have the baron here identify my subjects from his. I do need to retaliate, or he will judge me weak and press his advantage further. But in doing so, I do not want to provoke a war I cannot win."

Edgar waited patiently to learn what Malcolm would do. I had been studying him in turn, and judged him to be about 40 years old—elderly for persons in our time—fair in color, with flaxen hair, and clean shaven, an unusual fashion. His garb was elegant.

Then Malcolm seemed to make up his mind. "I planned to have the baron patrol in Northumbria as soon as the spring floods subside, to learn if Rufus has been engaged in the same land grant tricks there. And since Godric learned well how to scout opposition while on his pilgrimage to Jerusalem as squire with cousin Robert of Flanders, I need him to venture across the border into England and judge the strength of Rufus's garrisons. Baron, how soon can you go?"

"At any time, sire. The rivers are already shallow enough to ford this year," I replied.

"Good! Go as soon as you and your men are ready. You should be able to learn what we need to know and return by March. If Rufus has given me any cause, I am justified by Church and tradition to retaliate. And by May I can levy enough strength to mount a raid on his holdings in Northumbria that all England cannot halt while Rufus is abroad with his army. Brother, can you abide with us until Godric returns?"

"Alas, I cannot. I must return to tell Robert of the success of my emissary, giving him both news and hope. And Rufus will threaten the lands I still have there. But I will share with your clerk the secret script Robert and I share to write each other, so that you may write us in confidence, and we you."

"Fair enough—go. I will send you news when Godric returns. And Godric knows just the man to convey you back to France."

✠✠✠

I paid Thorsson another visit, this time with Edgar Ætheling, and paid well for a fast voyage to Normandy. It wasn't cheap, but it was Malcolm who was paying this time—with gold.

✠✠✠

A few days later, I set off on a patrol into Northumbria. My mission was to visit Malcolm's holdings, meet with the stewards, examine their accounts, and renew fealty to King Malcolm.

The region had been quiet of late, but that was about to change, for I found English barons living on Malcolm's estates, and knew it would intensify Malcolm's outrage against Rufus. I can still recall the history Father Thomas had taught me alongside the princes of Alba—it was their history and heritage, too, after all.

> *"Before he became King of Alba, King Malcolm was prince and heir to his father, King Duncan I. And when his father's cousin MacBeth killed Duncan in August of 1040 to seize the throne of Alba, Malcolm was just ten, too young to be a serious rival to MacBeth. So his mother placed him in care of her uncle, Siward, Earl of Northumbria, who raised him to knighthood there. Siward helped Malcolm defeat MacBeth at the Battle of Lumphanan in Aberdeenshire in 1057, and then Lulach, MacBeth's stepson and successor, to claim the crown of Alba in 1058. From Siward Malcolm inherited lands and titles in Northumbria, property that Malcolm owned before the Conqueror became the English king."*

It happened thus: one of the manors I visited—one the king had as his own personal property—was at Carham, located on the southern bank of the River Tweed a league west of the ford at Coldstream. The manor, the village and all the land around it were Malcolm's property, but he had not gotten revenue from it for two years, and Malcolm wanted to know why.

As usual, I led a patrol of a dozen mounted men-at-arms—and Cedric, of course. As we approached, riding the road through the village to the manor, there was a sudden flurry of excited agitation among the folk we passed. Now, there was nothing unusual about a small troop like ours riding the king's road, so the fact that it got the reaction it did made me take notice. And to my men I said, "Something's up. Be ready."

We rode into the manor yard. To a boy of about ten, I tossed a bronze half-penny and said, "Tell the steward that Baron Godric MacEuan, sheriff-at-large to King Malcolm, is here to speak with him." My list of the king's tenants told me the steward here was Gavin MacDomnall.

The lad gave me a wide-eyed look and ran into the manor. A few moments later, another appeared, a knight from his dress. The sword belt at his waist was hurriedly fastened, for he had not tied the customary hitch around the belt after fastening the buckle, and that led me to deduce our visit was both unexpected and unwelcome.

"I am lord here," he said. "Why are you on my land?"

"I am Baron Godric MacEuan, sheriff-at-large to King Malcolm of Alba. I am here to see the king's steward, Gavin MacDomnall. Who are you—and why do you claim to be lord of King Malcolm's manor?"

"I am Robert, Baron of Carham. MacDomnall is no longer here. This village and the land around it is mine, granted to me by Earl Robert de Mowbray of Northumbria for services to King William Rufus. This is Northumbria, and King Malcolm has no rule here."

I shook my head. "Nay! The King of Alba has title to this land. He owned it prior to the reigns of both King William I and II, and his ownership was reaffirmed by the Treaty of Abernethy. Did either your earl or king inform you that you usurp the personal property of the King of Alba?"

"Apparently they felt no need," Robert said with a smirk.

I was unimpressed. "What happened to MacDomnall?"

"He refused to acknowledge my title and surrender occupancy. Now he occupies a much smaller estate in the churchyard."

"Was he armed at the time?" I asked.

"I found him in my new bed, which he claimed he was too ill to leave. And when I compelled it, he was rude enough to bleed all over it and die."

Fury swept through me. For refusing to vacate, he had murdered a man sick in bed. I wanted to kill him then and there, but not by murder. A knight accused of wrongdoing had to be tried in a court or trial by combat. Mine was a mission of reconnaissance, not justice, and I still had much in Northumbria to scout. But I also had a duty to chivalry to challenge this wrong-doing, so I gave Robert a final choice.

"Baron Robert of Carham, by your own words before these men I denounce you here and now as murderer and thief. If you value your honor as a knight, draw that sword and face me here."

"I refuse," Robert sneered. "You have no authority here, Scotsman. And your accusation is an insult I must choose to ignore, since you outnumber me thirteen to one."

"No, just it is you and me. They will not interfere in a fight of honor."

"I refuse, nonetheless."

"Then my accusations stand. And with justification, to them I add coward. You will face me again, false knight," I said, "and Gavin MacDomnall will be avenged."

He seemed unimpressed, but I had no further time to waste on him. I turned my troop and we rode on. Robert's time would come—and soon.

✠✠✠

Robert of Carham was by no means the only baron on Malcolm's land. Cormac and I soon discovered that every estate Malcolm owned in Northumbria had been recently given to an English noble or knight; Rufus was that thorough. Malcolm was already inclined to harry the foresworn and the usurpers, confiscating stolen gains and driving them out. But when at the end of February Cormac and I returned to Dunfermline, and reported that English barons and knights had seized King Malcolm's personal estates and were living on them by right of deeds signed by King Rufus, everything changed again. The outright theft of his personal property drove Malcolm into a fury I had never before seen, and he ordered a general levy: All of our forces were to assemble at Dunfermline in the last week of April. All the English in Northumbria would soon feel Malcolm's wrath.

A boy from Leven found me in Cenachedne. He had been sent by Thorsson, just returned from hauling the English to Normandy. The boy told me Thorsson had something I wanted—news from Normandy. I gave the lad a silver penny, put him on a gelding behind me, and he rode behind me the two miles he had walked from the port.

Thorsson awaited me. "Thank'e for coming, sire. I thought you might want to know: William and Robert met at Caen and have come to terms."

"There was a fight at Caen?" I guessed.

Thorsson shook his head. "Duke Robert couldn't levy near enough men to match Rufus's numbers, and Rufus used gold to get other Norman nobles to join his side or stay out of the fight. So Robert settled instead. They met at Caen without a fight. Robert gave up some of his holdings in Normandy, and they came to terms."

I nodded, thinking it ended. "So is Rufus returning to England?"

Thorsson shook his head. "No. He has his entire army there, one he paid to fight for him. And gaining just a portion of Normandy isn't enough. Whatever Rufus has, it is never enough. Instead, he offered Robert concessions to join him on a campaign against their third brother, Henry Beauclerc, to take from him his holdings in Maine and Cotentin—land Robert sold to Henry earlier."

I shook my head. "Brother against brother. Could there be worse?"

Thorsson nodded. "They plan soon to march against Henry's castle at Mont St. Michel and put it to siege. They want to force Henry to surrender Cotentin to regain his freedom."

"So Rufus and Robert are friends now?"

"No, I think not. Many are beholden to Rufus, but none trust him as friend. And Rufus has no loyalties. Robert hates Rufus, but campaigning to perhaps regain some of what he lost is preferable to losing the rest. It will be Henry who loses. I wager he hates Rufus, too."

"I'll not disagree. Thorsson, I am grateful." I handed him silver.

He nodded and smiled. "Happy to do it, sire—as often as I can."

✠✠✠

Thorsson's news, when I delivered it, did not change Malcolm's plans a whit; rather, I think it reinforced them. Rufus had crossed the line twice—first in Cumbria, and now in Northumbria—with his expansionist provocations. Malcolm had good cause to think himself justified to retaliate, for both acts broke the status quo set long ago at Abernethy. Malcolm owed no fealty to Rufus, and since Rufus was still fully engaged in Normandy, the opportunity to harry Northumbria unopposed remained.

That Rufus and Robert had reconciled did not change this. Robert no longer played any part in the calculations. Malcolm could not expect support from Robert, but the fact that the two brothers were now besieging brother Henry meant Rufus would be engaged through the summer. For that long at least, Malcolm would be unopposed in taking revenge on Rufus.

✠✠✠

In Cenachedne we had had a good winter—neither terribly cold nor wet. The spring of 1091 brought us not only a bountiful birthing of calves, lambs and piglets throughout the barony, but also people. Following last year's wedding fair, my newlyweds did what all newlyweds do—a lot, it seemed. Since then, God and nature had brought to nearly every house, crofter's cot and hovel at least one newborn babe, and I had to send to manors and villages nearby for midwives, for we quickly overtired our own.

As soon as the midwives departed each birth, the new godparents would snatch up the swaddled infant and rush to our village chapel to christen the child—since many newborns often did not live long, we christened them quickly, to make up for a life cut short in this world by eternal happiness in the next. To keep up, our priest began baptizing newborns daily in batches at midday.

That year, the sight, sound and smell of babies was everywhere, by day and night. Every breeze carried the squalling of infants, as well as the scent of their irresponsibility. Wherever you looked, some woman had a babe stuck fast to a bared tit, sucking for dear life, even as she tended to her chores.

If babies bothered you, it was good advice to ride well clear of Cenachedne. But I did not mind, for once again I had people—happy, productive, thriving people—living on my land and helping make my bitter memories of what MacanFhirMhóir had done fade.

On my fifth attempt at a practical helepolis, we replaced the fixed box with a great box-shaped bucket, articulated by a heavy axle that acted as a bail. It looked marvelous.

When we loaded the bucket full of rocks and cocked the engine, the frame sagged under the great weight, which I calculated to be 4,000 pounds. Not much, just enough to make the combination of lower arm, bail, and bucket a bit too long. I did not realize that, though, until a moment later when I called "Loose!" and tugged the lanyard.

What a spectacular failure! The lower edge of the bucket struck the frame and burst it. Splinters and rocks flew everywhere. Only the fact that after our earlier mishaps, Cedric had insisted that we shelter behind protective mantlets spared us great injury.

As we surveyed the wreckage, Cedric sang impromptu lyrics to the tune of one of his little fife melodies:

"This thing is a mon-ster, I have to tell you.
Of ter-ri-ble pow-er, un-pre-dict-able, too!
Some stones they go straight up, while oth-ers go true.
I hope it don't kill us before we are through."

At that Carrick and I grinned, because we had to agree.

But only my reputation as a siege engine innovator was damaged, and my new title spread quickly and widely among Fife's commoners in compensation: "The Mad Baron of Cenachedne."

Oh, and that little tune, born then of mirth, soon grew into a siege weapon as fearsome as the machine that inspired it.

✠✠✠

FOUR

✠✠✠

On the first day of May, Malcolm marched south in command of an army of many hundreds of knights and thousands of men-at-arms and yeoman foot-soldiers, perhaps five thousand of us in all. I had command of Malcolm's scouts. On my advice Malcolm adopted the same seven-leagues-a-day pace that served so well Count Robert of Flanders's pilgrimage to Jerusalem. If you could travel thousands of miles at that pace, a few hundred would not trouble us.

Our line of march went by way of Stirling Bridge the first day, then southeast past Edinburgh the third day—where we left the queen (and Lady Aleine!) safe in Edinburgh Castle—and on through Lothian and the Borders, reaching Oxton on the fourth day and Carham the afternoon of the fifth. From my earlier patrol, I knew of a ford a half-mile west of Carham, and it was there we headed. We needed the ford to cross the Tweed into Northumbria. And I had a grudge to settle.

We intended to encamp that night at Carham, the king to stay in his own manor there, and as Malcolm and his lords rode into the manor yard, I hailed him and introduced a bedraggled knight, his hands trussed.

"Your Grace, I have the honor of presenting to you Baron Robert of Carham, who claims title as lord of Carham to your estate here. He wishes to protest your claim to the property, on the grounds that he holds title to it from King Rufus."

Malcolm dismounted and strode over to stare into the man's eyes. "Wrong. I own Carham from my youth, well before Rufus became king, and his crown grants him no rights to the property of another king. Rufus had no right to deed it to another; in this case, you."

I went on. "Baron Robert has another matter to answer for—the death of your steward, Gavin MacDomnall. In the presence of the dozen men of my patrol, he stated that MacDomnall refused to surrender your manor from his sickbed, so he killed him for it."

Malcolm's gaze was steely. "Is this true, Baron?"

There was a stubborn outrage in Robert's eyes, but fear as well, in acknowledgment of the truth. His mouth opened and closed twice, but he said nothing.

I said, "I believe Baron Robert would prefer trial by combat to hanging. I volunteer to serve Your Grace in that capacity—I have pledged to avenge MacDomnall."

"Fine with me," said the king. "Your choice to refuse, Baron."

Robert finally found his voice but his words did not serve him well. "I demand you take up this matter with King William! If he deeded the land to me in error, that wasn't my doing."

Malcolm shook his head and smiled. "Take up the false deed with William, I will. But this trial is for the death of my steward, who was under my protection as lord. For that you will answer now. Combat or hanging—choose!"

"I choose combat," Robert croaked, his throat gone dry.

"Very well. Half an hour from now, here in the courtyard. Page! Fetch my chaplain."

✠✠✠

Shriven of our sins and dressed for battle, Robert and I faced each other in a thirty-foot circle swept clean. Around it, an honor guard of Scottish nobles and knights stood impassively, blades naked and shouldered—a guard against treachery.

Robert and I wore full mail and helm, and fought with shield and sword. Robert was my height, but nowhere near as well-muscled—my reward for years of pounding yellow-hot iron.

The king himself, with bared blade—the blade I made for him—acted as judge. "This is a trial by combat to the death. No quarter will be asked or given. May God Himself defend the right, and have mercy upon the wrong. Begin!"

Robert was strong and well-trained, I'll give him that. He was cunning as well, and quick. He had a fair chance, for it was a fair fight.

But he was in the wrong, and I the right. We both knew it, and God did, too. And an instant later, when I parried his blade with my shield and stabbed for his face, he died with my sword through his left eye.

And at sunset that night, I visited the churchyard at Carham and prayed there for his soul, and that of Gavin MacDomnall.

✠✠✠

Now, the English had garrisons at Bamburgh and New Castle, but those forces were nowhere near large enough to challenge us, separately or combined. Instead, the king entrusted a quarter of his forces, more than one thousand knights and fighting men to his son, Prince Edward, to act as a flanking force between the garrisons and Malcolm's army. It was Edward's first major command, and he was proud to be entrusted with the responsibility.

Now, decades ago, when Northumbria—or Northumberland, as the English call it—was an earldom contested by both Scotland and England, the Conqueror brought his army through here and for months laid waste to everything, sparing not the innocents as he punished the rebellious nobles resisting his rule. He burned the villages and massacred everyone in them, burned their crops, slaughtered or took away the animals, and left those survivors he could not catch to starve. Many of these were forced to eat the dead in order not to perish. William called it "harrying the North." The survivors called it murder.

In the aftermath, with no one left to resist, William had appointed his own Norman earls and high nobles over the populace, and after the Treaty of Abernethy, Northumbria was ruled by England. But only those lords were Norman and English; the people they ruled were still Northumbrians with Scottish and Danish ancestors.

Malcolm was certain that the people of Northumbria had no love of their Norman masters, and would gladly welcome their departure. As he saw it, that was our task here and now.

So unlike the Conqueror, we did not harry the land—only the Norman English overlords. With the screening force under Edward in place, Malcolm divided the rest of us into companies, and we spread out to find Rufus's barons and knights and harry them—particularly those on Malcolm's estates. Them we did not kill—we took them as prisoners for ransom. But we confiscated their wealth, collected their stores to feed the army, gave half their animals to their populace, and took the rest to feed our men.

From the Tweed to Durham we purged the land. Only the castles at Bamburgh and New Castle we spared. For my king and my own professional curiosity, I scouted each of them.

Bamburgh castle, a great beast of stone and timber buildings and palisades—where stone was steadily replacing timber, section by section—was enormous and very strong. Indeed, Rufus himself later besieged it and could not take it. But with most of its garrison gone off to fight in Normandy, it posed small threat to us, so we left it alone, an impotent stronghold filled with English who would in time have to surrender or starve. And they did not come out to fight us, though that option was always theirs.

New Castle was a motte-and-bailey fortification Robert Curthose built to control and protect the Great North Road bridge across the River Tyne in 1080. There, a strong timber palisade surrounded an earthen mound, a timber tower built atop it to provide a strong fighting platform. On my earlier scouting trip in February I discovered that Rufus was raising a new structure there, building a square stone tower inside the palisade. Already it was tree stories tall and strongly built. Only my new engine might be able to conquer it—*if* ever I could get it to throw as I thought it could.

May passed, then June and much of July. Herds of animals and prisoners were sent north under guard while we marched south through Northumbria. Our treasure train grew fat as the wealth confiscated from the barons was brought in.

Our objective was Durham, southernmost city in Northumbria, and we reassembled our army as we approached it in preparation to take the city. But as we encamped outside the town of Chester-Le-Street just five miles north of Durham, in the last days of July, my scouts reported disturbing news. At my instructions, they had found a ship captain at the shipyard near Jarrow upon the Tyne with news.

I rode with them the five miles to Jarrow to meet the man and hear his news myself. It was more than worth the pound of silver he asked for it. Then we raced back to report our news to the king, who promptly called a council of war.

Malcolm opened the assembly of warlords. "My lords, our chief of scouts, Baron Godric, has news you all must hear. And then we must decide on our next course of action. Baron, tell us your news."

"My lords," I began, "I have just heard a reliable report from a Dane ship captain just put into Jarrow for repairs. He told me that he carried a company of English troops back to England from Normandy on the 22nd of July. From those soldiers he heard that King Rufus had intended to fight Duke Robert Curthose at Caen in February, but the two met and after Robert gave up some of his holdings in Normandy, the two made a treaty of peace. Then the two joined forces to campaign against their brother Henry, and lay siege to him in his stronghold at Mont St. Michel. After fifteen days Henry surrendered, gave up Cotentin and was allowed to go free into France. So Rufus and Robert returned to Caen to tend to regional business until 21 July, when they learned we had invaded Northumbria. At that news, Rufus rushed home with his army intent on saving Northumbria. And now Rufus is in England, reassembling his army and preparing to march north against us."

That news did not sit well with anyone. A siege of Durham was out of the question, and all prospect of keeping our territorial gains in Northumbria now depended on facing a much larger English army on soil they thought English, and overwhelmingly defeating them.

In the discussion that ensued, the lords from Cumbria and Northumbria—chiefly those who had lost lands to the English—declared that we should not tolerate continued English usurpation, and urged a fight. Others, those from the northern regions of Alba, thought we should retreat for the present, and await another opportunity to fight with better advantage on another day. Their fear was that since we were not fighting on our home ground and suffered defeat, there was nothing else in Alba to prevent Rufus from seizing the entire kingdom.

In the end, Malcolm declared that retreat was wiser than risking all in a head-to-head battle with a larger English army. We might well have won, for we Scots always outfight Englishmen when we are in the right. But it was Malcolm's kingdom and his decision, and I cannot fault his judgment.

So we retreated north again and harried the remaining English overlords we could find, rounding them up, confiscating their moveable wealth, and taking many with us as prisoners for ransom. By August we were home—in time for the harvest.

✠✠✠

Rufus was finally ready to march north in August. He brought a huge army against us by land up the Great Coast Road and sent a fleet of fifty ships along the coast, carrying the army's food stores, to rendezvous and offload food supplies as they were needed. This time, he intended to invade Alba and conquer it.

The news of their coming reached us late. The first I knew of it was when I got an urgent summons from the king.

"Baron, King Rufus marches north at the head of an army and intends to conquer Alba! I must call up the army to oppose them and we urgently need you to buy us time. Take your mounted scouts south. Lay waste to all in the land in their path. Burn the bridges, slow their advance, weaken their army, and starve them as best you can. They chose this late season so they could feed themselves from our herds and harvest. I would have them faint with hunger when we fight them, if it be possible."

"Aye, sire! We will do our best to make their way Hell on Earth!"

So I took a well-mounted force and raced south across Northumbria clear to Durham, where I discovered the van of the approaching English army on 10 September. Ahead of them we withdrew north, ravaging the land along their route, staying—sometimes barely—just ahead of their mounted horsemen.

Barns and manors filled with harvested grain I burned. With animal carcasses, of which we created a sudden glut, I fouled ponds, waterholes, and streams. Every loyal Scottish landowner and churl I warned to flee.

"There is an English army close on our heels. Go! Kill or burn what you cannot move, then take all the livestock you can and drive them north and west, out of English reach."

"But milord! We've only just harvested! Can it not be saved?"

I shook my head. "No! If you leave it, it will fill English bellies, not yours, and just make it easier for them to kill you! Burn it or drive it off! And hurry! You have little time left!"

They did not like it, those Scots, losing a year's work and substance like that. But neither they—nor we—could save it for them, and they were about to lose it all to the English anyway. Depriving the enemy of all that ill-gotten sustenance was much to be preferred.

And as I scorched the land of food the English hoped for, God fought for us at sea. On September 29th at Coquet Island, seven leagues north of the Tynemouth, He confused Rufus's fleet with fog and rough seas, so that the captains wrecked their ships, running them upon rocks or colliding with each other, drowning their crews and driving the wrecks aground. The commoners, in hatred of their Norman overlords, came down in droves to the shore then and looted the cargoes, taking all away. And they drove the English bastards who made it ashore back into the sea.

To this day I take considerable pride in the job we did. Without the food the fleet carried, the English march slowed considerably, because the army had to hunt for enough to eat, and ultimately they were forced to subsist on burned grain, spoiled meat and fouled water, which loosened their bowels, and the bellyache and diarrhea slowed them more. I tell you, you could smell that army from five miles off, and theirs was not the scent of lavender.

The weather, too, grew cold and stormy, as winter came upon us early. This was never the season for war. We were discomforted, but we could eat. The English had no such luck and suffered much the worse.

But Rufus would not be thwarted and pressed on without regard for his men, marching into Alba all the way to the southern shore of the Firth of Forth. There in mid-October Malcolm confronted him, with our entire army assembled for battle against an enemy larger than ours but weakened by sickness, starvation, and cold.

We were fighting for our homes and families, the English solely for Rufus's greed. We would have slaughtered them.

Dear God! How I wish now we had!

✠✠✠

The night before we fought, though, emissaries came to Malcolm urging mediation rather than war. Under flag of truce came Duke Robert Curthose of Normandy, Rufus's brother, together with Edgar Ætheling, a man Rufus hated so much he had banished him from both England and Normandy. I remember marveling at his resourceful resilience.

I was there with the war council and witnessed the negotiations. The discussions were too long and tedious to recount here, but

Robert and Edgar listened carefully as Malcolm recited a long list of grievances against Rufus, and demanded full restoration of all the lands Rufus had usurped in Cumbria and Northumbria.

The most memorable moment came when Malcolm said this: "I vow here and now to all of you, and to God Himself, that I will have justice, even if I have to cut my way single-handed through the entire English army to get it. I owe King William no fealty, so if he will have it from me, it will be only that which I gave his father, and only when he has pledged his sacred honor to respect both my property and my rights as King of Alba!"

Under the same white banner, Robert and Edgar rode back to Rufus, relaying Malcolm's words and Malcolm's demands. Back and forth they rode, through the night and well into the day that followed, trying to stop a war.

In the final event, the two men managed to negotiate agreement between the two monarchs. In return for making the same pledge of personal fealty that Malcolm had given William the Conqueror at Abernethy in 1072—this time to William Rufus—Rufus promised to honor all the same land grants, titles and promises the Conqueror had made Malcolm. In particular, Rufus pledged to respect Malcolm's kingship over Cumbria and his ownership of the twelve villages and manors in Northumbria that Malcolm had long owned. Malcolm agreed to give Rufus a king's oath of fealty and pay Rufus the traditional payment of twelve marks of gold annually for the twelve villages.

With that, in the presence of the two armies, and before the gathered nobles of both kingdoms, Malcolm and Rufus met face to face, and Malcolm made the traditional oath of fealty to Rufus that kings do. The two kings pledged friendship and then parted, to march their armies home again without further bloodshed.

Now, to this day, I regret that we parted in peace and did not fight then, but not for the reason you may think. Yes, we had our advantage at last, with armies of similar strength after Rufus lost some men at sea and I weakened the rest with starvation and disease. We would have slaughtered them, for we were in the right and the English knew it—for they only fought to serve their king's avarice while we fought on our land for our homes.

But the real reason we should have fought was because of what happened thereafter. For as you might expect by now, that greedy and treacherous little bastard Rufus reneged. I think he made his pledges then to avoid a fight he realized he could not win, yet still got some advantage over Malcolm with the oath. For after he was safely home, he refused to honor the terms he swore to keep.

And so, the peace did not last.

✠✠✠

During that long night of negotiation, I led the Scottish escort to the mediators, and had opportunity to meet and talk with Duke Robert, the nephew of my old patron, Count Robert of Flanders, and first cousin to his son, Robert II. He and I chatted about Flanders as we rode. Knowing of his battles against Rufus to keep his inheritance of Normandy, I asked him why he acted now to Rufus's benefit. His answer was telling.

"Baron, it is true I have little love for William, the little prick. He is greedy and ruthless and does not deserve to wear a crown, though he is in truth a better king than I would be. Yes, I act on behalf of my brother, but I do not do this for him. I do it to spare the lives of my countrymen and yours, all the men who will die tomorrow…" Seeing the faint glow in the east that gave lie to his words, he corrected himself: "…no, today—to settle a personal grievance between two kings, when they really should battle it out themselves in single combat. And between us, if they did, I would cheer when Malcolm killed the little turd."

With that, I found I liked Duke Robert very much!

✠✠✠

Duke Robert and Edgar Ætheling did not immediately return to England with Rufus, but lingered a few weeks in Dunfermline to visit with their kinswoman, Queen Margaret, and her family. And a chance event occurred then that changed my future, making all that followed possible.

During a dinner among them, I learned later that Robert had asked Malcolm about me and Malcolm told Robert and Edgar the story of my conquest of Dunnottar to defeat MacanFhirMhóir. Both men became very interested in the siege engines I had used, and expressed a desire to see them. Malcolm, too, had never seen them in action, so a day later, Malcolm asked me to demonstrate them a week hence.

When a king asks, the only answer is, "Aye, sire!" So I begged leave then and rode to Cenachedne, for I had much to do!

✠✠✠

The purpose for which the king and his guests would visit Cenachedne might have been to them a casual entertainment, but to us at Cenachedne, it was a huge event and a rare opportunity as well, one we would not waste. Not since Queen Margaret had surprised us by visiting Andrew's manor—now mine—five years earlier while trying to locate my poor mother had royalty visited the area. No one could recall if ever the king had even passed through the village. Now he would spend a day or more!

My big concern was weather, so I visited the priest at our village chapel—our new church was rising, but lacked both walls and roof as yet—and made a substantial offering for Masses to invoke the help of St. Kenneth, our patron, for three days of good weather before and during the king's visit. Fine weather was rare at any time, but good weather in Fife in late October would need a miracle!

I notified all my people of the pending visit and my intentions, and put the whole village to work tidying all. Muck was shoveled from the streets into the ditches. Wreathes decorated doors. Folk wore new-washed garb, and we set up a market fair, one not unlike our wedding fair, beside the demonstration grounds to take advantage of the rare mercantile opportunity. After all, when a king visits, many accompany him, and all would want food and drink.

Carrick and his smiths set up a booth to sell their best weapons, mail and other ironwork—and did brisk business, I later learned.

My onager and ballista had lain disassembled in storage for the two years since Dunnottar, so I was grateful the king had given me a week to get them assembled and ready. Fortunately, knowing mice would otherwise chew to bits the leathern skeins that powered both machines, I had stored them in sealed barrels, which preserved them quite well, so it did not take long to pull out all the timbers and reassemble the machines—after all, I designed them so I could do just that.

In addition to these, I had built a scorpio—a big, very powerful crossbow—mounted on a pedestal with an elevation pivot and a full-circle swivel to make it easy to point and shoot accurately. I truly loved shooting it, and drawing upon my skill as an archer, I found I could hit targets at its full range, which approached 300 yards. I certainly wanted to demonstrate it.

From storage I pulled mantlets, chevaux-de-frise, caltrops, gabion baskets, and so on, and from their chest I extracted my collection of miniature engines to display on a table.

My sixth helepolis was nearly ready. We put some hurried effort into finishing it. I did not have a suitable seasoned timber of the length I wanted for the throwing arm, so I was forced to use a shorter one taken from one of its predecessors. I knew I wouldn't get the power the right arm would give me, but it would throw well enough to impress anyone new to such machines.

I had an impressive array of engines to demonstrate, and wanted to do that well, so I had targets similar to those Demetrius used in Constantinople—panels of cloth held upright by poles and painted with images of military targets: charging knights, foot soldiers, archers, castle gates and other engines. I had built a wooden panel to serve as a target like a palisade or gate, and also a squad of strawmen on poles. These we set up in the pasture beside the market fair ground. A ruined croft in the center of the pasture would become our chief target. On it we hurriedly put a lattice of poles covered with sailcloth and sheaves of straw as a makeshift roof.

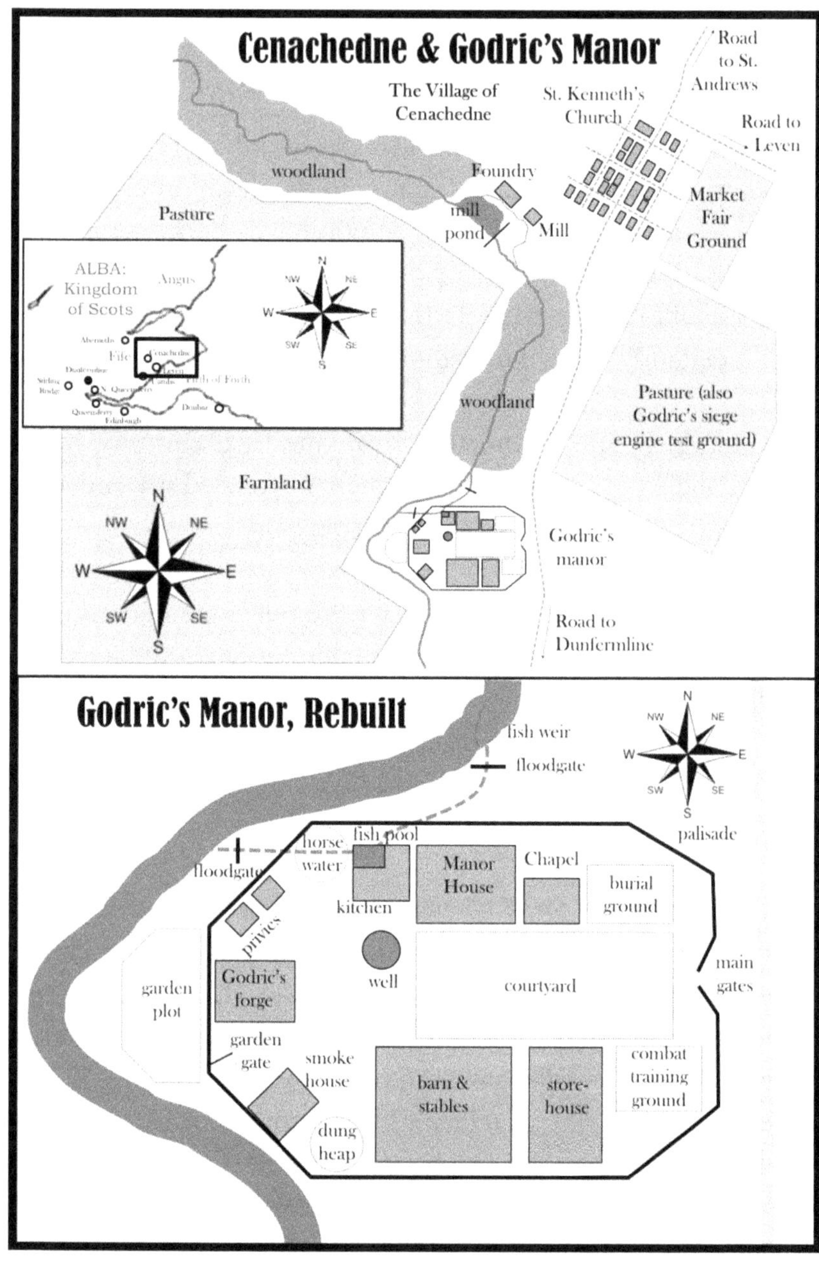

Figure 3: Cenachedne & Godric's Manor, Rebuilt

And behold! Whether it was the earnest efforts of our good priest, the affection St. Kenneth had for us, or the favor God had for King Malcolm, the miracle I hoped for came to pass. For three days, the skies cleared, and the low sun shone bright on Cenachedne!

✠✠✠

King Malcolm brought a sizeable party, for many in his court had heard of the demonstration, and there was much curiosity among his sons and military men. They in turn brought their squires and pages, and since the weather was fair, a party of ladies came as well, welcoming the rare outing. These included Lady Aleine and the queen herself on her first visit to Aleine's new home.

At my suggestion the royal party arrived the night before. I put the entire manor at their disposal, with the monarchs in my room, the princes and lords in the upper hall, and the squires and pages in the undercroft. For my own folk I had the barn emptied and swept, fires built in circular hearths in the middle for warmth and cooking—cozy enough for two nights and a day. Aleine and I retreated to the loft in my forge, which had been my home when I was a slave under Carrick, and had since been made comfortable as my personal hideaway.

For the first time ever, my stable was over-full with fine horses. Only my own warhorse, CiùinLùth, kept his usual stall—the rest had two nights under an awning.

This was an inaugural event for my manor, now largely finished inside, and all newly rebuilt. At the queen's request, I took the royals on a tour of the manor. Aleine had told her of my unique innovations, and Margaret wanted to see them for herself.

I can truly say that they were stunned and amused—and perhaps a little envious—to see me pull handsome trout from the fish pond in the kitchen with a dip net. “By God, I should have such as this for myself!” said Malcolm.

We had a splendid feast that night. I had an entire cow and hog roasted as meat. We had bread and cakes made with fine-ground flour from my new mill. My smoked trout was in much demand. There were tarts of apples and honey, and we drank ale and cider that my miller and brewer had produced.

And for those who were willing to try it, there was my first offering of Anselm’s spirit, made of fermented grain cooked in the strange little copper pot I had made to match his. It tasted different, because I had to use barley rather than his wheat, but it tasted quite well, and proved most popular with my male guests.

“Dear God, what is this?” cried Duke Robert, after choking and sputtering on his first swallow.

“Sire, we call it ‘water of life’—‘aqua vitae’ in Latin, and in our Gaelic, ‘Uisge beatha’. A priest in Count Robert of Flanders’s household taught me how to make it.”

“Whew! ‘Whisky beta’, you say?” Robert mispronounced it. “That priest should be burned alive, or sainted—I cannot decide which. Is there more?”

I just grinned and poured.

✠✠✠

The next morn, following a breakfast of oat porridge, smoked trout, hearty bread with good Scottish butter and honey, apples, and ale or small beer, I led the royal party through our new mill and foundry, both built beside the stream and powered by flowing water.

In the mill, a water wheel drove the millstones—two set vertically with one turned by the wheel and the other stationary. Grain fed by a chute into the center of the fixed stone was sheared and then powdered by grooves cross-cut in the stones. The meal and flour emerged at the edges and fell into a collection trough below it. It wasn't ideal, but we were too busy rebuilding the village to build the new cogs needed to set the mill wheels flat; but those would come soon, and it was still better than the previous mill MacanFhirMhóir had burned, because now we didn't need the wind to blow to mill grain, we just needed water from the millpond.

Carrick's foundry was even more impressive. A water wheel there turned a shaft bearing a wheel-and-belt. This powered a cam to pump the forge bellows, and another cam to lever up a heavy trip hammer above a stout anvil. With these we could heat iron yellow-hot, hammer in the charcoal that made it into good steel, and hammer-weld interleaved hard and soft iron billets that made our swords strong but flexible—crucial to make them reliable and effective in combat. And my metal-shearing machine made cutting plate for brigandines no chore at all.

The king had never seen such things, and was most impressed with the foundry, its products and the way we had harnessed water to make things work. The queen loved our clean streets, and wanted to know how and why they stayed clean. I told her that anyone caught tossing waste or night soil into the streets instead of the ditches spent a week shoveling the dung into the ditches, where rainwater washed it off into a pond to settle. And Earl Causantín voiced astonishment at how quickly we had been able to rebuild a community filled with such evident accord.

"Sire, I'm sure you regard marriage good for families. And it is good families that make for civil society."

It was Queen Margaret who answered for all, saying, "Amen!"

✠✠✠

Then it was on to the reason for the visit: the demonstration of my siege engines. I led the royal party to the pasture. There we had chairs set under an awning where they could rest and see all. I had asked my old friend Hamish to captain the onager crew, and squire Cedric the ballista. I would explain the logical target and use of each weapon, narrate and coordinate our actions, shoot the scorpio, and captain the new helepolis. Unbeknownst to the royal party we had rehearsed the demonstration the previous day before they arrived and knew just where and how to hit our targets. I did not want this to go badly!

I told them we would demonstrate each machine separately, and then fight a planned joint action against a mock attack. We began with the ballista and I was inwardly most thankful when Cedric—with his first bolt armed with a fire cage—succeeded to set alight the wooden target standing in for palisade and gate. Then he shot two bolts at—no, completely through—the cottage, and took down three strawmen with a single bolt.

With the powerful scorpio I picked off horsemen and archer targets at a range well beyond that of ordinary bows and crossbows.

The onager was next. On his first attempt Hamish was short, but after quickly raising the front of the machine with wedges, his second cast, a clay pot filled with burning Danish tar, set the cottage roof ablaze. Then he stove in the burning roof completely with three more boulders.

Finally it was time to throw with the helepolis. We had thrown several times the day before, and I was edified to see that this machine would hold together and throw properly. I realized it really wasn't much more powerful than the onager—my fear that the throwing arm was too short was confirmed. For that reason we were only throwing at targets 100 yards out. But the big bastard was impressive all the same: On the release command the huge counterweight dropped, the throwing arm whipped forward in a vicious arc, and the sling bearing the boulder arced high as just a blur. And though my onlookers were royal, they reacted just as the common folk did—with excitement and elation.

My first cast bounced a stone to the right side of the cottage, as I had told them it would, so they could see the big projectile bounce repeatedly and unstoppably out to 200 yards. Then we adjusted the point of aim, and the second throw hammered a hole a man could walk through completely though the cottage. The third boulder went through the exact same hole without touching the cottage. And that drew real astonishment from my guests—for accuracy was the real strength of the weapon, after all. But to prove its power, I then flattened the ruin with two more throws, one toward each end of the structure. And each time it threw, it drew cheers from the gallery of nobles and the crowd of servants and commoners gathered on either side, just alike.

And then together the machine crews fought the mock attack. The onager cast bushels of fist-sized stones at horsemen and archers, taking most of them down with several rapid throws. The ballista and scorpio killed the enemy commanders far behind the attack. And one just throw from the helepolis blasted a great furrow through ten ranks of the oncoming footsoldiers.

As I led Hamish, Cedric and my crews back from the pasture, we were greeted by a most unusual reaction. The king stood, looked around and addressed all, saying, "Most glad am I that you fight for us—and not against us!" Then he applauded, and the others took their cue, breaking into applause and cheers.

We bowed our thanks and pleasure, and I said a quick internal prayer of thanks, for it could hardly have gone better. I tossed a purse of silver to my men and waved them dismissed. Grinning widely, with quick bows they scurried off to spend some on ale.

The royals adjourned then to a tent for refreshment. Both the king and Duke Robert wanted to shoot the scorpio, so we walked down to it, and Cedric and I crewed for them as they shot bolts for an hour, both performing respectably, I must say. Neither could hit at long range, though, and I took much satisfaction from their regard when they realized the skill they found it took.

✠✠✠

After the demonstration, Carrick's booth was swarmed by nobles and fighting men, all keen to spend what they could afford on our blades and plate. Some nobles returned to the mill and foundry to learn what they could for their own manors and villages.

Both King Malcolm and Duke Robert kept me busy answering questions about how my engines were built, how they operated, and how they could best be used. And it was there and then my reputation as a siege master was first born.

And more than any other, this event shaped my future, for by it Duke Robert and I became known to each other and friends, as best baron can be with duke—although in each other we saw only the kindred soul of another fighting man. But more importantly, the duke discovered that I possessed an uncommon expertise in the warfare of sieges, and that skill he would call upon more than once in the years to come. And it was he who later nominated me to my role in the great commission we would together undertake: Siege Master for the Recovery of Jerusalem!

The day was largely spent. It being a full day's ride between Dunfermline and Cenachedne, I urged the royal party to spend another night with us and ride fresh in the morning. They consented, and we had another most enjoyable eve. We feasted again, there was music and dance, and the talk and merriment was lively. Both monarchs were most pleased with us, and said so. The king praised my martial innovations, the queen my care for my people and our civic improvements. Aleine and her family could not have been happier.

✠✠✠

From this visit my barony benefited hugely, the commerce alone like nothing they had ever seen. Word of our civic innovations spread among the minor nobles and brought many others to see what we had done. That recognition and pride of place, more than anything, built bonds among my folk, making us a community.

During the visit Carrick sold nearly every blade he had, and soon had orders for swords from lords and knights from every part of the kingdom. With his royal appointment as the Master of the Bladesmiths' Guild, Carrick's reputation was made and he truly came into his own. Equipped with good apprentices, better forges and water-driven tools, he and his smiths began producing steel blades and plate better than any ever yet seen. I taught him how to make Damascus steel, but lacking Martun's powder and unable to guess what its secret was, our steel was never quite that good. Reluctantly we gave up on it and reverted to what we knew. But from the Damascene steel billets I brought home, we made nearly 100 swords, each worth a half-pound of gold apiece.

✠✠✠

The Christmas of 1091 was more joyful than any we had yet known. My barony had recovered, and it was thriving. My people were prospering and happy with their rebuilt lives. My manor was rebuilt also, not only comfortable but—as my royal guests had said—as nice as, and in some ways better than, a palace. Carrick had his own house now, sited close by in the village, and Alice, with now both cook and serving girl to help keep it, was thrilled at her good fortune. She delighted in having us come there to dine with them and at our invitations to come feast in the manor. For us, life was truly good.

And so, it could not last.

✠✠✠

FIVE

✠✠✠

Baron though I am, I did not look it. I was stripped to boots and breeks, drenched in sweat and laboring hard as a few chosen men and I wrestled another large boulder into the sling on the tray. The day was uncharacteristically warm for spring of 1092, and we had been hard at it all morning.

With the sling in place and the sling's tail-hook on the release pin, we were once again ready, so I called for a rest. Now the fun and the danger were about to repeat, and it was best if we had all recovered first. I drank deep of a huge tankard of ale and passed it around.

"Wagers, anyone?" I asked.

Carrick squinted at the target, a mud-and-wattle hovel two hundred yards downrange. The building was a ruin, with a thatched roof that was falling in, but that was how it had been when we began. So far the structure was untouched. "This bastard is much more powerful than yer onager," Carrick said. "Even with the bigger stone, we'll overthrow again. And get in the way of the arm, counterweight, or boulder, and it'll crush every bone hit!"

Cedric shook his head. "This stone is double the weight of the one we threw too far. I think we'll be short."

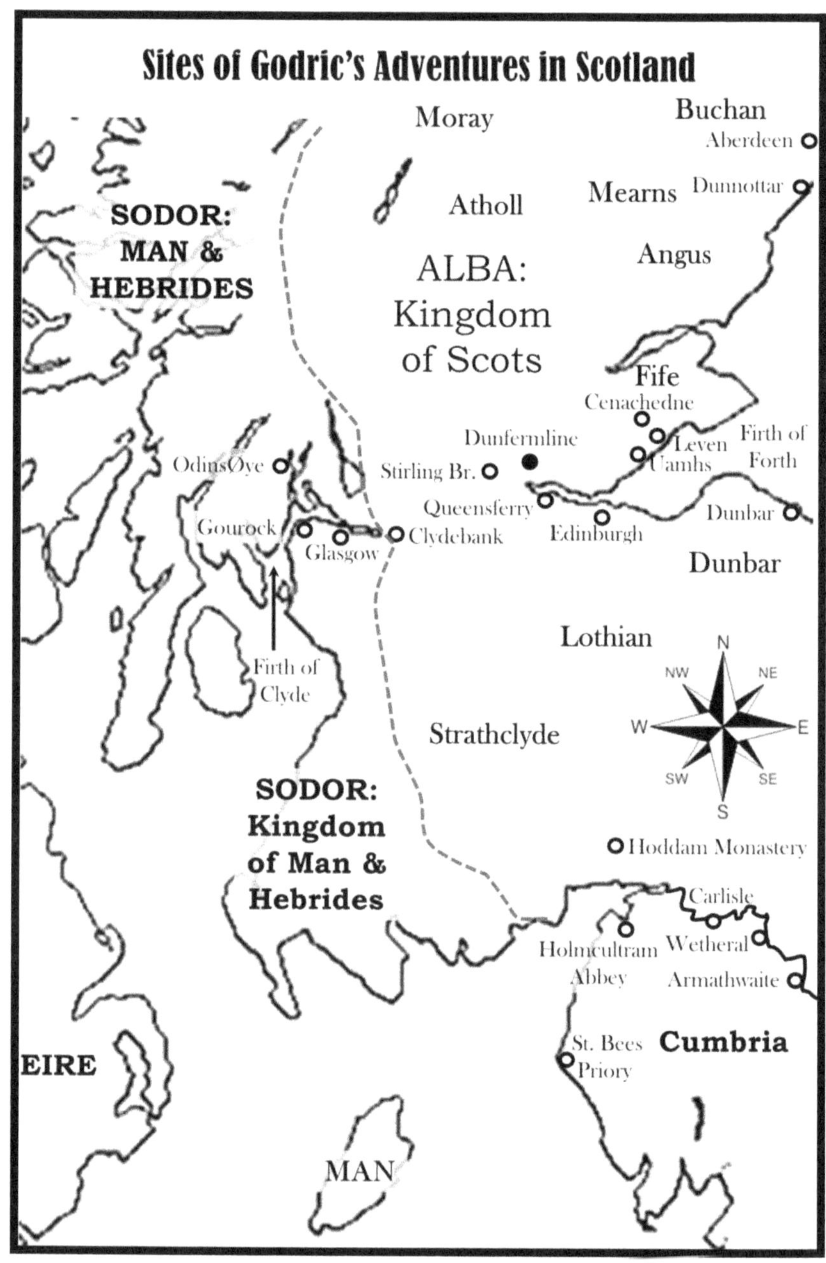

Figure 4: Sites of Godric's adventures in Scotland

Using a charred stick, I made a calculation and a notation in my little codex. I had been keeping track and had my own ideas.

"This one should hit," I said.

I squinted along the sighting sticks on the machine's frame and again verified that the aim was straight. "Right! The release is set. Everyone back! Cedric, remove the loading safety strap. Good! All clear?"

"Aye!" resounded three times, a correct count. All were ready and safe.

The cluster of gaping onlookers, watching from afar, exchanged eager looks as the count began again.

"Release in three… two… one… Loose!" I sharply tugged the release lanyard, and once again the great arm began its upward swing, pulled by the great box of stones. Underneath, the sling was snatched backward and then up, its cargo accelerating into a blur as the arm whirled it into the air in a great overhand arc.

As the sling passed above the release pin, the sling's tail-hook pulled free and the sling opened, releasing its boulder to fly free in a great curve up and forward toward the hovel. Then it began to plunge.

With a great crash, the stone slammed into the front wall of the hovel. A cloud of dust and splintered wattle-sticks exploded in all directions. The boulder bounced, and then burst through the back wall as well, leaving a hole large enough for a mounted knight to ride clear through the building.

"Yah-hah!" cheered both crew and onlookers.

"Well, damn me if we didn't hit it!" said Carrick, disbelieving his own eyes. "Why now?"

I said, "I needed all those earlier throws to calculate how far this beast could throw stones of given weights. Once I had that knowledge, I could choose the right weight for the distance."

"So that's why you used the scales to weigh and sort all these rocks. How do you plan to use all these paint colors?"

"We weighed and sorted them to find the right stones for a given range. If nothing else is changed, then smaller stones go farther and stones of the same weight will hit in the same spot again and again. Once we weigh the stones, we paint those of the same weight the same color, so we can quickly find a rock of the right weight for a given range. Here we can take our time, but in a siege we cannot, so we will weigh and then paint the stones beforehand. Red for a hundred-weight, yellow for fifty pounds, blue for twenty, and so on."

"It's a wicked kind of magic you do, son, with your figures and your scales... but I have to admit it is almighty powerful." Carrick shook his huge, shaggy head and grinned. "And I certainly wouldn't want to be trapped inside fortress walls while you had this thing nearby, and a big pile of these damned stones!"

I grinned back. I had been Carrick's apprentice too many years, helping the older man pound steel into tools and blades, to take any offense from familiarity. To me, Carrick would always be my second father. Besides, the man had a point: it was a wicked kind of magic, and I was proud to have mastered it.

Carrick pointed at the machine. "Well, that was first hit! What do you name it?"

I stepped onto the tray and poured the rest of the ale from the tankard on the great box of stones that formed the counterweight.

"In honor of Carrick the Eloquent, I name thee *Bone-Crusher*!"

✠✠✠

We were still throwing stones, pounding flat the remains of the hovel, when a messenger found me. The twelve-year-old page from King Malcolm had first stopped at my manor to inquire where to find the baron.

"My Lord Godric, the king requires your earliest attendance upon him! There is a matter his sheriff-at-large must deal with on the western borderlands, and it cannot wait!"

"And did his grace say what that matter might be?" I asked.

"Nay, sire, he did not. He just ordered me to find and summon you to Dunfermline."

"Well, thank you for riding so far on a warm day, lad. I will attend the king this evening. Climb down, eat, and have something cool and wet to drink."

The lad hesitated, no doubt under orders to come straight back. But my squire Cedric spoke. "Would you disobey the sheriff-at-large, boy? Besides, your horse needs rest and water. Eat something, boy, while I water the beast."

Grateful, the boy dismounted. I went to the stream nearby to wash off the sweat, and as the messenger wolfed down bread and mutton, he eyed the engine.

A square base of heavy timbers, reinforced by crossbeams between opposite corners, formed its base. From this, six timbers rose to form two tripods aligned with one of the diagonals to support a stout axle bearing a long vertical arm that reached twenty feet skyward. Its lower end suspended a rectangular wooden bucket filled with 5,000 pounds of rocks. Beneath it, a long wooden tray ran between the tripods along the diagonal.

From an eye on the upper end of the arm hung a leathern hawser, which widened into a mesh sling at the middle and tapered back to an eye at the free end. Mounted at the rear of the frame was a windlass—two iron posts supporting a concave horizontal drum between them, and cranks extending from each end of the drum. With it, two men could crank down the arm using a tagline wrapped several turns around the drum, while a third kept tension on the free end of the line. Once the arm was cocked, the free end of the tagline was removed from the windlass and secured around a cleat near the bottom of the arm.

The boy washed down his meal with small beer and said, "What is that thing?"

Carrick said proudly, "It's a weapon. Throws boulders that weigh more than you as far as the woods." He pointed to the forest's edge three hundred yards away for emphasis.

The boy squinted at the tree line. "And what do you call it?"

"*Bone-Crusher.*"

"It's a bone-crusher?"

Carrick frowned. "No, that's her name, not what she is. What she is doesn't have a name. We just built it. It's number… Lord Godric, what number is this one?"

"Seven!" I yelled, muffled by the tunic I was wrestling over my shoulders.

"Seven! Our seventh such one. Lord Godric says the Romans called them 'hell-apples', or some such, but to me it's mostly a big tree and a damn big box of rocks, so I think we should call it a tree-box!"

Nearby, Cedric held a bucket of water so the thirsty horse could drink, and said, "That's not a box like the others were. This box has a bail on which it hangs, so it swings and the rocks don't spill. That makes it a bucket. 'Tree-box' sounds stupid."

Carrick frowned. "You want to call it a tree-bucket?" Waggling his head, he considered it. "Well, 'tree-bucket' is better than 'tree-box!'"

I said, "No, no, no! It's a helepolis, which means 'city-taker'. Not 'hell-apples', 'tree-box', or 'tree-bucket'. *Helepolis*!"

Carrick shook his head. "Tree-bucket is better! I cannot say t'other."

Cedric grinned and nodded.

I ignored them and turned to the page. “So what did you hear in the palace about this urgent matter?” Palace gossip was usually reliable enough to supply the hint that the king had not.

“That a Northman from Argyll raids nunneries and monasteries to steal Church treasures and provisions, and that he kills all the church-folk wherever he goes.”

“That is indeed a problem! If fear of God does not stop him, there is little short of death itself that will. Come, let us ride to the manor. I’ll furnish you a fresh horse, and we will ride back to Dunfermline together.”

“Aye, sire,” the boy said. He asked with a frown, “Why have you built seven of these?”

I thought a moment, then replied, “The frame of the first wasn’t strong enough. The bottom of the box on the second was too weak, and the arm on the third too slender. The fixed box on the fourth spilled its rocks when we cocked it. The combination of lower arm, bail, and bucket were too long on the fifth, so the bucket struck the frame and burst wide open. That was fairly spectacular—threw splinters and rocks everywhere. And when we got all that right on the sixth, we found we needed to make the upper arm longer to get enough power to throw large stones. Hence this one: lucky number seven.”

“Aye, sire. But why build even one? On what would you use it?”

“Stone castles, lad.”

The boy's mouth gaped open. "Stone castles? Castles are built of wood! Only churches are built of stone…" Then he frowned as the idea of building castles from stone sank in.

I turned to Carrick. "We've had a damned good day. Send out your lads with the wagons to fetch in the machine. Just knock out the pins, and she'll come apart again easy enough. I built her that way to be broken down and stored for ready use."

Carrick grinned and nodded. "We'll pack her for transport and stand her next to the ballista. What do you want done with numbers one through six?"

"Now that we know what works, take what is usable from each and fashion replacement parts for *Bone-Crusher*."

"Aye, we'll do that. She's a fine one, this tree-bucket."

I glared at him a moment, and then grinned. "Aye, that she is. Cedric! Bring up our horses. Let's go see the king!"

✠✠✠

Stopping only to ask a page to inform Lady Aleine that I was in the palace and would attend her anon, I went to see the king.

King Malcolm was in the great hall, conferring with clerics and clerks when I entered. The king greeted me, saying, "A moment, Lord Godric. I'm up to my neck in monastic land disputes…"

True to his word, not a few moments later, the king waved them all away, saying, "Enough! We shall finish this tomorrow. You will have my decision then. I must put my sheriff on the trail of a devil! Baron Godric, come forward!"

As I paid homage, the king said, "Thank you for a most timely interruption. Those monks are so wearisome, droning on about rents, fees, and tithes they tell me I owe to various houses of God. Enough!" He took a deep breath. "What have you heard of a Northman from Argyll named OdinsØye?"

I frowned and said, "Your Grace, there is a Jarl OdinsØye, ally and kinsman of Godred Crovan, the proclaimed King of Man and the western isles the Northmen occupy." I thought on and added, "Beyond this, your court gossips of a Northman who raids Alban convents and monasteries, murdering the inhabitants, and making off with their herds, provisions, and ecclesiastic treasures. Do you believe them to be the same man?"

"They are the same man. *Jarl* is the Nordic word for earl, and Jarl OdinsØye rules Argyll for his lord and kinsman Godred Crovan, which makes him a powerful lord in his own right, with many men-at-arms at his command. He renounced his Christian name and faith for pagan ways, and named himself *OdinsØye*—Odin's Eye, after the one-eyed chief Norse god—having lost one of his own in a fight. He has a terrible hatred for the Christian faith, and particularly the religious men and women who devote themselves to serve the faith. He has vowed to root Christianity from his earldom and all the other lands he can seize."

Malcolm frowned. "Over the past year, while we have been busy with Rufus, he has filled his longships with raiders to strike by sea and raid into Alba, seeking out convents, monasteries and churches to loot and burn, sometimes after trapping congregants inside. The treasures taken he uses to buy service of more men, and the provisions stolen supply what they cannot grow or raise in their rocky holdfasts.

"These are crimes of easy success—they face no opposition and no defense. They commit heinous acts of rape upon the nuns and mayhem on the monks before killing them. It is time they suffer justice in kind. The difficulty is, we have no idea where to find him—he has hidden himself well."

Inside I blazed with fury, for there was nothing I hated more than men who used weapons in hate to spread murder, mayhem, and worse among defenseless people who did no wrong. But, as ever, I repressed my fury, to unleash it on deserving foes at the proper time. Instead, I spoke with a calm the king knew only too well. "I understand, sire. What would you have me do?"

"Start a war, if you must. Bring on a confrontation requiring all Alba to take up arms against Crovan and his Northmen. Let there be a war as never happened yet! Do whatever you must do… but hunt Jarl OdinsØye down to his lair and confront him. Accuse him of these crimes and confirm that he is responsible for their commission. Leave no doubt in his mind that with another such atrocity, I will bring every man I have to his very doorstep and destroy him. Is my meaning clear?"

I understood. The king and I locked eyes in an agreement that needed no other words. I nodded, saluted my king, and left—to hunt a man named OdinsØye.

✠✠✠

From before we had any recorded history of Alba, Northmen had plagued the kingdom. Starting in the late 700s AD, they came as raiders. After 870, they came and refused to leave, once they realized that no force of unified Scots existed to drive them out again. Since they came from the sea, they used the sea as their main defense. They first settled islands around which they could sail, thus ensuring they could not be approached by land or across tidal shallows. If the water was swift and deep enough to stop horsemen and foot-soldiers, it was barrier enough to stop their foes and give them a residence like their homeland.

By 1090, all the islands off Alba's western coast were held by Northmen, and they had kingdoms in the land of the Irish as well, the most notable Dublin, which they founded. Godred Crovan was said to rule Dublin and Man, while his kinsmen ruled many of the other islands: Iona, Mull, Jura, Tyree, Arran, and Bute. They held the islands called Hebrides far to the west, and the Orkneys to the north. Even Dunnottar, the rock MacanFhirMhóir had made his lair, had first been built into an impregnable fortress by Northmen. *Well, nearly impregnable*, thought I grimly, *though not to me; not with my siege engines.*

Having proven myself adept in dealing with the worst kinds of criminals, my judgment and resourcefulness had come to be held in high regard by the king. When my father rode as Malcolm's battle companion, the king had dispensed justice himself. Now, more often I rode in his stead. And it was precisely because he knew I would cope with Jarl OdinsØye without starting a war with the Norse that Malcolm gave me the task. His subtle warning against starting war did what tying my hands would not.

✠✠✠

I spent the night with my Aleine in our quarters in the palace, the room Aleine occupied as Queen Margaret's lady-in-waiting and companion. It was not unusual that we did so. I divided my time, seeing to the estate and enterprises of my barony at Cenachedne, and riding on the king's business as one of his sheriffs-at-large.

I loved Aleine deeply—I had saved her life more than once, and elevated her from blacksmith's daughter to nobility as Margaret's most favored lady-in-waiting and companion after my mother's death left that position vacant. Aleine loved me even more for precisely the same reasons. We had loved each other on sight and from childhood. The bond between us was as lasting as it was deep, surviving long separation during my travels to Jerusalem, my battle against MacanFhirMhóir, and many sorties to bring the king's justice to the fringes of his realm.

Before we rose, Aleine clung to me in our bed, and urged me stay yet a little longer. I was not opposed to this; indeed, since Lady Isabeau had taught Aleine the secrets of the harem, there was no place on earth I preferred. But duty as a knight drove me always, and good people were being slaughtered or worse by OdinsØye's bloody band. So I pleasured Aleine until the sun broke in, and then dressed for war and took my leave of her. As always, I renewed the promise she ever demanded of me.

"Yes, my sweet Aleine. I will return to you, as soon as I can."

Whether it would be in this life or the next I left unsaid, for as always, I had no way of knowing which.

✠✠✠

My first task was to learn where OdinsØye dwelt, a fact not known to the king, nor to any who served him. Reconnaissance was needed to discover that intelligence.

When I found him, Squire Cedric was ready, with horses saddled, arms sharp and bright, and a fortnight's supplies packed on spare horses. That Cedric knew to do this was no surprise. Indeed, it was our normal routine whenever the king summoned me—for a mission always followed his summons. Only the direction we would ride was in doubt.

Today it was southwest. I had a list of the sites Jarl OdinsØye was thought to have attacked, with rough directions to each, and I intended to visit each, determine how the raiders had reached it, and if possible, which way they had come and gone. I had faced a similar puzzle with MacanFhirMhóir, and had only found him after we gathered all the available details on each attack and built a crude map of the raiders' line of retreat.

✠✠✠

We followed the route we had ridden some five years earlier, when I rode as part of the escort for Princesses Edith and Mary on their way to Romsey Abbey in England, and in which Cedric was a young yeoman-at-arms. Along the way we had stayed in a string of monasteries and convents, which offered the best meals and accommodations to be had on the road. Since then, OdinsØye had raided, and in some cases destroyed, several of them.

Hoddam Monastery, Holmcultram Abbey, and St. Bees Priory—three of the most significant clerical institutions in Alba. Only a few years before, I had stayed overnight in two of them.

The southernmost of these attacks was on the nunnery at St. Bees in Cumbria. A convent there had been founded three hundred years before by a saintly Irish woman who had fled across the sea to escape a forced marriage to a pagan Northman. The priory sat on the coast above a sandy beach, and I gained our first useful clue from that. The raiders struck from longships just after dawn while the nuns were at prayer, and carried off everything of value. Most of the nuns survived by barricading themselves in the church crypt, but the young porteress who saved them by ringing her alarm bell to give timely warning of the attack was carried off and never seen again.

Holmcultram Abbey was sited on the banks of the River Waver a couple of miles above its mouth, a telling fact. Attacking from *karvi*—boats built like small versions of longships—in early morning, the brigands looted the church treasures and the food stores in a raid timed for the close of the abbey's fall-time market fair, the biggest alms-raising event of the abbey's year. All the monies raised were seized, and nearly a third of the monks were killed, with many others wounded, before the alarm bells brought enough armed townsfolk to threaten overwhelming the raiders. The Northmen swiftly rowed back to the sea, with their pursuers—ineffectually armed with axes and pitchforks—chasing them along the riverbank. As the boats pulled out from the river's mouth, the raiders insulted their pursuers with bare backsides and obscene gestures unmistakable in any language.

Hoddam Monastery, some ten miles up the River Annan, was robbed by raiders using similar karvi longboats. This time there were no defenders and no pursuit, for Hoddam sat inland in an isolated region. The Northmen slipped up the river in moonlight, and after a day of raiding, returned downriver in the same way. The stone-built monastery was left standing intact, but not one of the monks was.

These accounts Cedric and I built up by piecing together narratives from survivors, shepherds, river men, and townsfolk as we toured each site. Near the sea, we found places where Northmen—for it could be no others—had beached longships and left them under guard while the raiding party went upriver in the karvi they had towed behind their ships.

Each raid came from the sea. Each raid returned to it. And in each case, that was where the trail went cold.

But one critical detail emerged: all the longships had hulls black with pitch. And their sails, though unmarked, were blood red.

✠✠✠

There was another kind of information to be had in Glasgow, and before we rode, Cedric and I had emptied a certain trunk.

In a reprise of our earlier disguises as "Wilhelm of Flanders" and his companion "Rolf," we went through the waterfront dives of Glasgow and Gourock, buying ale to drink with all the Nordic mercenaries we found—and there were many of them. As Walther and Rolf we gave out that we were wanted men, sought by Scottish law for thievery, mayhem, and murder, and in urgent need of a new lord willing to pay well for loyal, unquestioning services. The kind of services didn't matter—bloody work was so much the better than hard labor—except maybe pulling an oar. Did anyone know of a lord who needed such men?

Both Cedric and I had the muscle, scars, and coloring to pass as Northmen, but did not speak much of the Nordic tongue, so we pretended to be Northmen of Flemish origins, enough like them to be seen as kindred souls, but from a land far enough away to excuse our weakness with language. And it mattered little, for Gaelic was spoken well enough by all. Dressed in mercenary garb and weapons as we were, we could stand up to scrutiny by the local Northmen.

"We heard Jarl OdinsØye might want men like us, but cannot find him. He rules lands in Argyll, don't he?" I asked as Walther.

"He might want men like you, but he doesn't want to be found. Go ask elsewhere." That was the answer we usually got, and pressing the question got nothing but suspicion, so we moved on.

And soon we ran out of taverns, inns, and dives without knowing more at the end than we had at the start. That is, until sitting that last afternoon outside a tavern in Gourock, drinking the last of our ale in a silence reflective of our lack of success. Suddenly Cedric sat more erect, and in a low voice said, "Look there!"

To the north, half a mile offshore, a ship sailed past, headed west. With rising excitement, we watched it turn northwest, and when the sun suddenly pierced a gap in the cloudbanks, dropping a shaft of light full on her, we saw she was a longship… with a black hull and blood red sail.

We watched her 'til she sailed out of sight.

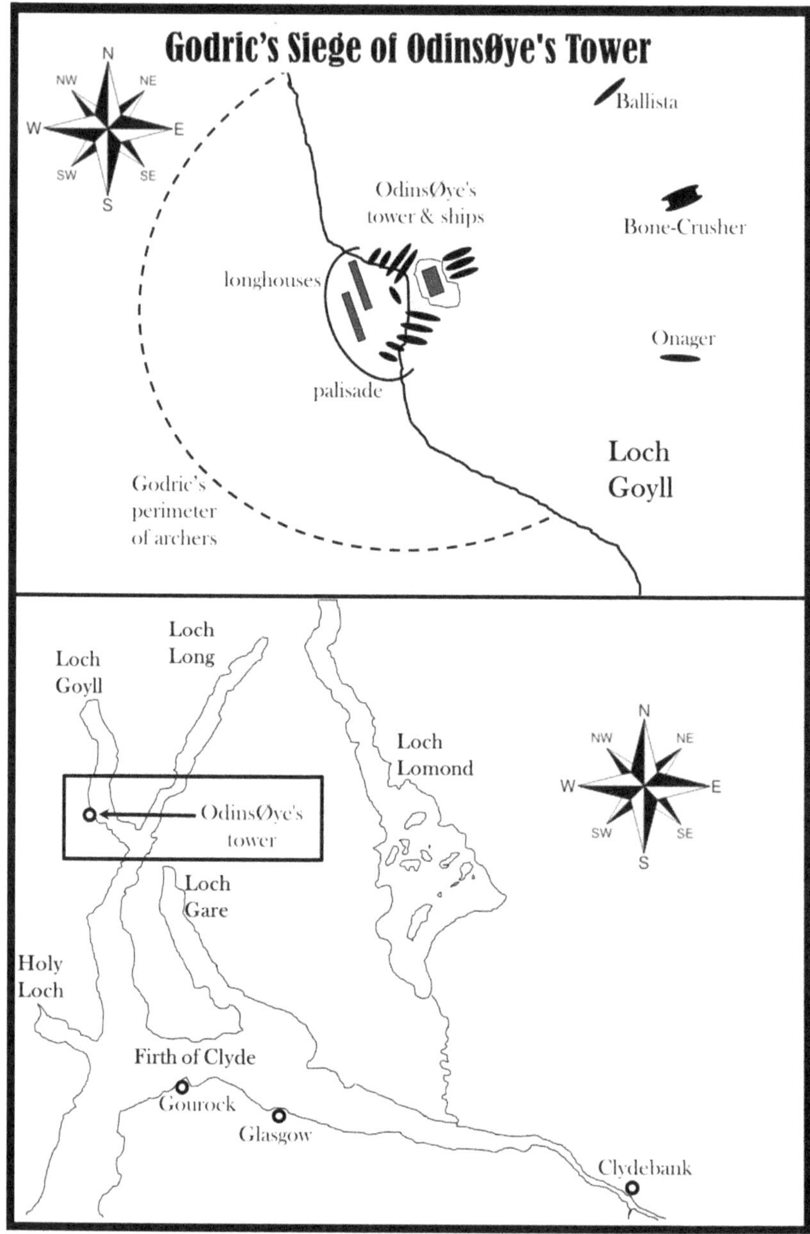

Figure 5: Godric's siege of OdinsØye's tower.

SIX

✠✠✠

Back in Dunfermline, I called for maps of the lands and waters around the Firth of Clyde. What I could get was vaguely drawn, and each map was contradicted by the next, so I chose what appeared to be the best of them and sent for Brother David, the monk from the abbey who had been of such great help a year previous in my effort to find the lair of MacanFhirMhóir. Brother David, Cedric and I began to build up a new map from the sources we had and our own recent observations. With the floor of the armory swept clear, we again drew upon the flagstones in chalk, and once again Brother David made notes and drawings upon parchment to record our results.

From where we had sat at the tavern on the point at Gourock, the Firth of Clyde tapered in a cone to the east and south to where the River Clyde entered the Firth, flowing past Glasgow Town seven leagues farther west. To the west and south the Firth extended, ever widening among peninsulas and islands, and emptying a hundred miles farther on into the Irish Sea. Due west of where we sat, a narrow loch stretched a league—but we had watched the longship sail past its mouth. Two long lochs lay north of our point of observation, one northeast and one northwest. We decided that it was into the latter of these the ship had sailed.

According to the only information we had, that loch, named Loch Long, ran north more than five leagues. Halfway along its length another loch, named Goyll, branched off to the north and west. Somewhere up the one or the other, that longship had been bound. And unless there was, unknown to us, another outlet to the Great Sea, the reverse route was the only way it could get out again.

When we finished, I felt confident I had a reasonable map of the waters of the Firth, one that would help us find Jarl OdinsØye's hidden lair. Knowing where to look was the critical first step, but the lands surrounding those waters were in Argyll, not Alba, so riding through them tempted attack by the Northmen. We would have to scout the lochs from the sea.

✠✠✠

Armed with new information on where to look, I had now another need—a small, fast ship, and a crew to sail it. I was no seaman, but I knew how to build well with wood and iron. Even more important, I knew men. So I set out to find the best of both that Glasgow had to offer.

Knowing Thorsson to be a skilled shipmaster from my return voyage with him following my squiredom, and that he sailed out of the new harbor at North Queensferry, I sent Cedric to find him with an offer of handsome payment in silver for his time.

In the meantime I rode to Cenachedne to look after matters there. True to his word, Carrick had retrieved *Bone-Crusher* and stored it loaded on a strongly built sort of wagon in the new barn next to those bearing the onager and the ballista. This wagon used the main timbers of the tree-bucket's frame as the wagon's frame. Tightly lashed to these timbers were two rear axles with massive wheels on each end to support most of the weight. Three throwing arms—a primary and two spares—extended to the rear, and two inverted rock buckets at the front formed a seat. At the front, two timbers with a pair of greased iron plates between them formed a pivot. The upper timber was lashed to the frame, while the lower formed a massive front axle with huge wheels at each end. From it a strong wagon tongue protruded, to which four horses could be harnessed.

It was a startling innovation and Carrick was very proud of it. "Took the notion from you. 'If one is good, two is better,' you allus say. True for everything but wives, I think. Needs a big space to turn, but four horses pull it well along if there is no great hurry."

"Well done, Carrick! You're a clever man. It's splendid, and just what I needed." I clenched the man's massive shoulders in a strong hug of praise and thanks.

Carrick gave me a sheepish grin. "About time I started using these ideas I have. Should have done so years ago, but until you came along, no one wanted new ideas and better ways of doin' things. Wait'll you see what I do with the new foundry."

"Do what you think right, man. I'll fund anything you like. You know what you're doing. Well done, indeed!"

✠✠✠

A week later, Cedric and Thorsson found me in Dunfermline. My promise of silver had lured the seaman to beach his ship. "My crew will scrape her hull clean—when they run out of money to spend on ale," Thorsson said with a wry smile, knowing his crewmen well. "What do you want of me?"

"I need a master who can sail me about the lochs and inlets of Clyde. I hunt a man who hides ships there somewhere. And if we find trouble, we need to get out fast."

Thorsson said, "Sire, I grew to manhood sailing those waters, so I know them all well enough. I know where I can get use of a North-built karvi for a time. When their hulls are clean, nothing sails faster, and they draw less than two feet of water, so we can get into any inlet or stream you like. I'll get a half-dozen men I trust to pull oars. It takes some skill, so I suggest we use those I choose unless you insist on your own men." He waited until I shook my head, then said, "Who is it you hunt? I won't raise my hand against my own kinsmen."

I said, "If you are kin to Jarl OdinsØye, I've misjudged you, for you are no devil. I intend to send him to Hell. Only cowards prey on defenseless folk who serve the Christian God—the same god most Northmen now worship—and Valhalla will not accept cowards. Is OdinsØye your kin?"

Thorsson shook his head, said, "No!" and spat. "I know of him and I'll go gladly. My kin are Christian, and have naught to do with his murderous pagan ways. Hell is where he belongs! When do you want to go look for him?"

"Send word to me here when you have the vessel and men. Here is silver to hire both. Make sure your men have no attachment to OdinsØye either, for I'll send a traitor to the bottom of the loch with a heavy stone as his last meal."

Thorsson took the proffered purse and nodded. "Have no fear, sire. These men are all my cousins, and Christians as stout as they come. I will send word soon." And with a smile and a wave, he was off.

✠✠✠

Within a week, a lad found me. "Thorsson sends me, my lord. He has both boat and men, and awaits you in Glasgow. I am to take you to them."

I called, "Cedric! Do you hear? We've a boat and crew. We'll ride as soon as you're ready. And this lad needs a fresh mount."

"Half an hour, sire," said the squire, and headed for the stables.

I tossed the boy a half-penny and said, "That will buy you a fast meal at the inn across the road. Go!" The boy grinned and bolted through the door.

✠✠✠

For twenty leagues and three days we searched. Most of the time the wind was of no help, so the crew rowed, covering a league an hour. It took a day to row the seven leagues from the boatyard at Clydebank, searching the northern shore to the top of Loch Gare, where we beached the boat and camped for the night. A second day and nine leagues it took to come back down the loch and follow the shoreline west to Arrochar at the top of the loch. In all that time we had seen much, but no signs of a fasthold suitable for a Nordic jarl, and nothing of his black longships.

It was midday of the third day when we rowed back down Loch Long to the mouth of Loch Goyll, our last hope, and started up its length. Two miles in on the western shore, there rose a stone tower unlike anything else we had seen.

I was wary of appearing too interested, so we maintained a course up the center of the loch and kept rowing. But from the corner of my eye I studied the building all the while, as Cedric scoured the shore with his keen eyes.

It was a new construction, rectangular in shape, and stood some fifty feet high, with dimensions that might have been the same in width and twice that in length along the shoreline. The lower portion was of mortar and rough stone to half its height, about three times a man's height. Above that, it appeared to be built of timber heavily covered with plaster or mortar to proof it against fire. It had not reached its full height yet, for men were working at its top, pulling up their materials with a gantry at the top corner of the tower. No door could be seen from the loch and the building itself stood on a rocky promontory sitting offshore, so its entrance had to be at the end of a causeway on the landward side.

As we pulled past, Cedric sighted an inlet, and through a screen of trees and bushes viewed a number of low dark hulls, their masts and yards lowered to reduce their profiles.

We did not slow or stop, instead pulling for the head of Loch Goyll. What we would find there we did not know, nor did it matter, for I was certain we had found what we sought. But I had always intended on only an initial reconnaissance to find the jarl, and then to return with sufficient forces to impress on the jarl the seriousness of King Malcolm's outrage. And although I considered immediately heading back to Glasgow, to do so would draw instant attention. I knew that as fast as the karvi and crew might be, we could not outrun a well-crewed longship. More importantly, we could not out-fight such a ship. Better to keep going, camp overnight, and come back out the following day. After all, karvis were common enough in Firth waters and used for fishing and trade throughout.

And so it was that we reached Goyll-head without incident and there encamped for the night, resting for an early start that would get us out before the jarl's castle—for only that could it be—awoke for breakfast.

✠✠✠

We nearly made it. By sunrise we were two miles past the castle, and once again approaching the mouth where Loch Goyll joined Loch Long, when two black longships pulled out from opposite shores to quickly come up on either side. Both ships had all oars manned by forty men or more, and there was no chance we could outrun them.

"Come with us or die here now!" called the captain of one ship, a huge Northman. "Our lord would know who you are, and what you are doing in our waters."

"Lead on!" I answered. There was no other good choice.

✠✠✠

Within the hour we beached below the castle where an escort of mean-looking brutes surrounded us, seized our weapons, and marched us into the tower.

On the ground level we passed between kitchens and servant quarters. The second floor housed the garrison troops in one huge barracks-style room. On the third floor was the jarl's great room, which put his quarters above it, and the treasury and weapons store on the highest floor.

Seated at the head of a table that seemed the size of a drawbridge, Jarl OdinsØye was stuffing himself with a vast breakfast from a score of dishes. Huge, blond, bearded and greasy, the jarl was garbed in leathern armor faced with chainmail, and a battle-axe the size of a shovel leaned against his chair. His left eye was missing, an ugly hollow crossed by a poorly stitched scar in its place, and his manner was as brusque and ugly as he was.

"Who are you?" he demanded in Gaelic of me, without ceasing to eat.

"I am Baron Godric MacEuan, sheriff-at large of the Kingdom of Alba. I seek Jarl OdinsØye, Nordic Chief of Argyll."

"And what do you want of him?" said the jarl, throwing a half-eaten chop to a nearby hound.

"I'll tell him when I see him," I said, knowing full well to whom I spoke.

"I am the Jarl OdinsØye. Now tell me why you disturb my meal."

"The King of Alba would have me stop your raids into his lands, to rob its holy places, and kill his people. Why do you do it?"

"I loot monasteries because they hold treasure I need. I hate the tree-nailed weakling they worship, and despise fools who think him a god. And my men need diversions. Raping nuns and killing monks pleases them well." Through all this, OdinsØye ate.

He belched, then said with a sneer, "*You* stop me? What makes you think you can?"

"I have a talent for it," I said.

"I think I'll kill you now," said the jarl, wolfing down boiled oats.

"That will certainly prove fatal to you, for King Malcolm himself will lead an army here to avenge me. He awaits my return with your answer. But I will gladly fight you, if death in combat is what you want." The former was a bluff, but I knew OdinsØye couldn't know it wasn't true. The latter I meant with every word.

"Hah!" laughed OdinsØye, and choked on the food in his gullet. Red with coughing, it took a moment for him to speak. Gulping air, he said, "Making me choke with mirth is the only way you could kill me, you pup! I have dogs older than you, and women more fearsome."

"I'm sorry to hear that. Old dogs and mean women! Is that what makes you so keen to kill?"

"It won't be me you fight, MacEuan. You fight my champion, Bjorn the Bear."

"*Baron* MacEuan. For the lives and freedom of those with me, and the right to bring my king your answer, I will."

"Only if you win. When Bjorn wins, all of you will die."

"Your oath to Odin and Valhalla on it, OdinsØye?"

"My oath I give," said the jarl.

"Then summon Bjorn. I accept."

✠✠✠

Bjorn the Bear was close to seven feet tall, and twice my weight. He came stripped to boots and breeks, and scars covered him, one overlaying another, more than were easily counted. Thorsson and his sailors exchanged uneasy looks, for they had not counted on any of this.

The great hall had been cleared of food, table, benches, and people, and the rushes swept from the flagstone pavement in a thirty-foot diameter circle. Only the jarl's great chair remained at one end, with his vast bulk seated in it, axe at his side, as ever. He was clearly looking forward to what would follow.

OdinsØye said, "You will fight in the Northmen's style: without armor, and with shield and axe or blade, as you choose. Bjorn?"

"I choose the axe, great lord." It was clear Bjorn had done this before and anticipated no difficulty defeating me.

"MacEuan?"

"*Baron* MacEuan. I choose short sword," I said, and with Cedric's help, stripped off to boots and breeks. In a low voice I said, "Give me a good cross-laid shield, and my short Damascus blade." Cedric nodded, fetching both from our confiscated pile of arms under the watchful eyes of the jarl's guards.

Bjorn took notice then of the scars I bore, and of the muscle under them. His boredom vanished.

I closed my eyes and raised a short fervent silent prayer asking Heaven to help me save the lives of my companions. And then I was ready.

As we entered the cleared space, all others moved back out of it, leaving the swept circle free. Morning sunlight streamed in through narrow windows and lit the space for all to see well.

Bjorn and I faced each other and took favored fighting stances. Both of us held our weapons in our right hands, and wore our shields on the left arm. Bjorn's axe had a wrist loop, worn to prevent having the axe pulled from his hand. Of that I took note.

The jarl said, "Begin!"

Straightaway Bjorn charged me, hoping to end the battle with a quick first blow. I dodged him, gave ground and circled right, carefully watching how Bjorn moved.

Big as he was, Bjorn was not slow. But big as he was, he wasn't as quick as me. So I kept moving, shield held ready against that fearsome axe, and kept my short sword tucked in when I did not use it to parry.

Bjorn tried all the tricks a long career of close combat had taught him: the sudden shove with the shield and roundabout blow at my head; catching the outer edge of my shield with his own to pull open my defenses; hooking his axe on the top of my shield to pull it down even as he struck at my head with the rim of his own shield. But I knew all these and more, and slipped clear, weapon always ready. After a time, Bjorn began to tire.

Bjorn was used to winning quickly, his battles half-won before they started by his intimidating size and appearance. This was not what he was used to. As he began to flag, frustration took over.

So he turned to power as his next tactic, trying to crush me under a hail of powerful blows. I kept a distance, forcing Bjorn to close the gap for each attack, and swing all the harder trying to hammer me down with that huge axe.

For my part, I had spent years as a smith's slave, hammering iron and working timber, and building my own muscles in the process. More years had followed, when daily I fought my knight, Jean de Bethencourt, and fellow squires in just this kind of close combat. Even now I and Cedric practiced each morning to keep me sharp and teach Cedric what he did not yet know. So I bided my time.

Bjorn was enraged now, and I knew the time was close. When Bjorn committed to a crushing blow, I raised my shield to catch the strike. As it fell, I suddenly pivoted my shield so the tail of the axe-blade bit deep in the wood and stuck fast.

With a twist of my shield, I forced Bjorn's axe-arm outstretched, and turned my whole body in against Bjorn's shield, pinning it against him with my shoulder. Then like a serpent's tongue, my short sword shot out, and I pulled it across Bjorn's right arm above the elbow. The blade, sharp enough to cut falling silk, sliced deep through muscle, nearly to the bone.

For an instant, Bjorn was frozen with shock. With a flick of my blade I cut the wrist thong and wrenched the axe from Bjorn's nerveless grip. Bjorn gave a scream of outrage and pain as he realized he could no longer lift his ruined arm. Blood jetted around the room as he panicked and tried to crush me with his shield. I slipped past the awkward attack, and with another slash at the back of his leg, I cut the calf, laming the Northman.

Crippled, the giant went down then, his death now certain. But in shock and outrage at the sudden and unexpected turn of events, OdinsØye cried, "Hold!"

I stepped back and guardedly said, "Do you yield for Bjorn?" In my mind, I rehearsed the throw of my short sword to nail the jarl's throat to his throne if treachery followed.

OdinsØye swore a dreadful oath. And then he said, "Yes, yes! I yield for Bjorn. By the gods, you all go safe and free. Now hold!"

Cedric and Thorsson went to retrieve their weapons. The guards allowed the retrieval when OdinsØye waved an impatient assent.

With that, I stepped to the side of the fallen giant, seized the wounded arm to pinch shut the wound. "Cedric! Bindings!" Cedric brought me cloth and a leather strap, both of which I wrapped tightly about Bjorn's injured arm and calf to stop the blood loss. Whether he would ever again use arm or leg was in God's hands, but Bjorn would yet live.

To the fainting warrior I said in a low voice, "You are a brave man and skilled fighter, Bjorn. You deserve a better master and kinder fate. I am sorry I had to do this. You have my respect."

Bjorn gave me a wry smile. "Thank you, but our skeins are already woven, and the Fates decided you deserved victory."

✠✠✠

It was clear OdinsØye regretted yielding to save his champion, and was already wishing he had not. But it was done, and a jarl could not violate his sworn word and still remain respected by his retainers, regardless of whether he was renegade or not. Break an oath to the gods in defeat, and his men would decide him cursed and abandon him. Nothing could be worse than that; so, however reluctantly, OdinsØye gracelessly set us free.

"Do not return to my waters or lands, for all of you will die when you do," he declared.

I replied, "You use that threat much too carelessly, Jarl, for a man just defeated by—what did you call me?—a pup."

Staring directly into OdinsØye's remaining eye, I declared, "For King Malcolm of Alba, I say this: if another monastery, church, convent, city, town, or herdsman's croft in his kingdom is raided, and I have cause to believe you or your men did it, I will return in force, destroy this tower with you in it, and paint its ruined walls with your blood. I, Baron Godric MacEuan, Sheriff of Alba, do swear it, and I will not be forsworn by such as you."

OdinsØye looked outraged, but said nothing more. And without looking back, I led my men from his citadel and back to our boat.

✠✠✠

On our return to Clydebank, unbidden I paid Thorsson and each of his men double what had been agreed upon. The risk of violent death had not been part of our agreement, and the additional coin was only fair. Nor did any of the men complain.

Thorsson said then with a wry smile, "You don't seem fearsome, Lord Godric, but damned if you aren't the most resourceful and dangerous man I've ever known. If you ever again have need of a sailing man, I'll serve in any way you wish."

I clasped his hand and said, "When I have need, Thorsson, I'll find you again, for I won't find a better mariner."

With nods of respect, the sailors bid us farewell, and Cedric and I rode for Dunfermline.

SEVEN

✠✠✠

Back at the palace, I reported to King Malcom, told him of discovering Jarl OdinsØye's citadel, and related an abbreviated version of the events there. The king was most curious to learn all I could tell him of OdinsØye, and concerned to learn the Nordic lord was building a stone fortress. But he thoroughly approved of the outcome, and my ultimatum to deter further raids without causing a war between Scots and Northmen.

"It is easy, Lord Godric, for men like OdinsØye to speak of death and war; that is what cowards do to hide weakness and fear. But speeches alone do not prevent war, and speeches cannot win them. Strength of arms does both. And when a foe believes you the stronger both in arms and in resolve, he will go far to avoid provoking war.

"Now that we know where to find him, we will closely watch Jarl OdinsØye and see if this deters him from further atrocities. If so, we will allow peace between us, since the people he has killed cannot be revived, and God Himself will punish their murderers.

"But! If he heeds not your warning and resumes his old ways, I order you to keep the oath you made in my name, and destroy him and his fortress utterly. I'm sure you already have thought about how you would do that, and I have seen for myself that you have the means. I will see you have everything you need. Bring away his slaves and captives, and take or destroy all he has of value. Bury him in ashes, and drop his walls upon him as a tomb so that, should anyone again ever speak of OdinsØye, they do so only in tones of horror and pity!"

I said, "I have indeed thought well about destroying that tower, and should it be necessary, Your Grace, I will be ready."

✠✠✠

At home in Cenachedne, spring had brought new growth and new life. For the first time in several years, fallow fields were plowed and planted and it did us all good to see our crops reappear in furrows of tiny green sprouts.

Warm weather brought outdoors the young of both human- and animal-kind. Little pink piglets foraged about, looking for more to eat than the troughs held, and with them frolicked tiny pink people—just as naked and mud-covered, so that it could be hard to tell the toddlers from the piglets. Still too irresponsible in their habits to stay clean, their mothers dispensed with dressing them in garments that would only need washing within the hour, and let them literally run amuck. After all, it was simpler to wash the muck from the child once than clothes all the day long.

✠✠✠

A month after my confrontation with OdinsØye, a rider the king expressly sent brought me news of a new monastic atrocity, by far the most ambitious raid: three monastic houses robbed in a single strike. So Cedric and I mounted up and ode straightaway for the western coast.

There we learned that a raiding party of Northmen had rowed more than thirty miles up the River Eden to the convent at Armathwaite, traveling at night and concealing themselves and their boats by day. Except for the town of Carlisle, the area was quite empty, and Alba had no garrisons there at all. Certainly in hindsight, this was the reason King Rufus thought he could seize the entire region.

As before, Cedric and I interviewed survivors, herdsmen, river men, and townsfolk as we toured each site. Through their stories we learned the raiders had slipped through Carlisle in the night and encamped between Armathwaite and Wetheral before dawn. Near Armathwaite, I found their camp—places where the karvi were hauled up on the bank, where the raiders ate rations cold, crushed down the moss and heather in sleep, and defecated indiscriminately around the edge of camp.

Hiding to rest through the day, they struck Armathwaite convent at sunset during Vespers, looting it and violating everything that moved.

They were back on the river within two hours. They swiftly rowed downstream five miles to attack Wetheral during midnight Matins. Taking the monastery treasure and leaving the monks dead in a lake of blood, the raiders returned to their boats, and slid another ten miles downstream, passing again through Carlisle in darkness, and then returning afoot to strike the Carlisle Priory at dawn's Lauds.

There they herded the monks into the refectory, barricaded them in and set it afire, counting on the flames to draw the townsfolk to the church as they ran back to their boats and escaped downriver.

It worked. The populace rallied to the fire and managed to save both the monks and most of the priory. The raiders went largely unnoticed; only herdsmen and farmers saw the little fleet of karvi slip downstream, ballasted to gunwales-awash by men and loot.

They made but one mistake. Their ships, moored at River Eden's mouth, were seen by a shepherd who described them to me.

"Aye, sire, I saw 'em clear. There was four of 'em, and they was long and sleek-like, with a single mast. And all the ships was black, and all the sails was red as blood."

✠✠✠

The shepherd's report left me in no doubt. For whatever reasons, Jarl OdinsØye had decided to ignore the warning I gave him, and had mounted another raid, this one his most ambitious yet. I sent this news by rider to King Malcolm, along with word of my plan to see Godred Crovan on the Isle of Man, with the intent of averting a war. Then I rode for Whitehaven on the coast and hired a boat to carry me ten leagues out in the Irish Sea to the Isle of Man.

I had little difficulty finding Crovan. There was only one town of any size, that adjacent to the harbor, and only one building of any consequence other than the church. And it was there I found the King of Man.

Upon learning that an emissary of the King of Alba had come to see him, Crovan received me most cordially. Crovan and Malcolm had always had generally amiable relations, despite the difference of cultures and the fact that they shared a disputed border of sorts. Moreover, Crovan had heard of me—my deeds apparently newsworthy well beyond my barony, and deeds like mine drew great interest.

The biggest basis for amiability between the rulers, however, was a common religion; for Crovan was, like most Northmen in these times, a Christian. I knew this, and indeed, it was the chief reason I came to see Crovan.

By the standard of our day, Crovan was quite old, and had ruled the Kingdoms of Man, the Western Isles, and Dublin for more than a decade. He was a ginger-haired man with a substantial moustache and sharply defined jaw made clear by the fact he was clean-shaven.

"Greetings, Baron Godric! Your fame precedes you, and we are glad to make your acquaintance. Welcome to our kingdom!"

"Greetings and peace to you also, Your Grace," I began, using the form of address reserved for the King of Alba and his equals. "I come bearing the friendship and well-wishes of the king, and in his name to seek your help in a matter that threatens peace and friendship between his realm and yours."

Crovan frowned and said, "What is there that could so threaten our friendship?"

"Sire, have you heard of the brazen raids in recent months upon Alban convents and monasteries by men from your kingdom? Raids that steal church treasures, leave the monks murdered and the nuns worse?"

"Worse than murdered?"

"Yes, sire. For nuns, rape is worse than murder, for it leaves them alive and haunted by evil memories, doubt, undeserved shame, and filled with a hatred difficult to forgive and harder to forget."

Crovan shook his head, sighed heavily, and said, "I suppose you believe these the acts of my renegade kinsman, Jarl OdinsØye."

"I do, sire. And despite my stern direct warning to him just a month ago, he has just committed another raid, this time on a convent and two monasteries. And in these attacks, the atrocities of rape, murder, and arson were more egregious than any of his earlier attacks."

I took a deep breath, and went on. "I am already ordered by King Malcolm and personally sworn to destroy Jarl OdinsØye and his raiders. But King Malcolm does not want war with you. So I have come to seek your advice and help."

At this, Crovan was much troubled. "You understand that Jarl OdinsØye is both my kinsman and a hereditary jarl. He inherited his rank and the lands of Argyll to rule, until recently a rare event among my people. You know also that, although he was raised a Christian like us, he abandoned our faith to live as a Norse pagan. He has since gathered a large following of like-minded retainers. Indeed, he hates all Christians, including me, and will brook no Christian in his service."

Sighing deeply once again, Crovan continued. "I condone neither his actions nor his crimes. He is a monster among us, bringing us disgrace in the eyes of the Church and our neighbors' wrath. I have no power or influence over him, and I cannot lift my own hand against him…"

Then Crovan thought a moment and said, "But I do not have to lift my hand to help him, either. And like you, I certainly do not want war.

"So, Baron, I can do this much. Deal with Jarl OdinsØye as you must, and you need not fear that I will take umbrage or raise arms in support of him. Tell good King Malcolm that your actions in this matter are condoned, and will not bring war between our two kingdoms. Convey to him our letter to that effect..." Crovan gestured to a clerk seated nearby keeping a record of the meeting, and the clerk bowed to acknowledge the order. "And you may tell your king that I will name as OdinsØye's successor a true Christian, well able to rule Christian lands in Christian ways."

With deep gratitude I paid King Crovan a parting homage that acknowledged this new accord between Man and Alba, and his letter in hand, took my leave, knowing that whatever happened next, it would not bring about a greater conflict. I only wish that horrid King Rufus had Crovan's wisdom and sensible policies.

✠✠✠

I immediately returned to Dunfermline, where I related to King Malcom the events of my meeting with Crovan and presented the Manx king's letter of friendship and assured non-interference. King Malcolm was much pleased with my diplomacy in the matter. Destroying OdinsØye now would remove a thorn from the flesh of both kingdoms, and Crovan's written assurance guaranteed it would not trigger a larger conflict between them.

"This is a great coup, one I highly value," Malcolm said, "and a further proof of my wisdom to trust you to settle these problems. But now I need to burden you with yet another task.

"You realize, Lord Godric, that your success in winning Crovan's stay of hand in the matter means that now we must fulfill our end of the bargain, and remove OdinsØye as a source of problems in this world by sending him on to the next?"

I looked my king in the eye and said, "Sire, for what he has done, and will continue to do to good nuns and monks until forever stopped, nothing could give me greater satisfaction."

"I thought you would feel that way," said the king. "Give me a list of whatever you may require, and you will get it. Oh, and when next you speak with Jarl OdinsØye, convey my displeasure with him in the strongest terms, then speed him into Hell."

"I'll be most glad to do so, sire!" I said, and deeply meant it.

✠✠✠

Later that day, I sent Cedric off again to find Thorsson and gain his help. Both returned within three days.

"Master Thorsson, good of you to come! I've a new problem with which I again need your help, for I couldn't think of another who could manage it as well. I'm sure you remember our recent friend, the Jarl OdinsØye?"

Thorsson growled, "Baron, I hope you jest when you call that man 'friend'. I'll never forget that… that…"

"Fat bastard?" offered Cedric.

"Aye! He's all that and more."

"Would you like to help me send him to Hell?" I asked.

"I'd consider it a great privilege to help you do so, sire!"

Then I thought out loud and explained our problem. "I plan to destroy him, him and his damned fortress, but it's a problem of terrain. OdinsØye built that mighty stone tower of his as a refuge and stronghold, and he built it where no ordinary siege can take it. It's made of stone, so we can't set it afire and burn him out. It sits on a great rock surrounded by water, so we can't undermine it. The tower controls the narrow strip of flat land adjacent, and the whole area is backed by mountains. Bringing a siege army there by land would take a year. And the tower is accessible by sea, so we can't surround it to starve him out, either."

I paused then, frowning. "We're going to have to lay siege to it from the sea."

Both Thorsson and Cedric stared at me in incredulity, their mouths gaping with surprise, for nothing of the kind had ever been tried, much less succeeded. "From the sea?" Cedric managed.

"I have three splendid machines with which I can reduce that tower to a pile of rock in a matter of days. But I have no good way to get them there except by sea, and no place to land them in order to use them properly. So I have to figure a way to use them from the loch…"

Then I grinned as I realized how it could be done. This was going to be fun!

"…and all the arrow slits face the land. Did you notice?"

Thorsson and Cedric looked at each other. They had not.

“Those walls are thick enough that we’ll have the place in rubble before they can pierce the seaward side with arrow slits. They can only fire on us from the ramparts. If we stay out of arrowshot, that side is helpless against us.”

Cedric shook his head. “But how do you lay siege from the sea?”

“We use ships as siege platforms and we moor them to seaward. Then we use our machines to tear the place apart. You saw what they can do at Dunnottar, Cedric.”

“Aye, the ballista on a ship, that I can see. It would be a fearsome weapon against other ships, especially with those fire-darts you used to fire the palisade. Put that opposite OdinsØye’s mooring inlet and all his ships would be doomed.”

“Now you’re thinking like a siege master, Cedric! That’s what we’ll do to neutralize his fleet. Bottle them in and burn every last one. That way, at one stroke, OdinsØye loses his chief means of fighting back and his chosen means of escape. All we need then is time to pound him to rubble with damn big stones.”

Cedric brightened at that, clearly liking the idea, then frowned again. “But can we put the onager on a ship?”

I said, “Yes, I believe so, if we remove the mast and throw over the bow. We don’t need the mast anyway during the siege, only oars. We point the machine by pointing the ship, and move closer or farther to adjust the range and point of impact. The ballista we will mount, point, and range in the same way.”

Cedric nodded slowly as these ideas sank in. But Thorsson was still clearly at a loss.

"Sire, I'm a sailor and no soldier. All this you say of sieges is beyond my experience, so I'm at a loss as to how I can be of aid."

I flashed him a big grin. "Isn't it obvious, man? You're going to build me a fleet and command them at sea!"

Thorsson gave us an astonished look and collapsed in shock.

✠✠✠

It took much of a day for Thorsson and me to design all the vessel modifications we thought necessary to build my special fleet. Although Thorsson was most dubious at first, as I explained what I would need and sketched out my ideas on parchment with charcoal sticks, he began to comprehend and to offer suggestions, most much better. By the time we finished, Thorsson was an enthusiastic supporter of the enterprise.

We concluded that if we bought old but sound ships—knarrs, cogs, or hulks—all of them common trading vessels with broad beams, shallow draft and substantial capacity, we could easily deck them over to support the siege machines and propel them with oars and sweeps, the form of propulsion they routinely used in ports, rivers, and lochs. And their stone cobble ballast would provide perfect projectiles for bombardment.

I provided Thorsson with a substantial sum to get it all done: Buy the hulls, timber, and shipbuilding labor to ready the ships within a month's time. It was already mid-summer, and time for a siege before winter weather set in was growing short.

✠✠✠

Yet another task lay before me. For this siege, I needed men. More importantly, I needed skilled and trustworthy commanders.

I had two such men in mind—men I could not trust more.

So I had written to each man a letter explaining the challenge and the king's authorization as a national priority. Then I sent Cedric off to recruit to the enterprise Sir Hamish and Sir Cormac, my two fellow sheriffs who had helped me destroy MacanFhirMhóir. Given their strong contributions to that success, I had every confidence that their help would ensure success with this one.

✠✠✠

With Thorsson on his way to Clydebank to ready our fleet and Cedric off to recruit the commanders, I headed for Cenachedne.

Things in the barony and among my folk were thriving. Carrick was well and quite the new man as Master of Bladesmiths, our foundry noisy and busy with men making mail, steel plates to armor brigandines, and good blades to fill the glut of orders our royal demonstration had brought in.

I spent time with him as I gave him instructions for tasks required to prepare for the siege. Together we went over the siege engines and decided on modifications necessary to mount them aboard ships. Carrick was most intrigued by the whole idea, and it was clear he wanted to participate. When the time came, we would see if it was possible.

In the meantime, I had him put the engines in good order and ready for transport—for it is one thing to take them out into the pasture on a fine spring day and hurl cobbles at targets, and quite another thing entirely to take them into war, where success is life and failure death.

✠✠✠

To Dunfermline I returned and reported to King Malcolm the progress on my siege preparations. Then I spent a full couple of days with Lady Aleine, to our great mutual enjoyment.

It was then that Cedric returned with Sir Hamish and Sir Cormac, both of whom were, it turned out, tired of long patrols through empty country and ready for, as Cormac put it, "summat wit' a wee bit more sport."

I greeted them warmly, and took them all to the inn across the road to "wash out the dust with ale." As we sat together, I told them of OdinsØye and his crimes, of the king's order, the jarl's castle and my plan to destroy it. Both Cormac and Hamish leaned closer at that point, for a good siege was sport not to be missed, and this one promised to be first-rate.

When I finished, Hamish asked the obvious question: "So what do you need us for?"

"I need a commander of archers to encircle the tower by land and hold the perimeter against breakout and escape overland. Could we employ here the same containment with archers, caltrops, and chevaux-de-frise that we used at Dunnottar?"

"Aye, that worked powerful well there. We could do that again," said Cormac.

"And I need at least one other commander for the siege boats. If I take one and Cedric another—Cedric, don't look so surprised; you wanted a command, didn't you?—I still need a commander for the third."

Cormac looked dubious at that, and said, "Then I'd better choose the archers. I canna' swim in chainmail, and like havin' solid ground beneath me."

I grinned, and said, "Cormac, no one can swim in chainmail. But if you don't fall into the water, you won't have to."

"Ahh, so that's what I've been doin' wrong!"

"Right then; so Cormac takes the land perimeter, and Cedric gets the ballista. Hamish, it seems the onager is yours."

Hamish grinned and said, "What we did at Dunnottar with that was truly a knight's recreation. I'll have a grand time. When can we get in some practice?"

"First gather your men. The king is paying and will pay well, so you will have no trouble. We'll need bowmen and crossbowmen enough for the perimeter and yet more who can pull an oar as well as fight with a bow from a ship. You know the kind we need. A hundred men apiece, you two. Any who served at Dunnottar is more than welcome. They'll need to be ready to take to the field after harvest at the end of August."

I thought a moment. "Bring them out to Cenachedne the third week in August and we'll spend a week sorting them out, getting in some archery practice and training with the machines. Then we'll march for Clydebank. We'll mount the machines on the ships and find some spot to practice bombardment from the ships for a day. Then we'll go kick in OdinsØye's door with damn great stones!"

✠✠✠

Late that week, Thorsson sent a message reporting that he had bought ships and hired a shipbuilder who had promptly started on our modifications, and firm promise to have them ready in three weeks. Thorsson said he would stay on to ensure that happened.

I sent Cedric back to Thorsson with a message to charter two other vessels with crews suitable to transport a hundred men and their siege supplies to Loch Goyll starting the first of September, and by him sent the money Thorsson would need to do it.

And so it was that—just when all was in hand and nothing could stop us—one fine summer's eve, a gang of four men lying in wait surrounded me in an empty street, pulled a coarse-woven sack over my head, and clubbed me unconscious.

EIGHT

✠✠✠

When I came around, I found I was trussed hand and foot, my head still covered by the sack. Through the weave I could tell it was night—but little else. But the jarring motion told me that I was in a cart or wagon headed somewhere over a rough track. And my head hurt, much as it had in another cart after the Battle at Demotika.

I lay still and listened, hoping to learn more of my attackers and their plans. I didn't have to wait long.

"Stirrin' is he?" said one. "Well, it'll do him no good. He never saw us clear, and once he's in the jarl's hands, he'll never be able to find us again."

Two men at least, then, riding on the seat of the wagon. How many more are there? Without moving, I began watching for shadows of any other men in the wagon, backlit by the lights we passed.

"Aye, he made an enemy sure when he tangled with OdinsØye. Wouldn't want to do that meself. That bastard carries a grudge like no one I've ever met, and I've known some purely mean men in my lifetime—worse even than tha bastard whose throat I cut for raping me mam an' makin' me!"

"What'd this 'un do?"

"Confronted the jarl in his own castle and beat his champion in a fair fight—a man bigger than any I ever seen, the size of a barn door and the weight of a prize bull. A man I know was there, and saw it all clear. And he did it as neat as anyone ever seen, bidin' his time, wearin' the big man down 'til he saw his chance, and then slashin' the big man's sword arm dam' near to bone. Then he goes and binds up the wound afore the big guy bled to death. And *then* he threatens the jarl with death and destruction if he attacks more monasteries like he had. Mighty queer, this 'un is!"

"So what's the jarl want him for? Revenge?"

"Nah. The jarl won't stop raidin'—he needs all that loot to build his castle and pay his men. So he goes an' raids three more at a single go. Then this 'un learns about it and goes to King Crovan and stirs up trouble against OdinsØye. So OdinsØye figures this 'un's gonna come after him—not that he could do much against that damn big stone fortress in any case. But why not just snatch him before he can? That's why we got hired."

"So what does the jarl want us to do with him? Cut him open, stuff a stone in his guts, and drop him in the loch?"

"That'd be a real good idea, and what I'd do! But the jarl wants him alive to bargain with if Malcolm brings an army against him. We're supposed to bring him breathin' to OdinsØye to get paid."

"And the two who helped us?"

"Cousins of mine in Dunfermline. Been watchin' him for days, to figure his comings and goings. Allus goes to check on his horses every eve in Dunfermline when the squire's away. That's how we knew when and where to grab him tonight."

You dolt! I told myself. *Walked right into it, thanks to habit. Well, it's just the two of them with me, then, on a long wagon-ride to the Firth of Clyde and a long boat-ride to reach OdinsØye's castle. Time enough to make something happen and figure out an escape…*

So what do I do…?

✠✠✠

I did not learn it until later, but up on his newly completed rooftop ramparts, Jarl OdinsØye was as angry and impatient as ever. He had hurried the completion of his defenses and then mounted his most recent raid in order to provoke a response from me—the jumped-up boy-sheriff—for I was the son of the man that OdinsØye hated most. And that was no mean feat, for OdinsØye hated everyone. But it was Baron Euan MacDougal, my father, who had taken OdinsØye's eye and left that horrid scar in its place a decade ago, when my father caught OdinsØye stealing cattle. And when he heard my name, OdinsØye decided to take belated revenge by forcing me to fight Bjorn. His defeat had been as unexpected as it was unfortunate. So OdinsØye had mounted the raid to try again.

But as I had not yet returned, OdinsØye had grown ever more impatient, hence the men he had sent to snatch me. And this time there would be no pretense, no stupid oaths, no delays. He'd load me with chains, lock me in a stone vault, cut the skin off me a square inch at a time, and rub sea-salt into the new wound. It would take months to kill me, and every day would bring agony.

The jarl liked that idea. Nothing brought him joy or satisfaction like the suffering of someone else, and the suffering of the men he hated most gratified him like nothing else could. Better still, those memories remained with him to enjoy always.

✠✠✠

I had only a small idea where I was, but I knew it would take two days to travel by wagon from Dunfermline, where I was captured, to Glasgow or Clydebank where they could finally take ship—and then another day's sail to reach OdinsØye's castle. I had no intention of remaining with them that far, nor any moment longer than I had to.

Whenever we passed a light, I tried to see through the sacking. Locating a weapon was my first priority, for I would immediately need one if I could free myself.

An hour later it began to rain, and with a sudden oath of surprise the driver halted the wagon. "Damnation! I've got a load of grain in the box for the jarl, as well as a trussed baron. If the barley in those damn sacks gets wet, some of it will malt and go to ruin, and he'll have my hide. I've got to get sailcloth over it now."

Muttering oaths, he ignored the comfort of his human cargo and dragged a cover, smelling as if it had once wrapped a corpse or a load of manure, over both barley and captive. I continued to feign unconsciousness. As the rain drummed down on the cover, the noise and visual barrier robbed me of hearing and seeing what my captors were doing, but it also gave me a much-needed opportunity, and I wasn't about to waste it.

From dealing with MacanFhirMhóir, I had learned more than one vital lesson, and one trick as well. The rogue had cheated death once with small blades hidden in his clothing. From that I had decided that the idea might prove useful to my own survival, so I had borrowed the idea. Now, I was sure it gave me a chance I would not otherwise have had.

As I had anticipated might someday happen, my hands were bound together behind my back and the rope then tied around my ankles. If I could reach them, I had a pair of flat blades—each the size of my thumb—hidden in little pockets inside the top of each boot. There were others in other concealments in my clothes, but those I could not reach, so these would be the vital tools.

Lying under the tarp with the sacks of barley in the rain, I began to try to recover one of the little blades. With a bit of strain, I succeeded, and managed to slip one from its pocket. Careful not to drop it, I was able to cut the thong that tied my wrists to my ankles, and then the ropes tying my ankles together. I was free to straighten then, and desperately wanted to, and ease my cramped muscles, but I dared not; to do so could reveal to my captors that I was escaping my bonds.

I nicked my wrist and cut a couple of fingers trying to get the blade to the wrist ropes, and nearly gave it up as impossible. But quitting meant death, so I tried again all the harder. Finally all the straining I did pulled the cord deep into my wrists but gave me a bit of slack where I needed it, and after a long struggle while my hands grew numb, I got a strand cut. After that, the slack grew as I struggled and soon my hands, too, were free. Carefully I rubbed blood back into them.

After the numbness receded, I ever-so-slowly eased my hands from behind my back and then the sack from my head, moving so slow I never seemed to move at all, and I managed to do this without attracting my captors' attention. I still had no weapon but the cord that bound me and the tiny blades. I had already felt about me to confirm that they had taken all my weapons, but they were probably in the wagon somewhere, so I tried to see them. I could feel that I still wore my mail, so I was largely impervious to *their* weapons. Every knight trained to face odds of two against one and more, so that posed no barrier to what I would need to do. I just needed to neutralize one of them as fast as possible.

The driver had been in a hurry and had not tied down the cover, just pulled it over his cargo. I could try to slip out and away, or I could jump up and try to overpower both men. Using the little blade to wound the driver with a neck cut might work—it would cause him big problems trying to cope simultaneously with a surprise attack, a team of draft horses on the move, and a serious wound. That would leave only the other man to overpower.

I didn't like that idea much, but these men took pay to kidnap me and take me to a certain death; they deserved no chivalry.

So I listened long and hard to learn if the two men still conversed. The conversation had stopped, so either the rider slept or the two men had run out of conversation. Either way, it was time.

But as I yanked back the cover and jumped up, a simpler solution came to me. With an iron-hard fist I punched the sleeping rider on the ear just as hard as I could, knocking him clear off the wagon. Then I punched the startled driver even harder on the side of the jaw, knocking him off the wagon and onto his head.

With both men floundering in the road, I scrambled onto the seat, grabbed the reins, and with a yell, whipped up the horses. The animals were already startled by the commotion and immediately leaped into a run.

Without looking back, I ran the horses a half-mile down the road, then pulled up. As I drove I had visually searched the wagon and located my weapons, so I quickly strapped them back on, feeling much better to have them once again. I climbed down from the wagon, cut free the two horses, climbed up on one and took the other by the reins, and then I turned both horses and headed back up the road the way I had just come.

A half-mile back, I met my captors again walking disconsolately. Hearing horses but not a wagon they were not expecting me, and when I appeared out of the dark, they stared without moving, then turned to run. But I was already on top of them. I clubbed the unfortunate rider down with another blow on the head with the flat of my sword, and held the driver at sword-point.

"Should you return to OdinsØye—which I don't recommend—I advise you both tell him I fought and you had to kill me and dump my body in the loch. He might believe you and let you live. I think he'll kill you all the same. Now enjoy the headache and the long walk, and don't ever return to Dunfermline."

Then I knocked the man unconscious and rode on for home.

✠✠✠

I learned later that because they took money for the kidnapping, failed to bring me back, and did not return to tell him so—two injuries compounded by insult—OdinsØye soon had them found, which wasn't too difficult, since they oh-so-foolishly returned to the same tavern in which his men had first found and hired them. And when they were brought to him, bound hand and foot as I should have been, they both told the same story, first separately and then together: that I had escaped my bonds and fought them; that they had in unfortunate desperation killed me—for which they were so sorry—and dumped my body, still in chainmail, into the Clyde where it sank forever.

OdinsØye half-believed them, for they were very sincere and very convincing; but although there was no way to prove it false, they had still failed him yet kept his money. So he had them killed and their bodies, like mine, dumped in the loch.

It was too bad, really; for if they truly had told the truth and I really was now feeding fish on the river bottom, OdinsØye would never get to enjoy the pleasure of torturing me to death.

And to OdinsØye, that was the real tragedy.

✠✠✠

As they pledged to do, Sir Hamish and Sir Cormac both arrived at Cenachedne in the third week of August, and brought with them two hundred archers and men-at-arms. They bivouacked in the meadow beside the village, and Hamish and Cormac quickly put them to work: setting up a proper camp; building chevaux-de-frise and wicker mantlets from withes and poles that I had had cut and hauled in from my timber groves; and engaging in combat practice of all kinds. We erected archery butts nearby, and all day men used them to sharpen rusty skills hitting a mark. The place buzzed with the shouts and laughter of men enjoying a rare bit of martial life.

In turn, the folk of Cenachedne lost no time in setting up a market fair to sell to the needs and wants of their army of guests. They soon earned a pretty penny from the trade. Carrick alone made a handsome profit as his smiths sold blades and arrowheads to men-at-arms and archer yeomen keen to buy good weapons.

Meanwhile, I had the three machines—the ballista, the onager, and *Bone-Crusher*—hauled to the meadow-turned-training range. There, Cedric, Hamish, and I picked three engine crews, and with their sweat set up each machine to hurl or shoot projectiles at mock targets, much as we had for the king's demonstration a year earlier. Downrange, cloth panels were erected between poles as targets. Not as satisfying, perhaps, as bombarding ruined hovels, but easier to replace as crews gained skill with their machines. And as skill and confidence improved, wicker hoops and wooden doors replaced the panels.

One at a time, starting with the ballista, I tutored each captain and crew: how to assemble their machine, and how to tear it down again and pack it for transport; the sequence of steps to correctly cock, load, and shoot each machine; the different projectiles each could shoot, and when and how to use each type; and finally the secrets of aiming and ranging each to hit their targets.

Then I gave command of each machine to its captain and went to teach the next crew, even as the previous team began to shoot for themselves and gain mastery of their weapon without my help.

The key to siege warfare, as I saw it, was not to pelt a city or castle helter-skelter with boulders and darts, but rather to strike strategic points repeatedly until I demolished a critical structure or breached an entrance into a citadel. Demetrius had drummed that strategy into me in Constantinople, and I had seen it succeed at Dunnottar. Now I would employ it against OdinsØye's castle.

So I incentivized the three crews by pitting them against each other, with prizes in silver for best performances at specific tasks: shooting fire-darts at wooden doors standing in for ship hulls, and hurling rock after rock through hoops representing doors, curtain walls, tower corners, and arch keystones. I praised fine shots and teased poor ones to incite jealous competition among the teams.

But in many ways it was no contest, for each weapon had an optimal mission, the reason I had one of each. Only the ballista could shoot a fire-dart like a crossbow, slamming a blazing cage of fire into a wooden door or wall and setting it afire. Only the onager hurled rocks rapidly, dropped fire-pots onto roofs, and battered in doors or walls with a series of boulders.

That said, it was still no contest. For when *Bone-Crusher* threw, it launched stones that outweighed the onager's ten-fold or more; when they struck, they punched huge holes. More importantly, as the skill of the crew grew, the stones produced a tight cluster of deep holes. Accuracy as well as power was its hallmark, and nothing could long withstand its blows.

Whenever *Bone-Crusher* threw, a crowd of onlookers quickly gathered to watch, thrilled by the power and wonder of the great engine and its remarkable accuracy.

For a full week, my little army trained and honed their skills. When they were finished—though I did not then know it—I had the most devastating military force in the entire world, for none had yet done what we were about to do.

We had reached the last of August. My army was assembled, organized, equipped, and trained. The engines worked better than I had imagined. We had a vile enemy to destroy and the means to do so in a dramatic new way. After this, warfare would change forever. But we could not finish until we began, and for that we still needed a fleet.

So it came as a great relief when a lad from Thorsson arrived in Cenachedne with a message that said in crude letters and strange spellings that the work at Clydebank had gone well and the ships would be ready and refloated by the time we arrived.

It was time to go to war.

✠✠✠

While the encampment was struck and packed, the engines were disassembled and loaded on their great wagons for transport. Tents, arms, baggage, military stores, and all the other provisions the king had supplied were loaded into carts and wagons. With the men afoot between wagons, our train stretched a quarter-mile.

The distance from Cenachedne to Clydebank was roughly twenty leagues. We marched seven leagues—twenty miles—a day. I had learned long ago, during my five-thousand-mile journey to Jerusalem and back with Count Robert, that this was an ideal pace to cover great distances without unduly wearing out my men and, more importantly, our draft animals.

When after three days the siege train finally reached Clydebank, I found that all Thorsson had said in his message was an understatement. Yes, the ships were ready and afloat, moored to the quay wall. But they were also splendid! The six hulls were old and hard-used, and the timber used to deck them was battered and marred by long previous use. For that, they did not look all that handsome—until you realized what they were: mobile, stable, floating fighting platforms. Each ship was well-suited to the size and weight of a siege engine, providing its crew ample room to load and launch their projectiles, and a cargo capacity that would easily hold three months' worth of projectiles—far more than I believed we would ever need.

In short order, I divided my men into three teams, and as each machine arrived, put them to work. With the engine captain and crew in charge, each team helped unload the engine timbers from the wagons and ferry them aboard the designated ship. Then the engine crew assembled the machine, and with the shipbuilder's carpenters, lashed and spiked the frame of the engine in place on deck amidships so as to throw or shoot over the bow. Meanwhile, other teams ferried ballast cobbles from the shipyard's stockpile and stowed them in the bilges of each ship. Atop this they stowed provisions, baggage, weapons, and great bundles of arrows.

Once the engines were mounted in place, I had men install the wicker mantlets made at Cenachedne, lashing and nailing them in locations that would afford engine crew and oarsmen protection from sling-stones and arrows.

When our work was done, the smallest and shallowest-draft vessel mounted the ballista, so that it could approach the inlet and attack the ships hidden within. The mid-sized ship carried the onager staged on the centerline to hurl over the bow.

The largest vessel was most unusual—two ships lashed and spiked side by side into one by heavy timbers supporting a single, solid deck that spanned both hulls from bow to stern. And in its center sat *Bone-Crusher*.

The sight of that ship struck awe into all who saw her, and as they finished their work, men gathered in clusters to stare at her. On the quay wall Hamish, Cormac, Carrick, Cedric, Thorsson and I stood entranced. Carrick broke the silence.

"Dear God Almighty, that thing is truly terrifying. Do you think she will work?"

I said, "If the shock of the launches doesn't rip her from the deck, I assure you, the stones she throws are going to do frightful damage to the jarl's stone tower. And if we can throw enough of them, that tower will collapse on him."

"And will this this thing hold together through all that? I canna swim, you know."

"She will, I'm certain." Then I turned to my commanders and grinned. "But Carrick is right. Just to be safe, all aboard this ship should probably wear just aketons and no armor. I can't swim in chainmail, either."

Thorsson bristled a little at that, and said, "She's got an entire damn forest of trees tying those two hulls together every other foot of the way from bow to stern. We spiked them to the gunwales and lashed them with hawser to the ship's timbers as well. And two layers of two-inch oak planks are cross-laid diagonally over those, just as you specified. Not much headroom for the oarsmen under it, but we checked that all can fit well enough. Dark as a tomb inside, so we need candles in lanterns below-decks. But she won't come apart, and I will gladly wear armor as a guarantee."

I clapped him on the shoulder and said, "Master Thorsson, I believe in you and implicitly trust your work. But some among us are nervous enough, at not only a new kind of warfare, but also a new kind of battlefield. A little humor only, to ease the fears."

Two other ships were moored nearby, transports for the bulk of my army—men-at-arms, archers, and crossbowmen who would create a perimeter encircling the castle by land. Into these ships we loaded tents, provisions, weapons, bales of arrows and bolts, disassembled chevaux-de-frise, barrels of caltrops, and wicker mantlets that would create an encampment, feed the men, and build a continuous barricade around OdinsØye's fortress.

Together Thorsson and I manned each siege ship with twenty oarsmen-archers, ten siege crew, the weapon captain, and the ship's master. Into each of the two transports went fifty archer-yeomen, their commander, and the vessel's master. The carters and wagoners were paid and sent back to Dunfermline to await another summons in the hopefully near future. Then the fleet unmoored and with the help of the river current and an ebbing tide, we began the ten-league pull to Loch Goyll.

✠✠✠

Rotating through the entire company aboard each ship at half-hour intervals, my vessels managed a most respectable league an hour. Even I and my captains took places in turn on the oars. This built respect and spirit among the men, who more readily follow leaders who take the same risks and put out as much effort as they require of their men.

Within three hours we were out of the river and into the Firth. I had the fleet heave-to then, so we could test-fire each weapon. Now was the time to learn if they would operate as I hoped, or if we needed to return to the shipyard and make alterations. First we summoned each crew topside on the ship's stern, lest some be trapped belowdecks and drowned if action of the machine proved disastrous.

I had no concern about the ballista, nor the onager, really. But *Bone-Crusher*, well, she was a monster, and both she and her ship were two new and untested ideas made into one. I prayed hard then that I knew what I was doing.

Cedric fired three bolts from the ballista easily, as if it was on dry land. Hamish threw big ballast stones three times with the onager, and while the ship bucked and wobbled a little with the shock, the action was minor. So far, so good.

Then it was *Bone-Crusher*'s turn. With the entire crew watching from the stern-quarters of the tandem-hulled ship, I cleared the area, called out the warnings, and tugged hard the trigger lanyard. The counterweight plunged and swung on its bail, and the great arm shot upward, whipping its sling in an arc, and a stone heavier than I was made a blur through the sky, and threw up a great pillar of water on impact close to 300 yards away.

The counterweight rocked fore and aft, waggling the great timber finger overhead. The ship pitched down and up, causing brief alarm among some in the crew, but that motion quickly damped. The deck itself held, for *Bone-Crusher* straddled both hulls from centerline to centerline, so that the deck timbers spread the load and shock entirely across the tandem hulls.

Twice more we cocked the great arm, loaded a boulder and threw it, to cheers from the entire fleet at the sight of power unleashed. By the third throw, my entire company grinned with anticipation, their confidence fully restored. We were ready.

✠✠✠

NINE

✠✠✠

Three more hours of hard pulling on the oars and we reached the mouth of Loch Long. By nightfall, we had reached Loch Goyll.

In a little cove south of the mouth and out of the castle's sight, we dropped anchor in the shallows, floating in a nest of vessels; as big as the ships were, all had a broad but shallow draft. A meal of lamb and barley stew was prepared over small fires built in firepots set on the ship's flagstone hearths, and I had ale shared out as both liniment and reward for the hard day's work. With watches set against tide, weather, and surprise, all of us got some well-earned sleep.

Up shortly before first light, I had a breakfast of oat gruel quickly served round to fuel the day. And then it was anchors up. Rowing at a swift pace, we quickly covered the remaining two miles to OdinsØye's castle.

It was still before dawn when the two transports quietly beached out of bowshot. One ship beached three hundred yards southeast of the castle, and the other three hundred yards northeast. The archers and crossbowmen crewing them swiftly went over the bow. Under Sir Cormac's direction, they established a defensive perimeter against a counterattack until all were ashore. Then groups of archers, bearing their weapons, a day's rations, and bundled poles for two chevaux-de-frise, swiftly made their way inland to enclose the castle in a semicircle, its radius just beyond the longest longbow range. After all, their job was containment, not combat.

As it was, OdinsØye's castle sat on a stony point jutting into the loch. Inshore, the land sloped gently up and away from it in all directions for three hundred yards before there arose a half-circle of steep hills and low mountains. It was this natural barrier that had made necessary my amphibious assault and seaborne siege.

Close around the castle a new ditch had been dug from shore to shore, forming a moat. Over it a new drawbridge had been built, its wood still white and unweathered, fresh from the cutting. A small, newly built timber bastion defended the bridge.

Just beyond the moat stood a new palisade, with a wooden wall-walk inside to support archers and slingers, stretched in an arc from the loch northwest of the castle to the loch southeast of it. Within it were three Nordic longhouses, necessary housing for OdinsØye's warriors, crews, animals and forage through brutal Scottish winters. In all, it was a compact but well-built fortress, well able to withstand the conventional assault of the age.

For timber to build these structures, OdinsØye had had the land cleared of all trees and cover out to the base of the hills, creating a killing field in the cleared land. And it was in the area beyond bowshot that Cormac posted his archers in small squads. His defensive line was six hundred yards long. As his men deployed, each squad worked quickly to erect their chevaux-de-frise by lashing six poles into three *X* shapes, connecting these with a long horizontal pole into a six-legged sawhorse, and adding sharpened poles angled like spears between the legs to create a wooden phalanx against charging horsemen. Placed end-to-end in a great wooden hedge, the archers then roped each chevaux to the next to create a continuous barricade of spears.

As some archers scattered handfuls of iron caltrops in front of this barricade to lame men and horses, others carried lightweight wicker screens called mantlets to their fighting positions, each screen affording two or three archers cover against incoming arrows.

Less than an hour from landing, the perimeter was complete. All this activity had not gone unnoticed, of course; the sentries on the castle parapets had seen the ships as the pre-dawn light grew and raised the alarm. But the invasion was so organized and swift that before OdinsØye realized his danger and did more than man his battlements, he was already surrounded.

✠✠✠

I had overlooked one thing in our planning, I realized, as the light grew. Close under the castle's covering fire, the jarl's fleet of ships were beached on the loch-shore or moored in the moat. Had I thought to do it, we might have sent a squad to fire them during the landing, and destroy the jarl's most valuable offensive asset before the siege even began. In this, my planning had failed.

It always bothered me when I realized my preparations had come up short, for I knew it might cause the deaths of men who had entrusted me with their single most precious and personal asset—their lives. I never feared for myself; indeed, my only real fear in life was failure, for failures that resulted in the preventable deaths of men I commanded would haunt me—they always did.

Nonetheless, the heart of my plan had always been a heavy and continuous bombardment, against which there was no defense beyond thick masonry already built. If OdinsØye sortied a force of fighters, my archers would fight to contain and kill their attackers. But I always intended that only my machines would do the hardest of the fighting, and force the jarl and his men to endure it in feckless impotency. And against that plan, the jarl's ships mattered little—unless they came out of their refuge to offer us battle at sea.

✠✠✠

For the moment, the jarl clearly had no such thought. As sunlight lit up the land and sea I could see OdinsØye atop his stout tower and watched him walk a full circuit as he surveyed us. *So the bastard had lived after all,* he must have thought, *and bought his promised army against me.* I was impressed by the speed and organization by which we established our blockade, and knew he had to be, too. Already he was completely hemmed in, as my siege ships moved in to complete the encirclement, and breakfast not yet ready in the castle kitchens. He watched us drop anchors fore and aft just beyond bowshot, my biggest ship the center of three. My strange contraptions, sitting ominously atop equally strange vessels, were a new puzzle, for nothing like them had ever before existed in Scotland. Were they some kind of bridging or scaling structures?

Later I learned what OdinsØye told his watch commander: "Well, sitting out there, they might pose a problem for my longships but they offer no threat to this fortress. Report any sign of those ships approaching any closer. If they get close enough, I'll burn them. Meanwhile we have our defenses in place, the cistern full, and the storerooms filled with enough provisions to last all winter if need be. These Scottish bastards will freeze long before we need aught else. We will wait and see what happens."

Then he went down to eat. On his way he told his castle steward, "Arm half our forces and man the palisade immediately. Feed the rest, then send them to the palisade so the first half can eat. Thereafter, divide the garrison into two watches. Four hours on, four hours off, day and night. Meals and sleep when off-watch."

Then he added, "They look like they may stay awhile."

✠✠✠

As the archers established their perimeter, I had Thorsson and the other masters move their ships into position, a longbow archer confirming that we were beyond the tower's bowshot by shooting at it and drawing arrows in return, all of those falling short.

As we moved in Thorsson had the masters sound the depths with sounding lines and discovered that an undersea ledge extended out from the castle's rock to give us good anchorage at a suitable depth. Thorsson told me the range of the tide in the loch could be read by the band of marine growth on the castle's rock, and it was slight—perhaps about a foot or so, no more—so the tidal current would be slight as a result. The anchors, backed by oarsmen if needed, would be quite sufficient to hold each ship in place.

With that, we were ready, so I promptly put my ships to work.

Each weapon had its targets. The ballista would start with fire-darts to set afire the beached boats opposite on the northwest shore. The onager would bombard the buildings, boats, and drawbridge just beyond the southeast beach. And I would unlimber *Bone-Crusher* to batter the tower itself.

✠✠✠

OdinsØye was just getting serious with his usual morning feast when *Bone-Crusher* hurled its first stone toward the castle. Once again I had the entire crew ondeck—not for safety this time, but rather to witness our first throw. I knew if they saw what we were about, I would win their heartfelt best efforts. And in battle, that is everything.

Without men at the oars to aim the ship, the pointing on the first throw wasn't ideal, so the stone went wide, missing the tower entirely. The defenders on the ramparts, who had watched us prepare with growing alarm, laughed and hooted with relief and derision as the stone flew harmlessly past, and taunted us with insults and bare arses. Only the watch commander realized peril had momentarily spared them and ran to where the stone fell. Sure enough, his worst fears were confirmed; a karvi, hauled out and lying bottom-up on the moat bank, now lay strangely—its keel shattered, the hull splayed wide and completely caved in.

Aboard our ships, the crews watched the stone fly, awestruck, and cheered the great crash they heard. Fully satisfied and keen to win, they readily went back to their posts—on oars, manhandling projectiles from bilge to deck, crewing the siege engines, and as archers guarding against counterattack by OdinsØye's longships.

I ordered the engine crew to recock the great engine, and chose a stone already marked for its weight with paint. As my eager men heaved the stone into the sling, I sighted along the aiming sticks and called for the oarsmen below to swing the ship two strokes to larboard. As the sticks centered on the tower and held, the crew removed the loading safety strap, and stepped clear.

I checked that all was in readiness, re-verified the aim, and called the warnings. Then I tugged the trigger lanyard, and *Bone-Crusher* threw her first warshot at the tower.

✠✠✠

The rampart watch captain wasn't eager to send down bad news to the jarl, for OdinsØye had a fearful temper well known among his men. The captain had witnessed what had happened to the two men taken after failing to bring back that baron alive—the same baron who now had them besieged. So he hesitated, hoping the weapon was as inaccurate on the second shot as the first. But his inaction proved more egregious than an unwelcome warning.

As a result, OdinsØye learned of the bombardment first-hand when *Bone-Crusher*'s second shot slammed squarely into the tower wall immediately behind him as he ate. His steward later told me what occurred.

A great hollow crash resounded through the building. Though the thick masonry held, dust sifted down in great clouds from gaps in the thick plank floors overhead, covering his breakfast with dirt.

OdinsØye jumped up in alarm, overturning his huge oaken chair, and ran up the stairs to the roof. Staring horrified at the siege engine even as we recocked it for the third shot, the jarl barely listened to the stammering of the captain before hurling him off the rampart wall to the cruel rocks sixty feet below. Every other member of the rampart guard shrank well back out of reach.

Jarl OdinsØye shouted at us then, hurling dreadful curses and personal insults over the water.

When he finally fell silent, I called back, “Now that you finally take me seriously, Jarl, I offer this: Surrender yourself to King Malcolm’s justice, and I will spare your castle, ships, and men. Refuse, and I will destroy all but the men who surrender. I give you a few moments to think and answer.”

In disbelief, OdinsØye did neither. Instead, he rushed to grab a bow and quiver from the nearest archer—spilling most of the arrows as he did—nocked one, elevated it, bowstring drawn to his ear, and took his best shot at me. And though his arrow flew true, it did not have the range to reach and struck the water twenty yards short.

I accepted his answer, and in reply, I launched my third stone.

Suddenly frozen with horror at the sight, the jarl watched transfixed as that great stone arced directly toward him. In the last instant it plunged, and struck the wall below him, powdering masonry with the impact. OdinsØye looked down at the two impact marks, and realized the second stone struck within a foot of the first. Worse, there was now a small, concave depression in the wall as shattered stone fell from it. With time and further impacts, the hollow would grow into a hole, and when the wall gave way to let in stones or fire, his once-mighty fortress would become his deathtrap.

With that OdinsØye suddenly realized that time was not on his side. Holding out until winter was not nearly good enough, but there was now damn little he could do about it.

✠✠✠

Even as I began to demolish the tower, Hamish and Cedric started wreaking destruction and carnage of their own.

On the southernmost ship, Hamish was cheerfully employing his onager—the Roman name for a catapult—to hurl stones and firepots at buildings, ships, boats, and the drawbridge. And he truly was having a grand time, picking targets and demolishing them. When war is one-sided in your favor, nothing is better.

On the northern ship, Cedric began shooting favorite projectiles at the beached fleet of longships. He truly loved the ballista—a giant crossbow, really, mounted on a stand that allowed the bow to be elevated and pivoted. Using it, he launched fire-darts: six-foot-long wooden shafts, each with a long spike as its warhead, backed by a steel cage filled with wool soaked in pitch, Danish tar, or flammable oil. Set aflame an instant before launch, a dart splattered burning liquid in a big patch on the target when it struck to set it afire. Cedric succeeded in setting a longship on fire, and planned to systematically burn all of them.

Suddenly, a hidden sally port at the base of the castle opened, and scores of heavily armed Northmen rushed along the beach to three longships hauled out there, and began to shove them into the loch.

As they did, archers on watch on the siege ships spotted them, and sounded the alarm with horns. Colored banners waved, spreading the warning among the siege ships. Quickly realizing the danger, I thought an instant.

"Carrick! Load a dozen blue stones into *Bone-Crusher*'s sling and make ready—quick as you can!"

"Aye!" the big man growled. To the crew he said, "You heard him. Jump!"

I called down to the oarsmen to swing the bow to starboard. Then, as crew cleared back and the sighting stick aligned with the longships, I tugged the lanyard.

Once again, *Bone-Crusher* spoke with authority, and a flight of blue stones sped toward the beach. With a great crash, one ship was holed even as she floated free from the beach and soon began to list. Another stone tore the prow from a second ship, ripping it open at the bow, and two other stones flattened Northmen as they struggled to get the ships afloat.

Meanwhile, Cedric took similar inspiration and with a fire-dart from the ballista managed to set the undamaged ship afire.

But the last ship was off the beach, and burning or not, the Northmen clambered in. Built without benches and lacking the sea chests that usually served as seats, the oarsmen had to stand to row. Forty of them thrust oars through the gunwale ports, another score crowded the centerline, scraping water from the bilge with helmets to extinguish the flames, and twenty bowmen clustered in the bow. And since the ship was now over-full, the remaining Northmen returned to the sally port, pounding on it to get back into the tower.

At the alarm on the siege ships, archers flooded up on deck and made ready to repulse the attack. By the plan we had arranged for this contingency, only one oar in four remained manned below to point the ships as needed. More than one hundred bowmen on the two northern siege ships confronted twenty Norse archers.

It was *Bone-Crusher* that posed the great threat to OdinsØye and had to be captured or burned. So as the Northmen pulled with a will toward my ship, the captains of archers on all my ships judged the longship's speed and distance carefully, and as each thought the target in range, called out the range and ordered volleys. Flights of arrows arced high and plunged into the longship, even as a score of arrows fell around the tree-bucket.

It wasn't a fair fight. Both sides shot arrows as thick and fast as possible, but my archers outnumbered the Northmen five to one, and so did the arrows. Within three volleys, half the Northmen on the oars were hit—for a man pulling an oar cannot hold aloft a shield. Those badly wounded dropped their oars, the trailing oars throwing the stroke into chaos, cutting the ship's speed markedly, and making steering difficult.

But unwounded Norse took the places of the wounded oarsmen, pulled all the harder, and their ship closed on *Bone-Crusher* still. Cedric's archers had to cease fire, lest their arrows hit men on my ship. Some of the Northmen readied grapples as others took up sword or axe, and shield. Only a third of our attackers were unwounded; but despite their wounds, another third remained determined to win victory or Valhalla; and those fifty-odd men were enough to overrun us.

But we had one more surprise for the Northmen. As the longship came in and grapples and throwing axes flew at us, the captain of archers cried, "Crossbows on deck! Shoot at will!"

Suddenly every other man onboard joined our archers, each bearing a crossbow. As the Northmen tried to clamber aboard, they were met by a wall of arrows from point-blank range. Only a dozen Northmen even reached the deck.

With sword and shield, I led a counterattack at the forefront of my men, and cut down two attackers myself. The fight at the ship's side was as brutal as it was short. The archers fell on the outnumbered Northmen with swords and seaxes, and promptly sent most of them to the Valhalla or Hell they had chosen in life. None of them surrendered but we took some of the wounded alive, too weakened to fight on.

The dead and mortally wounded went into the loch, their further suffering quickly abated by the burial usual to Northmen at sea. And after I had the prisoners stripped of weapons and wounds bound, we herded them back into their ship under heavy guard. The captain of the guard manned the oars with prisoners and they slowly rowed the ship to Cormac's battle line. They were, in truth, glad to be out of the fight—they had little love for OdinsØye after all—and they caused Cormac no trouble.

On my ships the wounded were also treated, but we had been fortunate: only two men killed by Norse arrows, one by axe, and a dozen wounded by arrow or axe.

With that lopsided defeat, OdinsØye had squandered his best chance. He should have led the attack, for whatever happened, it would have been better for him. But OdinsØye was in truth a coward as well as a brute, and no man for a real fight.

The attack and its aftermath had lasted less than an hour from start to finish. When it was over, signal banners through the siege fleet signaled resumption of the day's real business. Moments later, rock projectiles flew again, and the siege truly began.

✠✠✠

I resumed battering the tower, stone after stone to hammer at the dent in the wall. Cedric resumed setting all the longships, boats, and the palisade afire with dart after dart. Ashore, the Northmen were kept busy trying to extinguish all the blazes he was starting.

Hamish continued to hurl stones and firepots at buildings, boats, and the drawbridge. At Dunnottar, he and I had used clay jars filled with burning pitch to burn MacanFhirMhóir's longhouses. Here he worked to do the same.

The jars left a trail of greasy smoke through the sky as each arced landward, and exploded in a patch of flame wherever they burst on impact. Soon he had the steep roofs of two of the crews' barracks aflame, and they were too steep to climb while bearing buckets of water to douse the blazes. He hammered holes in the palisade near the water's edge, his stones snapping timbers like twigs with their impact. All the ships and boats he could see were ideal targets, and a single stone would put a hole through the bottom, whether the vessel was afloat or hauled out.

✠✠✠

As the sun set, I called a halt. As my hungry men ate in shifts throughout the fleet, Thorsson sent boats to fetch Cedric and Hamish. When they arrived, we all ate together and took stock of the day's success.

As things stood, beyond the three dead and the dozen injured in the morning attack, we had no more men killed or wounded, for we had stayed out of range of OdinsØye's weapons throughout the day. Our wounded were likely to survive and recover if fever did not take them.

To the north and south, the palisade had been holed or burned. Two of the longhouses burned fiercely, and the Northmen had been forced to abandon the palisade wall-walk nearby when the heat from the flames became too great. Cedric had burned two ships, Hamish had holed a ship and a boat, and one of the karvi was crushed—the victim of *Bone-Crusher*'s first stone.

The tower now had a great dent in its stone wall, a depression eight feet in diameter and two feet deep, formed as the great tree-bucket pulverized the masonry with great stones. Another such day, two at most, and we would punch into the great room. And then, when we hurled in firepots and fire-darts, the whole tower would burn, for only its walls were stone. The columns, framing, floors, furniture, stairs, walls and roofing were all built of wood.

So far, so good. OdinsØye had counted on formidable defenses to defeat any attack, and had not counterattacked because, frankly, his offensive options in this kind of war were poor. He was a seaborne raider, and had no heavy horse to charge his enemies. A shield wall had too many gaps my bowmen would exploit—unprotected faces and legs make good targets. A decent archer could put an arrow through any hole as big as his palm. All of my bowmen had been chosen because they were far better than that.

The jarl's Northmen were no doubt ruthless killers, but with only defenseless monks and nuns as their recent opponents, they were unprepared to face a well-organized army of crossbowmen and archers. And my siege machines had already destroyed more than walls and ships, for they were in truth weapons of terror. When the strongest castle in the land could be torn apart in hours by great stones and fire—against which there was no good defense

—it ruined an enemy's confidence, killing his will to fight and his hope for victory as well as his stronghold.

We four siege captains already knew what we would do during the night and on the morrow. So all through supper and the ale that followed, we debated the key question, which was this:

What could, and what would, OdinsØye do next?

✠✠✠

Our debate considered his options. And as the well-planned and well-constructed world he lived in was systematically demolished around him, Jarl OdinsØye had to be doing the same. And he could not like the options he had left or the conclusions they led to. I felt sure he had come to rue ever hearing my name, much less baiting me into this titanic duel.

He had never seen any of the machines now arrayed against him; indeed, he could never even have heard that machines like them existed—for mine were the only ones in all Scotland. And the fact that they floated on ships just out of his reach and dropped death and destruction on him with impunity had to fill him with outrage and frustration. That the too-young son of his enemy did this made it all the worse.

It came down to this: if he did nothing, we would soon set his tower afire or drop it on his head. Surrender might save his men, but it wouldn't save him. He could try to escape alone or with a few retainers, but our landside cordon was tight, and we expected an attempt, so he was unlikely to succeed. If he formed the men he had left into a shield wall to attack the landside perimeter, we would swarm in, surround them, yet stay beyond sword's reach, to simply kill or wound them all with arrows. And it wasn't clear if he could still get a ship or boat into the loch, given the damage we had already done to his fleet—everything on the loch shore, or outside the shadow of the castle, was already a wreck.

Still, a seaborne escape in the wee hours looked like his only choice left, and it would best use the fighting skills of his men. It meant abandoning all he had amassed to flee to kinsman Crovan or hide in Argyll or one of the western isles, in order to keep his life, which was all he had ever really cared about anyway.

But the fires that burned all around the castle cast far too much illumination, spoiling all opportunity for escape by dispelling the darkness. As it was, OdinsØye would have to wait for them to burn out so another night would provide the darkness for escape.

✠✠✠

I dearly wanted to keep up the bombardment all night, but my men had worked hard through two days and the intervening night, and badly needed sleep. And no one could sleep through the great groans of *Bone-Crusher* in action and the thundering crash of her stones on the castle wall.

So I chose prudence as a necessity and instead set night watches and sentries specifically to keep wary eyes open to acts of attack, treachery and escape. The whole castle glowed in the firelight, the scene was beautiful in a terrible way. So I gave orders to wake me for the midnight watch, rolled up in a cloak and slept in the tray of my great wooden mistress.

But before I fell asleep, across the water I heard Cedric play on his fife the same little tune he had played once before as a musical joke while we tested *Bone-Crusher*'s older brother. The tune was haunting, melodic but sad, almost a dirge. And then to that same tune, in a strong voice that carried clearly to the jarl's castle and echoed off its great wall, Cedric sang these words:

"We've brought up the army.
We camp at your door.
Our peace terms you refuse,
So now you'll get war.

"We'll cave in your rooftop
With boulders we cast.
With fire we'll burn all
So nothing will last.

"Come out now and fight us,
We'll entertain you.
And many will die here
before we are through.

"Your castle can't save you.
We'll never withdraw.
Until you surrender
We stay at your wall."

It gave me a shiver of fear to hear it, for it was very determined, very threatening, very ominous. I could imagine what the men it was meant for thought of it, and at that moment, I was very glad I was not among them. Nor was I the only one to think so.

My army was up before dawn. A hearty breakfast of mutton and barley stew washed down with ale was the reward for our initial success and liniment against the day's renewed aches. And as the sun rose, I sent OdinsØye an awakening in the form of a hundred-pound impact.

Cedric and Hamish had already smashed or burned their targets, so at my orders they moved their ships closer to mine, and Hamish began bombarding the wall also. His smaller stones were far less effective, but he could throw faster than I, and they began to add up. It wasn't much past mid-morning when cracks began to radiate from the impact crater, extending with each succeeding stone. Soon after, Cormac sent word that many of the Northmen were now clustered in the center of the palisade, too terrified to remain inside the tower.

And a curious thing occurred. Cedric's tune began to resound, whistled or sung, as my men used it to synchronize their work:

> *"Your castle can't save you.*
> *We'll never withdraw.*
> *Until you surrender*
> *We stay at your wall."*

At about noon, without warning, the center of the great crater gave way; stones fell inward and out, pouring down in a great cascade into a huge pile at the foot of the tower. A gaping hole, fully ten feet in diameter, replaced it. A great shout went up from the fleet. A moment later, Jarl OdinsØye appeared in its center, gaping in disbelief, for masonry more than three feet thick had been holed in sixteen hours by a machine without precedent, its only name—tree-bucket—created in jest.

I wasted no time. "Cedric!" I called, pointed at the ballista, and waved toward the castle. Cedric understood—he had it already cocked and loaded with a fire-dart. A moment later, he shot the flaming missile at that gaping maw in the tower.

A trail of black smoke marked the passage of the dart and ended deep inside the great room. But Hamish wasn't to be left out, so a firepot from the onager followed it in even before the smoke had dissipated. Two more darts and another firepot quickly followed.

In moments, firelight began to glow in the dark room, and smoke to billow from the hole. Both firelight and smoke rapidly grew, and men began to pour from the tower. Only the men on the ramparts now remained, trapped by the fire below. Soon they would be faced with a terrible choice: jump or burn.

Fortunately for them, one man was braver than the rest and risked the flames to reach the armory on the fifth floor, where he found rope. It wasn't enough to reach the ground, but man after man got down to fifteen feet before having to drop the remainder of the way. Nearby, they gathered as lamed but grateful survivors.

After that, nothing more was required—the tower was doomed. Both attackers and defenders stood in clusters watching the tower burn. Soon, a column of flame reached more than a hundred feet into the sky, rising in a strange twisting swirl that no one had ever seen before.

✠✠✠

I had myself rowed ashore, well clear of the palisade. Hamish and Cedric accompanied me while Thorsson and the ship masters remained in command. We were met there by Cormac, and after conferring briefly, we called upon the castle—or what remained of it—for a truce to parley.

Mixed answers came back, so I resorted to yelling my terms: All who surrendered their weapons and came out peacefully would live; all who resisted would die. And those who brought me OdinsØye alive would be pardoned and rewarded.

From inside the ruined palisade, I could hear the jarl angrily haranguing his men, but thought that it would be of little effect. And I guessed correctly, for soon enough, a parley flag appeared. When I granted the parley with an answering flag, a body of men emerged, peaceful and unarmed. There was only one discrepancy in their midst, for Bjorn the Bear bore an axe as he marched the raging OdinsØye ahead of him, the jarl's collar tightly gripped in one huge fist. And when the jarl struggled too hard to break free, Bjorn smacked him on the head with the flat of the axe.

To me they marched directly. Bjorn said, "Lord MacEuan, we have conferred among ourselves, and I speak for all but him. We surrender to you, every man, for all of us believe King Malcolm's justice will be fairer than this man has ever been. We know you do as you say, so we can trust your word. We hand this man over to you in mitigation of past acts, and give our word that you will have no further trouble from any of us."

I said then, "And I know that I can trust your word as well, Bjorn, for you are true as well as brave. Those who murdered nuns or monks or raped nuns must face justice. The rest will be pardoned and returned under escort to King Crovan to serve the lord he chooses. Fair enough?"

Bjorn looked around and said, "More than fair. You dealt with those men when they attacked you in the longship. OdinsØye used the threat of Malcolm's justice when he chose the men to send out in the ships."

"And those that returned via the sally port when we destroyed the ships?" I asked.

Bjorn replied, "OdinsØye had them locked in a storeroom for cowardice, and refused to release them as the tower burned. They cooked there first, as they now no doubt do for all eternity."

I nodded and accepted what could not really be proven otherwise. After all, it was just what OdinsØye would do.

"Very well, Bjorn, the siege is over. Bring all your people out, and let us treat your wounded first."

✠✠✠

What was left of Jarl OdinsØye at that point was hardly human, and well beyond all manner of redemption.

"Give me a sword and face me, MacEuan," he bellowed, "And in Valhalla I will dine tonight as you roast in your Hell, Christian fool."

Even in defeat, OdinsØye was full of pride and bluster, incapable of understanding, much less accepting, that silence is often wiser and much more becoming than empty boasts.

Disgusted, I had had my fill of the man. "I gave you that chance when first we met, and you declined. Indeed, you have always had the chance since. But not now. That time is past. You have no honor, so you do not deserve it."

To my men I said, "Gag him, and bind him hand and foot." Then I gave another order, one that got OdinsØye's attention at last, his lone eye going wide at its hearing: "Take him to *Bone-Crusher*."

A half-hour later aboard ship, all was in readiness when I had the gag removed. OdinsØye was spluttering incoherently, alternating between outrage and piteous whinging. Finally he was reduced to open weeping—and at that sound, all in Valhalla plugged their ears against him as cowardice damned him forever.

I addressed him then. "When I set out, King Malcolm ordered me to punish you for your many crimes against innocents, convey his displeasure with you in the strongest terms, and speed you into Hell. You go there now.

"I once warned you that if you continued your crimes, I would return in force, destroy this tower, and paint its ruins with your blood. I swore it then, and for that, you should have heeded me. As it is, for years to come, people will look upon this, your castle, and remember only this sight of you."

Then I pulled the lanyard once final time, and the tree-bucket—or *trebucket/trebuchet*, as it would come to be known—made one last throw at the ruined tower. The projectile screamed in terror through the short flight, the shriek cut short as OdinsØye created a large vivid red spot on his ruined tower wall.

In that way I provided OdinsØye a memorable tombstone. And *Bone-Crusher* earned her name.

✠✠✠

In the aftermath of the siege, we had much to do. We put the defeated—and now docile—Northmen to work pulling down the palisade. We dismantled our perimeter and reloaded war material and provisions on the transports. I called out the carpenters from among my men and the Northmen, and under Thorsson's supervision, and had the damaged ships repaired—we needed them to transport the Northmen to King Crovan's Isle of Man.

The unburned longhouse proved to contain a substantial cache of weapons and provisions; these too went into our transports. The tower had burned to a bare shell of masonry. After the ashes cooled, we discovered in them much looted monastic treasure. This we raked out and gathered into chests built from the planks of the wrecked longships. As was customary, four-fifths of the recovered wealth would be returned to its owners—in this case the monastic houses; the balance would reimburse the king his expenses, and reward the services of my men in its recovery.

When all was done, we raised anchor and my fleet rowed back to the Firth. There, the ships filled with Northmen parted company. Hamish and an escort would see the Northmen got to Man, and then return the longships to the Clyde shipyard to be sold; they were our prizes, after all.

With the Northmen I made one exception: Bjorn the Bear. The wounds I gave him months earlier had healed, and though the muscles were still weak, he was regaining use of them, perhaps because my blade was so sharp. A sharp blade cuts deep, but its wounds heal faster and cleaner, too.

Because he had helped bring OdinsØye to justice, I offered Bjorn another option: service in Alba. I had respect for his strength and courage and thought he deserved another life. So I gave him the option of returning with us and finding a better future. He was surprised but willing, and for that I was most pleased.

I had the siege vessels and transports return to the shipyard on the Clyde. There the troops unmounted the siege engines and helped ready them for transport to Cenachedne. Thorsson would stay behind to sell all the ships. With him I left Cedric in command of a squad of men-at-arms to see him—and the sales proceeds—safe to Dunfermline.

Cormac and I then led a long wagon train of provisions, treasure, engines and troops to Dunfermline. There, Carrick took charge of the wagoners and hauled the siege engines on to Cenachedne for storage while we delivered our treasure and cargo. With him I sent Bjorn; the man was mending, but there was no recuperation like working iron with a hammer to rebuild his strength, and this way he could earn good silver while he did so.

Cormac had the troops paid and mustered out while I reported our success to the king. I intended to give Malcolm a concise, unembellished report of OdinsØye's defeat, but Malcolm demanded details, and it won't do to refuse your king. So I spent an hour or more in his chamber answering his many questions, explaining how we had laid and conducted the siege, and the details of its outcome. He was most fascinated by the idea of *Bone-Crusher* mounted on a deck built over two hulls, and stated outright a wish to have seen it in action. In truth, I wished he had also.

At the conclusion he said, "Baron, once again I congratulate my wisdom for having given you this task. It could not have ended better. Not only did you handle the diplomacy with King Crovan well, but you have now fulfilled the treaty you made with him without making us more enemies of the defeated men. Very well done! How may I reward your service?"

Now, I have always been better able to bear criticism than praise —perhaps because I've had more of the former than the latter. Praise leaves me embarrassed to hear it—but I have to admit, I do relish it. And typically then, all I can do is stammer a thank you.

But in this case I did have a favor to ask. "Sire, I have all I need, so add my share to the others. But grant me this: Bjorn the Bear fought me honorably and lost. He helped bring a good ending to the siege. Now he needs new circumstances. I have engaged him to recuperate with Carrick at the forge to regain his strength. When he has, I ask he gain a position in your service. I believe he will be a splendid bodyguard, for yourself, or more particularly, for the queen. Until we fought he was undefeated, so I know his skill; yet I judge he has a good heart and quiet nature. Carrick will assess the man and confirm whether I am right."

The king nodded. "Your recommendation goes far, Godric. Very well. When he is strong again, send him with a letter to me and I will engage him. If the queen finds him to her liking, he will be her man. Otherwise, I will add him to my guard."

I thanked him then and took my leave. I sent a note conveying this good news to Carrick and Bjorn in Cenachedne, and then went to find my wife. It had been too long since last I held her.

The balance of the year was quiet and I spent much of it between Dunfermline and Cenachedne where we celebrated the Christmas of 1092. It was wonderful; all the more so for too many years, in light of the events that followed. But more on that in due course.

✠✠✠

TEN

✠✠✠

In early 1093 rumors reached King Malcolm that King Rufus had started building an English castle at Carlisle in Cumbria. Of course, this was disquieting news, for if true it meant Rufus had abrogated his oath to Malcolm within a year of acknowledging Malcolm's rule of Cumbria and agreeing to respect his lands and our realm in return for peace and fealty. Rufus was once again trying to steal Cumbria, this time by building a huge weapon of aggression—a castle filled with military might—in the midst of a region he had just sworn was Scottish. So Malcolm sent for me.

"Baron, I fear our treacherous neighbor to the south is back to his tricks. I am told he has a small army of men-at-arms and workers building a castle in Carlisle. I need to know if the rumor is true, and I need the strength of the castle assessed by one who knows how to destroy such fortifications. You are the best I have."

"I understand, sire, and go now. Do I leave it unmolested?" The question was both apropos and pointed because, at this stage, the castle would be highly vulnerable to destruction by fire.

The king thought aloud. "Much I would be pleased if it burned, but to the English it would be but a setback. Alba and England are at peace. I will not risk war until better remedies fail."

So I and Squire Cedric donned again our disguises as mercenaries "Wilhelm of Flanders" and "Rolf," and rode south to assess in secret the builders' progress. To our dismay, we discovered the rumors were true, and the castle well along. Using the skills I had learned as a scout for Count Robert, I mapped the castle; in particular, weaknesses in its defenses. And I taught Cedric how to do this also.

We found construction underway where legend said once stood a Roman fort. The English had already raised a substantial hill—the motte—by hauling to the center earth dug from a circular perimeter ditch—or moat, if it was later flooded by digging a short channel to the adjacent River Caldew. Inside this ditch rose the tall, stout timber palisade typical of a Norman-style motte-and-bailey castle. Against the palisade barracks, stables, granaries, storerooms, forge and kitchens were being built, while atop the motte was the framing and scaffolding needed to raise a large square donjon, or tower, of perhaps three or four stories. All were built of wood and, as yet, not fireproofed by any means.

Dearly did I want to burn the place, and with fire arrows could have set enough ablaze in a few moments to destroy many of the buildings at least. Most reluctantly, I had to let it stand, and construction continue unhindered. I regret now that I did not burn the place, no matter the cost to me, but correct decisions are always easy to make when looking back. Instead, we rode home and reported our findings to Malcolm. It was only to be expected that he was not happy to hear it.

Malcolm sent protests in writing against this new intrusion to Rufus, calling him a faithless rogue for failing to keep pledges of honor. The exchange of heated correspondence included renewed threats of war, which eventually led to a fateful decision for the monarchs to meet and settle their differences face to face. The meeting was set to occur in Gloucester late in the month of August 1093.

✠✠✠

Months spent toiling at a hot forge for hours every day, six days a week as once I had—had rebuilt Bjorn. The work and heat had melted away all the fat of sickly idleness, and his right arm was like the iron he pounded—even stronger now, he said, than before we fought. Standing all day had strengthened his calf muscle as well. But best of all, he found a new peace and focus in the work that burned away much that was sick in his soul.

Meanwhile my ship captains brought me word that Rufus had been struck down by fever in February of 1093, and came to believe he was dying. Filled with sudden panic that his unnatural appetites, great greed for others' land, and theft of Church revenues would make his damnation certain, he had a sudden change of heart—to the point of naming Anselm of Bec the Archbishop of Canterbury, a bishopric he had held open for years so he could keep its income. But Rufus was not dying after all, and after he recovered, he quickly reverted to his wicked ways. He also regretted appointing Anselm and so vehemently renewed his animosity to the Church.

His health restored, Rufus again invaded Normandy. But unlike his previous attempts, this year he made no gains before returning in August to meet King Malcolm.

Now, in all those years of chasing about the kingdom, I was often away from Dunfermline—and from my beautiful wife. Aleine and I were always happy together, and both our days and nights together were joyful. But until 1093 we had had no children.

Not for not trying, mind you—we did plenty of that. But never was there a blessing of our efforts as Heaven's reply until the spring of 1093. It came as a most pleasant surprise and a bit of a shock, then, that Aleine shyly told me she was with child. And I don't know who was happier—me, her or Queen Margaret, who despite ongoing illness had her motherly instincts reawakened by the pregnancy, and took special pleasure in Aleine's happiness.

✠✠✠

About Bjorn, Carrick gave me a good report. He had kept Bjorn close, and the two men came to enjoy working together, much in the way Carrick had enjoyed working with me. And at some point he said Bjorn started asking about the Christian faith—small questions at first, but he clearly liked what he heard as Carrick told him the stories he knew. Bjorn asked to attend Mass on those days we had a priest in Cenachedne, and stayed through the first portion—the readings from the gospel and the sermon, when heathens who sought to join the faith were permitted to be present.

And in keeping with Christian teachings and tradition, on Easter Sunday, Bjorn was baptized and given Holy Communion, Carrick standing at his side as sponsor and godfather. I made Bjorn a baptismal gift of gold, Alice and Aleine gave him new clothes, and it was a very happy new Bjorn that accompanied Aleine and me back to Dunfermline.

Queen Margaret soon liked him very much, and was most pleased to have him. Sick as she was, a strong man to lift her from bed to chair or back proved most welcome, and Aleine told me she could not believe a man as kind and gentle as he had ever been OdinsØye's killer.

✠✠✠

At the start of August, with Malcolm leading a strongly armed escort of Scottish nobles and knights numbering in the hundreds, we rode south. Since it was to be a peaceful meeting between kings, Queen Margaret accompanied King Malcolm, and my Aleine rode with her in a well-slung carriage.

Our route took us first to Durham, for King Malcolm was a great devotee of Saint Cuthbert, whose relics were enshrined there. And King Malcolm and Queen Margaret ceremonially set the cornerstone of the new cathedral being built to honor that saint.

We reached Gloucester on the twenty-third and the monarchs met on the twenty-fourth. I was among the nobles who attended the meeting.

Rufus had been in Gloucester for more than a week ahead of our arrival and had planned the meeting most carefully. A large pavilion had been erected on the open ground between the motte-and-bailey castle there and the great abbey, and in this we met.

As we entered, with King Malcolm the foremost, we saw Rufus seated in a large gilt throne at the far end. Chubby, red, and splendidly attired, he looked like a suckling pig wrapped in church vestments. The approach to the throne proceeded between thick ranks of English nobles forming a long avenue.

As Malcolm entered, Rufus refused to rise in welcome. A sense of foreboding swept through me, and with good reason, for in his greeting, Rufus was both insolent and disrespectful.

"Ahh, Malcolm, I see you have answered my summons. We have much to discuss—your insistence that you own our lands of Cumberland and Northumberland, your cruel dispossession of our subjects in those regions, and your unceasing demand for yet more lands and possessions in our northern realm. As a reasonable man and a generous king, I am, of course, willing to discuss these. But first I expect you to honor the oath of fealty you gave me two years ago. Kneel and pay homage to your king, as all these nobles gladly do, to acknowledge and prove your respect for our royal authority."

I looked about. All the English lords and knights I could see wore smirks. Rufus's immediate demand that Malcolm pay him an unwarranted homage as a subordinate vassal, here in this gathering of English barons, broke all protocols and violated all accords between sovereign kings. In fact, I believe Rufus always deliberately intended to humiliate Malcolm as a provocation, a way to create a pretext for a war he wanted—indeed, the war that followed.

King Malcolm remained erect and visibly bristled at the insult. "You misjudge me, William, if you think I will pay you homage here. For the sake of peace I gave you the oath of fealty between kings. If you want it renewed, we will do so, as ancient custom dictates between kings, as I did with your father: on our common border and in the presence of the principal lords of our kingdoms. Not here and not now."

Rufus oh-so-arrogantly rejected this. "No, my lord, no! The pledges made to you were conditional and always depend on your fealty. If you wish me to honor them, you will honor me!" He looked about the pavilion and said, "And I demand it—both here and now. Here and now!"

Now Rufus had already broken faith with Malcolm—the castle at Carlisle was proof. So his demand here could only have been made as an excuse to justify breaking his pledges to Malcolm. Malcolm's refusal to debase himself would give Rufus rationale to do it. But if Malcolm acquiesced, it would give Rufus as Malcolm's overlord the right to claim all of Alba for England. And Malcolm, Rufus and every noble and knight there knew it.

So Malcolm refused, and said instead, "For three years now, you have tried to steal our land. You sent your sneak thieves, men with false titles and charters, to occupy land you pretend to rule. You named a rogue the Earl of Carlisle and you build a castle there even now. You have invaded my kingdom three times in as many years, bringing armies over my southern border, pillaging my people and stealing their substance. But Cumbria is mine. My accords with your father settled that, and a year ago you swore an oath to the same terms. He could not take it from me, and neither will you, despite all your petty schemes."

At Malcolm's words, Ranulf Meschyn, the so-called Earl of Carlisle, took umbrage and stepped from the throng, a hand on his sword hilt. I moved between him and Malcolm, happy to cut him in half if necessary. But Rufus said, "Earl Ranulf!" and impatiently waved his earl back.

Malcolm went on. "Before I became King of Scotland, I inherited my holdings in Northumbria as a young man from my uncle

Siward. I declare that I retain my right to rule it to you and all who dispute my title. William and I settled our border with the Treaty of Abernethy in 1072. To secure that and my possessions in Northumbria, I gave him an oath of fealty. I gave you only the same oath on exactly the same terms. I owe you nothing more. And if you do not honor your father's treaties, your acknowledgement of my rights as king, and your pledge of peace to me, I owe you no fealty, and you deserve no homage."

Then Malcolm said, "If you want my land, bring an army. You are an evil little thief, not a king. A weasel, not a lion. I'll talk no more with you; it accomplishes naught."

Shouts of outrage rose from the English and we matched them, insult for insult. We might have come to blows then and there. However, the flag of truce under which we met carried penalties of everlasting dishonor and eternal damnation upon those who broke the truce, and neither they, nor we, would go that far.

Malcolm turned on his heel, and our ranks opened down the center to let him through and lead us from the pavilion. In leaving, no other Scot turned his back on the English. I was the last Scot out, and saluted them with my middle finger. A roar of outrage followed me out.

I am sure Rufus was delighted to achieve his purpose. He could disregard all his previous promises and act with impunity to invade our land without legal or moral hindrance now, not that those ever mattered to him. For our part, I know King Malcolm was completely unhappy and enraged, more by the turn of events than by any insult. He led us home, and promptly began to muster a tremendous army.

✠✠✠

ELEVEN

✠✠✠

In October of 1093, Malcolm led us through Northumbria intending to go as far as Durham. The night before we marched, he made clear to his council of war our purpose.

"Until now we have been content to share Northumbria and allow the English to control much of it. No longer! Rufus wants our lands, and brings an army to take them. But we will march first and empty Northumbria of the English before he gets here, and leave him nothing on which to base his claim to it."

Along the way we proceeded to ravage and lay waste every English stronghold there with fire and sword. We did our work well, and all through the region, columns of smoke rose by day from the manors we fired, and pillars of flame lit the night.

✠✠✠

T'was the 11th of November in 1093. The English Earl of Northumberland had built a wooden motte-and-bailey fortress named Alnwick Castle, and I was busy encircling it with a siege.

I began there as I had with Dunnottar and OdinsØye. At first light I surrounded it, and with caltrops and chevaux-de-frise cut off all reinforcement and resupply of its garrison. Opposite the gates we created bastions—improvised strongholds to protect us against a

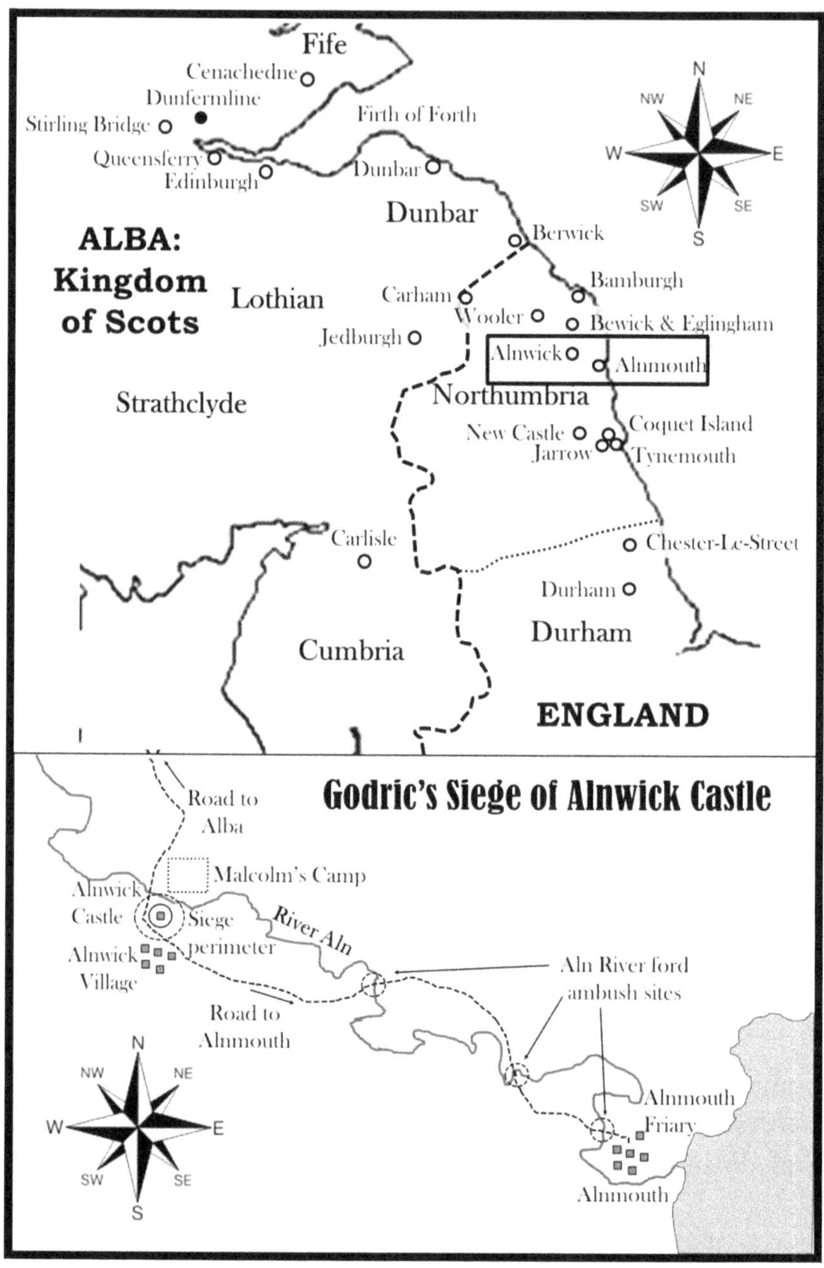

Figure 6: Godric's siege of Alnwick Castle

counterattack—from chevaux, mantlets, gabions, and strong placements of archers.

I had the castle completely isolated by midday. Since we gave the defenders no warning or means to gather extra food and forage, without relief their situation would soon be desperate, and with it surrender would come.

But we could not afford to wait, so I proceeded to burn them out. On the second day I used my ballista, brought from Cenachedne for just such a purpose, to shoot fire-darts and set a large portion of the castle's outer palisade aflame. As the wall burned, in spite of the defenders' best efforts to extinguish the blaze, my sappers worked to reassemble my onager. It was my intention to hurl jars of flaming pitch into the castle and set afire the buildings inside. In the interests of mobility—and no stone fortifications worthy of her—I left my tree-bucket, *Bone-Crusher*, in Cenachedne.

✠✠✠

On the third day of the siege, the 13th of November, while I was supervising the siege work, a party of English knights rode into our encampment, a half-mile north on the north shore of the River Aln, under a flag of truce. Sir Arkil Morel and Sir Geoffrey en Gulevant said they came on behalf of Sir Robert de Mowbray, the Earl of Northumberland. They said King Rufus had requested the earl to negotiate renewed peace with King Malcolm, but that Sir Robert was sore ill with fever and being treated by the monks in Alnmouth, not far downriver. They asked King Malcolm to return with them under a flag of truce to Alnmouth and negotiate peace with the earl. They swore on their honor that a full truce would exist throughout the negotiations.

King Malcolm agreed to the meeting, and sent to me a messenger directing me to suspend further attack on the castle under the terms of the truce. Then he rode off to Alnmouth with the English escort. With him he took his sons, Edward and Edgar, and several of the chief Scottish lords as his counsel: Earl Gospatric of Dunbar; his son Dolfin, the Earl of Cumbria; Mormaor Madach MacMeallmor of Atholl; Mormaor Gillebride of Angus; and Mormaor Malpender of Mearns. Many Scottish lords and knights rode in the honor guard, almost one hundred in all. Had I been there, I certainly would have also gone.

As customary during a truce, Malcolm's party rode in armor and armed, but with their helmets removed and tied to their saddle-bows. This allowed both sides to recognize the opposite party members. But, more importantly, knights without helmets are vulnerable, so it ensured both sides would refrain from combat.

When his messenger presented the king's order, I sent Cedric on a ride around the castle ordering all our bastions to suspend hostilities and remain in wary defense until further notice. Then I returned to the encampment to consult with the king.

But I reached it just after the king's party departed, to find all the Scottish leadership had gone with him. With king, princes, earls, and mormaers away, I was alarmed—for the safety of our camp and the strength of the siege lines. The negotiation might take days, or even weeks. And truce or no truce, I did not trust the English. So I sounded the alarm, gathered the men in camp and ordered all our unused chevaux-de-frise set up along the camp's perimeter in the direction of the threat posed by Alnwick and Alnmouth. This immediately incurred the mumbled wrath of our soldiers, who grumbled about "doin' unnecessary chores at the whim of nervous nobles."

I let them gripe; it really meant they were happy to have something to do. Unhappy soldiers are sullen and silent.

And we were just in time. Not a half-hour later, without warning, a force of English horsemen galloped toward camp along the forest-flanked road, yeomen and archers on their heels.

"Sound the alarm!" I cried. "Sappers! Caltrops in the road, now! Archers, kill everything English! Knights to horse! Attack their flanks! Every man of you, take arms and man the barricades! MOVE!"

My sappers flung caltrops by the handfuls into the road at the oncoming knights, creating chaos as those evil little spikes lamed their horses. Our knights and men-at-arms jumped onto horses and rode from camp by the north and west to hit the English on both flanks. I rode among the foremost on CiùinLùth, my warhorse. Most of us rode bareback, with only hack rope or mane for reins. It did not matter; we knights steer our horses with presses of our knees to free our hands for weapons and shield.

The attack of the English horsemen was already countered and foundering among the caltrops, so I skirted them and rode down the greater threat, the English archers and foot soldiers, cutting a path through them as a scythe mows grass. As protection from arrows and blades, CiùinLùth wore the barding I brought home from Constantinople. All the same, I made it a point to cut down all those who tried to kill my horse rather than me. A warhorse CiùinLùth was, but he was still just a horse. I was the enemy, not he, and all who made that mistake paid a steep price for it.

It was the first time I had used my Damascene sword in battle, and though I did not think of it at the time, it was superb.

Balanced and flexible, it cut through all but thick shields and plate steel: spear shafts, longbows, leather armor, cheap mail, collarbones, spines, forelimbs and skulls. All the years I had spent shaping yellow-hot iron with a hammer made the use of this sword nearly effortless. I enjoyed myself, and could have killed Englishmen all day.

But I did not have to. Their attack was a surprise, but they failed to catch us unprepared, and failed to bring a force large enough to overwhelm us. Instead, we killed more of them than they of us. So after a hard fight, they sounded retreat and withdrew.

A sudden attack during a declared truce—could anything have been more treacherous, or more evil? Its instigator was a self-damned soul, and I vowed then and there that if I could ever learn who he was, I would do my best to personally send him to Hell.

Just then, as I finally had a moment to wonder about the king, his horse trotted limping back to our camp, trying to rejoin our other mounts. And when I saw arrows in its shoulder and flanks, and the king's helmet still tied to the pommel, I was gripped by dread.

✠✠✠

Our king's horse stood before us, wounded and bearing signs of attack during the truce, just as we had been, for the king wore no helmet when his horse was wounded.

The sight stunned all of us, for it evidenced an act so treacherous that it violated all rules of chivalry and war. Still in command, I ordered all our knights, squires, and mounted men-at arms to arm and saddle to ride to the king's aid at once.

I had just mounted and we were just about to ride and when the survivors from the king's escort reached our camp.

A grim and bloodied knight among them spotted me and called out, "The king is dead, and many lords with him! The English ambushed us in a river crossing. Just as we reached the middle of the ford they sprang their trap. That bastard Morel spurred his horse and our English escort fled to the far side, donned helm and shield and rode back among us to attack us unprepared."

Then I saw they had brought Prince Edward with them. The crown prince—no, king!—was badly wounded from a spear or sword thrust and unconscious—a man rode on either side just to keep him in the saddle. He would not survive without better medical care than we could provide here. So we bound up his wounds, and a fresh escort with extra mounts then took him by horse-litter[8] immediately to the closest monastery at Wooler, five leagues northwest. Sore afraid for Edward as I was, I regretted I could not go as well in guarantee of his safety, but we had other missing nobles and men to rescue—that is, if any yet lived.

We mounted and rode to the ford, but we were much too late. All we found there were dead Scottish men-at-arms and horses, scattered in the stream. The English had gone, taking their wounded and dead with them. To our great grief, they also took the bodies of King Malcolm, Earl Gospatric, and our other dead nobles.

---

[8] Katherine T. Barkley states in *The Ambulance* (1990) that the Normans used horse-litters—a litter suspended on two poles between two horses. Not long after, in 1148, the seriously-ill Archbishop of Trier was conveyed by horse-litter to the Council of Reims.

Only much later did we learn that they had taken King Malcolm's body, a trophy of sorts to spite us, for burial in Tynemouth Priory. Earl Gospatric ended up in the new cathedral at Durham.

✠✠✠

The tale the survivors told was chilling. After riding through a wooded valley, they reached the River Aln to ford it where it was but a wide shallow stream. As they started across, Morel and his English escort suddenly spurred their horses and galloped across the stream and English spearmen, axemen, and archers sprang from concealment in the brush along both banks of the river to surround Malcolm's party. Flights of arrows flew from the banks, striking men and horses alike. Many struck Malcolm and his horse, which reared, tossing the king into the river; then the beast ran for our camp, with the king's helmet still tied to the saddle. Gospatric's horse followed, also with his helmet.

As herald and leader of the truce escort, Arkil Morel was a self-declared non-combatant, prohibited from drawing a weapon except in self-defense. And the purpose of the escort he provided was to ensure there would be no such attack. But now that his treachery had rendered his enemy trapped, surprised, and entirely vulnerable, that false knight led his escort back, all of them helmeted with swords drawn. They rode among the Scots to attack the mounted and fallen alike.

Morel himself sought out King Malcolm, who sat in the river, wounded by arrows and dazed by the fall. Without warning or quarter, he chopped the king down with cuts to the head and neck, severing poor Malcolm's spine. The king fell dead in the river.

Nearby, as Prince Edward tried to protect his father, he was badly wounded by a spear thrust. The Mormaer of Atholl rescued him by seizing his reins and leading his horse away as the prince clung to the pommel. Earl Gospatric was killed by an arrow through the neck, and many of the others, all without helmets, were slaughtered. Of perhaps a hundred in the party, just thirty Scots survived, Prince Edgar among them.

Upon our return to camp from the ambush site, we slaughtered all the English wounded and prisoners, their lives forfeit for their egregious violation of the laws of war: two attacks made upon us, without provocation or warning, during a declared truce. The just reward of treachery is death.

But upon a pair of their high-ranking knights we used techniques of great efficacy—born from brutal inhumanity—to interrogate them. From them we learned that King Rufus had ordered Earl Robert de Mowbray to stall us and, if possible, devise a scheme to lure King Malcolm away with a ruse and slay him. And despite protesting the loss of his honor, Robert did as Rufus demanded. He and his nephew Morel had planned their river ambush and the attack on the camp to coincide. Indeed, even as Morel massacred my king and his escort in a riverbed, it was the false knight Robert de Mowbray, Earl of Northumberland—never ill at all; that had been a lie—who had led the attack on our camp. Both acts came during a declared truce.

At that news I was very sorry I had not known to seek out and slay Robert de Mowbray that morn.

With the king dead, the crown prince wounded, and the war council decimated, the only decision possible was to abandon the both the siege and the campaign and return to Scotland. We retired, leaderless but undefeated, and we took our revenge on the English as we did, taking herds of their cattle and sheep, looting and burning all we could not carry. That damned earl would gain no profit from what was left. And the English neither followed nor attempted to hinder us in any way, cowering instead in their fortifications behind us.

The monks at Wooler could do little but pray for Prince Edward, so grievous were his wounds. So he was taken on horse-borne litter back to Scotland, to the Church hospital at Jedburgh. But he died enroute, just prior to reaching the hospital.

With that, it was unclear just who would be Malcolm's heir to the throne. Prince Edmund was next by birth succession, but with both king and crown prince dead, the settled succession was upset, and the potential claimants many.

The date of that great calamity was 13 November 1093. The English now call it a great victory, and claim that Morel defeated Malcolm in combat and defeated us with a surprise attack. They called the actions of Mowbray and Morel a ruse of war, but the use of a declared truce as a ruse to kill unarmed men is cowardly and dishonorable to the utmost degree. The men who planned it and the king who demanded it are cowardly varlets who justly deserve both our scorn and the eternal fires of Hell.

Prince Edgar was completely devastated by the loss of his father and brother; but he was just as aggrieved with concern for his mother, Queen Margaret, who had been ailing with prolonged illness for a year or more.

So Edgar sent for me. "Baron Godric, with heavy heart I must ask you to do something for me, a personal favor. My mother must be told of this terrible set of events, and of the deaths of the king and the crown prince. She loves you as much as she does me. I would not have her hear it from anyone else, and least of all as the result of rumor or gossip. I beg you, leave us, ride as fast as possible and break this news as gently as you can. She loved Father so; I fear for her when she hears it."

Believe me, it was the very last thing I wanted to do. I would have evaded the duty if I could have. But I had grown up with Edgar; he was like a brother to me, and the queen as dear to me as my own mother. And now Edgar was my commander, so his request, though begged, was still a command.

So I undertook the sad task of bearing the news to the queen. I left CiùinLùth with Cedric and rode hard then on a messenger's horse, bred for speed and endurance rather than strength, to get ahead of the rumors.

I found the queen in the castle at Edinburgh. As ever, my wife Aleine was there with her as the queen's companion and lady-in-waiting—just as my mother had been before her—and had been for several years. Before going in, I went to Aleine and told her my terrible news.

"Godric, my love, God has heard my prayers and kept you safe. But I fear so for the queen. She has been ever so ill this year, and is so weak that I fear what this news will do. Be gentle with her."

Indeed, on entering her chamber I found Margaret so weak, pale, and frail from illness that I could scarcely recognize her. I did not even get the chance to speak. She read the news from my face or demeanor as if it were written on me in great letters: "The king is dead and the crown prince as well."

Upon seeing me she fell into a swoon, from a shock too great for her kindly nature. Aleine summoned the queen's physicians, but they could not rouse her. With Aleine beside me, I sat with the queen for a time and held her hand as she slept, speaking of good times in our past. She may have been aware of me then, for once or twice she seemed to stir and squeezed my hand. But she died two days later, on the 16th of November, without ever regaining consciousness.

Aleine and Bjorn were devastated, of course, but not ever so much as me. She had always been good to me, and when I lost my own mother at eleven, she had filled that void. Even her sons, the princes Edward and Edgar had told me that Margaret had always loved me as one of her own—just as I had loved her.

And ever since, I have borne a deep sense of guilt for bringing dear Queen Margaret the tragic news that caused her death. It became a principal reason for my return to Jerusalem: the act of offering up my life and suffering in the struggle to reclaim the City of God as means to atone for my sins—and chiefly this one.

✠✠✠

TWELVE

✠✠✠

The news of the death of King Malcolm and Prince Edward spread far and wide, as if carried by the wind, and the news was certainly not regarded as tragic by some. For indeed, no sooner had Margaret passed than the mount upon which great Edinburgh Castle stood was surrounded by many hundreds of highlanders led by Malcolm's younger brother, Domnall Bán mac Donnchada —Donalbane MacDuncan, the English called him.

I met the man once when I was a boy, when relations between Malcolm and his brother were warm. They seemed much alike, though I liked Malcolm better, and sensed Donalbane a much lesser man.

Donalbane had always coveted his brother's throne and made little pretense otherwise, thinking he had more right to it than did his nephews. Now Malcolm's death offered him the opportunity to take it at last, so he swiftly gathered a band of highlanders willing to help him, and hurried to Edinburgh. The highlanders had always opposed Malcolm's rule. Now they would choose a much-preferred successor by removing his rivals.

As during the earlier campaigns, Malcolm's sons Edmund, Alexander, and David had stayed in the castle with their mother. Edgar had followed me as swiftly as he could, arriving just before Margaret died. So now all four princes were trapped inside, their

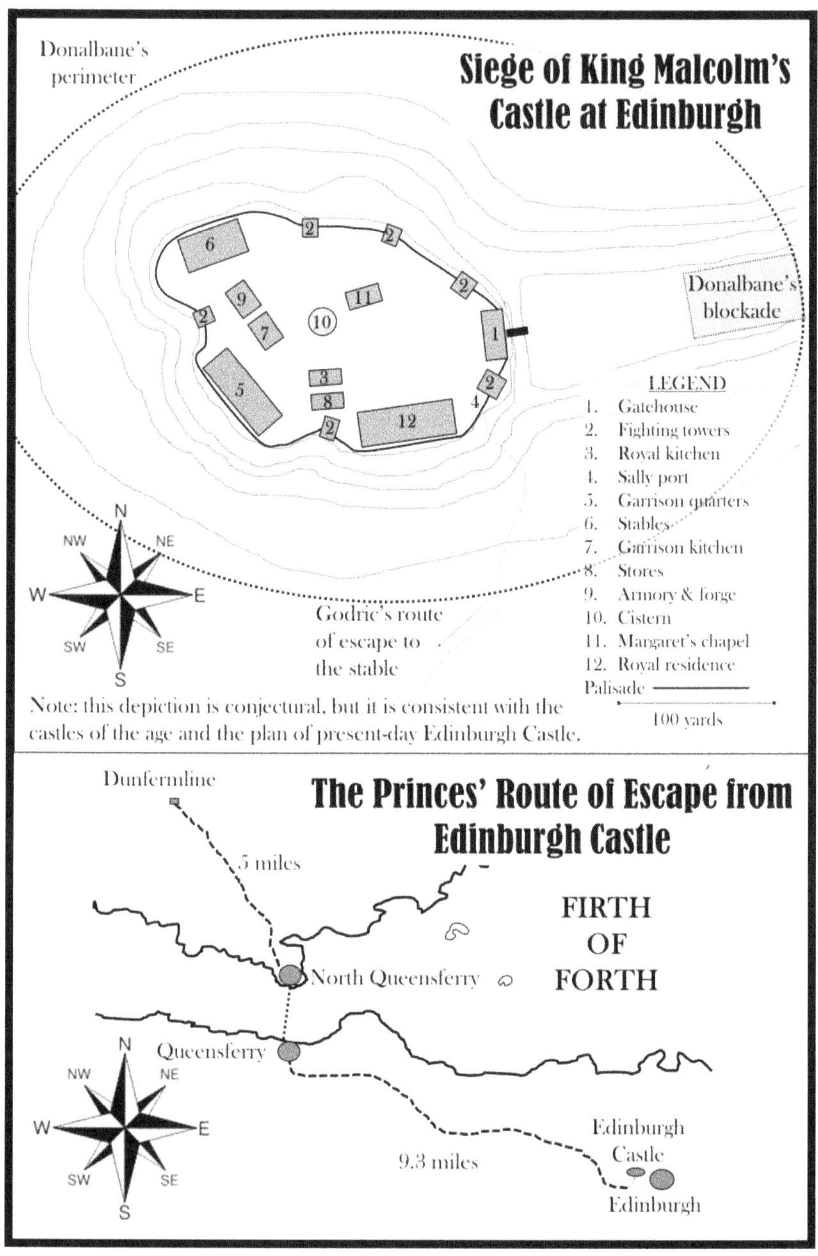

Figure 7: The siege and escape from Edinburgh Castle

lives suddenly in grave danger. Each of them posed a threat to Donalbane's ambition so long as he lived. If the castle fell, all four would be thrust summarily into gaol; or, more likely, graves.

Now Edinburgh Castle is the strongest in all Alba, Malcolm's principal stronghold. In Dunfermline he had constructed a stone tower as his treasury, but that capital was indefensible and solely intended as the king's residence in times of peace.

Not so Edinburgh. Upon the highest portion of the great rock Malcolm had built a royal residence for his family while he was away at war, built of timber, stone and plaster with a roof of slate. There was a chapel for Margaret, storehouses, kitchens, stables and an armory and barracks for the garrison.

Edinburgh Rock rose steeply along its north, west and south sides—too steep for horse or men to charge, and of a height so great that no machine-thrown projectile or arrow could crest it. Only squads of skilled climbers might be able to make an ascent. Against this, along the edge of the precipice, Malcolm had raised a stout timber palisade, topped with a wooden wall-walk as a fighting platform for crossbowmen, archers and hurlers to pick off such attackers.

The castle could only be approached from the east, along a great natural ramp of rock and earth. So, across the narrowest part of this neck—perhaps 200 feet—Malcolm had dug from side to side a deep ditch, backed by a rock-faced earthen mound studded with a phalanx of sharpened stakes and topped by yet another stout palisade fully twenty feet high. It, too, had a fighting walkway for defenders, great towers at either end, and a central gate tower to protect the drawbridge across the ditch—now raised, of course.

The fortress had a large cistern kept filled by Alba's frequent showers, and grassland atop the plateau to feed domestic animals. It could outlast a long siege. And provided it had a substantial garrison, without machines like mine, it would be impossible to take before now-imminent winter put its own end to the siege.

But our garrison was small—perhaps a hundred men; most had gone south with Malcolm. But now that army was disbanded, and no help in any case, for we were cut off completely.

Donalbane knew all this, which was why he intended to capture Edinburgh. Doing so would remove at one stroke all his rivals—Malcolm's sons—and gain him the crown.

✠✠✠

All around the palisade ramparts, Prince Edgar and I surveyed our foes. Although Prince Edmund was now the oldest, he had never been particularly inclined—or gifted—as either warrior or monarch. Edmund had always liked being a prince but had never shown aspirations to be a king. Third brother Ethelred had always been spiritual and was now in a monastery. But Malcolm's royal bloodline was all readily perceived in Edgar. While Edmund had stayed safe in Edinburgh, younger Edgar eagerly campaigned with us. So now, as ever, Edmund again deferred to Edgar, who took command—and in doing so, became Malcolm's next heir.

With a smile at the irony, Edgar said, "Well, Baron, for the once you are *inside* the siege. What do you think of our opposition, and how do you rate our chances of survival?"

I shook my head. "Sire, I think we are in serious trouble. We can hold them off for a while well enough, but with each assault we will lose men to death or wounds. And without relief—or a winter freeze—we cannot last forever."

Edgar nodded. "Precisely my thoughts. Moreover, there is no good reason to stay, if leave we could. Donalbane already has his army of support, while we have none. We cannot raise an army to counter him from here and no other has the means to do it for us, with so many mormaers and nobles dead in the Alnwick ambush.

"But leave we cannot, for uncle or no, the man would gladly prefer to slit our throats and spill all the royal blood that could raise opposition to his coronation. For that reason we need to find a way to escape this place—and quick!"

I had to agree. A castle is useful as a base for military operations, or a temporary refuge against them, but without the immediate support of the nobles loyal to Malcolm, the princes had no power to oppose Donalbane's claim. So they had to flee—to live, raise an opposition army, and fight to reclaim the throne another day.

"You must, sire. There is no merit in staying. Do you think it worth attempting to negotiate your freedom with Donalbane?"

Edgar shook his head. "I don't think I could trust our lives to any agreement. Anything promised to open the gate would only make it easier to end the entire issue with a stroke of the seax. We must slip out of here when we can. If we can."

I nodded. "I will study the place, sire, and look for a way to get the four of you safely out."

"You forget Mother. We must take her with us, get her to Dunfermline and see to her burial in the abbey church."

I frowned at that, and then had a realization that came as a shock. I had to get Aleine out with them—there was no way to know what would happen here when Donalbane and his savages got in, but I knew I did not want her here to find out.

"The queen's body—and Lady Aleine—then. I will search for a way to get all of you out."

Edgar nodded, and added, "If it can be done, Godric, I know you will find a way."

You have more faith in my ability to produce a miracle than I do, I thought. But I kept it to myself, for he was counting on me to do just that.

✠✠✠

I went to see the castellan, a knight named Robert MacDuncan, to learn what I could about secret ways out. Every castle was faced with need to get messengers—and sometimes their lords—out. There had to be a way to get the princes out of this trap.

And I was not disappointed. MacDuncan had an answer for me.

"Aye, Baron, there is a hidden sortie gate—of sorts—in the base of the southern palisade tower. It opens just where the tower meets the vertical rock face below the palace, and allows us to slip out a man unseen behind a screen of scrub there. 'Twas meant to send out messenger in case of siege, like now, or to sortie a small party for counterattack. The ground just at the base of the palisade is just wide enough."

"What way down exists from there to the level ground beyond?" Both sides of the eastern ramp fell away sharply, and there looked to be no safe way down.

"We keep cordage in the tower, a stout knotted rope that enables a man to descend from the sortie door to the base of the rock. The slope is steep, but manageable with the aid of the rope. From there he must make his way through the forest to a stable we have in a low building 300 yards south. We keep six horses there, guarded by trusty men-at-arms garbed as stablemen."

This was good news in most respects, but I still had two big problems: a very pregnant wife and a dead queen. Neither could well manage a rope-assisted steep descent.

"Thank you, Sir Robert. Do personally see the rope is in good condition. The princes may have urgent need of it very soon."

"Aye, milord. That I will do now."

✠✠✠

I was conferring with Prince Edgar when a messenger brought in news. Donalbane had sent emissaries under a flag of truce to the far end of the drawbridge. Their message from the Pretender was unequivocal: Surrender forthwith the castle and the princes, or all within the castle would die when it fell to him.

And it was the castellan himself who personally delivered an unmistakable reply. He clambered to the top of the gate tower and displayed his bared buttocks to the emissaries below, calling down, "Take it if you can, you blue-faced mutton-rapers!"

"...and that was rather less cordial than they were used to," he added with a grin when he reported it to Prince Edgar and me.

We had not yet been attacked, but they were in no hurry and were taking their time. Hemmed in as we were, we could not leave and there was no one who knew of the need to come to our aid. Every attack they mounted was going to kill far more of them than us. Donalbane might have been willing to buy his crown with their blood, but the highlanders were used to close combat in open fields, not assaulting a damned great fortification defended by skilled archers, so they weren't ready to throw themselves at it. They had no siege machines, and no company of archers to pick us off. Had I thought help would arrive to take them from the rear, I would have preferred our chances remaining inside.

But no help would come, and getting the princes out would end the siege without killing the garrison—there was nothing to be gained by continuing once the prize was lost. Escape was the best—and the right—decision.

The princes and I were fit, trained knights, well able to descend the slope and make our way to the stable. Not so the queen's body, which the princes unanimously declared must go with them to be buried in Dunfermline, so someone would have to carry it. And then there was my very pregnant wife; a descent like that was well beyond her skill or condition. She would need to be carried as well.

You may ask why I thought I should go. I'll tell you. First, Edgar expected it. Baron I might be and not a mormaer or earl, but the princes had precious few of those remaining, and every noble counted at this point.

Second, as sheriff-at-large I had ridden and knew every road and route between Edinburgh and Dunfermline as few did, and a desperate ride at night would demand that knowledge.

Third, Dunfermline wasn't the end of the princes' journey—it was the start. From there they needed to flee Alba, and going to Duke Robert and Edgar Ætheling in Normandy was their best chance for safety. But they needed a ship to do that, so again I was the man who knew which captains to trust and where to find them.

And last, I would not leave my wife or brothers—for I had been raised with the princes all my childhood and they regarded me and I them as brothers—I would not leave my wife or brothers to face the danger Donalbane posed them, either in here or out there without my strength and sword as their protection. My duty was to them, wherever they went.

And dangerous it would be. Not only the descent, which would kill anyone who fell. We then had to slip through the cordon that encircled the rock. It was not tight, for they did not have the numbers of men necessary for that. Nor had they built barricades as I would have. But they had parties of men spaced around the perimeter and sentries, no doubt. We would have to avoid—or silence—all we encountered.

And finally, we then had to find the stable, obtain horses and slip away to the west and north in darkness without raising an alarm. Escaping undetected meant having much of a night's lead on any pursuit. If we got to Queensferry, and I found Thorsson there, we might reach Dunfermline before Donalbane knew we were gone.

All that was to the good. But how could I bring out Aleine and her dead queen? Aye, that was the problem I wrestled.

✠✠✠

I am not much of a praying man. I pray to convey my thanks for God's many favors, of course; but only rarely would I pray to ask for help. Some men do, and I do not fault them for it. It's just that I always felt that God knew what I needed, even when I did not, so asking Him for help was superfluous. I am a knight, trained to press ahead with what I thought right, and trusting in God to aid me as He saw fit. Hence, my frequent thanks.

But this was different. Others with lives at stake were depending upon me, and for once I didn't know what to do—I had only half a plan, a most risky one at that. So I went to Margaret's chapel and prayed, asking help of the saints to save those I loved.

Of Saint Cuthbert, patron saint of good King Malcolm, I asked for help saving Malcolm's sons. Of the Blessed Mother I asked help to save my wife, soon to be a mother herself. And in the hope that both Malcolm and Margaret—especially Margaret—might already be in Heaven, I asked them to help me save their children by aiding our escape if they could.

I prayed hard for an hour, and as I did, an idea was sent to me—one that seemed a bit daft, perhaps—but I felt much better for it. So I said a hurried but devout thanks, and set off to put it to work.

✠✠✠

I have not told you much of the princes at that time, so I must do so now. Crown Prince Edward, the oldest and my age at twenty-three, was—as you know—now dead. Prince Edmund was about a year younger, about twenty-two. Ethelred, the third, aged twenty, was already a monk in the monastery at Dunkeld, where he would eventually become the abbot. The fourth son, Prince Edgar was nineteen, and in my view most able of the lot after Edward. The fifth son, Alexander, was fifteen and a new squire, while the sixth, David, was still a boy of just ten, in training as a page. Alexander and David had been regarded as too young to campaign with their father, so they had remained in Edinburgh with the queen. And Edmund—well, Edmund was never quite right, which is why the royal succession was now contested.

So Edmund, Edgar, Alexander, and David were the four princes trapped inside, whose escape I had to engineer. Now night was approaching and we had no time for further delay. My plan might work now, but once the siege turned from standoff to combat, our chances for success would diminish quickly.

I found the four princes gathered together, and to them I related my idea. Their immediate outrage was quickly damped by the reality of their situation, and the difficulty of the task ahead, and in the end, there was no real alternative. So finally Edgar agreed, and the others all followed his lead, although it seemed to me Edmund was unusually quiet and almost disengaged—as ever.

With their assent I went to find Aleine. I needed her help with the queen, I needed her to understand our situation, and I needed her willing to risk the danger I was asking her to share. The task took some persuasion, but she came to realize the necessity, and to her credit, once Aleine made a decision, she never later regretted or vacillated on the choice.

With the queen's other maids-in-waiting, Aleine then undertook to prepare Queen Margaret's body: washing it, redressing it in a white burial gown, and binding and wrapping it in a tough linen shroud. The indignities of transport I could not avoid—the reason the princes were so upset. But the queen I loved would reach Dunfermline with us ready for eternity—provided we made it.

Aleine, too, had preparations to make, and it was for her sake I was so worried. Had she not been heavy with child, she might have enjoyed this as another of our childhood adventures—such as when we sneaked off to swim and frolic together, or when I stole one of Andrew's mounts to joyride double.

But she understood the risks she faced. I was well-known to some of the highlanders outside, had confronted enough of them to expect no good treatment, and was known a favorite of Malcolm, which would do me no good now. And as my wife, if the castle were sacked Aleine would be singled out for worse than the other women in the castle—after all, Donalbane wanted this fine castle for himself, and knew it unwise to mistreat women who could always later poison his food.

There was one other whose help I had to have, so I went to find Bjorn the Bear. On him much would depend.

✠✠✠

It was midnight, I judged, when we began our escape. The night was overcast, which was more than I could hope for, because it would hide our movement with darkness. But as the hidden sally port in the south tower was opened, I realized my prayers had been answered—the entire castle rock was wrapped in a mist so heavy it was almost fine drizzle. Dark as it was, you could barely see your own feet, and certainly not further.

Against my preferences, Prince Edgar went first. We could not risk lowering or tossing the rope down the slope, hitting a sentry or alerting one with the noise—so instead we lowered him, carefully paying it out as he slowly walked backward down the steep face on the end of the rope. It would be up to him to silence any sentry he found, and that was why I wanted the task. But he rightfully pointed out that I had a greater duty and he was next best-suited for the task. Reluctantly I had to agree.

We had arranged silent signals using a seax haft to tap on the rope, causing sensations that could be felt along its taut length without making much noise. Other than that, this operation was conducted in silence.

I followed him, with Aleine wrapped in a wool cloak and seated in a sling of strong linen on my back, her large belly against the small of my back, and her arms linked over one of my shoulders and under the other. She weighed more now with the wee one, but she had always been built slight, and no great burden. It was the best way I could think of to get her down safely.

The slope was slick with the moisture from the mist, and I had to proceed slowly, taking care that each foot was well-planted—a single slip could kill the three of us. What took moments seemed an hour, and the strain on me was great, but with hard-grit teeth I struggled backward down the great rock, a careful step at a time, and we reached level ground in the trees below safely enough.

Edgar steadied me as I landed, and whispered, "No one close. But there is a campfire and voices nearby—southeast, I think. I smell smoke."

In silence, then, he helped me extricate Aleine from the sling, and while I seated her for the moment beneath a tree close by, Edgar tended the rope. Alexander was to follow and assist David.

To my whispered inquiry, Aleine replied that she was well, but I could tell she was strained and tired by the late hour and the extra exertions.

Moments later Alexander and David arrived safely, and I sensed David was grinning, delighted by the rare adventure. I moved them to where Aleine awaited us.

Next down the slope arrived Bjorn the Bear, with the body of Queen Margaret wrapped in her shroud bound tight about him with strong linen over his right shoulder and left hip, her head against his chest and lower limbs at his back. The stiffness that came after death had passed and made it possible to carry her so. Not very dignified, perhaps, but the only practical way we could find to carry her after several tries. Bjorn needed both his hands and legs free to negotiate the steep slope, and although her long sickness had wasted her to a mere slip of a thing, Margaret's body was still an awkward bundle.

Bjorn did not mind though. He had become very devoted to her, and I was amazed and grateful to God that had planned this very strange chain of events to just this purpose, for only Bjorn could have managed that feat.

As eldest, Edmund was to descend last. But Bjorn whispered to Edgar and me that at the last moment Edmund had declined. "He is not coming. He said to tell you to go. He intends to stay, delay as long as possible discovery you are gone, and negotiate with his uncle for the future of his family and the lowland nobles."

I strongly doubted that story, but kept my silence. Edgar did as well, for I could see he was outraged, and he was about to re-ascend the slope when I stopped him. "Sire," I whispered, "it is to no purpose. We must get you and your brothers away if Alba is to have a future. Edmund has cast the dice and made his choice. We are not safe yet and you have far to go. Let us go now."

Reluctantly, Edgar nodded. Then I cut a ten-yard length from the rope, and after signaling the castellan to retrieve the rest of it, we went to join the others.

✠✠✠

Although we knew where we were, and had studied the route to the stable from high above, once down in the thickets, especially at night and in misty fog, we had little we could use to guide us there. But I had earlier estimated the distance to the stable at 300 yards—300 paces—and decided that bearing southwest from our starting point would bring us there.

With whispered instructions I had the others take hold of the rope to keep us in a single file. I took the lead, followed by Aleine, Alexander, Bjorn, David, and Edgar at the rear. The rope was meant to keep us from being separated, the single file to aid us as we maneuvered quietly and carefully through thickets and trees. To go quietly, we had to go painfully slow. Still the darkness and fog were as good as invisibility. Only noise—or bad fortune—could betray us now.

I judge it took us an hour to cover that 300 yards. I had to use the line behind me to steer by. Having started off heading what I judged southwest, whenever forced to veer left or right from that direction, I tried to veer back the same amount in the opposite direction as soon as I could. It was all I could do.

Our foes were clustered around fires and nearly all were asleep, with just two men awake on watch to keep the fires burning and count the hours. In dense mist there were no stars by which to judge the passage of time, so they talked, and this is what allowed us to detect and avoid them.

We had just one truly close call, when a sentry decided to relieve himself just as we skirted one of those fires. I had veered wide to avoid all the men on the ground sleeping in sodden cloaks around it, and to avoid them as well he had come our direction. I could hear him staling like a stallion—and puffing from the exertion—not five yards from where I crouched. Finally he was finished and stumbled, cursing, back through the bracken to his fire—just a low glow in the mist. Carefully we moved on.

It came as a great relief when at last we came to the rock wall that ran around the stable. I knew where I was then, and quickly found our way around to the building. The castellan had given me a password, so in a low voice I hailed the building and spoke it—and got no answer. I tried again without result. I shook the door, which was latched from within, and tried a third time. I was about to have Bjorn pull on it with me to wrench it open when a light showed through cracks in the wall. I hailed once more with the password, got a proper reply, and the door opened to admit us.

The stable sentries were much abashed and apologetic for being asleep, but we had no time to waste on vituperation and still far to go, so I ignored it and ordered them to have every horse saddled, even putting Alexander and Edgar at it and saddling one myself. Aleine was faint with weariness, so I assigned the largest horse to Bjorn, the second biggest for myself and Aleine, the smallest to David. To carry both Aleine and me, I chose for us a messenger's saddle, which lacked any pommel and had only a small cantle—in truth it was little more than a thick pad with stirrups. The queen's body got her own mount—I had her lashed over a saddle like a grain sack, I regret to say—but we had no better recourse. She was coming to Dunfermline with her sons, and we needed to ride far and as fast as we could now.

Within perhaps a quarter-hour we were ready, and tarried not at all. I got everyone in the saddle, mounted my own beast and had the stable guards lift Aleine into my arms, where thick burlap sacking gave her some added padding from the jolts of the road. She was faint and trembling from chill but gave me a sweet smile as I hugged her close, and snuggled closer against my chest. And then we were off.

✠✠✠

Now you may think we ran those horses to get away quickly from the danger of Donalbane's horde, but we did not. We walked those horses, their footfalls softened by drizzle on earth to the faintest of thuds, away from Donalbane's army along the track headed west. Half an hour later we hit a road headed north, and followed it to Queensferry Road—named for Queen Margaret, who brought both road and ferry into being, and the very queen we now carried with us. Aleine slept against my chest, snoring gently in her curled position.

Another two hours brought us to Queensferry. It was perhaps three hours to sunrise at this time of year. No one was stirring in Queensferry, but I knew where the ferryman dwelt. I hammered on his door in the name of the king with the hilt of my short sword until he appeared, blinking and half-dressed, irate at being roused in the night.

"I am Baron Godric MacEuan, sheriff-at-large of Alba. My party has urgent need of your ferry—now! Stir yourself, and I will pay double your fee in gold. Vex me, and I will pay you with steel."

That got his attention. He waved a hand and vanished and I could hear him inside, kicking his crew awake. In moments they all appeared—six of them—disheveled and bleary, staggering out into the cold morn, and shivering with chill I had long forgotten.

Stumbling down to their vessel they began to bustle about preparing to sail. The ferryman beckoned us to board and we led our mounts over the broad gangway and into the crude stalls ranging down the vessel's centerline. As we did, the crew cast furtive glances at us. They were no strangers to nobles—for who better could afford to use the ferry?—but even so, we were most unusual, both for the richness of our attire and for the oddness of our journey, and they were trying to work out who we were.

The Firth of Forth is only a mile wide between the ferry landings, and thanks to the miraculous mist, there was no wind and only small waves—no hindrance at all. The six men manned sweeps and rowed the shallow-draft barge across the water, which took about an hour. As they did, I carried Aleine into a shelter, gave her small beer and a little sweetbread from my satchel to eat, and let her rest there. Edgar, I noted, never took his eyes from the crew, and stood guard, but he needn't have worried, for Bjorn did the same, and none on that barge was daft enough to cross him.

It was growing light when we reached North Queensferry—dawn was perhaps an hour away. We docked and disembarked without trouble, and before we mounted and rode, I paid the ferryman the promised fee—then held up another gold coin.

"Spend the day here. Do not return to Queensferry for any reason until tomorrow. Tell any who ask you needed to make repairs. None of you left your beds today until sunrise. You did not see us. You did not carry us anywhere. You don't remember us or even my name." Then I added this: "Remember—I know who you all of you are, and where you live. Understood?"

By keeping the ferry and ferrymen here instead of returning to Queensferry, I was buying the princes time. These men were the only people outside Edinburgh Castle who knew where we went —we told the stablemen nothing of our plans. Donalbane might discover our flight and guess it was to Dunfermline, so I did not want his followers to be able to use his ferry to follow us. By land it was two days' travel to Dunfermline over Stirling Bridge.

He swallowed and nodded. So I smiled and gave him the coin. "My thanks for your good service, and may God treat thee well."

✠✠✠

The weak winter sun was just a half-hour high when we completed the five-mile ride in Dunfermline. We were slumped in our saddles and near dozing by the time we reached the palace and its neighbor, the abbey.

At the palace the porter greeted us with astonishment. I said, "Their highnesses need food and rest now, and immediate preparations for a long journey, traveling light. Their lives are in danger. See to it!" He nodded and darted inside, and almost immediately servants and pages poured forth to usher the royals inside and care for them. Stablemen, too, appeared to take charge of our mounts—all except the one bearing the queen.

I sent for messengers and gave quick instructions. One I headed off to Cenachedne to alert Cedric to make travel preparations for Aleine, Cedric and me. Another rode to North Queensferry, where Thorsson would be found, to request an urgent voyage. A third headed to the abbey to request the monks make preparations for a requiem Mass and the burial of Queen Margaret. Bjorn followed, leading the horse bearing her body.

I myself took Aleine to our chamber in the palace and saw to her, bedding her down for some decent rest. The exertions of our flight had taken a toll on her, but she was safe. Then I lay down beside her and for a couple of hours slept like one dead.

✠✠✠

At midday, a Requiem High Mass was celebrated for the souls of Queen Margaret, Prince Edward—his body had been returned to Dunfermline the day before—and the memory of King Malcolm, whose body the English had stolen. The Mass was well attended: by her sons—refreshed as I had been by a few hours' sleep and a meal; by Lady Aleine and me; and by many from the palace, noble and common, for many regardless of station loved their monarchs. The ceremony was made most wonderful by the harmonious voices of all the monks raised in glorious chant. At the conclusion, the body of the queen, her shroud overwrapped by royal burial vestments, was interred before the altar in a floor vault she herself had arranged—a year earlier, Aleine told me—and that of her son Edward on her left. I have no doubt that someday the Church will declare her a saint. And later, when in due course their son Alexander became King of Scotland, he succeeded in recovering his father's remains from Tynemouth Priory, and buried good King Malcolm on her right.

✠✠✠

Their duty to their parents done, the princes now had a duty to Alba: this time to flee, live to fight another day, and when they could build the followers and strength to challenge Donalbane, to return to recover the throne.

My messenger found Thorsson at home, and though the season was late, and the storms that made winter voyages risky overdue, he was willing to sail once more for me on a fast voyage to Normandy. So he sent word—by the same messenger but a fresh horse—that he would have his ship in North Queensferry harbor ready to sail with the tide at dawn on the morrow.

Bjorn had again come to a turning point—the loss of the queen had hit him hard. What had begun with a royal favor had grown into a relationship, for Margaret was that kind of woman. Aleine told me later it was hard to tell who was caring for whom—he for her, or her for him. But it wasn't hard to tell that Bjorn loved the queen and grieved his loss of her. He wept openly and without shame during the Requiem Mass, and afterward knelt to kiss the stone covering her vault before leaving her there.

So I approached him and sat with him. "Bjorn, thank you for helping me save the queen, her sons and Lady Aleine. How can I repay you? Would you like to return to Cenachedne? Carrick would enjoy having you there once again. Or you can join me. I go to Normandy to see the princes safe with their uncle Edgar Ætheling and Duke Robert. Your martial skills would be most welcome!"

Bjorn shook his great head. "Thank you, Lord Godric, for all you have done for me. You took me from being a murderous pagan and made of me something better—a Christian man who served a saintly queen. I can no longer go back to that old life. Indeed, the song of the monks appealed greatly to me. I wonder if they could make a monk from a bear?"

Then he smiled and said, "But I would go to Cenachedne. Carrick and I are good friends, and I truly need a good friend now that—" His speech ended in a sob as he choked back his feelings.

I hugged those great shoulders then, and said, "I understand. Off to Cenachedne you go. Carrick will be thrilled. And I would be ever so grateful if you could see to the safety of my family—Lady Aleine, Carrick, Alice and the others—and do for them as you did so well for Queen Margaret."

Still speechless, he nodded, great head bobbing—as a bear does.

✠✠✠

That afternoon, once all I could do was in hand, I sat with Aleine and held her close. Since I had left with Malcolm to march into Northumbria—was it just a month ago?—we had barely had a moment together. Now both of us were stunned and saddened by this swift chain of events, which had destroyed the order we had always known.

The loss of Queen Margaret, who had been like a mother to us, came as a huge shock to me, and to Aleine even more than me, for Aleine had lived with the queen during much of the past eight years. Now in just a matter of days, all that had been swept away. Malcolm, Edward and Margaret were gone. A new king had de-facto control of the kingdom. And now I was off to Normandy to save the princes. It was all so overwhelming to her, all she could do was cling to me and weep, and all I could do was hold her and assure her that I loved her with all my heart.

Cedric arrived before sundown, and with him Carrick, driving a cart. He would take Aleine to Cenachedne where she would stay with her parents and deliver our child. I dearly wanted her to come with me, but the escape to Dunfermline was already too much risk for a woman so late in pregnancy, and more travel danger would do neither mother nor child any good. The midwives in Cenachedne were well-practiced these days, so she would be safer there than anywhere. Donalbane might now have a grudge against me, but it violated all Christian and chivalric principles to attack wives and children, and it was a bad notion in any case—especially if later the tables were turned. I might lose my barony and my manor, but in Carrick's house Aleine would be safe—especially with Bjorn there.

Aleine's tears were spent, but sadness lingered, and she clung to me tightly and kissed me sweetly. Then I lifted her up onto the seat next to her father, wished them all "Godspeed" and watched them head off down the track to Cenachedne. When I would see it or them again, I did not know.

✠✠✠

THIRTEEN

✠✠✠

Thorsson had indeed had his ship ready to sail and waiting in North Queensferry when we reached there at dawn on the 19th of November. Hamish led the strong escort that accompanied the princes and me back—just in case Edmund or fate had betrayed us to Donalbane. But there was no sign of his highlanders—it seemed they were still outside Edinburgh, ignorant of our escape.

I had asked the castellan to give us at least a day, and ideally two, to get the princes out of Scotland. I did not want his garrison killed fighting for the lives of royals who were not there, but I knew it would take two days to be sure they would be out of Donalbane's reach. I hoped he, and perhaps Edmund—though I had my doubts—would be able to bluff the highlanders into holding off an assault with a pretense of negotiations for the princes' safety and freedom. And it seemed to have worked.

But Edgar and I had told the castellan that he was to open the gates and surrender peacefully after 48 hours. By then we would either be beyond Donalbane's reach, or already in his hands and dead. Either way, Donalbane would have no choicc but to spare the castle garrison and residents from a sacking, should he ever wish to use that castle for himself thereafter.

✠✠✠

We sailed for the tiny port of Ouistreham, closest port to Caen. At this time of year I expected to find Duke Robert in the castle his father had built there. Robert was a strong friend of the princes' uncle, Edgar Ætheling, whom I felt I could trust with their safety, and Robert and I had begun our own friendship in 1091. So now I thought we would be well-received and that the duke would agree to shelter the princes. But if not, I had another I knew would: my brother in battle, and the knight I had served as squire, Baron Jean de Bethencourt.

The voyage to Normandy was rough, cold and sorrowful for me. The events of the past week had come fast, one piled on another, each demanding so much of me that I had only time to react, not reflect. Now the enforced confinement of the voyage gave me too much time to brood on all that evil and ill fate, so that I was swallowed by a black despair. Even the weather and sea seemed to share my mood, for the sea was violent, the weather miserable.

In a single week I had lost the king and queen who were more my parents than my monarchs, and a prince who was like my brother from birth. Grief and rage filled me. I felt personally responsible for not being able to save Malcolm and Edward, and for bringing death to Margaret. I vowed to avenge them someday, although how I did not ponder. I also had no idea what the future held for me. The entire order I had always known had suddenly been swept away, like a wagon by a flash flood. Now the kingdom was upside down in turmoil and a new band of men in control. A man who might be my enemy was about to gain the throne, and could sweep away all I had in the process. All I could do was my best as a knight, and trust that God held me in His hands.

Five days later, Thorsson saw us safely ashore in Ouistreham, a tiny village of a hundred souls or so—families of the men who fished for the oysters that gave the place its name—at the mouth of the river that flowed through Caen, ten miles upstream.

Thorsson was eager to return home straightaway for Christmas. As I paid him for our passage he said, "Sail with me, Baron. You delivered your princes to safety here. Your duty is done," he said, and the princes nodded in agreement.

But I knew it was not. "Nay, I cannot. If Duke Robert does not welcome them, if Edgar Ætheling wants nothing to do with them, or if those two are elsewhere, not in Caen, then they are not safe." To the princes I said, "I will not have the ghosts of your parents haunting me, nor your souls on my conscience. When I *know* you are safe, then will my duty be done and I will head home..." And I added with a rueful note, "...if I can. I defied Donalbane, likely now the king, to spirit you out of his reach. He knows that by now. And for that treason, my life may now be forfeit in Alba."

The three princes nodded somberly, and then Edgar said, "Now perhaps, but not forever. My brothers and I are greatly in debt to you for the risks you have run on our behalf, and I pledge here and now—for all of us, on our sacred honor as princes—that our brother Godric MacEuan shall always be welcome and honored in our kingdom. So say I!" And Alexander and David added, "So say we all!"

Thorsson nodded. "So be it. I sail for home, but I will return on a trading voyage and put in here the last day of January with news of Donalbane, your family and Cenachedne, and give you the chance to sail for home with me if you are willing and able."

I clasped his hand and nodded my thanks, and as he returned to the sea, we five headed inland.

Ouistreham's only tavern-keeper was happy to rent a two-horse cart and driver, a young deaf-mute idiot who grinned at us and drooled the whole trip, but had a magic touch with his horses. Edgar rode on the seat beside him. Alexander, David, Cedric and I sat on our baggage in a cart-bed that stank of fish. It was not all that pleasant, but much better than walking all ten miles to Caen.

The castle was not difficult to find. The road along the west bank of the river Orne led inland directly to it, and as we approached, I could see the princes struck with awe—for this castle was built of stone. Had I not seen greater in Constantinople, Nicaea, Antioch and Jerusalem, I would have been also.

As it was, this was the most impressive fortification I had ever seen in all the western world. It stood inside a great ditch forty feet across and half as deep, shallowly filled with rainwater, making its bottom a deathtrap morass. From there great walls of stone rose forty to fifty feet to form a great square, 200 feet on a side, with circular corner towers. A single entrance was reached by a bridge with a drawbridge just outside the gatehouse tower. I guessed the walls were at least ten feet thick. Nothing could take it but starvation—*and Bone-Crusher*, I thought to myself.

We announced ourselves to the sentries and, after a short delay for word to reach the duke, we were readily admitted. The walls inside the castle were lined by wood and plaster buildings—kitchens, garrison barracks, stables, storerooms, chapel, armory, and the like, while the duke had a house in a rear corner. And in the center rose a great square tower under construction. Already it was two stories in height and strongly built—but incomplete.

With that all my doubts were dispelled and my faith rewarded, for we were indeed welcome. Duke Robert was most pleased to see me again. Even better, Edgar Ætheling was there to spend the Christmas season with his friend, and he proved most willing to see to his nephews' welfare.

✠✠✠

December and the Christmas season was bittersweet for me. The time passed quickly, with a whirlwind of activities always ready to distract from thoughts of home, for Duke Robert loved his manly leisure pleasures, even as brother King Rufus loved his unnatural ones. Every other day offered a ride or a hunt—of birds with falcons, or boar, or deer. We also enjoyed exhibitions of martial arts and contests of combat sport—duels with blunted weapons, archery contests, and lancing contests against quintain[9] or a variety of suspended targets—rings, fruits, and the like.

Evenings featured a feast, music, drink and gambling; the duke was a keen wagerer, and his was a particularly strong vice. Once he admitted to me that on occasion he had foolishly wagered his attire, lost and been forced to stay in bed for want of clothes. But since there was an indication that he had female companionship for the occasion, I discounted the full truth of the tale. Still, the unfinished tower outside his door spoke to a spendthrift tendency and a shortage of money, so I knew there was at least some truth in the story.

Now while all these entertainments were most enjoyable, I could not escape worrying for Aleine and our child—born by now and healthy, I hoped—for Carrick, Bjorn, the manor, and my future. For stealing the princes from Donalbane's grasp, I was probably

[9] A lancer's training device consisting of a swinging arm on a vertical post, with a small target on one end of the arm and a counterweight on the other.

now a wanted man, perhaps even declared an outlaw with a price on my head.

Robert and Edgar tried to assure me otherwise, that I was safe and welcome here in Normandy. Both had faced a similar fate at one time or another, and were wise in such matters. Edgar even suggested I return with him and the princes to Rufus's court. I knew that was a bad notion—I had poisoned that well with a single uplifted finger the previous year, and many English nobles would want revenge for that insult. Not least of these would be Rufus, I was sure.

But unable to act or otherwise allay my worries, I did the only thing left to me: I bided my time. Thorsson would bring news—good news, I hoped, but any news was better than the frustration of uncertainty, which kept me twisting in the wind like a hanged man. Any news I got from him would at least free me to act in some way: to go home; to sneak in, extricate my family and flee again to build a new life here; to do *something*. After all, the only thing I cannot do is *nothing*.

✠✠✠

At the beginning of January I took advantage of the season and proximity to borrow from Duke Robert three horses in need of exercise, and ride the 25 leagues east-northeast to Sigy-en-Bray. There lived my friend and master, Baron Jean de Bethencourt, his sweet wife Isabeau, and his ever-expanding brood of children. Cedric, now in his fifth year as my squire, accompanied me as ever. He had met Jean and Isabeau at my wedding years before, and I thought it best to get him away from the constant drinking and sport in Caen before he abandoned all his remaining virtues for Duke Robert's freely available vices.

Jean and Isabeau had a handsome manor at the end of a track a little more than a half-mile north of the village of Sigy-en-Bray. A spacious stone house with a three-story tower, kitchen, stable, barn, storehouses and quarters for the domestic folk formed a cluster of buildings built of stone or timber-and-plastered-wattle, the whole surrounded by a fifteen-foot palisade within a ditch. Around it stood spacious patches of farmland, pasture and woods.

Our reunion was joyous—we had not seen each other since my wedding, and we had much to say, much to catch up on. I met a half-dozen of their children of both sexes and descending ages—like stair-steps they were, and I never got all their names right. I was constantly being corrected—for either mispronouncing or guessing wrongly—who was Jean, Robert-pronounced-'Robear', Guilliame, Marie-Claire, Isabeau, and tiny Basilie.

To all of them I was introduced as "Uncle Godric," and it became immediately clear they had all heard stories of me, for I was promptly: bombarded with questions three at a time; climbed on; fought over; sat beside; and pulled hither and yon to see the baby pigs, the mean goose, the big horses, the apple trees, and so on. Cedric was hugely amused and he became just as popular when it was learned he could make whistles from goose bones. It was noisy—goose whistles!—chaotic, frantic, and great fun.

From the walk built around the upper level of his tower, Jean pointed out his holdings. "My lands extend from the north there..." he pointed, "...south around the village of Sigy-en-Bray all the way west all to Bosc-Asselin over there. That land to the east over there supports the Abbey of Saint Martin and Saint Vulgain in Sigy-en-Bray—see it over there? I owe fealty to the Duke of Normandy and Count of Rouen, Robert, whom you call Curthose. My grandfather went to England with his father, Duke

William, and died in 1066 at the battle at Hastings—you didn't know that, did you? Had he lived, I might be English!" He punched me in the shoulder as he had when I was his squire, and I realized then how much he missed our adventures together. And while my adventures never ceased, it seemed, I realized I, too, missed the ones I had had with him.

That first evening, when at last their children were bedded down and the four of us sat together, sharing wine beside the evening fire, I explained to Jean and Isabeau how Cedric and I had come to be in Normandy—how Malcolm and Rufus had warred, how our monarchs had suddenly died, how we had spirited the princes out of Alba, and how we were now probably outlawed traitors in our own land for doing so.

As I concluded, Jean said, "This is not the first time you've stolen something precious and had to flee an angry ruler in a hurry. At least you had no arrows or Turks in pursuit this time!"

Cedric cried, "What's that? I haven't heard this story! Tell me!"

And we three grinned.

I said, "Cedric, you are too young, and your squire-ly character unready to hear of such deeds. Even now I fear it will warp your soul to hear it..." But Jean and Isabeau ignored me. Both jumped into the tale, and enjoyed reciting it—telling parts over one another, and getting it wrong, so that I had to interrupt as well: '*stark-naked*' wasn't right, Isabeau had worn a diaphanous bourka—this time it was Isabeau who punched *Jean's* shoulder at that; and it was *five* Turks I took down—five, and let the *sixth* flee.

I'm not sure Cedric heard the story right, as tangled as was its telling, but we all enjoyed reliving the way those two lovers met. And it made us long again for the adventures we had shared.

We did not know it then, but our adventures together were by no means over; they were merely in hiatus.

✠✠✠

I am neither farmer nor herdsman, nor ever will I be. Were I not a knight, I would be a smith or a builder, for there my God-given talents lay. Jean, however, was, and took pride in the crops, herds wine and cheeses his estates produced, boasting that they were the best in Normandy. And Cedric and I were forced to admit he was right: we had not had better elsewhere.

With no combat to be had, and a domestic life full of family and farming, Jean worked hard alongside his domestic folk—both to keep fit, and see his estates improved. He invited us to join him, and it was only right that we earn our keep, but that toil ill suited me, so while Cedric helped him, I put myself to work at his forge.

And was there smith-work for me? Very much! His horses needed shoes, his weapons sharpening, his farm tools repairs, his kitchen utensils mending. Isabeau needed brackets for shelves, hooks for clothes, and hinges. And on a manor, there is a never-ending need for nails. I had no lack of items on which to work.

As I worked, I noted small faces ever peering at me from nearby corners, big brown eyes full of curiosity. Without words, I would beckon them in, but not too close; a line in the dirt marked the range of my sparks, and they were shooed back when they came any closer. I would let the bigger ones—those who could lift the hammer—try striking orange-hot metal and wonder at the force it took. Jean, the oldest at nearly six, I put on the bellows, puffing air into the coals to increase the forge's heat. His siblings loved picking up the new nails I made with wooden tongs and dropping them into the quench bucket, grinning at the *psshhht* each made as it hit the water.

But Jean needed his martial skills sharpened, too, and Cedric still had much to learn. So for an hour daily we three would take turns, man-on-man and two against one, in combat exercises with blunted sword and shield. Jean taught Cedric new sword tactics I had forgotten. I taught Jean the tactic I had used to defeat Bjorn—and to keep his guard up, when he got careless. Cedric taught me yet again that he was a sneaky bastard not to be trusted as a foe; Cedric had begun his military career as a yeoman-at-arms, and he knew foul tricks no knight should know, but which could save your life and were well worth knowing all the same.

And so went January. With each day that passed, pleasant though they were, my need for news grew. I began to itch to return to Ouistreham, and there learn whatever Thorsson might be able to tell me. I prayed, too—mostly that it would be good news.

At last the time came, and we bid Jean and Isabeau and their stalwart band of little ones adieu, hoping we would see each other again, and soon. And as we rode off, our departure was saluted with a fanfare of goose whistles.

✠✠✠

Thorsson returned as promised, and we were there to greet him. "How goes the voyage?" I asked.

"Well! Thank'e, sire, very well. My outbound cargo of Scottish wool was well-valued, and I'll do better from the sale of Norman wine and cheese I took on in Le Havre. And wind and weather have been better than I expected. It was most worth the effort."

Then he paused, and I tensed, for I sensed the news wasn't good.

"Baron, I wish I had better news for you. It's not all bad, I know I cannot tell you what you wish to hear." He stopped a moment to think, and then hurried on.

"The good news is that Lady Aleine is well, and that you now have a healthy daughter she has named Margaret Alice. Both mother and child are well—I saw them myself in Cenachedne. They are safe and thrive, as do your in-laws, the Baileys.

"And Causantín, the Mormaer of Fife himself, has declared them under his protection. He values you, and says what you did for the princes was not done as treason against Donalbane, but out of knightly duty and love for Malcolm, Margaret and the princes. He defends your back now when you cannot, and will stand by you as his side of fealty requires." Then he paused again, and I knew what was coming.

"But you cannot return. Donalbane is now crowned King Donald III of Alba, with Prince Edmund at his side as his named heir and co-ruler. They are not terribly popular, either; they have support from the highland nobles who never loved Malcolm, but for all that cannot now really rule them. And they banished the nobles who supported Malcolm in order to appoint their own favorites in their place. Now these appointed lords are forcing themselves on folk, demanding taxes and shares of crops, flocks and goods, so they can enrich themselves while they can. It's breeding much resentment and not likely to make Donald III popular."

I nodded. It was just what Rufus had done, and I had seen how that had gone. Donalbane was making a great blunder, destroying support within his kingdom even before he ever really had any.

"Is there a price on my head?" I had to know.

Thorsson looked glum. "I cannot truly say. Causantín is one of the few who was spared. His support within Fife is solid and he is very influential among the highland nobles, so Donald does not wish to cross him; and outwardly Causantín is neutral, so he does not have to. And because of that you too may be spared."

Thorsson shook his head. "But you are not safe either. I hear that Donald was outraged to learn the princes had escaped, and when Edmund told him how you had got the other princes out, Donald swore to hang you. So you are ill-advised to return for now..."

Then a thought struck Thorsson, and he brightened. "...But you may not have to wait long! I've just realized something. In Lundene I learned from a wool merchant who sells to the court that King Rufus is not happy with Donald on the Scottish throne. He would prefer his own choice on the throne: Duncan, Malcolm's oldest son by his first wife Ingibiorg Finnsdottir. Duncan has been in the English court since 1072, when he became the hostage guarantee of peace between William and Malcolm.

Thorsson nodded then, affirming certainty in his hunch. "Now, in return for fealty, Rufus plans to make Duncan the loan of his army so he can go overthrow Donald, and take the throne. If that happens, you may able to return home before year's end."

Thorsson grinned then, happy he had good news to offset the bad after all. To him I was a valuable source of silver-for-news.

I thought for a bit. Year's end was a long time away. But much better than never, especially with Causantín protecting both my family and barony. I could be free much sooner if Duncan defeated Donald in a mid-year fight. In any case, I could make it work—and in the meantime, perhaps benefit from my enforced stay in Normandy.

"Thorsson, my thanks as always. If you can tarry a bit, I'll write a quick letter to Aleine and Carrick to deliver to Cenachedne. And then I'll ride for Caen. I may have noble passengers for you to transport on your return voyage."

Thorsson nodded. "They have good oysters here. I'll go eat some now and have my crew load a cargo of them to take with us. I can wait a day, and sail the morn after tomorrow, if any wish to go."

An hour later, my unpracticed scrivening was done. The letter bore both good news and sad to Aleine, but above all, my love to her and our daughter, and my promise as ever to return to her. I gave the letter and a gold coin to Thorsson for all he had done, and Cedric and I were off to Caen.

✠✠✠

Knowing I had fresh intelligence of importance to Duke Robert and Malcolm's sons, we did not spare the horses, and cantered much of the way there, reaching the castle within an hour. I found

Edgar Ætheling and gave him a quick summary. In turn he sent for the princes and requested the duke join us.

"My lord," Edgar Ætheling began, "Baron Godric has discovered much of importance to us all. I pray you hear what he has to tell us. Lord Godric?"

And with that introduction, I related what I had heard from Thorsson, adding that I found his news ever timely and reliable.

Robert and the princes listened carefully—particularly Prince Edgar, I noted.

Then Edgar Ætheling spoke. "Robert, you told me you protested to your brother at the end of the year that he is not keeping his pledges made to you. Now he has intentions of sending his army north to drive out Donald III, and install Duncan upon the throne of Alba. I do not know if he will come here again this year to make peace or war with you, but if he sends a large army north, he cannot campaign against you as strongly as he has in previous years. We may both have a new opportunity here: you in Normandy, and I to place the princes in positions that will eventually aid them to regain the throne of Alba."

Robert nodded, and said, "That is true. I did send a messenger to William Rufus at his Christmas court in Gloucester, and said I would renounce all peace conditions unless he promptly fulfil then terms stipulated in the treaty. I called him a forsworn liar, devoid of truth, unless he adhered to our treaty. I requested we meet here in Caen in March, and I expect him to come. Whether peace or war will come from it, I cannot know, but knowing him as I do, I expect the latter more than the former."

Edgar nodded. "William Rufus and I are on good terms now, and I hope to use that to the benefit of the princes here. If I can take them to England and place them in the court, Rufus may think they offer him both advantage over Donald, and leverage with Duncan. I will offer to march with Duncan against Donald, and bring Edgar here beside me. By that means we may be able to establish Edgar as the tanistic[10] heir and successor of Malcolm following Duncan. In time then, Edgar, Alexander or David may reclaim their father's throne."[11]

I could see Edgar and Alexander liked that idea. David was a boy as yet, and so probably did not care—he wasn't really listening.

Robert was only half-heeding Edgar, as his next words showed. "Rufus cannot be in both places and prevail. So if it is not peace he is willing to commit to, I will get a new opportunity to recover some of my losses to him, particularly my lost castles."

Then Robert paused, and with a grin, said, "For that I could well use the skills of a talented siege master, especially one stranded here in Normandy and in need of gainful service. What say you, Baron? I've seen you in action. Do you want the commission?"

With a grin, I nodded. "I would relish it, sire!" And then to the two Edgars I said, "If you wish to go to Lundene, I have a ship ready and waiting to convey you."

✠✠✠

---

[10] Under the Gaelic tradition of tanistic royal succession, the king's successor was not necessarily his first-born male child (as in the primogeniture system of England), but rather one chosen by the chieftains or nobles as being of royal blood, adult age, all his faculties, and free of blemish in mind or body.

[11] As it happened, all three brothers in turn became kings of Scotland.

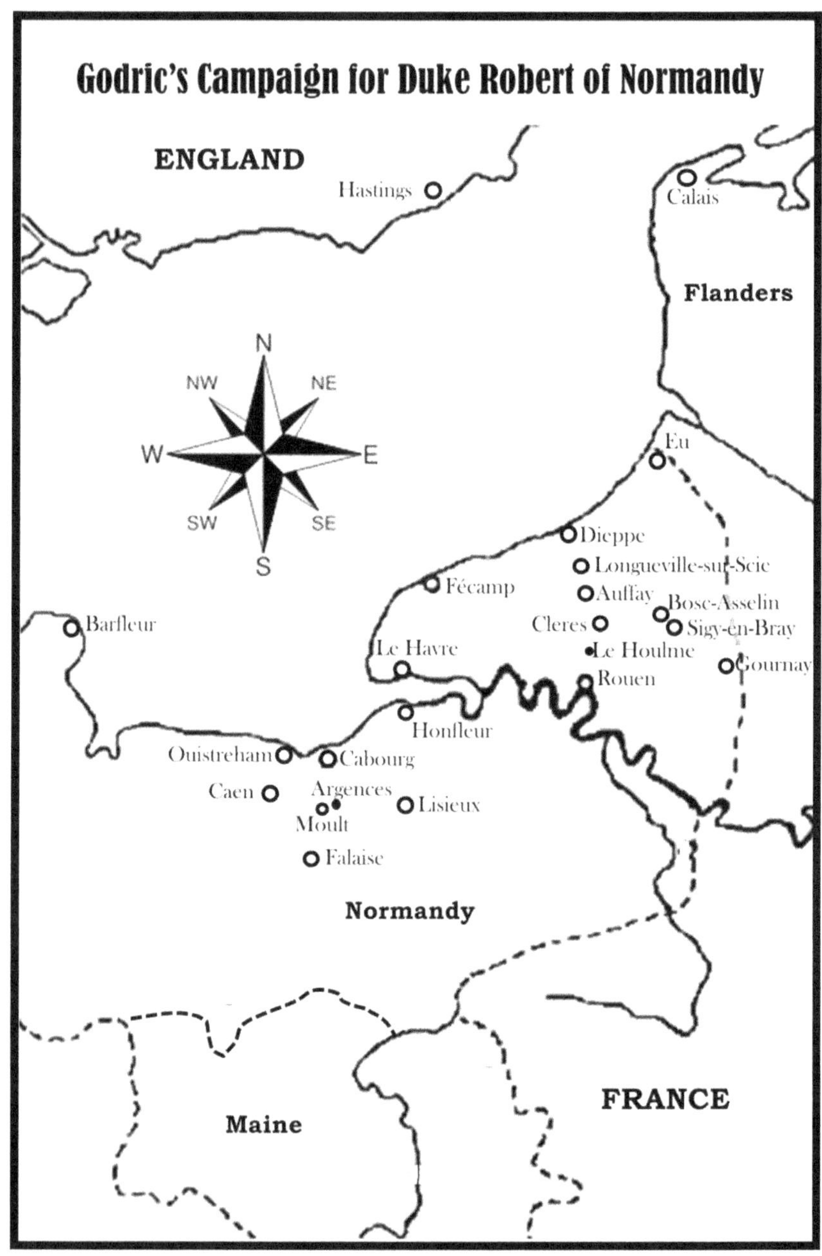

Figure 8: Godric's campaign for Duke Robert of Normandy

FOURTEEN

✠✠✠

I was not a witness to some of the events that followed, but heard of them later directly from witnesses or participants, and relate here what I heard.

Edgar Ætheling and the three princes did indeed avail themselves of Thorsson's ship, and sailed immediately for England. They found King Rufus in Hastings, and Edgar was successful in pleading their need for sanctuary to the king. Rufus, of course, saw it only as opportunity to shape three more potential kings of Alba as allies who owed him fealty, so they were welcome enough. And as Rufus was already preparing to send Duncan north with an army to seize the crown from Donald, he readily accepted the offer Edgar Ætheling and Prince Edgar made to assist Duncan in that campaign. Plans were laid to march with the return of good weather after Easter. Alexander was made a squire and David a page in the royal court, so for the time being they were safe and able to develop as princes should.

But content with having furthered his interests in gaining control of Scotland, Rufus then turned his attentions again to the thing he wanted most: rule of all Normandy. On the 19th of March, 1094 Rufus returned to Normandy to meet with his brother Robert. In preparation, Robert had summoned the Norman nobles who had witnessed their Treaty of Rouen in 1091 as sureties to again attend and serve as witnesses to what had been agreed.

To me, Robert said, "I am certain William seeks to renege on our treaty. He is already busy seducing nobles here who owe me allegiance and fealty to support him, bribing them with estates and titles in England and gold stolen from the Church. I need all my witnesses here to confront him with his own words and oath."

I had to agree. "Sire, I saw him do the very same with King Malcolm—use surreptitious means to steal or cheat his way into Malcolm's realm, and then create an excuse to void his promises. I have no reason to believe he will behave any better for you."

Nor were we wrong. Although Rufus and Robert first met privately in peace and with civility, it did not end that way. Rufus refused to be bound by the terms of the treaty, stating that Robert owed him fealty—ah, that same old evil trick!—and no subject owing fealty could bind his liege lord to any obligation. I forget the exact nature of the contested terms now—Robert's lands and revenues for his inherited estates in England—but Rufus clearly did not intend to honor them. Robert accused Rufus of seducing William, Count of Eu, to abandon his fealty to Robert in favor of William and demanded that Rufus cease these hostile actions, restore Robert's lands in England, return the twenty castles Rufus had taken in Normandy, and swear a new oath to abide by the treaty, this time with eternal damnation as consequence. That stipulation so outraged Rufus that he refused. Robert called upon the nobles at Camp Martius outside Rouen and made public his accusations and demands.

"Noblemen of Normandy, I ask you, when this treaty was made just three years ago in your presence, did you hear King William here vow to restore and respect my all holdings and rights, and refrain from further incursions upon my Normandy inheritance?"

"Aye, lord, we did," came the resounding reply.

"And did King William then and there give his oath to honor all the terms specified in this treaty?"

"Aye, lord, he did!"

"You have heard me lay out his violations, and know them from direct knowledge to be true. Has he given you any proof that I have also broken the treaty?"

"No, lord!"

"Yet now without cause he seeks to renege on it in your presence. These acts make him a foresworn and faithless liar! Do I owe fealty to any lord or king who violates his word and honor?"

"No, lord! He is a false knight, and a king without honor."

Although Rufus was outraged and furious at hearing this, yet he still refused to recant or swear to honor and abide by the terms of their treaty, so stubborn and greedy was he. Instead, he rose to leave the pavilion, and as he did, he shook a fist at his brother, saying, "Then we have no treaty and you will have no peace."

"So be it. Let there be war, brother, and all its blood be upon your soul," said Robert.

And with that, indeed, there was once again war between them.

✠✠✠

Later I learned that Rufus had already imposed a heavy tax upon his people and the Church to pay for a campaign of reconquest in Normandy—which meant he had never intended to pursue peace with Robert. Instead, he withdrew to his new stronghold in Eu with William, Count of Eu. There he gave instructions and paid the lords and soldiers in Normandy loyal to him to fight Robert, and returned to England.

Within two weeks—that is, in April—Rufus's forces surrounded Robert's castle at Bures with a siege and took it in little time, for the castle had had no warning nor time to prepare; it was spring, their winter stores were already entirely consumed, and there was no replenishment to be had. Rufus had those knights captured in Bures who could pay a ransom brought to England and there they were held prisoner until he extorted from them ransoms of money or deeds to their land. As I say, Rufus was ever greedy.

In turn Robert levied an army from his nobles and his ally, King Philip of France, sent a body of knights and men as well, producing a combined force of nearly 5,000. It took nearly a month for them to gather, for it could only happen once spring planting was done.

In the meantime, Robert told me of our possible targets. "Rufus has a large garrison of knights in a castle, just ten miles south-southeast of here at Argences, and it is my principal concern. It sits astride the route between my castles at Caen and the castle my father built in my capital of Rouen. It is one of the deepest penetrations Rufus has made into the duchy, and the first I need to retake."

Robert frowned. "He uses it as a base for further encroachment. His mounted knights and men-at-arms raid the area around it to subjugate the local knights and nobles using bribes or force to get them to violate their oaths to me and give fealty to Rufus."

I had to agree. "That is a favorite tactic of Rufus, one he used against Malcolm in Cumbria and Northumbria. He establishes a large force in a rival's territory, fortifies the place with a castle as a base of support, installs chosen nobles with deeds and grants in the surrounding area and then forces the local knights and lesser nobles to give him fealty. When challenged, he claims sovereignty over the region because of that fealty, and says he only acts to protect his fiefs."

I shook my head. "It's diabolical. Rufus used castles at Carlisle and New Castle to seize lands from King Malcolm. The only way to counter him is to take the castle. For that, though, you must have the larger army, and we never did."

Robert grinned and said, "Aye, but we will. Loss of his garrison at Argences will cost Rufus much, and go far to recover some of what he has taken. If it can be taken, I greatly want to do it."

I nodded and met his gaze. "Let me go see it, sire, and I will tell you if I think it can."

"Good man!" said Robert. "Take it, and I'll give you a tenth of the ransom, and a barony anywhere in Normandy you like."

✠✠✠

With Argences as our first target, it was only prudent to scout it, so Cedric and I borrowed garb, weapons and leathern armor from Robert's armory to disguise ourselves as mercenaries and went off to see what we faced.

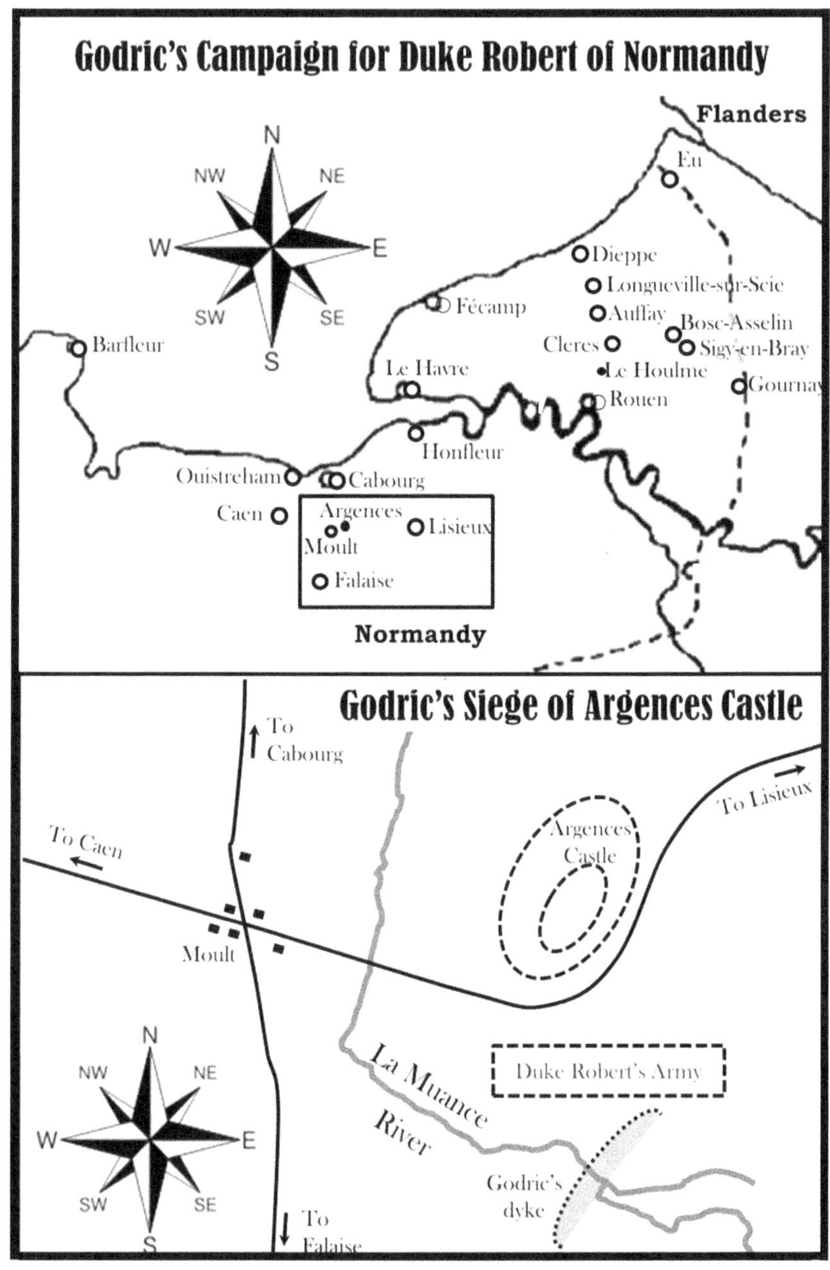

Figure 9: Godric's siege of Argences Castle

Robert had told us the castle at Argences was close—ten miles south-southeast of Caen and a half-mile southeast of the village of Argences on a great hill. We found it by traveling east on the road from Caen to Lisieux. At the crossroads with the north-south road from Cabourg to Falaise sat a little tavern, the first we had encountered outside Caen, amid a half-dozen hovels. We stopped and sat outside the tavern, where we drank ale and made idle talk with its owner. It was a good spot for a rest, for from there we could clearly see both hill and castle just a half-mile away.

Our host told us we were in the village of Moult—although 'village' was too grand for what we saw—and that the folk there called the hill "La Hoguette." He did not know what 'hoguette' meant, but the Danes in the highlands at home call 'haugr' what we Scots call a great hill—so perhaps it meant "little great hill." The hill itself was perhaps 300 feet high, rising from the southern end of a north-south ridge. It was the highest ground in the region, and natural for fortification.

Like most Norman castles of the age, Argences Castle was a motte-and-bailey fortification, but one of unusually great size. In truth, it was more a fortified encampment than a castle like Carlisle, but it was undeniably well-built and well-defended. Its most distinct feature, a great wooden tower of multiple stories—three or four, I do not entirely recall now—stood as a command platform and final redoubt atop the great hill. The base of the hill was entirely encircled by a ditch, mound and wall. A twenty-foot wooden palisade was built along the crest of an earthen ring mound inside a ditch ten feet deep and twenty wide. The whole defensive wall formed a great oval fortress more than 150 yards across and 250 yards long. Every 100 yards around the perimeter, wooden archers' platforms of 30-foot height rose.

Our host was happy to talk, and not just for sociability's sake. We were spending good silver, and the longer we sat, the more he earned. I hinted that we were interested in whether we could join the garrison, and when I offered to pay for information as well, he was all too willing to earn it. From him we learned that the garrison comprised 700 knights and maybe three times that many footsoldiers, under the command of Roger of Poitou.

As we drank, we watched, and noticed a cluster of longhouses around the tower at the top, no doubt where the knights and men-at-arms resided. The lower slopes were covered with tents for the footsoldiers.

Argences Castle was strongly fortified and well-garrisoned, and I was hard-pressed to see how we could take it without sacrificing many men that Robert could ill afford to lose. But Cedric had always had keen vision—better than mine, certainly. And after a bit he noticed something important, and nudged me.

"Barrels," he said. "They have lots of them, everywhere."

"Ale. They're English, so they need ale—lots of it," I said, too dismissively, and Cedric nodded, but with no conviction, which irked me just enough to ponder on the barrels.

And then it struck me: Some 2,800 men and 700 horses or more, were all encamped on or around that hilltop fort. Where did so many men get water? There wasn't likely a spring or well up that high, so they must have to haul in water… and for that they would need… lots of barrels!

"Sorry, Cedric, you are right," I said in a low tone. "Some are ale, but many more are for water. Where do they get the water? Let's go find out!" I paid the tavern-keeper well and we set off to see.

A short ride east and south gave us our answer. Our host had said a little river called La Muance flowed northward between his tavern and the castle, and we found it with no trouble. It was hardly a river; at home we would have called it a stream. But the horse tracks we found along its banks south of the castle told us all we needed to know. Here was where the squires watered the horses, and where yeomen filled the water barrels. There were some doing just so when we passed by, and though they eyed us, we paid them no attention and rode on unhindered.

We rode south following La Muance upstream. What I needed to find now was a place where we could dam or divert the water. If we could cut off their supply, the siege would be short. Men and horses need a lot of water, and after three days without it, men and horses start dying. Without water, a siege ends in days.

An hour later, we had found what we needed. So we turned our horses and rode straightaway for Caen.

✠✠✠

In May of 1094 Robert's army was ready. We marched from Caen in two bodies. The larger body, 4,500 men, headed the same route we had taken—directly for Argences. They marched by night, reached Moult at dawn and arrayed themselves for battle. On the flat plain south of the castle along the eastern banks of La Muance, companies of footsoldiers formed a great line of battle, while squadrons of mounted knights protected the center and flanks. Outnumbering the garrison by half-again as many men, Robert offered battle on the plain outside the castle. But Roger of Poitou knew his advantage was the castle, one he would throw away by leaving to confront a greater force on open ground outside it.

Meanwhile, just behind the main army, I led a body of 500 men, yeomen who until levied had been farmers, woodcutters or builders. We followed the same route until we reached the crossroads at Moult, where we turned south. And when we were a mile south of the castle, I put my men to work.

The bulk of them I had dig a long ditch across a flat ground on either side of the little La Muance stream, building a mound on the northern—downstream—side of the ditch, and gradually curving it south on both ends. It was spring so the ground was soft. I spaced the men ten feet apart and each man dug ten feet of ditch. The mound they raised was only about three feet high, but it was unbroken and formed a great dam, able to hold back a huge volume of water for long enough. We did not cut the ditches into the stream yet, however.

As they dug, a smaller team of woodcutters cut trees and dragged them with teams of horses to build a dam across the little river—only five yards wide at the point I chose. My masons brought to the dam-site cartloads of rocks collected from the rock mounds nearby where local farmers had piled the rocks cleared from their fields. And with timber and rock, we started damming the stream, building our dam to the height of the earthen mounds.

Finally, when dam and dyke were well along, we cut the two ditches into the stream, and by rocking shut the last gap, diverted the water along the ditches. With that, no water flowed toward Argences, instead flowing to fill the ditches and then backing up in a great shallow puddle behind my dam and dyke. Downstream the water level in La Muance fell. By nightfall only a tiny trickle remained, in small muddy puddles and basins in the streambed.

With that engineering feat, Argences was doomed. The following morn Duke Robert called for parley, and under a truce led Roger of Poitou to the banks of what had been La Muance.

"I give you this choice, Sir Knight," Robert told Roger. "You can all come out to fight us, the greater force, or you, your men and animals can die of thirst inside your wooden walls. I won't waste my men's lives trying to take your stronghold when thirst will do all the hard work of killing you for me. But I vow this: none of you drink again until you surrender that castle and all in it to me."

And with that Roger realized he had no choice—he lacked the men to win a battle, and could not withstand our siege without water. Disgusted, he handed his sword to Robert then and there, surrendering himself and all his men without a fight. In keeping with what Rufus had started, all 700 knights were forced to pay a ransom[12] to Duke Robert and King Philip to regain their freedom.

And Robert kept his word on the ransom. He had to divide it with Philip, of course, but he argued that each of them owed me half my promised share on the grounds that I had done all the work that had won it. Philip assented, so I did very well by it. For his part, I gave Cedric a tenth of my share, enriching him much, so that he not only gained enough to equip himself with excellent weapons, armor and horses, but also to buy his own land, house

[12] The actual record of a knight's ransom from the Battle of Poitiers (1356) reports he paid 300 gold florins, worth $42,000 today, plus additional gold and silver items for his freedom; perhaps $50,000 in all. 700 knights at $50,000 would have earned Robert and Philip the equivalent of $17,500,000 each, Godric $3,500,000 and Cedric $350,000!

and more. Since he was an excellent squire and would be a fine knight, he deserved it—though it would never do to tell him so.

Later, credit for forcing the surrender of Argences was given to King Philip, "who took Argences in a day with a stratagem." Those words were clearly written by English clerks to spite Duke Robert and flatter Philip after he changed sides. But Philip never left Paris, and that stratagem was mine.[13]

✠✠✠

What ensued in the month of June following the fall of Argences was a period of manic activity by Duke Robert—always a man of excesses. We relocated to his castle in Rouen, one his grandfather had begun and his father enlarged and strengthened. Then, with a large army at his disposal, he set about scouring his dukedom of nobles and magistrates who had taken Rufus's gold to switch sides. From town to village to manor, he sent companies of men-at-arms commanded by loyal knights to seize these men and punish them with impoverishment for their betrayal, using many of the same tactics Rufus used to force them to switch fealty in the first place. Those refusing to comply he burned out, destroying their manors and sometimes villages belonging to them as well.

In this I had no part, for Robert was most enthused by our success at Argences, and keen to know what other strongholds we might take, and kept me busy considering possible targets. He and Philip had high hopes of drawing Rufus into a single fatal battle, or alternatively trapping Rufus in a siege at Eu. To do either we

---

[13] True! That's how the history reads, and probably why. What the stratagem was is not reported, and the site of Castle Argences is lost, so my version is as good as theirs.

would first need to take Rufus's castles along the line of march, starting with Le Houlme—bypassing an intact castle allowed an attack from the rear, the worst of all possible military blunders.

To see if we could take the castle at Le Houlme, I needed to see it, so Cedric and I planned another scouting mission. Just as we were to depart, at the end of June, Robert and I each received letters, newly written and sent together from Alba. His came from Edgar Ætheling, and mine from Prince Edgar. By now, Robert and I were good friends, and shared contents relevant to the other.

From Prince Edgar we learned this:

"King Donald has been unable to build any support in his new realm. The highlanders supported him to take Alba's throne, but they never intended to be ruled by him; rather, they wanted to end rule by Scoto-Normans like Father and ourselves—they see us as foreign invaders, even though we have as much Scottish royal blood as Donald, and the highlanders are no more than half-blood offspring of Celtic women and Danes. In the lowlands where he does rule, the landowners and Church officials all loved Father. So Donald has gained the throne of a land that preferred Malcolm, not him, and not of the men who helped crown him.

"And then upon taking the throne, Donald immediately made two mistakes: first, his attempt to eliminate us as rivals has angered many; and second, he exiled nobles like you, who earlier supported Malcolm—for they too have supporters, and none of them favor this new regime. But he did not know this until too late, for he was focused on the trappings of kingship, and not on building lasting support for his reign.

"So when in May Donald learned that my older-half-brother Duncan was marching north leading an army of Northumbrians that Rufus lent him in return for an oath of fealty, and with the Earl of Northumbria, Edgar Ætheling and me at his side, he sent out an order to call up an army to meet us. Only then did he discover that lowland Scots refuse to comply and that he lacked both time and means to raise an army of highlanders instead. He was a king without power.

"We reached Edinburgh at the start of June and would have trapped him as he did us in the castle there, but he knew he could neither fight nor outlast our siege, so he has fled north, deep into the highlands. Our wretched brother Edmund has gone north with him, for he had convinced Donald to name him heir, and now he fears what Duncan would do with him. Duncan has been crowned "Duncan II" and is now the new king of Alba.

"I have ensured that your family and lands are safe. Earl Causantín, Mormaer of Fife, declares he is your good friend and vows they will always have his protection. And know that I and my brothers will always be in your debt for our lives."

And so it was I learned that Alba had another new king, that my life as outlaw was over, and that when my present commission as siege master to Duke Robert ended, I could return to my life in Cenachedne. I might not continue as sheriff-at-large, but I was still *Baron* Godric MacEuan.

In turn, from Edgar Ætheling we learned more:

"The loss of Argences has hit Rufus hard. Bringing to Normandy another army to take more of your inheritance from you is an expense he can ill afford. Moreover, he realizes he cannot win against the allied forces of you and King Philip, so he has resorted to yet another infamous trick.

"First, he used his power to mobilize the Fyrd—the whole of the military-eligible men of England—to levy an army of 20,000 from all the burghs and shires in England. He knows each burgh and shire must pay each levied man 20 shillings for his expenses in service.

"Then, as the 20,000 men mustered at Hastings to embark for Normandy, Rufus had his faithful Justiciar Ranulf Flambard collect ten shillings from each, saying the payment would spare him the risks of the crossing and war in Normandy, and give him a safe-conduct home.

"In this way Rufus got 200,000 shillings, all of 10,000 pounds[14], to spend on his campaign at no cost to himself. And these funds he has used to pay a huge bribe to King Philip of France to cease support of you, his ally. If you have not learned this yet, you need to know—before you engage Rufus in a major fight—that King Philip has changed allegiance, and will not support you further."

Robert was outraged, of course, to learn of his brother's sneaking scheme and Philip's betrayal. And the warning came just in time, for Robert had grand notions of engaging Rufus in a single great battle to finally decide the future of Normandy. Without the aid of Philip's army, Rufus was almost certain to win. And there was a further risk Philip might be further bribed to join the fight on Rufus's side. Ah, the wicked machinations of kings!

Angry as he was, though, Robert still had a grudging respect for his brother as a warrior and a king, if not as a human being. And

---

[14] £10,000 then is worth £5,326,933 or $7,528,554 today.

he openly showed it when he shook his head and said, "Brilliant! That cunning bastard of a brother is damned brilliant. Greedy, conniving and completely immoral, of course. But he is brilliant. There is no denying that Rufus has a gift for wicked tactics. Hell holds few who can exceed him."

✠✠✠

FIFTEEN

✠✠✠

With his plans for a major battle to draw out, engage and defeat Rufus forever in Normandy in shambles, Robert fell back on his hopes to besiege Rufus at Eu and pressed ahead with his efforts to purge Rufus's supporters. He urged me to find a way to take Rufus's castle at Le Houlme, for it controlled the most direct line of march between the two opponents' chief strongholds at Rouen and Eu, and therefore became a critical buffer—whoever held it had the advantage in the contest of conquest.

So once again Cedric and I donned our mercenary disguises and set out to scout the castle at Le Houlme.

✠✠✠

Le Houlme is a village sited in a narrow valley ten miles north of Rouen. The most direct road to the coastal towns of Dieppe and Eu runs through that valley, and then on by way of Cleres and Auffay to Longueville-sur-Scie, our next target. Rufus used these ports as his favored beachheads to bring forces into Normandy, so throwing him out of the duchy required taking back his strongholds, one by one, until we also regained these ports.

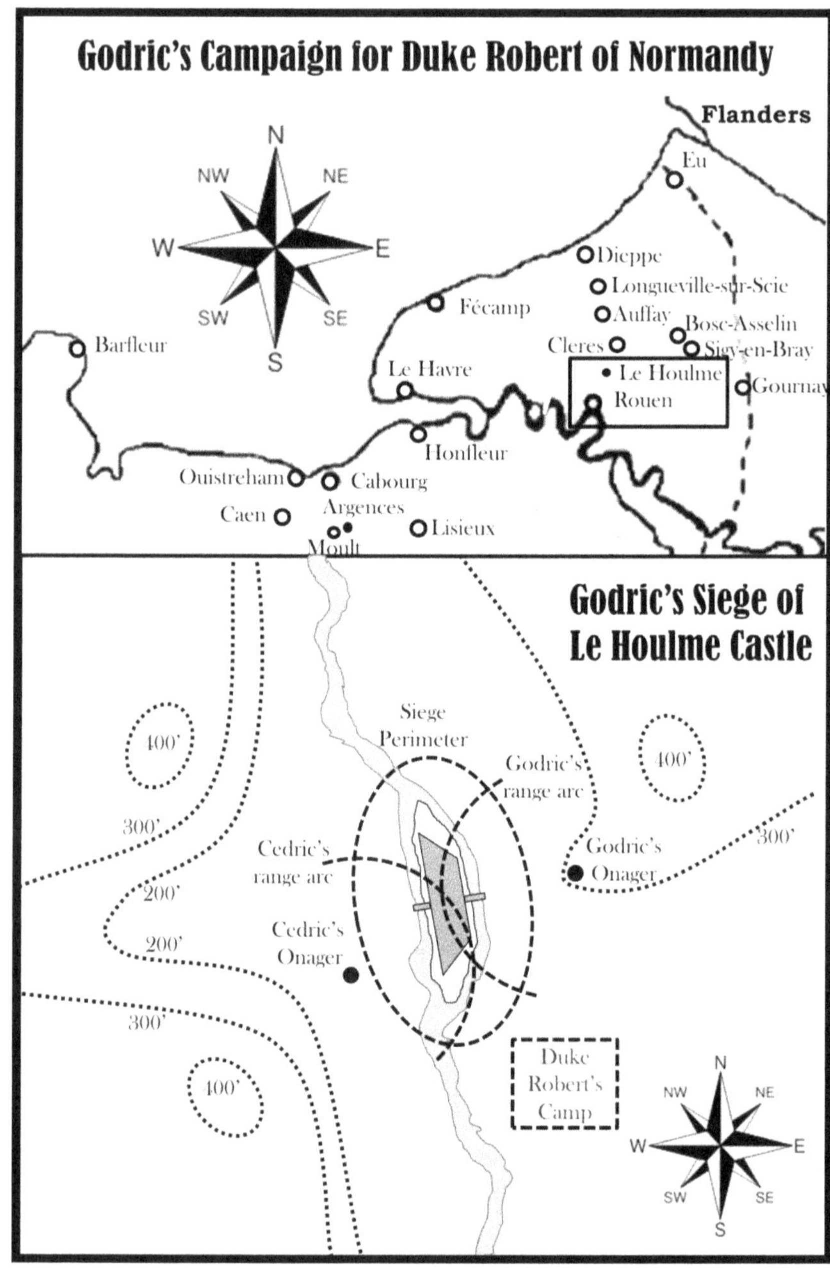

Figure 10: Godric's siege of Le Houlme Castle

Once across the Seine by way of the Rouen bridge[15], Cedric and I took a circuitous route; for although Le Houlme was only a short distance away—just three hours at a walk—Robert had told us the valley was narrow, and the garrison wary of armed men coming north from Rouen, too likely thought to be Robert's men.

Instead we rode another route: the fifteen miles northeast to Sigy-en-bray, where we were welcomed, and spent the night with Jean, Isabeau and their pack of tiny rascals, who were overjoyed to see us. But our strange garb had Jean and Isabeau puzzled, for we could have passed for Dane raiders or English footsoldiers.

"Have you taken up Duke Robert's ways? Gambling and losing?" Jean asked with a smile. The duke's vices were widely known.

Knowing Jean was loyal to Duke Robert from our earlier stay, I concluded it was safe to discuss our mission. In any case, I knew I could always trust both Jean and Isabeau with our lives.

"We are scouting a castle held by Rufus in Le Houlme. I need to know what it is like before I can devise a plan to take it," I said.

"You besiege castles here now?" Jean asked, for this was news to him. "Dunnottar and OdinsØye gave you an appetite for sieges?"

"He took Argences in a day without a fight by cutting off its only source of water, capturing 700 knights and 2,100 men-at-arms at a stroke," Cedric said—with impudence and pride, for which I cuffed at him. Knowing it would come, he ducked, and I missed, so I scowled at him.

---

[15] Yes, it existed. The Rouen bridge over the Seine was built in the early 11th century.

"My apologies. This scoundrel is too forward and too used to my ways. Time he was knighted, and forced to take on a squire of his own as a pain in his..." I left the site of said pain unspoken.

Jean nodded. "I completely understand. I had a squire like that..." He looked at Cedric. "The bastard constantly upstaged me. I should have drowned him, but I owed him both life and wife."

Cedric said, "I have the same problem, sire. I tried to drown him once, but he bit me on the—Ow!" This time I did not miss.

Jean grinned and said, "Did you really take Argences as he said?"

I nodded. "*We* did. At Argences Rufus had a motte-and-bailey on a hilltop without a cistern, its garrison so great they thought they would never face a bigger foe or a real siege. But Sharp-Eyes here discovered they stored their water in barrels. We diverted its source so they could not withstand a siege, and they knew they lacked the strength to defeat the 5,000 men of Robert and Philip together."

Then I added, "But I don't think Le Houlme will be that easy."

From there the talk moved to who supported whom—which barons backed which overlord. It was complicated. Jean preferred Duke Robert, but avoided getting entangled in war. Jean's noble neighbor to the south and east, Baron Gerard de Gournay, was one of the first Normandy barons Rufus subverted with English gold, for which de Gournay turned over three castles to Rufus's use. Jean said he was one of the few who was an enthusiastic supporter of Rufus, periodically trying to cajole or press Jean into supporting Rufus as well. But Jean feigned neutral indifference, as indeed did most barons until forced—or heavily bribed—into choosing a side. There simply was no merit to choosing between feuding brothers for any lesser reason. And Jean was determined to keep it that way, for the sake of the charming little squirrels who clung to us as we tried to take our leave the following morn.

✠✠✠

We approached the valley of Le Houlme from the high ground to the east, and from a distance of just 300 yards and a height of perhaps 300 feet, we were able to look directly down on—or rather into—the castle of Le Houlme.

Along the eastern side of the valley ran a stream called Le Cailly—these French folk call every little trickle 'river'—which flows south into the Seine, a real river, at Rouen. In the midst of the valley, the stream divided to flow around an island, and upon the island was the castle.

Le Houlme was of an irregular shape matching that of the island: it had four straight sides, but the western wall was about 1,000 feet in length, the eastern half that. Against the long wall stood half-timbered barracks, stables, storerooms, kitchen and refectory for the garrison commoners, while along the eastern was a long hall for the lord and knights, a chapel, kitchen, armory and forge. At the ends stood two greater towers; in the middle the stub of a stone donjon, under construction and already a story in height.

As at Argences, this stronghold was built largely of wood, and except for the stream, much like it. Along the banks rose an earthen mound, topped by a twenty-foot palisade with a fighting platform encircling the top. Wooden towers stood every fifty yards around the perimeter as platforms for longbowmen. Gates were set in the eastern and western walls, a gatehouse around each, and at each a drawbridge across the stream.

For most purposes this was a very strong castle, and with skilled archers—which it had, for we could see archery butts for training against the end walls—it would be very costly to take. But they had not anticipated the war I could bring. And after Cedric and I compared impressions of what we saw, I knew how we could take it.

✠✠✠

Back in Duke Robert's castle in Rouen, we had preparations to make, and I had siege engines to build, but first I had to win Duke Robert's support of my plans, for it was his money I would spend. After Argences, on top of the earlier demonstration of my machines in Cenachedne, that wasn't difficult. "I have every faith in you, Baron. Do what you think best."

So with the help of hired smiths and timber-framers, I built two onagers, two ballistae, four scorpions, and a substantial number of fire-darts for both of the latter types of engines. For a wooden castle, fire would be my best weapon, and I bought wool, clay pots and Danish tar to that end. But we also filled wagons with round cobbles and river stones, for an onager has more than one use. And as ever I needed caltrops and chevaux-de-frise in plenty.

By mid-July we were ready, and Duke Robert lost no time. He still had contingents of King Philip's men with him, for the ruler of France was gluttonous, lazy, and entirely consumed with the pleasures of the table and the bed of Bertrade de Montfort, wife of Count Fulk of Anjou, the paramour for whom he had been excommunicated. And while otherwise obsessed despite the bribe he had taken, he had not yet ordered them to withdraw, so Robert was determined to use them while he could.

It was a twelve-mile march to reach Le Houlme: four hours by foot, but it was only an hour's ride. So at midnight of July 20th, Cedric and I led a small mounted contingent of picked men, mostly archers and crossbowmen to reach the castle in darkness ahead of the main body.

We dismounted at a distance and slipped in on foot. I sent skilled archers to points opposite the northern and southern towers, where I estimated the sally ports would be, and others opposite the gates, their mission to kill any messenger sent out to summon help from Rufus in Eu.

To Cedric I gave command of the party for the western gate while I led the eastern. Dressed in dark garb, our faces and hands darkened with charcoal, and without helmets to shine or weapons to clink, we slipped through the darkness to a hundred yards of the castle. Each of us carried a leather bag filled with caltrops. We spread out, working silently from closer to farther and right to left, placing these a foot apart in a belt fifty feet deep along the road to each gate and out ten yards to either side. Within an hour, we had surreptitiously filled the roads to both castle gates with caltrops so that every horse riding through that belt would be lamed. Thus we could defeat a mounted charge by Le Houlme's knights before it reached our lines.

Then we drew back to wait for Robert and the army to arrive. And an hour before dawn it did. Up the valley it came, dividing south of the castle into two columns to march up both sides.

An alarm was sounded in the castle when the sentries heard the noise of thousands of men, horses and wagons on the move, but we had them surrounded before they could see well enough to assess their danger and formulate a response. And the messenger sent from the base of the northern tower was captured after my archers felled his horse.

The slopes of the hills on either side of the valley were more than 300 yards from the castle, a very long bowshot indeed. It was here we established our siege lines, putting our men generally out of range of Le Houlme's archers. The job of this army was to isolate the castle rather than assault it, while I used long-range weapons—my siege engines—to breach or destroy it with fire.

We had the garrison vastly outnumbered. Unlike Argences, Le Houlme had, I had estimated, perhaps 500 men-at-arms. Robert commanded ten times that number, but the defenses the castle offered neutralized our advantage. Without my engines we would have had to attack a well-fortified position across open ground; many more of us would die doing that than they.

Now, around Le Houlme there were three points of high ground, formed where two side valleys joined the one where Le Houlme stood. The point to the northwest was too far at 700 yards, but the ones to the west and east were inside 400 yards of the castle. That made them beyond bowshot but just within the longest throws I believed I could achieve, for I had learned that from greater height I could achieve greater ranges. From those points I could only attack the southern flanks of the castle, but it would take only one big breach to doom the place, and that was what I had prepared to do.

So while I put my teams of siege engineers—many the same men who had helped me cut off the flow of water to Argences—to work hauling the disassembled engines up onto the high points, Robert called for a parley with the castellan, Sir William Peverel.

Sir William was made of stronger stuff than was Roger of Poitou, for he was not about to surrender an intact castle simply because he was vastly outnumbered. And the demand that he surrender, I heard later, he rejected in the strongest terms possible, suggesting that Robert go do something King Rufus was already well-known for. Robert then promised he would shortly do it to William. And with the niceties done, both sides settled down to a proper siege.

William chose to save his arrows and men for the desperate and dangerous close-in killing that castle assaults always required. That we did not immediately attack may have had him puzzled, but it did not prompt him to foolishly attack us. I am certain he felt he had food and water reserves to outlast us, and chose to save his arrows—the usual most critical shortage of a siege—until they were truly needed.

By the end of a generally quiet first day—a few desultory arrows ineffectually shot in both directions, to judge distances more than hit, and many obscene verbal volleys and gestures—Cedric and I had the onagers ready to throw from the southern promontories. A fortnight earlier we had trained both crews on them in Rouen, both to test the new machines and to give our men experience using all the machines. But it would be up to Cedric and me to direct loading and aiming to hit targets at such long ranges.

As Cedric and I had been up and hard at work for most of two days and a night, we got some sleep at sunset, ate a much-needed meal, then as planned set to work at midnight—after the castle thought the day's work over and lay down to rest.

Bombardment by night was unusual in sieges, and generally whenever we used siege engines we did so by day since we needed to see the fall of our projectiles to adjust our aim. But my siege of Le Houlme was different. During the afternoon I had set pairs of whitened stakes as sightlines to mark the point of aim for various castle targets—the knight's hall, armory, gatehouses, and the like. All I needed do was align the onager's aiming stakes with a set of sightlines, adjust the tension on the skein for range, and throw. And this night we used illuminated projectiles.

Since we had together besieged OdinsØye, Cedric and I had used signals to communicate and coordinate attacks across distances, using flags by day and torches by night. This time there was a distance of 800 yards between us, but we were high and could clearly see each other's position and such signals. For complicated messages, we could also send mounted messengers—squires who carried our messages in writing or memory. But that took longer.

Now I had my signalman send Cedric: "Commence." And to my own crew, working by torch and firelight, I said, "Cock and load the spoon. Three firepots."

From a nearby fire where they had been heating, my crew took round clay pots filled with Danish tar—pine pitch cooked into a viscous liquid and shipped in barrels from Daneland—usually for use in caulking ships. Tonight it had another purpose.

With a torch I set aflame the hot tar in each pot, and when they burned well, I checked my sight alignment one final time.

"Stand clear!"

"Aye!" resounded five times—once from each crewman.

"Loose!"

As fast as an eye blinks the onager's spoon whipped forward to slam with a great *whack* into the stop. The firepots made arcs of fire through the sky. Plunging, they burst on impact, splashing three great puddles of fire on the streambank ten yards short of the castle. And, as if in answer, fiery arcs from Cedric's position achieved similar results on the opposite side of the castle a moment later.

"Add one full twist to the skein," I ordered, and my crew used long poles as levers to tighten the leathern bundle a full turn on each side of the throwing arm. This increased the torsion on the skein, adding power to the arm and distance to the throw.

Greatly alarmed, the sentries in the castle sounded a call to arms on hunting horns and rapidly the darkened castle boiled again with activity: shouts, horn signals, torches hither and yon in the castle, and more torches hurled across the stream to light up the oncoming night attack. William evidently thought our firepots were intended to light our way for a night assault upon his walls, for men quickly lined the tops of the palisade.

From the darkness, unannounced, Duke Robert materialized at my elbow. "Baron! Why did you not send for me? Would you have me miss this fun?"

"Welcome, sire! We thought you preferred sleep." To my crew I called, "Cock and load. Three more firepots." When they were ready I handed Robert the torch. "Care to do the honors, milord?"

Robert ignited the pots and again we repeated the drill: check the alignment; stand clear—I had to pull Duke Robert back, for he was both too eager and too close—five ayes, and loose!

And fireballs again arced through the darkness, and Duke Robert watched intently. My crew as well—all this was new to them too.

This flight of fireballs crossed the stream. One burst on the roof of the armory, setting the thatch—*thatch!* A very bad idea—afire. The second created a pool of fire in the castle yard. The third broke at the top of the rampart, splashing burning tar on palisade and men alike, to create several human torches, running, falling, screaming and writhing in the castle yard.

Cedric had increased his torsion as well, and had managed to get firepots into the castle too. Within the walls there were calls for water to quench the flames, and soon every defender was running wildly with buckets, pots, kettle helms—anything that could hold water. The trouble was, we could start the fires more easily than they could quench them.

The defenders had managed to quench the armory roof fire, so again I set it ablaze, and again they struggled to put it out. To the duke's unspoken question I said, "I hope to burn all their arrows. No arrows, no defense, we win."

He gave me a grin that expressed not only approval of my tactics but also a great enjoyment of the entire spectacle. I saw the same grins on the faces of my crew. Despite the hard work, they were truly enjoying this. And then I realized I wore one, too.

God, forgive me—I truly love a siege. And this was ever the best.

They began to empty the armory of its stores, so I shifted targets to set aflame the knights' hall, forcing them to save it instead. Cedric had the roof of the barracks burning also, and all our overshots had spread fires in patches all over the castle yard.

We continued to throw as quickly as we could—three pots every few moments or so. Within half an hour we had fires burning everywhere in the southern half of Le Houlme.

Now I signaled Cedric with "palisade" and we shifted targets again. I added another pot to each throw to reduce the range of each slightly, and four pots slammed against the palisade itself. Three more throws and we had set the great wooden wall afire over a large area behind the armory. With all the other smoke and flame, and the defenders driven back from the walls, this was soon burning fiercely.

Again, to Duke Robert I explained. "We need a breach. Even if the fire does not burn completely through, it will weaken the palisade so further bombardment can punch a hole in that wall."

His nod told me he agreed. "I brought 5,000 men here to take Le Houlme, but your dozen men may be all I needed. Well done!"

I nodded my thanks. "I intend to keep them busy all night. They may not be able to endure much more by morning. If they refuse to surrender, they may instead send out a sortie in force in hope of destroying these machines to save the castle. I would ask you to be ready to stop them."

"Baron, that would be the least I could do in return. Count on it." Then he clapped me on the shoulder, and left us to our work.

Through the night we kept them busy. They saved the knights' hall, but lost the fight for the armory and the barracks. Through the night columns of flame reached high into the darkness. We ceased our efforts, then, to let the fires do deadly work for us, and all of us got a few hours of much-needed sleep.

✠✠✠

In keeping with Scottish custom, King Duncan was crowned at Scone and ascended the throne of Alba in the summer of 1094. And while the supporters of Malcolm in the lowlands accepted him well enough, not all did. There were some who rebelled at his coronation. Others resented the presence of the English army that won him his crown, and had remained. They were needed to help him keep it as long as rival King Donald was at large in the highlands, where he was busily building support to retake it from Duncan. But the army was certainly neither liked nor welcome, for the soldiers demanded shelter and subsistence in peoples' homes and largely took what they wanted by force. For allowing this, Duncan never achieved more than tenuous rule of the lands south of Edinburgh.

Now, King Duncan then was about 34 years old. He was married to Ethelreda, the daughter of my comrade at Alnwick, Gospatric, Earl of Northumbria until Rufus deposed him and gave his lands and title to Robert de Mowbray. Ethelreda provided Duncan with a son named William Fitz-Duncan, who was in 1094 a boy of twelve. And this soon came to matter, for he was too young to rule a kingdom, so under Alba's tradition of tanistic succession, Prince Edgar became Duncan's heir instead.

By fall Duncan was faring as poorly as had Donald before him. He had lackluster support and growing opposition. The prelates and the landowners joined the outright rebels to protest the acts of the English occupying army and demand its ouster. Duncan was forced to consider the choice of dismissing the army that kept him on his throne or fighting the people he hoped to rule. Knowing the latter wasn't possible, he sent the English soldiers back into England, hoping that would win him the support and favors of the protesting lowlanders. But alas, it did not; it only showed weakness that fueled further disfavor.

I did not learn all this until later. It happened as I wrestled away Rufus's castles for Duke Robert. But it affected my kingdom and soon came to matter to my life directly, nonetheless, and for that reason I relate it here.

✠✠✠

I was up at dawn. As soon as the daylight grew sufficient, I studied the castle from my elevated perch and assessed the effects of our efforts, both the damage to Le Houlme and Peverel's countermeasures. Then I mounted and rode down to Duke Robert's headquarters for a meal and council of war. I signaled Cedric to come as well so we could confer with the duke on our results and formulate fresh plans. We took a moment to compare conclusions before we entered his headquarters tent, located south of Le Houlme where our forces had divided to envelop the castle with our blockade.

Robert greeted us with high spirits and unusually manic morning energy. He, too, was up, cheerfully eager to be about the day's business. Truly, war campaigning suited him as a stimulant even better than did revelry with wine, women, and games of chance.

"A good morrow, gentlemen! How did your night's efforts fare?"

"Well, sire," I said. "Both the armory and barracks are largely destroyed by the fires. The palisade behind each is charred and greatly weakened. We saw a line of perhaps a dozen bodies laid out in the castle yard, shrouded for burial. And Peverel has men pulling down timber from wherever it can be taken to reinforce his defenses. He is not ready to surrender, but they lost much last night—many must sleep outdoors after this."

The duke nodded and started to speak, but the sound of our alarm horns cut off his words, and we rushed outside to see why.

A mounted messenger galloped up, frantically reining his mount to a skidded halt. "Sire! A mounted sortie from the east gate!"

We leaped into our saddles and raced northeast, up the eastern side of Le Houlme. To save time and distance, we raced across the deadly ground inside arrow range, at about 150 yards from the castle. I was hit—twice, I think—by arrows, though saved by my mail and brigandine. My horse took a shaft in the left hindquarter—meant for me, I am sure—but in spite of it carried me to the site of the sortie where a wild melee was in progress.

From the eastern gate, fifty mounted knights and men-at-arms had charged, headed upslope toward my engines. Forewarned of this possibility, Robert's archers reacted swiftly and shot freely, as fast as they could. The heavily armored knights would have ridden straight through them, had they not ridden straight into my hidden belt of caltrops.

Suddenly the lead horses, wounded by sharp spikes driven deep into their hooves, were screaming, rearing and plunging, pitching off their riders. The horses following them collided with them and floundered, tripped or fell, adding more downed animals and fallen men as obstacles. Others further back veered away, only to find caltrops for themselves, for we had sown a wide semicircle reaching far beyond each side of the road. And into this chaos our archers continued to shoot, felling horses and men alike.

As we reached the scene, so did Robert's knights, riding to meet those who evaded the melee and escaped my trap. Duke Robert, Cedric and I joined in, meeting our foes with sword and shield.

The fight was short, brutal and pointless, for the surprise was gone and the sortie broken, most of the English already down. Robert himself engaged the boldest knight, and with his war hammer smote such a blow to the knight's helm that it suffered a dent the size of my fist. Stunned or killed—who could tell?—the knight fell from his saddle like a grain sack. At that, my own opponent realized he was the last knight still ahorse, dropped his sword and held aloft an empty hand, yielding the fight. I ceased my attack and the sortie was over.

Arrows shot from the castle ramparts continued to fly at us until Robert waved a white cloth of truce. At that, both sides withheld further shots so that the wounded and captives could be taken from the field and the grievously wounded horses dispatched.

Once more, Duke Robert called for a parley with Sir William Peverel to demand his surrender. Sir William rode forth with one other, and the two commanders met. At this, I was present as Robert's second.

Now, I had never met Sir William, so I studied him as the parley continued because it is important to know your foes. He was then about 55, ten years older than the duke and thirty years older than me. He was well-armored and well-mounted, clearly wealthy. The arrogance of the earlier parley was gone, but the defiance was not. He would not be easy to defeat.

Said the duke, "Well, William, now you have seen what we are capable of. If you surrender, you will save the lives of your knights, men and women. We will treat all of you with honor, accept your pledges of ransom, and upon receiving an oath not to further support Rufus in war against us, grant parole and safe conduct to all who swear. If you do not surrender, we will renew our assault with even greater vigor, and continue until none are left to resist us from the ashes of your castle. What say you?"

While he listened to Robert, William had been studying me. This I found surprising until I realized that he already knew Robert, and I was the foe he needed to know.

William ignored the demand. "Is this your siege master, Robert?" I wondered at the familiarity between them; first names implied a long relationship of peers.

The duke replied, "He is. William, I present you Baron Godric MacEuan of Cenachedne in Alba." To me Robert said, "Baron, this is Sir William Peverel, my elder half-brother, and my father's favorite bastard son. He owns—how many is it, brother?—162 manors in England, nearly as many as darling brother Rufus!"

William ignored his brother and to me said, "My compliments, Baron. You gave us a hard night. I expect no sleep tonight either, and that soon, when I do sleep, it will not be under a roof."

Then he turned attention back to the duke. "No, brother, I do not yield. Rufus expects much for his gold and goodwill, but honor demands yet more of me." To me he said, "Do your worst, lad."

I said. "As you wish, Sir William. No sleep for you by day or night. Count upon it!"

The parley was ended. With a parting salute we turned our horses and as we withdrew to resume the siege, I said, "You must battle your half-brothers as well as your brothers?"

Robert grinned and said, "And how did you get along with your half-brother, Andrew?"

At that I smiled and replied, "Touché!"

✠✠✠

SIXTEEN

✠✠✠

Following the parley we conferred to make fresh plans. In planning Peverel had it easier: react and endure was all he could now do. He had sacrificed a tenth of his garrison on a gamble to reach and destroy my engines, and added to his earlier losses to arrows and fire, he had, I estimated, lost between a tenth and a fifth of his garrison. At ten times his numbers, we were largely untouched. Unless I did something stupid, or a military miracle brought here an army from Rufus, we would defeat him yet. But how best to do it?

Still, we had just started this fight, and we were well along on winning it. Sieges usually go on for months—a few arrows back and forth every day, occasional desperate attempts by one side or the other, but mostly both sides sitting, waiting for the other side to eat the last of their provisions. Depending on who ran out first, either the defenders surrendered their castle or the attackers gave up the siege.

What was different here was that I had engines able to reach in and inflict serious damage to both structures and men. That tilted the balance in our favor, and there was nothing William could do to stop me; he knew it, and knew I knew it, too.

✠✠✠

I resumed my attack of the castle with firepots from the heights; my crews up on the promontories were now experienced enough to do this without help from Cedric or me. This left me free to focus on breaching the castle palisade, so I had my ballistae and scorpions assembled, and from Robert's ranks chose crews of skilled crossbowmen for each, as they were already experienced shooting smaller versions of these machines. After training them to load and shoot each, I sent the scorpion crews off to practice. I learned later they chose the tower sentries as practice targets, and with glee picked off several from a range of 250 yards, forcing the others into concealment. Nor could I disapprove, for their role would be to do this against all archers on the towers and ramparts as we assaulted a breach.

Now as we worked I heard, from here and there, snatches of a familiar tune—Cedric's. And as I listened, the words, murky at first, began to become clear. There were sung from our lines, variously in English and Norman French, at our beleaguered foes:

"We've brought up the army.
We camp at your door.
Our peace terms you refuse,
So now you'll get war.

"Climb over, dig under,
Or pound a way through.
We'll use every weapon
To bring death to you.

"Your towers will tremble,
Your garrison fall.
Your ramparts will tumble,
Starvation for all.

"We'll cave in your rooftops
With boulders we cast.
With fire we'll burn all
So nothing will last.

"Come out now and fight us,
We'll entertain you.
And many will die here
before we are through."

But now one quatrain had become a refrain, to a new tune.

"Your castle can't save you.
We'll never withdraw.
Until you surrender
We stay at your wall."

And one quatrain of lyrics was new, one that drove me into fury.

"Your loot we will plunder
And your daughters too.
We'll give them fat bellies
So as to spite you."

Now, we had earlier planned to attack the drawbridge and gates. But another idea hit me, more likely to gain us victory, so I found Cedric and gave him a task.

"Go find out where the streams around the castle can be forded. That little trickle cannot be that deep. Interrogate the locals. We need to know where we can get men and horses across."

He grinned and said, "Aye, milord!" a term he only used when being impudent, which only happened when he got a task of great appeal to him. Good soldier that he was, he did not ask how. I thought he would ferret out the information—I certainly did not expect otherwise—but I should have, for I knew him well.

But I was not finished. "By the way, I heard today a quatrain of your song I like not at all." And I repeated the words of which I spoke:

"Your loot we will plunder
And your daughters too.
We'll give them fat bellies
So as to spite you."

I shook my head. "Siege is an ugly kind of war. But for knights that is beyond the pale of just warfare. I am furious and ashamed that you are my squire."

At that Cedric looked distressed. "Sire, I did not compose those words, nor half those the men sing. I taught some the tune and the verses I knew. But now they are adding their own, and calling it *The Siege Master's Song*. Sire, I beg you to believe me!"

Just what I needed: A song the lyrics of which I hated was now named for me.

But I realized then that what Cedric said was true. It was the kind of song soldiers like: sing-able as they work, ominous, bold, and outrageous. It was just the kind of song that they would adopt as their own, and then adapt to suit their inclinations, good and bad.

I nodded. "Very well. I believe you. I retract my condemnation. I would not hear those verses again, but..." and here I sighed, "...we cannot control all that is done in our name." I clapped him on the shoulder and added, "And it is a most engaging song."

✠✠✠

Meanwhile, we hauled two scorpions and a ballista to a point opposite the eastern gate, where the raised drawbridge served as a protective outer wall in front of the gate, and set it up 300 yards from the castle, shielded with flanking mantlets to protect the crew from arrows. This proved most prudent since, as soon as it was noticed, every archer on the eastern wall began to shoot at us. Most fell well short, for it takes a damn strong bowman to reach out that far. But enough fell close to have me send back to safety all but two well-mailed men-at-arms to help operate the engine.

We loaded the ballista with a dart bearing an iron cage behind the spike tip, both set on a long, light wooden shaft. The cage was filled with wool soaked in hot tar, creating a fire-dart. I had used these against Dunnottar and OdinsØye, and favored them to set wooden targets afire. Now I would burn the drawbridge to get at the gates.

After consulting my codex, I aimed for the great wooden panel, set an elevation suited to the range, put fire to the cage, checked that my crew was clear, and then tugged the lanyard.

With a *snap* the bowstring shot the dart downrange, a tail of black smoke arcing up and down again marking its passage. It struck the gatehouse just to the right of the drawbridge and set it afire. I noted the smoke trial drifted right, too, so as my men recocked and reloaded another fire-dart, I nudged the machine slightly left to correct for the breeze.

Snap! The second dart struck the drawbridge this time, and fire splattered in a patch on the great panel. Since the drawbridge was beyond the gatehouse there was no easy way to douse the flames, and my scorpion crews took joy in shooting at all those brave enough to try. Three more darts followed in short succession, and the drawbridge was soon engulfed in flame.

Elsewhere the defenders fought fires inside the walls all that long day, and if he slept at all, Sir William had to do it where we could not reach, up at the north tower. And inside Le Houlme, all who tried to sleep were serenaded by the lullaby my soldiers sang:

> *"Your castle can't save you.*
> *We'll never withdraw.*
> *Until you surrender*
> *We stay at your wall."*

✠✠✠

I was awakened from the rare little sleep I was going to get that night by something wet splashing water on me. It was Cedric. The idiot was sodden and shivering, and stood over me while he considered whether to wake me. As I sat up, he said, "I have your answer, sire. Do you wish to know now or in the morning?"

I frowned. "Does it rain, or have you been interrogating fish?" Through my tent door I saw it was still dark. I was awake and now wetted, too. "Tell me now."

"Come and I'll show you," he replied.

"First put on dry clothes, you dolt," I retorted, and summoned a young lad to fetch him hot mutton stew. "Bring two!" I added. I would not likely get sleep again, so the food would help make up for it. An old military saying goes thus: 'Never pass up a chance to eat, sleep or relieve yourself, for in war these opportunities are always in short supply.' *And Sir William is learning this*, I thought.

An hour later we stood opposite the southeastern wall. Dawn had come and there was now light enough to see. Fires burned still at the drawbridge and within the castle, the smoke forming a pillar like God had once raised for Moses.

"There," he pointed, "where the wall is burnt. Outside there is a stretch of shoal that is fordable. There we could create a breach we could ride through, for there is no building on the other side."

"How do you know?" I had a good idea, but he deserved the chance to say it.

"I searched the waters from the high points, looking at the water flow." Cedric always had keen vision. "Then after dark I stripped down to dark clothes and under a black cloak I crawled in. It took a while." That was an understatement.

"You got wet crawling across the meadow?" I knew otherwise.

"No. I slipped in and swam across the stream—crawled it, to be truthful. I did not want others to be put at risk trying to cross water too deep to ford."

Too true—you cannot swim wearing sixty pounds of mail.

“Well done—well done, indeed! Let us go find the duke,” I said.

✠✠✠

To Robert I said, “My squire has found us a point to breach, and I will have that breach made for us on the morrow.”

That got Robert’s attention. “What! The fourth day? Other than Argences, I’ve never known a castle to fall in less than a month! How did we find this miraculous spot?” This last he said intently gazing upon the squire in question.

“Cedric exceeded both his task and my expectations by spotting a suspected shoal. He then crawled through darkness to the spot and crossed the stream to the castle wall to confirm it.” I have to admit I took more than a little pride in relating the deed to his commander.

Robert stared at Cedric. “Did he indeed?” Cedric wilted under the gaze. Like me he was used to rebuke, not praise, and not a little unsettled by the phenomenon. I was damned proud of him.

Robert said, “Look at me, lad!” Cedric met the duke’s eyes. “When this castle falls, if I still can, I will knight you myself in its courtyard and be proud to do it. Well done, Squire Cedric!”

Squire Cedric’s eyes welled up with tears of gratitude at that. I barely got him out of the headquarters tent before the dam broke.

✠✠✠

From the eastern promontory Duke Robert, Cedric and I studied the condition of Le Houlme. The buildings along the southern walls were roofless, mere burnt-out shells. Only the stables along the northwest palisade were intact. They had since been cleared out and the horses were now penned in the northern triangle so people could use the stable as shelter. The eastern drawbridge was a wreck, although the gatehouse around it had been saved. Here and there the ramparts were charred by fire, and had been reinforced with timber obtained by tearing down some of the archers' towers. And it appeared William expected an attack on the eastern gates, for he had built a stout barricade of timber and debris in the courtyard behind it, forming an inner wall behind the gate.

"We need a diversion," I told the duke. "If I turn my attention now to the southeast wall, they will reinforce it, and—if I were William—plant a phalanx of spears behind it to kill knights and horsemen coming through. We need to draw their expectations elsewhere and only breach there at the last possible moment."

"I agree," said Robert. "Since they already think the eastern gate is our aim, let it become the diversion instead."

"Aye. I was thinking the same way. We should start massing men opposite the gate. I will bombard the gates and gatehouse with firepots. And meanwhile I will prepare to breach the southeast wall in this way..." And I described what I had in mind.

"Godric, you are a devil!" said Robert. Cedric just grinned.

✠✠✠

At my direction Cedric oversaw the move of the western onager to the eastern gate, and with it began hurling firepots to set the gates and gatehouse ablaze, while my eastern machine hurled cobbles down on the barricade. This would keep William focused on defending and reinforcing the eastern gate. Meanwhile I used a makeshift forge and the aid of blacksmiths from Robert's army to fabricate a new kind of dart for the ballista. These I would need to make the breach. As well, I had Robert's foragers obtain for us another commodity, and I am told they raided the entire Rouen waterfront to collect as much as I requested.

We planned to begin the breach at "prima luce" or first light, when predawn light grows, offering visibility before sunrise. That would allow us to attack in daylight but not reveal our plans with enough time for William to counter them. And to wear our foes out, my onager crews kept them awake much of the night by hurling firepots into the castle. A half-hour before first light we ceased, so that William's defenders collapsed into a sleep that left them groggy and hard to awaken when we attacked.

In darkness we had moved a ballista and a pair of scorpions into position opposite the breach site 150 yards out, largely silently and without torches. We laid out our breaching materials, raised wicker mantlets to shield machines and crew, and then we were ready. As we worked, suspicious sentries shot a few arrows out in the dark, but they could not see us and after hitting nothing that cried out, sounded no alarm.

Duke Robert had his part to play, and in darkness moved the men of his army to the eastern side, leaving their night fires burning in the care of a few men for each fire. The archers were placed to the south and east of the castle, well back until the attack began. The knights chosen for the breach were given chance to confess their sin and obtain absolution by their chaplains, as many of them might not survive the fight.

As soon as it was light enough to see the site of the breach, a charred section of the palisade just beyond the shoal, I shot a first dart, an arrow-like shaft to confirm I had the range and pointing right. It struck in the middle of the charred palisade, a little low, and after a quick correction I knew we could proceed.

The dart I shot next bore a heavily barbed point like a fish-spear. Welded to it was an iron ring through which a strong cord was threaded. As it flew, it pulled a loop of cord as two strands from two tubs. The point stabbed deeply into a palisade timber two-thirds of the way up the wall, where it became an anchor of sorts.

As I readied the ballista to fire another dart, Cedric took the cord from one tub, cut it, and tied the end securely to a stout rope. A man-at arms took the other tub back to a team of men behind us. At Cedric's signal, they began to haul on it, pulling the rope out across the field to the palisade, through the ring and back to us. This gave us a way to pull on the palisade itself.

As this happened, I shot another such dart similarly equipped, anchoring a second rope line in an adjacent timber. The process repeated, and my men pulled out another rope.

Now all this had not gone unnoticed by the castle sentries. They first sounded the alarm, and then began shooting at us. A few arrows quickly became many. But as my fires of days earlier had burned away the fighting platform behind the breach—a key reason I had chosen this site—they could not reach our ropes and cut them.

In a matter of moments, we had five ropes set into a section of weakened palisade about ten feet wide—enough for two mounted knights to pass through abreast. All ten ends of the ropes were quickly made fast to whiffletrees pulled by pairs of harnessed horses, putting the power of twenty draft-horses into the task of pulling open the breach. Men seized the ropes as well, adding yet more traction power on the ropes. We were ready.

"All together! Heave!" I cried, and men and horses pulled as one. The breach section of the palisade bent outward: at first a bit; then more and more, until it bent so badly it could not resist long.

"Sound the ready!" I ordered, and a squire blew the signal on his horn, alerting Duke Robert and his knights that breaching had begun. At that, they rode forward from the wood in a column, and prepared to charge.

From the first dart not much more than a few moments had passed. Several very brave defenders scrambled over the wall and tried to reach the ropes from the outside to cut them. My scorpion crews, there for just that reason, cut them down instead.

Arrows flew at us in a torrent now—whatever remained in their store of the missiles was being used as fast as men could shoot. But the range was long, and not many of their archers could reach us. Robert's archers countered then, running forward at the ready horn, and shot arrows in high arcs as they did to down the enemy on the wall-tops and in the courtyard. Le Houlme's defenders were outnumbered ten to one, so it wasn't a fair fight. They ceased loosing the high volleys just before the knights reached the breach, but continued to shoot at archers upon the wall-tops.

Suddenly, with a great *crack* the palisade broke and the shattered timbers were pulled across the stream and up the bank. I was greatly relieved then. I had feared the timbers at the breach might break away separately leaving the breach plugged by a few. But there was enough strength in the cross-braces to carry away the intervening timbers as well, so that the whole section failed entirely, leaving only stumps a good warhorse could jump. I prayed quick thanks to Saints Michael and George, who protect men in battle and give the deserving victory.

At that Robert needed no signal. His squire sounded the charge and off they went—100 knights or more in a column of twos, off at full gallop across the open ground.

Slowing only enough to negotiate stream and mound, the column bolted across the shoals, and then up through the breach. I dearly wanted to be with them, but my job had been to get them in—and now it was done.

The mounted knights and squires of the breaching company bore shields and crossbows. As they entered, each was instructed to shoot an archer or pike-man trying to stop the breach, drop the crossbow and draw a sword. Not to be dissuaded from the role, Duke Robert led the charge and was first man through the breach.

The fight inside, the duke himself told me later, was vicious but short. The crossbows—an idea Cedric had put forth—made a great difference, for each knight shot down a critical defender at close range, clearing the way for others.

Many of the defenders were down from arrows, and perhaps only a quarter of William's men unwounded. Faced with the certain death of his entire garrison, Peverel did the only thing he could: he handed Duke Robert his sword and had the gates opened in surrender.

Le Houlme had fallen. And, like Argences, it fell to me.

✠✠✠

Later that day in the courtyard of a badly damaged castle, two men underwent a ceremony generally conducted in more courtly settings. At the site of the victory each had helped make possible, a squire who rode through the breach and my squire, Cedric, were each knighted by Duke Robert. The squire had saved Duke Robert when a pikeman impaled his horse just beyond the breach, using horse and sword to drive back the breach defenders, and shielding the duke as he freed himself from his fallen mount. Cedric's deed—finding the ford that made the breach practical—I have already related.

The ceremony was brief but eloquent. In a circle of knights and nobles, Duke Robert recounted the man's heroic deed, declared him worthy of knighting, and then performed the *accolade,* as the French call the dubbing that signifies knighthood, in this case a colée, a blow with a naked fist on the side of the head, the same way William the Conqueror knighted Robert 25 years earlier.

I had first met Cedric in November, 1085, when we rode together, carrying King Malcolm's young daughters to their aunt's convent in Romsey to be educated. Cedric then was a young yeoman-at-arms in the Dunfermline palace guard, while I was entering squiredom with Robert the Frisian, Count of Flanders. When I was knighted in 1089, I chose him as my squire, and he had performed bravely and well in our adventures together. More significantly, he had mastered siege warfare with me, helped me build my skills and commanded siege engines for me against OdinsØye, Alnwick and Le Houlme. I taught him much, but I learned from him, too.

Sir Cedric MacUilleam of Dunfermline. I could not have been any more proud of him that day.

✠✠✠

One more event of note happened at Le Houlme. Robert's army was busy gleaning the battlefield: burying dead men and horses; recovering arrows—you can never have too many, and repairing them was easier than making them—and scavenging all of value against our next objective—food, forage, and the like. And my crews were disassembling my engines for transport. I had hopes of using them again, God willing, against Rufus at Eu.

After the knighting I toured the wreckage I had made of the fine, proud castle of Le Houlme. The southern half was a ruin. The northern end had not gone unscathed either, for the defenders had dismantled much, stripping away all the nonessential timber to reinforce the southern defenses. Half a castle is no castle at all.

And it was as I made my way about, assessing the effects of my weapons to learn from the results, that I met Sir William Peverel once again. He had been given parole, of course, and dejectedly sat in a chair taken from the once-fine knight's hall while his servant stitched closed a sword cut to his right forearm.

Seeing me, he nodded—a tribute of sorts—so I went to him.

"Come to gloat, have you, Baron?" He hadn't spirit to put any sting in it. It was just a sad acknowledgment of a reality.

"Nay, sire." The honorific carried sincere respect. "You made a tough defense. I came to see what else you had in store for me. The stake-filled pitfall between the gate and the inner barricade was inspired. I never suspected it. Had we come through the gates you would have shattered our attack, cost us Duke Robert, and won the siege." I meant every word, and he could tell.

He shook his head, and in that act he looked much less the proud warrior, much more the tired old man. "A tough defense. Hah! We should have been able to withstand you for months, yet you took this place in a week." He looked up at me. "I have been a warrior for forty years, fought in a half-dozen lands, yet I know of nothing that can hurl fire 400 yards, nor shoot pikes nearly that far. We could hardly reach any of you, yet you could pound us night and day with impunity. With what? Where in Heaven or Hell are there means to do it? Was it sorcery you used?" And I could see he really thought so.

"Perhaps. But I used nothing of Hell. I have mastered the art of ancient siege engines the Romans once built, and improved them where I could. There are no others closer than Constantinople. They gave me great advantage here."

Now, I had engines like these stored in Cenachedne, so I spoke a lie; but it was a small one. My point was: *no one else* had them.

"Well, I suppose that *is* a blessing. I underestimated you, and that was my great mistake. It's no pleasure being trapped *inside* the bonfire. You cooked us, and kept us running to fetch water and douse new fires. And you kept your word, for I had no sleep since our last parley. That damned song your men sang crawled into my head and stayed there, haunting me all night long.

"But for all that, I thought fire was all you had." He sighed then. "I suppose this will end wooden castles. We'll have to build them of stone."

I shook my head. "I felled a stone castle as easily. Castles are not the answer. Kings and nobles need to rule honorably, so castles are unnecessary. King Rufus needs that lesson; King Malcolm could have taught him much."

William looked at me then. "Malcolm is dead. Rufus reigns on."

I nodded. "And for that reason I will never lack employment."

✠✠✠

After taking Le Houlme, we marched north, following the roads through the villages of Cleres and Auffay toward the fishing village and port of Deupa[16]. Just eight miles short of that town we reached the village of Longueville-le-Giffard,[17] where stood the castle of Walter Giffard, Lord of Longueville. Giffard was a celebrated battle companion of William the Conqueror in his conquest of England and fought beside William at Hastings. Lord Walter was dead ten years hence, but his son, also named Walter, now held the castle and had taken gold to abandon Robert and support Rufus. Robert wanted the castle if not the castellan.

But it was here that King Philip finally received—or acted upon—his bribe, and withdrew all further support of Robert. As we were about to begin another siege, half of Robert's army, with the personal apologies of the commanders, turned about and headed for Paris. At that, Robert found himself lacking enough men to press his campaign. Doing so risked losing a last battle to Rufus.

Disgusted by Philip—his feudal lord and supposed ally—and filled with outrage and begrudging admiration for brotherly guile,

[16] Dieppe today

[17] Now called Longueville-sur-Scie

Robert reluctantly concluded that the campaign to regain his lost lands was over—for now. So we turned about and marched back, all the long way we had come, to the safety of Rouen.

✠✠✠

With that ill fortune, my service as siege master to Duke Robert came to an end. Although he planned to renew his campaign the following year, that was months away and fraught with uncertainty—for if Philip would not support him, there was no way Robert could again challenge Rufus in a head-to-head fight. Hence, further sieges were unlikely.

But I had a more pressing reason to end my service here. With Duncan now King of Alba, the threat Donald had on my life was over, and I was free to return to my beloved wife Aleine, Alice, the daughter I had never even seen, and my own barony. I had been away in exile here for most of a year, and I was keen to go home.

For his part, Robert had fallen back into his old ways. War was thrilling to him; when there was none, he reverted to food, drink, carousing and gambling. Of those I had had my fill, but not he.

Nonetheless I had made a lasting impression with him. As we parted, he clasped my hand and said, "Godric, my young friend, you are as brilliant in sieges as is brother Rufus with trickery. When next I campaign in a way requiring a siege master, you are the man I will seek out to aid me."

✠✠✠

Cedric and I gained further benefit from the ransoms due for the capture of Le Houlme, and in lieu of other payment from Duke Robert, I took my engines, for I had learned something from Sir William Peverel. Engines like mine afforded special advantage to those who had them, one I had not fully appreciated before. Once they became available to unscrupulous men like Rufus, they would gain added power and advantage to do as they wished rather than what they should. I needed to keep them from the hands of men like Rufus. With that realization, I had them hauled out of Rouen and burned them. Then Sir Cedric and I rode to Honfleur, took ship, and sailed for home.

But I did take home one new weapon: *The Siege Master's Song.* Peverel had taught me that, too. That song had proved itself to be a weapon as powerful as my tree-bucket *Bone-Crusher*, a tool for demoralizing castle garrisons and inducing surrender before more violent means were used. If I could get a castle to fall with a song, it was far better than by killing its inhabitants.

It was a lesson I would call upon again and again, and for that reason I came to treasure *The Siege Master's Song.*

✠✠✠

SEVENTEEN

✠✠✠

We reached home at the start of September, 1094. Harvest was in progress, and despite the turmoil in the country caused by the struggle among kings, life in Cenachedne was unroiled and the place was thriving.

So too were Aleine and little Margaret Alice. Aleine was even more lovely than I remembered, in part perhaps because motherhood brought with it certain changes fathers appreciate as much as do babes. Margaret Alice was a tiny wonder: pink, fat and perfect, with her mother's looks and none of mine. A great advantage for a girl in that—not to look like me.

Well, too, were Carrick and Alice, though I did not see them for a full week after reaching my manor. Instead we handed the babe to her wet nurse and told the entire household that any who disturbed us unbidden would stop a crossbow bolt. And Aleine meant it when she said it—holding up the weapon for emphasis.

For nearly a year I had routinely worn mail and brigandine, other than while Cedric polished the mail or I doffed all for a wash. Now Aleine called for hot water, had a tub filled, acted as my squire to help me remove my armor, gave it to a house-girl who staggered under the 60 pounds of weight, chased her from the room, and bolted the door. Clad only in a linen shirt, I felt I might float away on the next breeze.

While I bathed—awkwardly, for the tub that easily held all of her was much too small for me—she burned my linen. When I had finished, I asked for clothes, but Aleine smiled, shook her head and said, "Nay, milord, you shall not need them for some time."

It was then I learned what Duke Robert meant when he confessed to being stuck in bed for want of attire. And truly did we enjoy it.

✠✠✠

For two months all was peaceful in my little corner of the world, but I was, for the first time in my life, without a meaningful form of employment. It wasn't a question of money—I had more than I needed. It was a matter of purpose, a purpose to my life. I no longer had any role meaningful to my sense of self.

I entertained thoughts of going to King Duncan, offering homage and seeking renewed service as a sheriff-at-large, should he wish it. But Aleine was so happy to have me home, and I was content to be free of turmoil for a time, so I did not go.

And then, suddenly, everything changed again.

In November, without warning, Donalbane, the recently-deposed King Donald III, came south from his refuge in the north with an army of highlanders and Prince Edmund by his side to challenge nephew and rival King Duncan. A battle was fought the 12th of November, 1094 at Monthechin near Kincardine. The survivors among Duncan's men called it an ambush, but clerks record what the victor says. This time it was King Duncan who was slain—one day short of a year since King Malcolm too died in ambush. Duncan had been king just seven months.

How he died was as suspicious as the nature of the "battle" itself. Among those named as his killer were: Donalbane himself—unlikely, as he was thirty years older than Duncan, quite elderly; Edmund—even more unlikely, for I had known Edmund all my life, and knew he was a schemer, not a fighter; and Máel Petair, Mormaer of the Mearns—he was my choice, the most likely, and probably acting on Donald's wishes.

Some described it since as a murder rather than death in combat. As I was not there, I have no way to know how it was done. But whatever happened, Duncan was dead and Donald was free to reoccupy the throne, as he immediately did. And with his return as king, so returned the threat to my life and my family.

I could not flee abroad again. Aleine urged it, but this time my honor rebelled. For my family's sake, it was time I ended it—for better or worse.

✠✠✠

Before I went to Donald, however, prudence suggested I visit another: my liege lord, Causantín mac meic Duib, now the Earl of Fife in his own right. So I mounted my warhorse CiùinLùth—how I had missed him in Normandy!—and rode south four miles to the coastal village of Uamhs—the English say "Weems"—after our Gaelic word for its caves, where stood the earl's new wooden castle. Of late, Uamhs is being called "Castleton" for that reason.

The earl's title was new, though he had filled the role as regent for ten years. In 1093, at age 20, Prince Ethelred had decided to abandon life as a prince in order to become a monk, and had entered the monastery at Dunkeld. Malcolm then elevated faithful Causantín to be the Earl of Fife, as had his father before him.

Ushered into his hall in mid-morn, I found the earl engaged against a young squire in a novel form of battle, a most popular new game called chess, played with carved figures on a checkered field. It seemed the squire was finding it difficult to avoid defeating his lord.

"Baron Godric, old friend! It has been long since I've seen you. Welcome! How did you fare in Normandy?" It appeared my arrival came at an opportune moment, allowing an earl to escape defeat, for both seemed grateful when the squire begged leave to return to his duties, freeing his lord to attend his guest.

When Donalbane became King Donald III—the first time—and thought to punish me for helping his rivals, the princes, escape his grasp, it was Causantín who blocked all efforts to move against my family and barony. The highlanders who supported Donald had swayed him to expel all the Norman lords Malcolm had appointed, but Causantín was a Scot with royal blood, the grandson of King Cináed mac Duib, who ruled Alba a century ago as King Kenneth III—followers called him "MacDuff." In truth, Causantín had a claim to the throne as valid under tanistic succession as Donald's.

As a lord, Causantín was both competent and popular, powerful through his Gaelic blood ties as well as favor with those he ruled —like me. Donald could not move against him without losing all support of Fife—and where Fife led, others followed. For that I was most grateful, and realized there was a way to use his power and our friendship to reconcile myself to Donald.

Hence, my visit today.

"Lord Causantín, I came to offer you my deepest thanks for all you did for Lady Aleine and Cenachedne during my absence, and to bring you this."

A gift is always welcome, and this was one of the finest I could give: a new sword, done in the Norman style with the best steel Carrick could produce, its scabbard dressed in black leather overwrapped with gold wire, producing a quilted appearance, and the throat and frog in gold. So too the grip—dressed in black leather and gold wire. The pommel was dipped in gold and highly polished. It was a sword easily worth twenty pounds of silver. Carrick and Cenachedne had come far of late.

"My word! A truly handsome weapon! I am much indebted." Causantín beamed, impressed as well as pleased.

"It was made with your sea-coal, sire," I added, as he drew blade from scabbard to examine it closely. Castleton had a pit from which coal was dug where the sea cliffs had exposed the vein. And when I found it burned hotter than charcoal and made better steel, I began buying it from Causantín for our foundry. Knowing his coal was critical to its production would give him a sense of added pride, it was as if he had hammered the steel itself.

"I have brought with me its equal as a gift for King Donald. I would ask if you would present it to him as a gift, a sign of fealty and homage from me, one of your vassals and his. I have need to reconcile with the king, but hesitate to approach him directly, for I know not how I might be received."

The earl nodded. "I understand, and knowing your circumstances, I think it both wise and generous. I will be pleased to present it on your behalf. And I think King Donald will accept it, for it is a rare and wonderful thing. If he does, you are accepted as well, safe from further peril, for not even a king can accept such a gift and condemn the giver. And one such as this is hard to reject."

I nodded. "Sire, that is what I hope for. Do tell him this: I never sought to defy his rule—only to ensure the safety of the princes, with whom I was raised as a brother. I had just lost my king, my queen, and the crown prince who was a better brother to me than my own kin. I could not bear to lose the rest. But I raised no hand against him, and have no desire but to live in peace on my land."

The earl smiled at that. "Well said! Donald may think otherwise, but rescue is not rebellion. Nor treason—for he was not yet king when you acted, and as the man who crowned him at Scone, I know. I remain high sheriff through all this turmoil of kings—four now in just one year's time!—so as chief judge my view is beyond assailment. You will be safe at home."

"I thank you most profoundly, milord," I said, and I meant it, for with that I knew that, whatever Donald thought, I was safe.

"However," the earl added with a knowing smile, "you, Godric, have never been one to 'live in peace on your land'. You live in a saddle, longing for adventure. I have no sheriff-at-large to rival you, nor anyone who can replace you. Malcolm cherished your faithful service, and I never feared that you would overstep your authority. We gave you the hardest problems we had, and never once did you fail us..."

He paused in thought then. I wondered what would follow.

"So here is my price for this errand to the king. I think you will find it agreeable. Remain my sheriff-at-large. I will again affirm your commission, and give you such assignments as I see fit, and you accept. I cannot afford to lose you, and will use that as final sway with the king. What say you?"

Somewhere inside I had hoped for this, but had not dared to ask. Whether the reluctance was mine, or for Aleine, I could not say.

What I did say was, "I would be honored and proud to serve you again, sire, to the best of my ability."

Causantín took visible pleasure at that. "Splendid! I hoped for nothing less. Is there any other service I can perform for you?"

"Yes, sire. I need a new squire. Cedric became my squire when I was knighted in 1089, having been a yeoman-at-arms beforehand. He completed his training in Normandy, and Duke Robert knighted him for heroism before Le Houlme. I would be grateful if you could send me a page you think would benefit as my new squire. Any you think fit will undoubtedly be suitable."

Causantín nodded. "Done! Now, let us drink to it and, if you do not mind, do tell me the news from Normandy. Sarah! Bring us wine! What have Rufus and Robert been up to?"

✠✠✠

After Donald III returned to the throne in mid-November of 1094, the kingdom calmed for a time; all in it were tired of the turmoil, so life settled back into something like normalcy.

Donald, despite whatever he thought of me, did not refuse my gift, and appeared to accept both my explanation and my homage. Prince Edmund may have helped, for Causantín later told me that Edmund did corroborate that I had acted solely out of concern for the safety of the princes, and only because Donald had encircled the castle as if for siege. For saying so, I came to owe a debt of gratitude to Edmund. But afterwards I was, as Causantín had predicted, both safe and free to live in peace upon my land.

Edmund had clearly found favor with Donald, and was now his co-ruler and designated heir. Donald had no sons, and, at the age of sixty, he was unlikely to produce one. Edmund had found his route to the throne after all.

But not for long. Christmas of 1094 came and went. I celebrated with my family in Cenachedne. King Donald did so in the palace in Dunfermline, and King Rufus in Lundene. But when the festive fortnight ended in January, my faithful sources among the ship captains returning from Lundene told me that Prince Edgar intended to claim the throne. Rufus had decided to support Edgar just as he had Duncan, and offered him the loan of an army—in return for the usual pledge of fealty, of course. Whatever his personal feelings about his father's enemy, Edgar kept it to himself, accepted the offer, made the pledge of fealty, and began to make preparations to come north against Donald.

At that point, I was glad enough to stay out of it. I would prefer Edgar on his father's throne for many reasons, but it would not be as quick or easy as it had been for Duncan, and I had no stake in the contest. Rather, I had matters of more import to worry over.

✠✠✠

In Cenachedne, life was pleasant and peaceful. Carrick and Alice were their old selves, pleased to have Aleine and Margaret Alice near them. The manor and village prospered, and I with it. Life was good—for all but me.

In all Cenachedne, there was only one discontent person: me—although I hate now to admit it. But after all I had seen and done, I began to find the place stifling. I began to long for something more. I loved little Margaret Alice, Aleine, her parents and Cenachedne. But my heart told me I was made for something else—something greater, something more. I began to ache for… I knew not what.

Aleine noticed, of course. She was heartsick for me and offered me comfort and consolation as best she could. For her love I was grateful, but it only made me feel all the more guilt that I was not content with all I had. I fear I was less than I should have been.

Instead, I used the time I had at home to find a kind of solace out at the forge, working metal to dull my personal pain. Sometimes I slept in the loft—I had rebuilt the smithy much as before, but better, and the loft I made into a kind of personal retreat.

But sleep was hard to come by. Often was I was haunted by troubled dreams, in which I relived painful events of the past dozen years again and again. Some nights I helplessly watched Andrew kill my mother. On others, I witnessed Andrew burning my manor with all my people locked inside, and then had to again dig up their living corpses. Some nights I took OdinsØye's place on that horrific last ride. And then there was the horror of being trapped again in the flooding cistern. I began to dread lying down to sleep altogether.

It was as if part of me could not—would not—forgive or forget acts my mind told me I had. I am afraid it was my conscience.

In many ways I felt grief for the fact that I could not keep death away from the people I loved. Had I hanged Andrew myself, my people would yet live. Had I slain OdinsØye after I fought Bjorn, three houses of religious folk would not have been massacred and robbed. Had I been there to defend my king and stop the murders of Malcolm and Edward, Margaret would not have died of shock.

But despite my best efforts, many I loved had been crushed by tragedy or death, and I could not help but feel responsible—that it was either my doing, or my failure to do, that had brought about all those tragic outcomes.

And so, as so often I had, I went back to the smithy to cope with my grief by hammering yellow-hot steel. And as I worked there with my old friend and father-in-law Carrick, verbally regretting my failures, he listened as he always had, and then said this:

"Godric, you've always had a strong sense of duty, and it's this that's eating at you now. You feel guilt for failing to prevent their deaths, though you could not have done it, for God intended it and you are not God. You are not to blame. You cannot change things either. But you still have duties, and they matter. You can go after the men who did it, can you not? You're still a sheriff-at-large, aren't you? Go then, do your duty. Go punish the men who killed the king."

And in that flash of insight, I realized Carrick was right. I was an officer of Scottish law. Would-be kings struggled over the throne, too busy fighting each other and trying to build their power to truly rule. They were doing nothing—indeed, *would* do nothing

—to see that the murderers of Malcolm and Edward faced justice. Instead, they profited from their deaths and were instead already beholden to the man who had instigated the murders: King Rufus.

But a sheriff I was, and it was within my charter to hunt down killers and punish them for murder. These men were Englishmen all, and I had no authority in England, but the men they killed were Scottish. The laws they broke are the same in Alba and England, based on God's law: Thou shalt not murder. Someone needed to send them off to face His judgment—just as they had summarily done to Malcolm, Edward and Margaret. If no one else would seek justice for my monarchs—indeed, my family, for Malcolm and Margaret had been like parents to me after I lost my own—then the duty to avenge them fell to me, now their eldest living son.

Sir Robert de Mowbray, English Earl of Northumberland; Arkil Morel, his kinsman, Steward of Bamburgh Castle and Sheriff of Northumberland; and the king who demanded acts of treachery from both of them, King William Rufus of England. These were the men who murdered King Malcolm, Crown Prince Edward and Queen Margaret by treachery. I had no doubt their hands were bloody because I had I witnessed it all. And I knew all too well that punishment for willful, treacherous murder was death.

So the verdict and sentence were settled, and the criminals had been sentenced in absentia. Let the punishment begin…

✠✠✠

EIGHTEEN

✠✠✠

Three men and two questions. Robert de Mowbray, Arkil Morel, and William Rufus. Where do I find him? How do I punish him?

It was spring of the year 1095 AD, and I was hunting men, a skill I had acquired over the past few years and at which I had become adept, especially when my purpose was to send them to Hell. My list had these three names on it, all English, and I would not stop until all met with justice. Whether God's or mine did not matter, for both suited me.

Had he been able, my old tutor Father Thomas would have told me that vengeance belongs to God alone, and that I should leave that work to Him. But I had already had this conversation with my conscience, so my reply to him would have been, "These men murdered my good king by treachery, and violated the laws of God, chivalry, and war to do it. Acts of king and God have made me the tool of justice, and punishment is my duty to perform. In this matter, I act to bring them the vengeance of God."

My king had made of me an instrument of justice, but it was God who willed that it happen. And so, God help me, it is for this very reason that I must now see justice done, no matter the cost, for now, no other can do it.

✠✠✠

Robert de Mowbray. Where do I find him? How do I punish him?

The first question was not hard. Mowbray moved about among his castles at Bamburgh, Alnwick and New Castle in "Northumberland," as the English call our Northumbria. Since King Malcolm was not there to stop them and there was no other opposition, King Rufus had the earl hard at work solidifying his control over Northumbria. I doubted, no matter who eventually became King of Scotland, that he would ever get it back.

With Mowbray, it was the second question that was the harder. Find him, I could. But surrounded as he was by an army of vassals, I would need an army of my own to confront him. Challenging him to single combat would not do. I had heard that in the ambush of Malcolm the earl claimed he only acted on King Rufus's order under protest, decrying 'prostitution of his honor'. But it was a hollow protest; no true knight would have done what he had, king's orders or otherwise. So a challenge of honor would not be enough to induce him to face me in combat, since a knight without a true sense of honor would not fight to keep or regain what he did not have. He would instead foist off a brave vassal as his champion, declaring himself innocent and too valuable to the earldom to risk his life against a ridiculous charge, or some such nonsense. I would need to find other means.

✠✠✠

Briefly did I consider seeking out Earl Causantín of Fife, High Sheriff of Alba to disclose my plans and seek his approval and advice. But after careful consideration I decided against it. If he approved, he could do so as well after the fact. If not, I did not want to find myself having to violate his command to abandon my mission. Worst of all, if he approved but the king did not, I would entangle him in my actions and take him down with me. I certainly had no desire to do that.

My father told me this: "Never ask a question to which you do not wish to hear the answer." I always thought it good advice.

So I decided I would act alone, and trust that God would lead me to do what was right. If not, I would bear the guilt myself. But I could not do this without help. So I went off to the manor chapel and there laid out my thoughts and intentions in prayer, asking for guidance and a sign that it was right to do this. Within a day my mind was cleared, my concerns dispelled and a plan sent into my mind.

When choosing messengers, God has a sense of humor—for of all people, it was Thorsson who brought me the sign I sought.

✠✠✠

In January 1095, Thorsson sent word that he was in Leven with news for me, so I rode there to meet him in the little tavern there.

"I have news about your favorite people," he began with a grin. He knew 'favorite' would irk me, and irking is what men do to their friends.

"Must I guess, or do you plan to tell me?" I said with a scowl. For form's sake, he who has been irked must give an irked reply. But he had my attention. 'Favorite people' could only mean Rufus, Mowbray, or Morel. I couldn't be angry at him for that.

"It seems that while you were away adventuring in Normandy last summer..." Thorsson was enjoying himself. "...on orders of Earl Robert, Sheriff Arkil Morel of Northumbria found an excuse to seize four fully-laden merchant ships that took shelter in a Northumbrian harbor to escape a storm. And despite the owners' protests, the sheriff and earl confiscated their cargoes and vessels on some pretext, sold off to others the cargoes and the ships, and kept the proceeds."

"And how do you know this?" I asked. I had a good idea, but I needed to speak to the victims if I was to confirm the truth of a crime.

"Because all four Norse merchant captains are my relations, who live in and sail out of ports in Alba. No one in England will give them satisfaction, because those who should are the thieves. I told them I would speak to you because—how did I put it? Ah, yes! 'Lord MacEuan will do something'."

Ahah! The fact that the merchants were my countrymen gave me both grounds and authority to act on their behalf.

"Can we arrange to meet with them? I will do something, as you promised, but I will need signed letters of complaint to justify my intervention, and take the accusations to higher authority."

"Sire, I thought you would. Each has produced for you such a letter, with the circumstances of the confiscation and an inventory of cargo and vessel. Here they are, signed and sealed."

"Tell them I will act. I may not be able to recover their losses, but I will have the men involved punished severely for their crimes."

With that, I thought we were through. But Thorsson said, "Wait, sire. I have more! These same men—Mowbray and Morel—are planning a revolt against King Rufus. I haven't many details but learned they want to replace him with a rival and the number of co-conspirators includes the present King of Alba."

Now that took my breath away. If this was true, I now not only had a legal basis to act against Mowbray, I also had the means to destroy him. God had heard me and had indeed sent me a sign.

✠✠✠

From my earlier forays into Northumbria I knew many men there with loyalties to Scotland—men who had no affection for their English overlords, were in positions that would hear things, and were willing to report on the actions and whereabouts of Morel and Mowbray. So I spent silver among them and hired several of them to act as my spies. Each week riders brought me fresh news.

Most of their information was little more than gossip, but it kept me current on their whereabouts and led me to realize that Mowbray had no love of King Rufus. In fact, when the Conqueror died a year after naming Mowbray an earl, Mowbray had sided with Robert of Normandy against William Rufus as King of England. Once Rufus secured the crown, he had forgiven Mowbray and allowed him to keep his earldom, but there was no love for the other in either heart. Indeed, it may have been the very reason that King Rufus ordered this earl to use treachery against King Malcolm, and I realized that this mutual dislike was a way to punish both Mowbray and Morel.

I also was able to get a better understanding of Mowbray the man. Those who knew him described him as courageous but proud; harsh with his vassals, cold and distant among his peers, and arrogant with his liege lord. And to all that I could add this, from personal knowledge: position and power mattered far more to Mowbray than honor, for no true knight could be seduced, convinced, or forced to do what Mowbray had done, even by a king.

But what emerged as well was that Mowbray was dissatisfied with what was happening in Scotland following Malcolm's death. I think he had hoped that through the fights of the several rivals—Donald, Duncan and now Edgar—he would gain new territory, and that hadn't happened. I think he never wanted Rufus as king, and since Duke Robert hadn't managed to gain England's throne, he was looking for another to put on it. The name most often mentioned as Rufus's intended new rival was Count Stephen of Albemarle, a cousin of Rufus and one of his faithful retainers. Stephen was a nephew of the Conqueror by a half-sister married to Count Odo of Champagne, so there was basis for a royal claim.

And the circle of conspirators was growing. Among them were: Count William of Eu, who had recently abandoned Duke Robert for Rufus, and was now switching allegiance again; Judith, wife of Robert de Mowbray; William of Alderi, the king's steward; the paternal uncle of Stephen; many other barons of distinction, and perhaps most notably, King Donald of Alba and his heir, Prince Edmund.

As far as I could discern, their plotting had not reached a point of action, but it was well-enough defined to count as treason against King Rufus, and that was all Rufus would need to act.

✠✠✠

I began with a letter to King Rufus on behalf of the Nordic merchant captains reporting the piracy with a full inventory of ships and cargoes seized, the signed testimonies of the aggrieved, and naming the culprits as Morel and Mowbray. Acting on behalf of aggrieved men with no other recourse, I signed it in my own name and title as "Sheriff-at-large of Alba."

I also sent an anonymous note informing Rufus of the conspiracy and, without naming all the conspirators, did name Robert de Mowbray as leader and Count Stephen of Albemarle as his rival.

And with these two correspondences, I set Rufus upon Mowbray, thereby using one of Malcolm's enemies to destroy the other.

My letter reached Rufus in Rockingham in February at a council called to try to settle his ongoing dispute with Anselm of Bec, now the Bishop of Canterbury and the chief prelate in England by Rufus's own hand. Rufus had been feuding with Anselm since he had appointed him over Rufus's usurpation of Church revenues, his unnatural and gravely immoral lifestyle, and other matters.

In that matter the council was a failure, but I learned later that Rufus had received my letters and promptly noted that the Earl of Northumberland was not in attendance. So Rufus sent a letter to the earl, demanding that he appear or make restitution in the case of the ships and cargoes, and summoning him to attend the Curia Regis—the King's court—in Winchester at Easter, which was March 25th that year.

✠✠✠

Easter came to Winchester, but not Earl Robert. The earls were expected to attend, since the king took council from them as he wished and announced to them his decisions and policies in the various matters of the kingdom, whether diplomatic, legislative, financial or judicial. To fail to appear demanded good reason, but to decline a summons, only death, natural or otherwise, would do.

So Rufus, already suspicious of Earl Robert, now had a solid basis to believe the rumors of a conspiracy of rebellion were true. Furious with Mowbray, Rufus ordered Robert to appear at the Curia Regis in Windsor at Pentecost, the 20th of May, to answer my charge against him and Arkil Morel of having stolen the ships and cargoes of four Nordic merchantmen.

Now, had Robert appeared at Easter in response to the first summons, he might have allayed Rufus's suspicions, or at least deceived the king about his loyalty and bought his conspiracy time to act. My understanding of Robert's character, however—especially the bit about being 'arrogant with his liege lord', the king—led me to think Robert would disdain both summonses and orders, as indeed he did!

So Pentecost too came, but Robert did not. The entire council was present to attend the king at Windsor except the Earl of Northumberland, who instead sent the king a letter in which he declined to appear upon grounds that the king gave him neither hostages nor any guarantee of safety or assurance of freedom to subsequently depart the council.

I ask you: if charged with a crime, could you write a letter any more certain to convince your king you were guilty—and almost certainly plotting against him? I think not!

Neither did Rufus, as it transpired. To my great surprise, Rufus made restitution to the four merchants from his own coffers, no doubt intending to recover the expense from Mowbray. But whether or not the piracy angered him, Rufus was otherwise convinced by Mowbray's odd conduct that the earl was plotting against him, and that was all he needed to decide to act. I know this because the young Scottish princes I saved—Alexander and David—were present in the king's court on all three occasions to tell me of it later.

Rufus immediately called for troops, and at the start of June he and his army marched off to Northumbria to deal with its recalcitrant earl.

✠✠✠

At home in Scotland, things were relatively quiet for me. True to his word, Earl Causantín sent me a splendid new squire, a cheerful, strapping lad named Colin MacDuib, who came from Saint Andrews in Fife, and had served King Malcolm and Queen Margaret as a page. Aleine already knew and liked the boy well, so he proved a welcome addition to the household. I introduced him to Carrick and Bjorn, and assigned him to them for two hours a day. There, Colin would learn to forge iron and steel—an always useful skill for a future siege master—while pumping bellows and pounding hot iron would build muscle faster than any other discipline.

The first few weeks of this, Colin would return limp and sore, so I used the balance of our training time each day teaching him his duties and the less physical aspects of life as a knight: caring for horses, polishing mail, sharpening weapons, making camp, cooking, manners in court, courtesies to women, and so on. Only after he could return without evident sign of fatigue from his toil did we begin his training with weapons.

I rode on patrols and attended to lesser matters of justice for Earl Causantín—theft of a sheep or pig, delivery of charter papers to monasteries, robbery of a church poor-box, and the like—but little of import transpired that you might care to learn. Colin I took with me, and though initially I found myself doing as much of the squire's work as he did, it was good refreshment of my training as well as development of his. He learned fast and well, and before long, I had little to criticize.

Meanwhile, in the south of Scotland, a war of proxy was taking place: Prince Edgar, backed by King Rufus, was warring for control of the kingdom against King Donald, who was in turn supported by Earl Robert de Mowbray. Edgar had not succeeded in driving Donald into the highlands as Duncan had, but he was making gains against Donald and by June he had already gained control of Lothian—control he never again lost.

While Donald and Edmund were too busy fighting Edgar to rule, Earl Causantín was effectively Alba's monarch, with me in his service—so I was left in peace to pursue my secret agenda.

✠✠✠

Rufus began his campaign against Earl Robert de Mowbray well enough by besieging the earl's castle at New Castle, where Earl Robert's brother mounted a stout defense. Had I the task of taking it, it would have been mine in a week, but New Castle managed to withstand Rufus's siege for two months. And after Edgar prevailed against Donald and Earl Robert to the north and his brother fought his battles for him in the south, the earl and Arkil Morel stayed safely in Bamburgh Castle.

Finally, in August, able to take no more, New Castle surrendered. Rufus had the entire garrison bound and sent off to imprisonment in the south, replaced the garrison with trusted men and marched on with his army to lay siege to Bamburgh Castle.

✠✠✠

Now, Bamburgh Castle was then perhaps the strongest castle in all the land. William the Conqueror had rebuilt it, repairing and strengthening damage done by the Danes nearly a century earlier. It stood on a great rock outcrop, not as high as Edinburgh or Dunnottar, perhaps, but sufficient to allow its attackers to reach and overtop the walls. Two concentric timber palisades exceeding twenty feet supported fighting walkways around the perimeter, and inside these stood a great square wooden tower, as well as the usual collections of other structures around the walls: kitchens, garrison barracks, stables, storerooms, and so on.

Since its reconstruction by Rufus's father it had never been taken by force—nor would Rufus be able to do it, for that matter, as he well knew. Without an engine like my tree-bucket *Bone-Crusher* to hammer holes in the defenses, the cost to Rufus in lives and treasure to take it by force was simply too great.

So he had the castle encircled by his troops to blockade it, so that time and starvation would accomplish what arrows and fire could not. Outside its main gate he built a wooden castle he named with sly humor, "Malvoisin," the Norman French for "Evil Neighbor." And the two forces bombarded each other with profane words and taunts while days passed and Bamburgh's stores dwindled.

In September Rufus learned that the Welsh had taken his motte-and-bailey castle at Montgomery, located a mile inside the Welsh

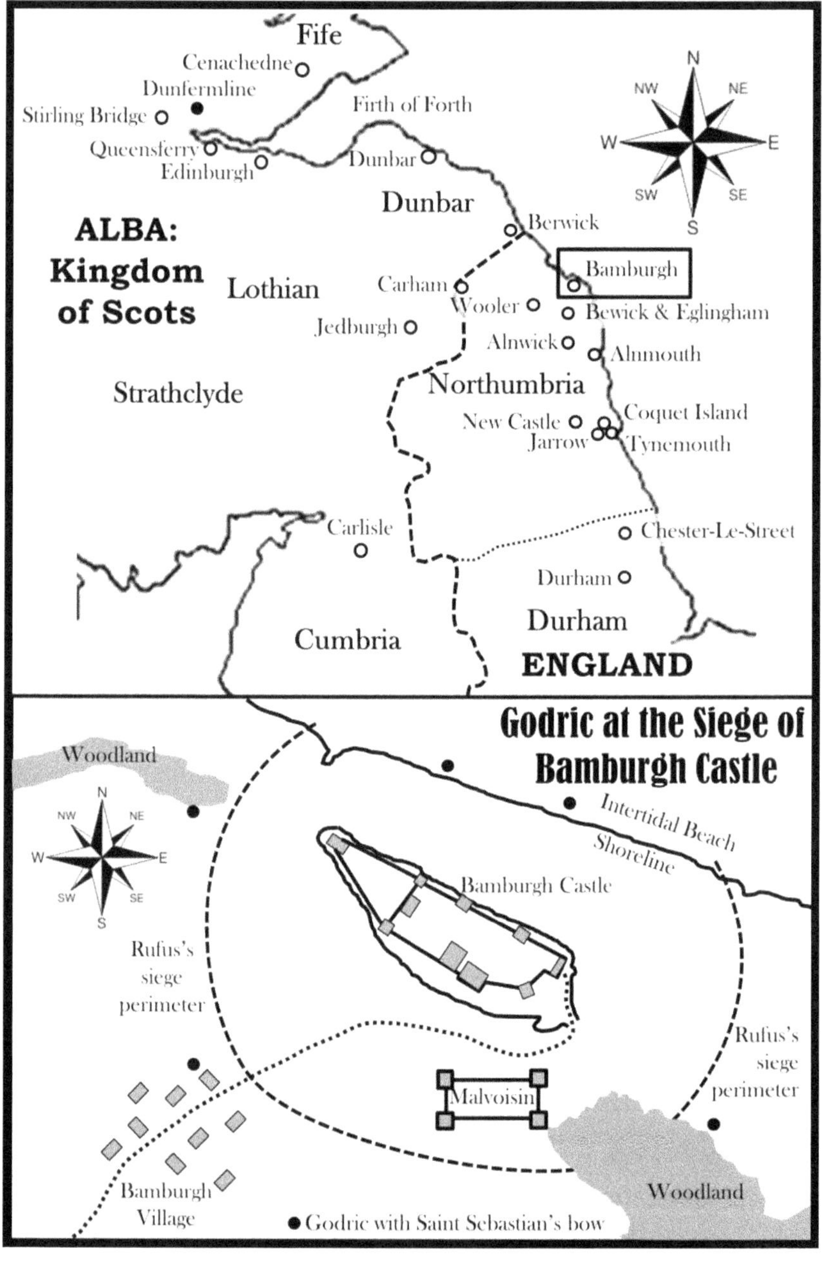

Figure 11: Godric at the siege of Bamburgh Castle

Marches from the contested border with England—with Rufus, all borders were contested.

Determined to go take it back, Rufus left at Bamburgh a force strong enough to maintain the blockade and prevent any breakout by the garrison, and marched off with the rest for Wales. He levied additional men on the way, and spent the months of September and October taking Montgomery back. And Robert de Mowbray and his nephew, Arkil Morel, remained trapped inside Bamburgh Castle.

✠✠✠

In October I rode a patrol into Lothian on judicial business for Earl Causantín. Lothian then spanned the southeastern portion of Alba from the Firth of Forth to the as-ever disputed border with Northumbria, which the English now call "Northumberland." Lothian had been ruled by Earl Gospatric of Northumbria until his death beside Malcolm. Now his son Gospatric II was the Mormaer—or Earl—of Lothian, Dunbar, Berwick and Jedburgh.

In Jedburgh I found Prince Edgar. It was late in the season for war. King Donald had already withdrawn to Edinburgh Castle for the winter, ceding Lothian to Edgar, who had made Jedburgh his capital and now occupied a strongly fortified manor while he had a wooden castle built nearby. Donald might see this as consorting with his enemy, but to me Edgar was family. I wanted to stay neutral and friend to both sides throughout this conflict if I could.

Our reunion was merry. I had not seen Prince Edgar since he left Normandy for England with Edgar Ætheling, who was here with him. His brother, Squire Alexander, was present also, assigned as courier between Edgar, King Rufus and the siege commander at Malvoisin outside Bamburgh.

Over a private dinner in his hall, we—that is, Prince Edgar, Edgar Ætheling, Prince Alexander and I—exchanged news of friends and events on both sides. In my case, I told them news of Aleine, little Margaret Alice, Duke Robert and my sieges of Argences and Le Houlme; Edgar in turn told me of his strange journey from a refugee from Donald, to guest of the English court, and now as King of Scots campaigning to regain Alba from Donald.

"You are King of Scots!" I said.

Edgar nodded. "Uncrowned as yet, but recognized as such. Last month Rufus issued a charter at Durham, and in it he named me "Edgar, son of Malcolm, King of Scots, who possesses the whole of Lothian by the gift of William, king of the English, and kingship of the Scots by paternal heritage." Edgar might then have been a king without kingdom, but he was proud to have earned the title, and was determined to see it fulfilled—as indeed he did, two years later, while I was gone on campaign to recover Jerusalem from the Islamites.

As I hoped, in the course of our conversation my discussion of Argences and Le Houlme led us to talk of the siege of Bamburgh, and then to my efforts to avenge King Malcolm. I described my evidence against Mowbray and Morel—this was safe to do since they were clearly in the disfavor of the English court. But I left out the fact that King Rufus had instigated the entire plan; that I kept to myself, for he was their present sponsor, and my intent to act against Rufus needed to remain my secret until I completed it.

"...So, you see, the truce Mowbray and Morel declared was a lie, a ruse intended to lure Malcolm, Edward and the rest of the noble escort into their ambush. And as you know, that violates all rules of war. Morel himself murdered Malcolm—after he was unhorsed and helpless from his fall. News of the catastrophe in turn killed your mother with shock. So Mowbray and Morel are criminally guilty in their deaths, and those of Gospatric and the others in the escort as well. I intend to see they face justice," I concluded—and saw solemn approval from both Edgars and surprise on Alexander's face.

"But that just happened again!" he blurted out. "I was there—riding in attendance to the royal party up the Great North Road. We were about to ford the River Aln when Gilbert fitzRichard de Tonbridge suddenly rode alongside Rufus's horse, seized his reins, and stopped the beast. Gilbert then threw himself from his own mount and fell prostrate before the king, begging him not to enter the ford, for an ambush had been set there by Mowbray and Morel to kill King Rufus by treachery—attacking him without warning while Rufus was unprepared to defend himself. Gilbert confessed being an accomplice to the plot, but begged the king's pardon in return for the warning—a pardon Rufus granted."[18]

I said, "Then this is proof that Mowbray and Morel arranged the death by ambush of King Malcolm, for apart from the truce, the place, tactic and target are the same. God has sent me a sign that I am right to seek justice for Malcolm by revealing proof of their guilt. They have now acted treacherously, not just toward their king's enemy, but in just the same way with their own king!"

---

[18] True! Gilbert disclosed the ambush and confessed that Mowbray and Morel had planned a trap essentially identical to Malcolm's ambush—proof they had already done the same with Malcolm. Its actual location is unknown. I put it at the same place because it is an ideal spot and worked well for them the first time.

"And we are here now because you sent the accusation against Mowbray and Morel on behalf of the Nordic merchants?" Edgar Ætheling asked me.

"Yes."

"Did you also send Rufus warning of Mowbray's conspiracy?"

I simply smiled.

"You canny devil!" said Prince—nay, King!— Edgar, with not a little admiration. "You called down the full fury of the King of England on one of his highest lords in order to avenge my father. Malcolm could not have found a better champion! It is a shame that Mowbray and Morel sit safe in Bamburgh Castle—for now."

At that point we started thinking aloud. I do not remember now just who said what, but it went this way:

"How do you lure a man to his doom?"

"Offer him something irresistible—the thing he wants most."

"How do you get him to believe the offer is real?"

"Have it offered by someone he trusts."

"Who does Mowbray trust?"

"His brother, King Donald, and maybe the Count of Eu."

"What proof would he need?"

"Maybe none if he is desperate and the offer compelling."

"Such as?"

"Such as that the Northumbrian barons have risen up to depose Rufus and offer Mowbray the crown if he will lead them; or that Donald is bringing his army to join Mowbray and his garrison at New Castle; or perhaps both together."

I said. "Mowbray *will* be hoping Donald will come to his rescue, and he is arrogant enough to believe his barons would make him king. But I still need a way to get a letter into Bamburgh, and an image of King Donald's seal I can reproduce."

At that, Edgar Ætheling frowned. "Donald's seal? No. Donald is illiterate—he cannot write, or even sign his name. His clerks do it for him. And English kings affix seals, but Scottish kings do not —though that may soon change," he added, smiling at Edgar.

I nodded. "No seal, then, and his signature in any hand—that I can manage. How do I get it in? Their conspiracy used messages. Does Bamburgh have a secret tunnel? Could I bribe a messenger to carry one in through the secret tunnel?"

Alexander said, "Aye, we think it does, but we have yet to locate its exit—it's that well-hidden. And they are keeping it in reserve by not using it; we have been watching for couriers either way."

Edgar said, "Why not wind a letter around an arrow? Shoot it in."

I shook my head. "We have English bowmen with longbows on both sides of this siege. If I were Rufus's siege master, I would have set my perimeter at 300 yards, outside longbow range from Bamburgh."

Alexander confirmed it. “Aye, that’s just where we are.”

“So to shoot a letter into Bamburgh by longbow I must get inside Rufus’s lines to do it. That won’t do! I need a bow that shoots farther than a longbow. And there is no such bow.” I shook my head. “If I had my scorpion here, I could shoot all of 400 yards, over Rufus’s men from outside his blockade. But the only scorpion in the entire land sits in Cenachedne.”

Edgar gave me a wry smile, and said. “Ah, well! Rufus will stay here 'til winter is full upon us, and if Bamburgh does not fall this year, he will return in spring. He may settle Mowbray’s account for you. But I have a notion, brother, you will find a way.”

We four talked late until the ale did what it was supposed to, and then retired. And during the night Saint Sebastian, patron saint of archers, appeared to me in a dream. He was young, handsome, pierced by many arrows; and he came to show me a strange bow.

✠✠✠

That bow was a strange thing, unlike any I had ever seen. The vision of it stayed with me the following morn, and I realized I was supposed to build it.

At breakfast I told Edgar an idea had come to me, and without a question he gave me leave to use whatever I needed. From his armory I obtained two very different bows. One was the biggest longbow he had. The other was small and light, the sort of bow pages and ladies use to hunt birds for sport, but one which had taken a set, curving in the direction it was strung; a poor bow as it was, but perfect for my needs. These I took to Edgar’s smithy to work on them.

Working from the vision, I built a 'shoe' of sorts to hold them so that their bellies met at the handgrip, their strings farthest apart, and lashed them together with leather thongs. I fashioned three bowstrings: the first to normally string a longbow, the other two each run from a nock on the small bow to the corresponding nock on the longbow. Thus, as the main bowstring was pulled back, it pulled as well on the other two strings, flexing the second bow against its set. This increased its draw weight—the power of the bow—to in turn increase the distance it could shoot an arrow.

Curious to learn how it would work, I took the bow and a bundle of arrows into a pasture to see if it worked. Seeing me go out, Edgar and Alexander came along to watch.

It was a beast just to string. And it took my utmost ability to draw —which meant few men could do it, for I had pulled heavy bows since childhood, worked iron and wood daily for years, and yet more in daily combat drills. Both Edgar and Alexander tried to draw it also, doing no better than three-quarters to the cheek.

It was time to see what it could do. I took sight on a cottage a half-mile distant, nocked an arrow, and in a smooth quick act, drew, elevated to half-vertical and loosed the arrow, which arced high and vanished downrange. I shot a dozen more in just the same way and then set off to find them, pacing off the distance to where they landed. Edgar and Alexander followed, of course.

I found my arrows in a cluster, all fallen within thirty feet, the nearest at 370 yards. This bow was miraculous, for with it I could shoot over the English army into Bamburgh.

King Edgar grinned at me boyishly then, and said, "Did I not say so? You found a way. From whence came this wondrous bow?"

Sheepishly, and with not a little hesitation, I told them then of my dream. And its other-worldly origin made us stare awe-struck at the thing—Saint Sebastian's bow.

✠✠✠

A week later, within Bamburgh, a servant girl laying out washed linen to dry upon the green found an arrow with a little letter wrapped tightly around the shaft and lashed with scarlet cord. Indeed, it was the scarlet that caught her eye. Nearby, she found two more identical to it.

She took them to Arkil Morel, the steward of Bamburgh Castle, who discovered the letters were identical copies, all addressed to the earl and read thus:

"To my brother, Robert, Earl of Northumberland: The news of your plight at the hands of King William Rufus has reached us. In keeping with our pact, I am determined to come to your aid with my entire army. Rather than assault William and his forces at Bamburgh with but half our strength, I have sent messengers to summon your vassal barons to assemble an army at New Castle on St. Crispin's Day,[19] to be led by you if you can escape to lead it. I will move to strike William from the north as you come at him from the south. And if God grant that we be victorious, you will be crowned the King of England by All Saints' Day. Your friend and brother, Donald III, by the grace of God King of Alba."

By now you will have realized how they got there. To be clear, I chose a moonlit night, wore dark clothes, and crept to positions

---

[19] St. Crispin's Day—25 October—A tip of the hat to another day famous for archers—the Battle of Agincourt.

Alexander scouted for me outside the English lines—a grove southeast of the castle, a knoll on the beach northeast of the castle. From each site I loosed a half-dozen message arrows, my goal to get at least one or two inside where they would be found. Suffice to say, I succeeded.

I cannot be sure what transpired in the earl's chamber, nor what discussions he had with Morel and Robert's new bride Mathilda. I am certain they agonized over whether the letters were true or a ruse. They had no way to obtain news of New Castle, nor any way to determine if Donald was indeed gathering the barons in revolt against Rufus—facts I counted on. In the end, Earl Robert had to decide whether to stay safe inside until starvation finally forced him to surrender, or gamble that the letters were true and the crown of England was his to win.

But my missive offered succor to his desperation, and a true prize appealing to his vanity. And as I expected, Robert was seduced.

He never knew that I wrote that letter, or that I sent a warning to Malvoisin as well. Indeed, there never was any intent by Donald to intervene or the other nobles to rise at all. It was, as Mowbray himself was known to say, a 'ruse of war'.

✠✠✠

On the night of 24 October, Earl de Mowbray left his new wife and nephew Morel in Bamburgh, and with a bodyguard of thirty picked knights, slipped out a postern gate hidden in the base of the northern tower by dark of night and in a blinding rain, mounted and rode hard, bursting first through the thin line of men along the beach, around the bulk of the English army unseen, and south down the Great North Road to New Castle. And moments later, when news of the escape reached Malvoisin, another mounted party quickly set off on horseback in pursuit.

Mowbray and his men did not spare their horses—they had expected pursuit and so pressed hard. By alternating from walk to trot to canter, they managed to cover the intervening 45 miles to reach New Castle about dawn.

They should have been safe. Had my letter been true, they would have been. Alas, when the gates of New Castle opened, no cheering nobles awaited them—just Rufus's garrison, warned earlier against the possible attempt by Malvoisin.

Still mounted, Mowbray and his men fled to the only possible refuge left to him—the Priory of St. Oswine in Tynemouth, to which he had been a generous benefactor. The monks there could not refuse him, but had cause to regret not doing so, for war followed hotly, and the monks themselves were forced to flee as soldiers poured into their priory to displace them.

For six days, Mowbray and his knights made a stand, assailed on all sides by soldiers from the New Castle garrison and the pursuers from Malvoisin. They barricaded themselves in the church, and finally just its tower, fighting on until all were killed or wounded and could hold out no longer. Suffering from a serious crossbow wound in the leg, Mowbray was unable to flee again, and was finally taken prisoner.

✠✠✠

For my part, once I delivered my 'poisoned sweets' to Mowbray and Malvoisin, my purpose was accomplished, so I returned to

Cenachedne to let Mowbray's inevitable catastrophe play out. From King Edgar I learned what soon transpired.

King Rufus had been off subjugating Wales for two months, but in early November he returned to Bamburgh and found Mowbray had been captured. Within the castle, Morel and Mathilda had no idea that neither his army nor Donald's was coming to break the siege, nor that Mowbray was now Rufus's prisoner. Their first news of Mowbray's fate was when Rufus had him paraded before the gatehouse battlements with an executioner by his side.

Rufus's herald called out, "Bamburgh! Your lord has returned. Surrender the castle now, or watch as his eyes are plucked out, here and now, in your sight! You have an hour to decide."

Mathilda was a new bride, married to Robert less than a year, and certainly disinclined to see him maimed. Nor was there any reason for her to continue to resist, however Morel might have wanted it otherwise. So it took her no time at all to surrender.

And with that, the siege of Bamburgh was over. Mowbray was rightly judged a traitor, not only for the ongoing rebellion, but also for the evidence of treason my letter provided—proof that Mowbray was willing to conspire with King Donald of Alba and lead an army against Rufus to seize the crown of England. Mowbray promptly lost his earldom, lands, castles, wife, and freedom. He spent the rest of his life first a prisoner in Windsor Castle for the balance of Rufus's life and after Rufus died, as a monk in St. Albans Abbey. In his case, justice was done, and Robert de Mowbray gained much time to think on his sins and make amends—far more than he'd given Malcolm and Edward.

Arkil Morel, ever the epitome of knighthood, saved his skin by turning on his own uncle and patron, attesting to Mowbray's treason, revealing the full details of the conspiracy, and naming all the participants. His life was spared, but he was exiled forever from England. Morel returned home to Scotland, where I found him soon thereafter, living with kinsmen.

Rufus's recent favorite host in Normandy, Count William of Eu, was castrated and blinded for his treachery. Many of the Northumberland barons were betrayed by Morel, though not all of them were actually guilty—Morel's way of spiting his enemies. Rufus's own godfather, William of Alderi, king's tailor, was scourged in the churches of Salisbury and then hanged. The king's uncle, Ode of Champagne, and Philip of Shrewsbury were imprisoned. Earl Hugh of Shrewsbury managed to buy his way free of prison by paying a huge ransom.

On the other side, King Edgar gained favor with King Rufus for blocking Donald from rescuing Mowbray and for helping expose the plot. I got no credit with Rufus for destroying so many of his once favored supporters, but did not care. I had avenged Malcolm and Edward against one of their killers and was content. King Edgar, for his part, remembered my deeds well, and I won favor with him and his brother—the future King Alexander of Alba.

✠✠✠

Morel was far more straightforward prey. It is one thing to kill an unarmed, wounded man lying helpless in a river. Killing a determined knight on equal terms in battle is quite another. As Sheriff of Northumberland, he was my peer. Charged face to face with his crime and challenged to single combat, he had to face my challenge or live denounced as a false knight and a coward, worthy of only disgrace and damnation. No knight, true or false, could bear that. So Arkil Morel would die in single combat, or I would—it was that simple. I only needed him outside Bamburgh.

✠✠✠

In December 1095 King Edgar sent me word that Morel had gone into exile in Dunbar, East Lothian. Morel was twice my age, of Scottish forebears. Indeed, he came from Fife, and not far from Cenachedne. When his uncle Robert de Mowbray found favor with the Conqueror and became Earl of Northumberland, Morel became his most indispensable man. Mowbray appointed him Sheriff of Northumberland and Steward of Bamburgh Castle, and gave him estates at Bewick and Eglingham, just three leagues from Bamburgh and two from where he murdered Malcolm.

When I rode to confront Morel, fellow sheriffs Sir Hamish and Sir Cormac accompanied me as witnesses to what would follow, and I took Colin, of course, as my squire. We found Morel in the household of his daughter, Sybille de Morel, Countess of Dunbar, married to Gospatric II, son of the very same Earl Gospatric who had been slain at the River Aln at the hands of Morel. I doubt either daughter or son-in-law knew Morel had engineered the murder of their father until I appeared.

Walking up to him, I said, "Arkil Morel, I am Godric MacEuan, Baron of Cenachedne and sheriff-at-large of Alba. I accuse you of the treacherous murder of King Malcolm of Alba, as he lay helpless, wounded, and unarmed during a truce you declared. I accuse you as well of planning the treacherous ambush during a truce that led to the deaths of Crown Prince Edward of Alba, Earl Gospatric of Dunbar, and many other Scottish nobles.

"You are a treacherous murderer and a false knight, and I demand that you face me in single armed trial by combat on the morrow. On a field of honor you will, by God's grace, either prove your innocence or die for your crimes." Then I backhanded him across the face as hard as I could, an insult no knight could allow to go unanswered.

My blow staggered him and bloodied his lips, and his kinfolk bristled, but I had no fear of them. The laws of chivalry were clear, and only Morel could answer my challenge. Besides, I could hold my own against men like these. But to them I said, "If any of you wish to prove me wrong, you too may face me on that same field of honor, but it will only be after Arkil Morel answers my challenge." That stopped them.

Morel wiped blood from his mouth and snarled through split lips, "I will meet your challenge, and I will crush your skull as I did Malcolm's, you young pup."

To the rest of the Morel kin, I said, "He has a habit of treachery. He has already betrayed my king, his king, his own uncle, and his daughter's father-in-law. He will behave no better for you. So I hold all here responsible to see he meets me tomorrow. If you allow him to flee me during the night, I will burn your houses and drive all of you, impoverished, into exile forever in England."

I meant it, and they knew it.

✠✠✠

Outside the new stone castle old Earl Gospatric had built beside the sea in Dunbar there was a greensward, well-suited for knightly training and tournament. It was there we met to settle my challenge. Sir Hamish acted as marshal, setting the time and place for this site at midday. The younger Gospatric acted for Morel, although we clearly saw that he had no taste to do so and acted only for his wife's sake. I knew he had loved his father, and certainly now despised his father-in-law, Morel.

We faced each other in full armor: helmet over mail coif; chainmail hauberks worn over gambesons; mail sleeves; mail leggings over breeks; and boots and gauntlets. We carried sword and shield, with a seax or short sword as a second weapon. My hilted Damascene short sword was sheathed in my right boot, easy to reach and fast to draw.

The contest was simple: pure combat man-to-man, to the death. No assistance or interference from others permitted; no rest; and no quarter. If weapons broke, we fought on with whatever still we had—shields, helmets, knives, and hands. God would judge the contest, and He alone would determine the outcome.

The grass in the center of the greensward had been mowed with a scythe, and a fifty-foot circle had been marked by a hawser on the ground. A crowd had formed around its perimeter. Sir Hamish drew his own sword, and in a loud voice grimly promised to slaughter anyone who interfered by entering or throwing anything into the circle before the contest was settled, or either combatant who tried to flee before the trial ended with death. As if one, the crowd backed away several feet, for none doubted him.

Sir Hamish stood between us, raised his sword, and looked at Morel. "Ready, Sir Knight?" Morel was grim and oddly white behind his nasal, and he replied with a nod. Hamish looked to me.

"Ready!" I said.

Hamish stepped back, said, "May God reward truth with victory!" Then he slashed his sword downward and cried, "Begin!"

Morel rushed me then, hammering at me, trying to win quickly by overwhelming my defense with furious blows. We were evenly matched in size and weight. Twenty years younger, I had strength and vigor on my side, while he had more experience. But other than murdering defenseless men from horseback, I wondered when last he had fought.

I caught his blows mainly upon my shield, or deflected them with my sword, and studied him as I let him burn off all that furious energy. He would tire before I did, I knew. As he did, I started to take the fight to him, varying my blows to strike high and low, left and right, seeking holes in his defense.

He was strongly right-handed, preferring hard chopping blows all up and down my left side, rarely crossing over to strike from his left—my right, where I had to use my sword to stop the cuts.

Mailed as we were, our armor stopped cuts that got by our shields. Victory would not come by chopping our way through all that armor and padding. Instead, it would be the consequence of a fatal error: a slip, a trip, or a gap in the defense that let a sword-point in to find flesh. As my mentor Sir Jean de Bethencourt had often said, the point always beats the edge.

So I concentrated on my footing, and watched his eyes to read where the next blow would fall—his eyes betraying him by looking to where his blade would go. Then I began to take him apart.

We trampled down that fresh green grass as we fought throughout the circle, moving left and right, advancing or backing, and circling each other to gain advantage, each seeking to get past the other's shield and strike home.

I could sense that he was tiring, and the furious power of his initial blows faded. Instead, desperation began to creep in and he became more cunning, trying to surprise me with new tactics. More than once my mail saved me as he slipped a blow past my guard.

Suddenly he stumbled, stabbing his sword-tip into the turf! He instinctively ducked down and threw up his shield to cover himself as I sought a vulnerable spot to strike. But he grasped his sword by the blade rather than the grip, pulled it free, and before I realized what he did, swept it in an arc to hook the hilt behind my left ankle. Then he jerked hard and toppled me onto my back.

As I lay stunned by the hard fall, he sprang up, stepped on my sword blade to pin it, kicked my shield away from my body, and straddled me. I could see joyous triumph in his expression, and he stood tall over me, panting hard from exertion. He cast his shield away, and shifted his grip to hold his sword in two hands—the right reversed on the grip, the left around the blade at the hilt. Then he looked around the circle of onlookers.

"This pup, this jumped-up squire, accused me of heinous crimes and challenged me to trial by combat to the death. Look at him now. As God is my witness, he dies a liar, for God gives me the victory I deserve."

As he raised his sword to stab down, lightning struck close by, the first bolt from an oncoming storm, and thunder roared right behind the flash. In that instant, I did as I had done a hundred, no, a thousand times, in practice with Sir Jean. I drew up my right knee, pulled the short sword from my boot, and stabbed twelve inches of hard steel deep into Morel's unprotected groin. With my other hand, I drove the blade to the hilt into his guts, and then used both hands on the grip to topple him over my head.

He screamed as I did it—a high-pitched shriek of horror and pain like that of a terrified girl. And I noted in an abstract way the crimson and amber beads that seemed to hang in the air as a trail of blood and piss droplets made an arch marking his trajectory. I held onto my weapon, and as he hit the grass, he curled into a ball. Hands buried in his crotch, he continued to sob and wail.

Unlike Morel, I neither gloated nor hesitated. I got up, put that blade under the point of his chin, and drove it in along the base of his skull, severing his spine. His keening stopped and he died with a look of surprise and terror on his face, no doubt as he suddenly met Satan face to face.

Sir Hamish then spoke: "God has awarded victory as He saw fit. Sir Arkil Morel is guilty as charged, and has now paid the earthly price for his crimes. May God have mercy on his soul."

Now you may wonder, with all the armor we wore, why Morel was vulnerable. The answer is simple: our armor was designed for horseback. The long chainmail hauberk we wore was slit up front and back to allow us to sit in the saddle, and our mail leggings encased each leg to the top of the thigh. Mounted, our saddle pommel protected the groin. Afoot, we had shields.

But for a fallen knight on the ground, the unarmored groin of his opponent was a natural target. Jean and I had practiced that strike endlessly as a final defense. Now that drill had saved my life.

As I arose, I looked at the faces around the circle. Only Morel's daughter was upset, shocked no doubt by the sudden reversal in her father's fortunes and the terrible nature of his death. Her husband, Gospatric, nodded at me, for I had just avenged the death of his father. Then he led her away as servants came forward to recover the body. The other onlookers seemed not at all upset by my victory or Morel's death, and quickly fled the oncoming rain. Then Hamish and Cormac swept me off to a nearby tavern to drown my post-battle nerves in ale, and Colin followed with my arms as fat raindrops struck in a torrent.

✠✠✠

And what of the third, William Rufus, King of England? He deserved no knightly challenge, ordering as he did his vassals to murder his rival by treachery. He wore a knight's spurs and a king's crown, but at heart he was no knight and no king; even his own lords and subjects said it, though not to his face. Rufus deserved to die from an arrow in his back. If I could not do it, God would find another archer for it.

Rufus was safe in England with thousands of vassals and knights to protect him, but he deserved death and his time would come. I had made a vow and would fulfill it one day. So help me God.

✠✠✠

NINETEEN

✠✠✠

After the past two years of turmoil, Christmas of 1095 was a rare time of peace. Cenachedne was thriving. My businesses—the foundry, mill, tavern and market—were prosperous, and my estates blessed with bounteous produce and growing herds. Aleine was happy, sweet little Margaret Alice a delight. Carrick and Bjorn had become best of friends—kindred souls despite their vastly different past lives. I could not have been more blessed.

I reported to Earl Causantín that I discovered evidence tying Mowbray and Morel to the ambush of King Malcolm, Edward, and our nobles in their second identical plot against Rufus. I told him of my role in luring Mowbray to his doom, my challenge to Arkil Morel to trial by combat, and his death. If he did not entirely approve of my initiative, he did not say so. He agreed there was no question that the two men were guilty of killing our king, that justice was due, and that it had been done. In the end, he concluded my judgement was correct, and my conduct right.

Alba still had two kings in contention—Donald and Edgar—but their conflict was contained to Edinburgh and its surrounds, and their war suspended by winter. Donald had not the support to levy troops for a sustained campaign, and Edgar's borrowed army had gone south with Rufus once Bamburgh surrendered. It was Peace who reigned—for now.

With painfully awkward penmanship I corresponded with Edgar, who was, despite my official position of neutrality, my preferred monarch. King Donald had done nothing against me, but nothing for me, either. Edgar was my brother-in-spirit, born of our long acquaintance if not by blood. And I knew he would be a far better king than king Donald or Edmund, his chosen heir, could ever be.

Edgar wrote me too, saying Rufus planned to again campaign in Normandy in 1096, and that for now he would have to be content to hold Lothian as the extent of his kingdom against Donald, but that Rufus promised him troops again in 1097.

And then at Christmastide, there came to me a letter from my old friend Father Anselm, borne by a young monk from Dunfermline. The Benedictines provide mail service between abbeys in return for donations. No doubt Jean told him where I could be reached.

The letter revealed the sad news that Count Robert "the Frisian," my patron when a squire, had gone to God on 13 October 1093, a month ahead of King Malcolm. His son Robert II was now the Count of Flanders in his stead; he had been made co-regent when we went to Jerusalem on pilgrimage back in 1086. Anselm reported that Count Robert, Baron Jean, his wife Lady Isabeau, and Anselm himself were all well and sent their affection. Jean and Isabeau had children now, both boys and girls. True enough, I knew—goose whistles!

Then Anselm quoted a letter that Emperor Alexios of the Eastern Roman Empire had sent his friend Count Robert I, unaware that he had died. Anselm said he knew of it since he handled all Count Robert II's correspondence. It said, " *Of our lands, we have little left but Constantinople, which our enemies threaten to take also in the near future, unless speedy help from God and faithful Latin Christians reaches us. The emperor runs from one city to another before the Turks and Pechenegs, who violate and murder all Christians alike, even children, youths, women, and girls. Emperor Alexios would rather put Constantinople into the hands of Latins than pagans...*

"...Therefore, hasten with all your people; hurry all your forces, lest our relics and treasures fall into the hands of the Turks and the Pechenegs. You have seen our relics, which I list here: ... Endeavor while you still have time so that the Christian Empire and, still more important, the Holy Sepulcher, be not lost; that you may have in heaven not doom, but reward. Amen!"

In the last part of his letter, Anselm told me that in March 1095, an ambassador from Emperor Alexios came to Pope Urban II at the great Council of Piacenza—attended by so many Italian, French, and Burgundian bishops that it had to be held outdoors—to ask for help against the Seljuq Turks overrunning the Byzantine lands in Anatolia. And recently—since November—Pope Urban had preached everywhere, urging all Christendom to go to the aid of Constantinople, saying, *"All who die by the way, whether by land or by sea, or in battle against the pagans, shall have immediate remission of sins. This I grant them through the power of God with which I am invested. ... Deus lo vult! It is the will of God! It is the will of God!"*

Anselm said that in response to these appeals, Count Robert II had decided to go to the aid of the Emperor, to rescue that Christian Empire and free Jerusalem from the infidel Islamites. Our mutual friend Baron Jean de Bethencourt had also decided to go. He, Father Anselm, would accompany them as chaplain.

In closing, both lords entreated me to go with them, for my unique skills in war would be greatly needed. They were both raising money and men to march the 1st of August of 1096, and begged me to join them with whatever I could bring.

I never expected to return to Jerusalem, for Scotland is my home. But God planned my destiny, and made me for war. He shaped me into a siege master, a tool of battle. And when He called me to the Crusade, He knew I would not fail to hear and heed Him.

I must go.

✠✠✠

The Siege Master's Song:

We've brought up the army.
We camp at your door.
Our peace terms you refuse,
So now you'll get war.

Come out here and fight us,
We'll entertain you.
And many will die here
Before we are through.

Climb over, dig under,
Or pound a way through.
We'll use every weapon
To bring death to you.

Your towers will tremble,
Your garrison fall.
Your ramparts will crumble,
Starvation for all.

We'll cave in your rooftops
With boulders we cast.
With fire we'll burn all
So nothing will last.

Your loot we will plunder
And your daughters too.
We'll give them fat bellies
So we can spite you.

Your castle can't save you.
We'll never withdraw.
Until you surrender
We stay at your wall.

✠✠✠

Want to hear *The Siege Master's Song*?

You can. A free music video is available here:

https://youtu.be/aKypcrA_qos

I'm neither Ridley Scott or John Williams,
but a guy can dream. ☺

Author's Notes

✠✠✠

The preface notwithstanding, this is a work of historical fiction, not one of history. In the interest of full disclosure, there is no manuscript; Baron Godric MacEuan of Cenachedne is a fictional person living amid many actual persons. But there was a real man or men, now unknown, upon whom he is based: the medieval military engineer who built and used the siege engines of the Crusades, particularly the counterweight trebuchet, the most devastating weapon as yet created at that point in history. To date no one has undertaken to tell that story beyond the bare facts. It is, I believe, a worthy achievement and a fascinating tale, so I created Godric and gave him the task and title of Siege Master, the prototypic medieval military engineer, as a way to tell it.

Until exothermic agents, starting with gunpowder, empowered cannon to replace them, nothing in battle was more awesome than siege engines, especially their pinnacle, the counterweight trebuchet. Even today, siege engines in action inspire excitement, whether they hurl pumpkins across the farmland of Delaware or boulders at real castle walls. If you doubt this, rent *Kingdom of Heaven* and watch Saladin use trebuchets in his effort to take Jerusalem. I do not think anyone with a pulse could fail to enjoy the sight of a flaming piano arcing through the sky hundreds of yards to splintery destruction, except perhaps sons of Steinway.

After I wrote *Call to Crusade,* I wrote *March to Nicaea* as the intended second book in the *Siege Master* series. To cover events of the seven years that intervene between those two stories, I included much of the material in this book. My beta readers told me they thought that portion of the story-line was too condensed and convoluted to read well, and made the first half of *March to Nicaea* hard to follow.

Meanwhile, I wrote a third-person novella named *Bone-Crusher* to answer two important questions that arise during those seven years: By the time Godric arrives at Nicaea in *March to Nicaea,* he has extensive experience in siege warfare. So where, when, and how did he gain such expertise? And since he successfully debuts a novel siege engine, the counterweight trebuchet, at Nicaea, just where, when and how did he develop it?

So as I set out to fix *March to Nicaea,* I came to realize another intervening novel was really needed to tell the story properly. To do so I tore off the first half of *Nicaea,* incorporated the story from *Bone-Crusher,* and rewrote them into this novel. I hope it will now continue Godric's tale smoothly and seamlessly from *Call to Crusade* into *March to Nicaea,* as it always needed to do.

✠✠✠

The siege engines that Godric studies, experiments with, draws, and measures in Constantinople in *Call to Crusade* did exist then, and that was the best place on the entire planet to learn of them—the key reason why Godric needed to accompany Count Robert on his pilgrimage to Jerusalem in 1085-1088 AD, as it turns out. Using this knowledge and his natural engineering skills, Godric then builds and uses his own conventional siege engines on the natural fortress of Dunnottar at the end of *Call to Crusade*.

But the counterweight trebuchet did yet not exist there and then. Its actual origins are lost in historical mist, but according to trebuchet historian Paul Chevedden, the machine suddenly appears for the first time, fully developed, at the siege of Nicaea.

So who first built and used it there? It's a mystery. Anna Komnena gives her father, Emperor Alexios Komnenos, credit for its invention, and says he supplied it to the Crusaders; and to that Chevedden is inclined to agree. But I became skeptical. Would Emperor Alexios give his greatest weapon—the only machine capable of taking his capital, Constantinople—to men he clearly feared and did not trust, concerned as he was that they might soon use it against him? And he did not need to make the gift, because the Byzantines were secretly negotiating with the Nicaeans to surrender the city, using the threat of the Crusaders as the stick, and sparing it from being sacked as the carrot. I concluded otherwise, decided another invented the machine and set out to make Godric my avatar for that man.

I maintain that a man like Godric foresaw that gravity could better do what it had previously taken dozens or hundreds of men pulling together to do with its predecessor, the traction trebuchet. So in this novel, I set about postulating how Godric did it, just as that unknown man must have actually done.

Regardless of its origins, the Crusaders put their siege engines to such good use that Nicaeans were terrified by their effects, and chose to surrender the city to General Boutoumites, admitting Byzantine troops the night the Crusaders breached the walls and were about to sack Nicaea at dawn. When the sun rose the next morning, the Crusaders were astounded and furious to see the Byzantine flag flying above its ramparts—their hard-fought prize stolen in the night by supposed allies.

So someone among the Crusaders had to have the engineering expertise and experience to build and use that terrible engine for the first time in recorded warfare. Since no one can say who that man was, I have given Godric the credit for it in his place.

✠✠✠

This story makes good use of real history as well as pure fiction, and I think it is always important to report which is which. Jarl OdinsØye is pure fiction. I like my villains black-hearted, so he had to become the murderous pagan thug who, I'm sure you agree, deserved his final fate. But a real Nordic jarl did rule Argyll under the historic King Godred Crovan, though he was probably a much better man, for he in fact caused no trouble with Scotland or her religious houses. Wicked OdinsØye commits yet another crime by standing in to fictionally slander him here.

Should you wonder why I keep using "Danes," "Northmen" and "Nordic" instead of "Vikings," I should point out that calling these men and women "Vikings" did not begin until many centuries after their age, and that the terms I use are correct nomenclature used in their time. But yes, today we would call them "Vikings."

For OdinsØye's castle, I borrowed Carrick Castle, which sits today where I say it did and looks now much as I describe. According to Wikipedia, "The present ruin is possibly the third occupant of this location. The first may have been a Viking fort. The second structure, and first castle, is believed to have been built in the 12th century. Allegedly a hunting seat of the Scots kings, Carrick was originally a Lamont stronghold." So you see, a Nordic fort with a stone tower built on that spot by a Nordic jarl is not such a stretch, after all.

The raids on the monasteries I describe are fiction. In truth, the historic raids on monasteries ended some one hundred years earlier, and by 1090, most Northmen were just as Christian as the Irish and Scots they ruled. But rule they did in the lands I describe, and they would continue to do so for more than another two hundred years. And we should not forget that Henry VIII did far worse to the Catholic monasteries and convents of England and Scotland, including those very same ones, five hundred years later than ever did any Viking. Indeed, similar crimes and horrific atrocities against Christian religious persons occur routinely in several Islamic countries today. Godric is needed now more than ever.

✠✠✠

Could you lay siege to a seaside castle as I describe? Study the actual spot using Google Earth and tell me how, without cannon, you would do better. And what better place to set a siege worthy as a showcase for *Bone-Crusher*'s power?

✠✠✠

A word about the maps. One of the critiques my beta readers provided for the first novel was that it should have contained maps depicting the places and routes described in the story. They were right, of course, for only the one I drew of Dunnottar was included; and when I publish a second edition I will add all those missing maps. But the criticism spurred me to add many maps to this novel. I drew all of them and all their errors are my own. With a few minor exceptions, you should find every significant location mentioned here shown on at least one map, along with detailed maps for the several sieges. They are built from Google Earth image, so the basic cartography is reasonably accurate—I drew real navigation charts during my Navy years and have some experience doing it. The fictional events (e.g., OdinsØye's tower) are depicted from pure conjecture on my part. But this novel also reports actual history that took place nearly a millennium ago— the sieges at Argences, Le Houlme, and Alnwick in particular — real events for which neither maps or detailed accounts still exist, if they ever did. As a result, I have done my best to reconstruct what happened and where from the few facts available. To whatever extent I succeeded and failed, there is no other to praise or blame but me.

✠✠✠

In many ways, writing historical fiction is a much bigger challenge than writing pure fiction, inasmuch as one must interweave a fictional narrative through the most significant and exciting actual scenes in a series of larger historical events. The need to research actual events, historical details, and geographic settings is continual. For this, the invention of the Internet and several key websites remain invaluable, particularly Wikipedia and Google Earth. To these, my gratitude is everlasting.

As an example, to find a route for Godric's ride south with the princesses in *Call to Crusade*, it was necessary to locate monastic houses all over Britain; determine which were extant in the late eleventh century, an era predating foundation of most British monasteries; and choose those along roads that actually existed in the eleventh century because they were originally built by the Roman army. It took a week of research to piece all that together just to keep history-smart readers from crying, "Anachronism!"

Indeed, writing stories of knights in the late eleventh century is problematic. All the classic medieval tales feature stone castles, enormous monasteries, and knights in plate armor, and in result, most readers have come to expect these as fact. I could have taken that route, too. But this tale takes place at the dawn of the High Middle Ages. The few castles that existed then were motte-and-bailey constructions of earth and wood; most of the famous monastic houses are still decades in the future; and all knights then wore chainmail or gambeson coats; plate armor came into use a century or more later. So writing truthfully against that real timeline required abandoning the popular medieval conventions.

Other authors I admire have done wonders to bring dusty history from other eras to life, in some cases to the point of filling the air around my reading chair with the stink of battle: of gunsmoke, blood, and shit. Notably, Bernard Cornwell has done this with the Napoleonic War, Poitiers, and Agincourt, while Patrick O'Brian did so with the Royal Navy during the selfsame Napoleonic War. Edith Pargeter, writing as "Ellis Peters," did well with Brother Cadfael in twelfth-century England. Ken Follett wrote of England a bit later in *The Pillars of the Earth*. As yet, none but historians have written much of the First Crusade, and certainly not as fiction. I hope my muse and I can do it justice.

✠✠✠

Though Godric is fiction, other characters in this novel are real, and I have tried to keep them true to their historical nature. King Malcolm III and Queen Margaret are historical figures, and Margaret was not only a great queen but also a real saint. Her husband might have been more ruthless than I have portrayed him, but I think that reputation may have been more due to later English propaganda than reality.

King Malcolm III was known as Malcolm Canmore (Canmore is

Gaelic for "Big Head," which suggests a physical deformity to some. But another meaning is more appropriate: "Great Chief"). In fact, Malcolm reigned thirty-six years at a time and place where keeping one's crown three years was a true achievement.

Of Scoto-Norman origins, Malcolm was the son of King Duncan I, who was killed by Scottish rival King MacBeth to gain the throne. Malcolm had a son he named Duncan, by his first consort, Ingibiorg Finnsdottir. Son Duncan was taken to the court of William I of England in 1072 as a hostage for his father's good behavior under terms of the Treaty of Abernethy. Duncan grew up in William's court in England, only regaining his freedom in 1087 when William died. He remained by choice in the court of King William Rufus, and late in this book he appears as the Prince Duncan who becomes King Duncan II and reigns Alba for seven months before being killed on 12 November 1094.

When Margaret became queen, she set about civilizing her husband and his kingdom. A saintly woman, she entreated the king to bring Benedictine monks to Dunfermline in order to build an abbey in his new capital. Margaret also had inaugurated a ferry across the Firth of Forth, known as Queen's Ferry, to enable pilgrims to reach more easily the abbey from Edinburgh.

In *Call to Crusade* we first meet Cedric, Thorsson, Sir Hamish, Sir Cormac, Carrick, Aleine, and MacanFhirMhóir; and most of them will return in *March to Nicaea.* All of them are, alas, fictional, yet have managed to become good friends all the same.

✠✠✠

Princes Edward, Edmund, Edgar, Alexander, David, Duncan and Princess Edith are historical figures, as are Counts Robert I and

Robert II of Flanders, Duke Robert of Normandy, King William Rufus, Arkil Morel, Robert de Mowbray, and Emperor Alexios. Fathers Thomas and Anselm, Sir Hamish, Sir Cormac, Carrick, and Aleine and Isabeau are fictional, but Jean de Bethencourt, Sir Lethold, and Sir Engilbert de Tournai are fictionalized real persons.

✠✠✠

With the exception of the siege of OdinsØye, the events of 1090-1093 I describe actually happened, though I admit to fleshing them out and embellishing them. King Malcolm's difficulties with William Rufus are a matter of history. As the English began to take Cumbria and Northumbria, Malcolm contested the expropriation. When Rufus expropriated lands to which Malcolm personally had title, Malcolm indeed marshaled his forces.

Subsequent events—the meeting at Gloucester, siege of Alnwick, the fight at the encampment, and the murder of Malcolm are based on actual events, but as I had nothing more than skeletal facts to work from, all the speeches and descriptions of events are my conjecture.

The killings of King Malcolm and Prince Edward are historical fact, and Margaret did die of shock—or more likely, a stroke triggered by shock—when the news reached her. Malcolm and Edward did die; how—whether by battle victory or treacherous murder—is uncertain. The English still claim Malcolm's death resulted through battle during an ambush by Morel, and ignore whether a declared truce achieved it. A thousand years later, the matter remains so controversial that it seems whitewash is still needed to protect the reputations of William Rufus, Robert de Mowbray, and Arkil Morel, the most recent by the BBC, according to the following source. After reading every account I could find, the version I used, the most compelling, draws upon a reconstruction attributed to "Iolaire" or "Niall" posted on a Scottish Web forum at:

http://www.badeagle.com/cgi-bin/ib3/cgi-bin/ikonboard.cgi?act=Print;f=35;t=1165.

However, Gilbert fitzRichard de Tonbridge is a historic person, and his role in saving King Rufus from Mowbray's ambush is reported as fact by Orderic Vitalis, the contemporary historian monk who lived in that age and subsequently documented extensively the histories of Robert Curthose, William Rufus and Henry Beauclerc. Gilbert lived on, is said to have accompanied Rufus on a certain later fatal hunt, became a favorite of King Henry I, and lived on to die at last in 1114.

Now the simple fact that Robert de Mowbray and Arkil Morel are independently associated with two nearly identical ambush plots against two unarmed and unsuspecting monarchs makes me certain that my account of Malcolm's death is essentially truth. I wrote the original account of that ambush two years ago, and just recently discovered Gilbert's confession, which confirms the same men committed an identical plot. So you can choose to accept another version of Malcolm's death if you prefer. But the second incident proved to me I had the first right. We military men have a saying: "Once is coincidence, but twice is enemy action."

✠✠✠

A word about sheriffs in Scotland and a "sheriff-at-large":

"Sheriff" is a contraction of "shire" (county) and "reeve," the

Anglo-Saxon term for the local magistrate responsible to keep the peace in a county on behalf of the king.

In Scotland, the existence of shires began in the ninth century as an innovation adopted from Anglo-Saxon England, first in the English-bordering regions like Lothian, and later expanded to the rest of Alba by King Malcolm III and sons Edgar through David.

King David I (ruled 1124–1153) was the first to begin codifying Scots law. To understand what law enforcement looked like before him, I could find little information, and so was forced to reverse-engineer a plausible construct for this story. Any errors found herein are my own.

It was Malcolm III who created the office of sheriff, as a judge or officer of the law responsible for peace and order in his shire; but the nature of their actual duties and function is occluded history today. In Scotland today, sheriffs are judges. Were they then? In the eleventh century, Malcolm certainly had need for judges, and I believe they certainly had that duty. But who performed the other law enforcement duties we associate with police and sheriffs today—investigation, detection, arrest, and punishment? My own county in Virginia has sheriffs, serving as the enforcement arm of the county courts; not an accident, I think; rather a legacy from an English legal system we kept despite American independence.

In consequence, I came to think that the duties of an eleventh-century sheriff had to include police functions as well as judicial ones. At the time, barons governed baronies, with bailies as deputies, while sheriffs served the shires. Together these worthies would have handily dealt with local crime, local disputes.

But in an age long before Scotland Yard or the FBI, who would have investigated, tracked down and either brought to justice or directly punished far-ranging criminals like MacanFhirMhóir and OdinsØye—men who struck in multiple shires and fled to hidden lairs in other realms or jurisdictions? I could not identify such an eleventh-century functionary.

Were all criminals of the age only local? I could not believe it. Border raiders, cattle thieves, renegade highlanders and swift-striking Vikings are all stock-in-trade villains in Scottish fiction, and so must have their roots in truth. And indeed, in searching for actual examples, I found and bought a yet-to-be-delivered book on just this topic and timeframe: *Outlaws of Medieval Scotland: Challenges to the Canmore Kings, 1058-1266* by R. Andrew McDonald, published just last month (March 2016)—too late to be of any help now, but which may yet cast light on my dilemma.

So I crafted the title and role of "sheriff-at-large" to fit the far harder task Godric faced than did a nominal sheriff of the age. I placed my three sheriffs-at-large—Godric, Hamish and Cormac—under the command of King Malcolm and his historic High sheriff, Earl Causantín of Fife. They would have acted as higher-order officers of the law, armed with the king's authority to operate across jurisdictions, the wit and judgment to deal with complex crimes, and the right to use capital force if required. Think FBI special agents, Scotland Yard chief inspectors and, of course, the licensed-to-kill 007.

This will not trouble most readers, who willingly suspend belief when reading fiction for the sake of a good story. I may have reason to tremble before sentencing by Scotland's present sheriffs and history professors, but my defense is this: If I got it wrong, where was your learned treatise that would have set me right? ☺

✠✠✠

The seizure of the four Nordic merchant ships by Mowbray and Morel is a recorded fact, as was Mowbray's conspiracy. Report of the piracy did indeed lead to the siege of Bamburgh Castle, capture and imprisonment of Robert de Mowbray, and the exile of Arkil Morel. Mowbray was indeed lured out of a perfectly good castle, and absent any actual details I was challenged to find both the lure and the means to do it. Since no historic agent is known to have acted to bring Mowbray down, I took advantage and gave the credit to Godric.

The historic Morel is a direct ancestor of many English royals and others, including King George I, Winston Churchill, President James Garfield, and Princess Diana. My treatment of Morel in these pages may be frowned upon by his descendants, but if Malcolm was murdered during a truce by the man who declared it, he merits the disapprobation I heaped on him.

There is a good deal of historical and genealogical fog around Morel. He is given various birthdates as early as 1015, which would make him a most improbable 80 years old when the Aln River ambush occurred. Other accounts give him birthdates in 1050, 1054, and 1074, putting him in at least three different generations. To do his role as Sheriff of Northumberland and Steward of Bamburgh Castle justice, I chose a realistic middle ground, a birth year about 1050-54. Ironically, although Clan MacKay claims Morel is their progenitor, Morel is also claimed by Clan Dunbar because of the marriage of his daughter to Gospatric II, son of the same Earl Gospatric who was slain with Malcolm in the Aln River. All of these are historic figures, too.

Morel did die in combat in 1095, the only available detail that he was killed by an unnamed squire. At least I made his adversary a noble and knight.

✠✠✠

After Malcolm died, Donalbane and Donnchad did contend for the crown as I described. Donalbane did lay siege to Edinburgh, yet the princes somehow made their way out, off to Dunfermline where they buried Margaret and off to Edgar Ætheling, who did take them to England. Whether they went to Normandy or not is unclear. Edgar Ætheling did associate with both Robert of Normandy and William Rufus. In England, the princes did gain the favor of William Rufus, who did support their efforts to recover the Scottish throne as I have related. And I believe he did it for the nefarious motive I ascribe to him: personal gain.

✠✠✠

The letter from Basileus Alexios to Count Robert the Frisian is also controversial. Although there are references to the letter in other surviving contemporary accounts that indicate it existed, no actual copy survives to this day, and some historians doubt it ever existed. Whether it—alone or with others—induced Pope Urban II to call for Christians to go to the aid of Alexios is moot. An appeal was made, and the appeal was answered overwhelmingly; no one maintains that the First Crusade was spontaneous.

✠✠✠

Historical records say that my wife's earliest ancestor, Sir Jean de Bethencourt, joined Duke Robert Curthose of Normandy and Count Robert II of Flanders in the First Crusade. Little else is known of his life, but the Bethencourt coat-of-arms ("*argent, a lion rampant sable, armed and langued gules"*) is identical to that of Count Robert II except for a silver background vice Robert's gold, which suggests a relationship. Those arms are also identical at core to those of Orchies in Flanders.

For those reasons, I gave Jean de Bethencourt a key supporting role in Godric's saga, and deservedly so; for after all, he was in fact actually there.

✠✠✠

De Re Militari ("Concerning Military Matters") is a Latin work by Publius Flavius Vegetius Renatus written around the year 450 AD on Roman military matters. In four volumes he discusses military recruiting and training (Book 1); the organization of the army (Book 2); campaign operations and tactics (Book 3); and siege machines and techniques and naval warfare (Book 4). A copy of this book exists today in the British Library from the collection of Robert Bruce Cotton and dates from the eleventh or possibly late tenth century. It was widely read from the fifth century until well after the introduction of gunpowder, and considered the most authoritative treatise on warfare known in Medieval Europe. It would have been a vital training manual for a siege master during the Crusades, or so I believe. For this reason, I put a set of the books into the hands of Godric to inspire and authentically shape his natural engineering talents. It is also the means by which I judge whether Godric might or could not know of various military tactics and solutions to the problems of warfare in his age.

✠✠✠

The term “league” has been used to describe a measure of distance since Roman times, and throughout European history, although the distance it defined varied. My working definition is the distance a person or horse generally walks in an hour, which seems to be the underlying basis of most of the definitions. I chose the general English value of three miles to a league, which generally worked since the many French versions varied around that. I wasn’t terribly slavish about the calculation; this is fiction, not rocket science. I hope it suffices.

✠✠✠

Cenachedne is real, the eleventh-century name for Kennoway in Fife. I traveled all over Scotland, during my years with the U.S. Submarine Force in the mid-1980s and since, from Galloway to Shetland, but never to Kennoway; I have visited it only virtually. I chose the town for its proximity to Dunfermline, because it had an interesting name and history, and because it fit the needs of my story well. Most of what I wrote of it here is pure fiction, but it is at least consistent with the truth of the place. The geography of my maps is built from Google Earth images, so that is at least true to present-day reality. St. Kenneth was in fact the major saint of the region in that age, and today St. Kenneth Parish Church stands in the town. I hope none of Kennoway’s residents ever think I have slighted them; that was never my intent. But it was fun to reimagine their past, and give them such fictional glory as I could.

Godric’s manor is purely imaginary, yet modeled as accurately as I could manage on the actual history of eleventh-century estates, architecture, agriculture, defenses, and everyday life. One telling detail I borrowed from real life: Four decades ago, my bride and I honeymooned in Portugal, and visited the monastery at Alcobaça, begun in 1154. The eighteenth-century kitchen there did in fact utilize a weir in the Alcoa river and a canal to divert live fish into a stone pool inside the kitchen. Today the kitchen is not used, so the weir has been removed; but the water still flows. I could not resist having Godric do the same thing six centuries earlier. Could it be that's where the monks got the idea?

✠✠✠

The escape from Edinburgh Castle, although fictionalized here, is based on real events. Donalbane did besiege it, although no attack is recorded. There is indeed a surviving account of a heavy mist through which the princes did escape, bearing Queen Margaret's body, slipping away to Dunfermline to bury her in the abbey. Exactly where they went after that is not clear; both France and England are mentioned. Edgar Ætheling is reported to have had a hand in it all, and who brought the princes to King Rufus's court. I merely reconstructed a plausible story on this skeleton.

I did make one alteration. Edmund is said to have escaped with his brothers; yet just months later, with his brothers in France or England, he in fact succeeded in striking a deal with Donalbane to become co-ruler over half the kingdom and Donalbane's heir. Thereafter, his brothers, and particularly Edgar, regarded him as a traitor and later punished him for it. If he had escaped with his brothers, this actual chain of events could not have happened, so I had him stay behind in Edinburgh and bargain with Donalbane. And I think that is in fact what happened.

✠✠✠

A little about medieval hours of the day:

Long before clocks came to exist, ancient peoples measured time in hours, determining time by the movement of the sun during the day, and the moon and stars at night. The first reference to "hours" is found in the Bible, in the book of Daniel. Later we hear from Jesus Christ Himself, "Are there not twelve hours in the day?" (John 11:9 KJV).

In the Middle ages this system was still in use, and here is how it worked: An "hour" was an increment of time equal to one-twelfth of the daylight part of the day. Thanks to Earth's tilted axis relative to the sun, daylight is extended in summer and shortened in winter, so medieval summer "hours" were longer than winter "hours," although there was no practical way for most people to measure and therefore know this. The only folk with time-keeping devices were monastic houses, which used sundials, hourglasses, and rudimentary clocks to keep the hours for prayer, and it was their tolling of bells that marked the hours for most folk. As a practical matter, minutes and seconds did not exist.

The day began with the first hour at sunrise, approximately 6 to 7 am on a present-day clock, as follows:

First hour: 6-7 am
Second : 7-8 am
Third hour: 8-9 am
Fourth hour: 9-10 am
Fifth hour: 10-11 am
Sixth hour: 11 am-12 pm

Seventh hour: 12-1 pm
Eighth hour: 1-2 pm
Ninth hour: 2-3 pm
Tenth hour: 3-4 pm
Eleventh hour: 4-5 pm
Twelfth hour: 5-6 pm

There are an equal number of hours, and counted the same way, through the night. So the first hour of night began at sunset, about 6-7 pm and the last or twelfth hour of night would be during the pre-dawn at about 5-6 am.

✠✠✠

The events of 1094 in Normandy are based on fact. Robert did accuse William Rufus of subverting his nobles and failing to keep the treaty, and the two brothers did revert to war. Rufus took Bures, and Robert did take Argences and Le Houlme. Godric's role in these sieges is, of course, fiction. There are no surviving accounts of the sieges, nor even remnants of those castles, so the castles and sieges I describe are also fiction.

Historical sources confuse the site of the castle Roger of Poitou held; some call it Argences, others Argentan. The two towns are close to Caen, but not certainly the same, and neither has any evidence of an eleventh-century castle to resolve the confusion. After studying both sites, I concluded Argences, located at a major crossroad and closer to William's stronghold at Eu with better logistical lines, was the more logical. The hill named La Hoguette is real, located where and as I describe. I fortified it as the Normans would have. It is, in reality, less what we think of as a castle today—more a fortified camp like those the Roman army built. But it is just what existed as castles then. It will be Rufus's brother, Henry, who ten years hence begins replacing motte-and-bailey castles of timber palisades and wooden towers with stone walls and towers to create the stone castles we know today.

Argence's fatal flaw—no source or reservoir of water—only became apparent to me when I began to think about taking it, as historical accounts say, in a single day with a "stratagem." Denial of water was a practical tactic at Argences. Having such a large garrison of mounted knights and men-at-arms there would have deterred attack, so having to fetch water from a nearby source outside the castle wasn't really a blunder; that is, until a much bigger army appears to offer battle or siege—and then it was, as we have seen, fatal.

Historians are also all over Normandy on the location of "Hulme Castle," which a few sources link with Le Houlme, a real town sitting in the valley just where I describe it. If it existed as I have supposed, my Le Houlme castle would have been a powerful gate across the direct route between Rufus at Eu and Duke Robert at Rouen—the seat and power center of dukes of Normandy since Count Hrolf (popularly called "Rollo the Viking").

What is clear is that Robert's campaign with Philip the summer of 1094 was a thrust from Rouen northeast at Rufus in Eu, and my Le Houlme would have been a critical first obstacle. Their next named destination, Longueville-sur-Scie, is directly beyond Le Houlme along the route taken by the modern French roads D927, D155, and D3, which probably follow earlier roads.

Robert did besiege and take that castle. Sir William Peverel was indeed its castellan, and was a very wealthy favorite of William the Conqueror, one named in the Domesday Book many times. Because it makes the story more interesting, I chose to adopt an unproven historical allegation that Peverel was the illegitimate son of William the Conqueror and the Saxon princess Maud Ingelrica—which would make him Duke Robert's bastard older half-brother, as I alleged.

✠✠✠

For those unfamiliar with St. Sebastian, he was a third-century (died ~288 A.D.) captain of the elite Praetorian Guard and a Christian saint martyred by order of Roman emperor Diocletian's for protesting the emperor's persecution of Christians. He was shot full of arrows, but survived. After he recovered, he again accused Diocletian, who had him beaten to death with clubs. He is patron saint of soldiers, archers, and those afflicted by plague.

"St. Sebastian's bow" is real, though hardly heavenly, and is called variously the Penobscot or Wabanaki bow. The Wabanaki confederacy of native Americans have a tradition of using such bows, and legend has it that one of their chiefs used such a bow to kill a Viking chieftain at a long range of several hundred yards. Since the bow would have been contemporary with Godric for such a deed to occur—even if 3,000 miles distant—St. Sebastian let Godric adopt it. After all, saints can do as they think right.

✠✠✠

Godric has already endured much, but he is still a young man of twenty-five when Pope Urban's call in late 1095 triggers the Crusades. He does not know it yet, but he is a siege master, and the First Crusade cannot succeed without him. And so Godric must answer the *Call to Crusade,* and in the next book, he must *March to Nicaea.*

CALL TO CRUSADE: An Excerpt

✠✠✠

*If you liked what you read in **The Siege Master's Song**, you will need and want to know how it began and where it will take you. Here is another taste:*

✠✠✠

One morning in my fifteenth year, a man-at-arms we had never seen before rode in. I watched him from the smithy where I worked at the forge on brackets for the tower. He conferred a bit with Nessan, then came our way.

"I have heard that fine swords are made here. Is that true?" he asked. He was a leathery sort, scarred and stringy, about my size and missing half his teeth. But he wore a gambeson of the best quality under a full suit of close-linked chainmail—coif, shirt, and leggings—made of riveted rings as good as any we made. Clearly, he had money, though from the look of him I suspected he had taken it from corpses.

Carrick replied, "We make swords we are proud of." From his indifferent tone, I could tell that Carrick did not like him either.

The man's eyes roamed the smithy, then studied us. "May I see one?"

"Our swords cost dearly."

"If they are worth it, I will pay what you ask."

Carrick and I exchanged looks, then he nodded. I put my bracket in the fire to reheat, went to the storeroom, and returned with a sword wrapped in oiled deerskin. I removed the leather and handed him the sword.

Made of our best steel, it was shaped in the Norman form, more tapered than those of either Saxons or Danes. A yard in length, it was double-edged, with a fuller down the blade that kept it light and strong. It was counter-balanced by the pommel so that the balance point was a hand-width forward of the cross-guard. The guard was straight and about the length of the hilt. Best of all, it flexed to the side a bit, rather than breaking on a hard blow. In the light of the forge, it gleamed.

His eyes widened, betraying his astonishment. He looked down the blade for straightness, eyed and felt the keenness of the edge, balanced the forte of the blade on a finger, waggled it to judge the handling, and took a few cuts in the air and felt it flex a touch. He stared at it in his hand. Then he assumed an indifferent air.

"A good sword, but I've seen better."

Without looking up from his work, Carrick said, "You lie."

The man bridled at that, but knew we knew better, so he smiled. "I lie. This is in truth the finest sword I have ever seen, fit for a warlord, even a king. How much do you want for it?"

Carrick said, nodding my way, "Ask him. He made it."

At that, the stranger's mouth fell open. "But he's a boy! To make a sword like this…"

I took the sword from him and finished his sentence. "You have to pound steel for years and make thousands of blades. I have, and I did. I am no boy. I am a man now, and that sword will cost you six pounds of good silver if you want it."

"Six pounds!" he protested. "My gambeson and mail together are worth that much, and the best made! I offer four pounds."

"You insult me. A good sword is worth five."

"I'll give you five then."

"'This is in truth the finest sword I have ever seen, fit for a warlord, even a king,'" I mimicked him, and shook my head. "Buy elsewhere. This blade is not for you." In truth, I did not want to sell it. I had made the sword for myself. Carrick might have suspected it, but did not let on, and we never talked of it.

The stranger's greed for a bargain collapsed, and only lust for the weapon remained. "I haven't got that much silver with me."

I considered a bit. "You say your mail and gambeson are worth six pounds. I agree; I make mail and yours is that good. If you want the sword, give me both."

That idea had not occurred to him. He said, "I need to think on it."

I nodded and re-wrapped the sword.

"Who are you and why are you here?" Carrick demanded of him.

"I am Brian O'Hugh of Dublin, mercenary soldier. I came because I heard Sir Andrew was recruiting fighting men. I wait for his return."

I smiled wryly. "You may well wait awhile. Sometimes we don't see him for weeks… when ale and women are aplenty." He did not notice the scorn in my words.

"Ale and women—I like them both. The ride to see Sir Andrew may yet prove worthwhile."

I said, "Well, ale you can find here, if you see the miller. Leave the women here alone."

"I will do that," he replied, "and think more on that sword."

He wandered off to the mill, and Carrick said, "Your sword is worth more than his armor, you know."

"I could make another sword as good, but a full suit of mail and gambeson… that, I cannot."

We did not see Brian again until late afternoon. When he returned, he wore only an aketon over his tunic, and carried both gambeson and the mail. "I want that sword. I know I will never see another as fine, and with it I can always get more mail."

Reluctantly, I took the armor, then unwrapped and handed over the sword. He admired it again and then thrust it into the sword frog on his belt, and with a nod, he sauntered off, chest out. Back to the miller's, I thought.

✠✠✠

Later that night I awoke to a commotion in the smithy below. From my pallet, I could hear the voices of a man and a young woman.

"Hold still, my girl. Stop struggling if you know what's good for you." It was Brian, and he sounded drunk.

"No, no—you mustn't. Let me go. I'm a good girl, and no whore." That was the voice of Aleine.

"Doesn't matter to me. I take whatever I catch. Spoils of war, so to speak."

The smithy floor was faintly lit by the damped fire of the forge and moonlight, but my loft was buried in darkness. Quietly I rose, took down the yew bow from its hiding place in the loft rafters, and strung it. I notched an arrow with a bodkin point, then stood where he could not see me in the darkness.

"No, don't—leave me be!" She was crying as she struggled. He hit her then, backhanding her hard, and she cried out in pain. Then he was atop her, struggling to get through her clothes.

"If you wish to live, let her go and leave now!" I said in a grim voice.

It startled him, and he rolled off her and jumped up. "Who's there!" he demanded. "That you, blacksmith?"

"It is. Let her go, or die." My voice was flat and stern.

"Hah!" Brian laughed, backed to the wall, and drew the sword. "I think not. Come down here, boy. I kill people for a living. I will kill you first and then have the girl. Take back my armor, too. You can't beat a real fighting man armed with a sword like this!"

In the Norman tongue, I said to Aleine, "Keep down!"

I drew the bow to my ear and stepped into the half-light. "Your last chance. Flee now!"

He saw me and realized his mistake, but he did not run. Instead, he looked down at Aleine, thinking to stop me by threatening her. I did not hesitate then. The bodkin punched through his aketon, breastbone, heart, and the oak wall, pinning him in place.

He gaped at the arrow and then at me as his sword arm fell limp. I felt no pity. "You are no fighting man, Brian; men do not rape. You should have kept your armor. In truth, you needed it more."

The air left him and he died, still hanging from the wall.

I jumped to the smithy floor and picked up Aleine. "Keep your eyes shut, girl. You don't want to see this." And I carried her from the smithy and headed for the undercroft.

"How did he get his hands on you?" I asked her.

She said, "I was headed to the, um… privy. I tripped over him in the yard." She was embarrassed but not hurt, and I was glad.

I pounded hard on the undercroft door and Carrick opened it, a hammer in his huge hand. "What's happened?"

"Aleine is here and safe. Give her to Alice and come with me."

We walked back to the smithy and I pulled down the corpse. It was a struggle to free the point from the wall. Carrick gaped. "Sweet Christ!"

I told him then what had happened. He wrapped me in a fierce hug that left me embarrassed. "Thank you, Godric. If anything had happened… Alice and I worship the girl."

"So do I," I said, and meant it.

"What do we do with him?"

"Wake Nessan and tell him what happened, then bring me a horse. I'm going to strip him of all but a cheap tunic, take him to Andrew's favorite tree, and hang him there, wearing a sign that says *Rapist*, as a lesson to all like him. Andrew can make of it what he wishes."

And so it was that Andrew's tree gained a new decoration. It was weeks before Andrew returned, and by then vultures and ravens had left nothing to see. But around the manor, people looked at me with new respect and real affection afterward.

✠✠✠

ABOUT TOM VETTER

✠✠✠

Those who can, do. Those who cannot, teach . . . or better still, write. Tom Vetter has done both, living it first and writing about it later. As a naval officer, Commander Vetter served more than two decades and sailed 100,000 miles in submarines during the Vietnam and Cold Wars. He piloted submersibles and Navy bathyscaph TRIESTE II (DSV-1) on dives as deep as three miles to find aircraft, shipwrecks and pilots lost on the seafloor.

After several lives' worth of adventure at sea, Tom retired from the Navy to work a second career in information technology, operating a successful IT architecture business for more than a decade. When his wife's declining health required another retirement in 2012 to care for her, writing and publishing became his third career. Since then, Tom started Tom Vetter Books, LLC, a Virginia-based publishing business, wrote *Thirty Thousand Leagues Undersea*, a memoir of true tales about his undersea adventures, and *Call to Crusade*, first in the five-book *Siege Master* historical fiction series, which retells the saga of the First Crusade as the recollections of a noble Scottish siege lord.

Tom lives with his wife in Dumfries, Virginia, and as caregiver duties permit, he writes every day.

✠✠✠

Absolutely Free!

Sign up NOW on

http://www.tomvetterbooks.com/join-us/

for my email updates and offers.

I cherish my readers, and I'm thrilled you have become one of them.

As thanks for signing up, I'll send you my FREE e-Books, and offer you special discounts on my novels and e-books for as long as you like.

I hope that's forever!

www.ingramcontent.com/pod-product-compliance
Lightning Source LLC
LaVergne TN
LVHW010934100826
845153LV00001B/32

* 9 7 8 1 9 4 1 1 6 0 1 9 0 *